FOR HEAVEN'S SAKE:

The Dreams Continue

FOR HEAVEN'S SAKE:

The Dreams Continue

William Porter

ISBN-13: 978-1-944662-69-1

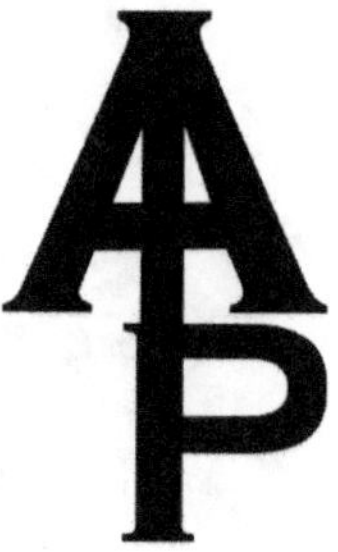

Affirmation Press Publishing date: 09/30/2021

Cover Design by Michael Scott, MASGraphicarts.com

Acknowledgments

A debt of gratitude is extended to the following for the work done on this project:

Michael Scott, Front and back cover producer

Mary Louise Smith, Cover drawings

Diana Henderson, Editor

Affirmation Press: Drew Becker, Publisher

Contents

CHAPTER ONE
MAGGIE'S BACK HOME

Ring, Ring, Ring!

"Who in the world is it this time of the morning?" Maggie whispered to herself as husband Fred was still sound asleep. "My, my! Does anything keep that man from sleeping?" she added in a sarcastic tone of voice.

"Well, it's no use both of us being awake this early in the morning anyway, so let me get up and see who it is," she said to herself softly. She got out of the bed trying not to disturb Fred, mumbling to herself, "Who could it possibly be this early?"

Her efforts to keep Fred from waking were unsuccessful. Her activity plus that continually ringing telephone roused him from his slumber to react to the situation.

"For heaven's sake, Mag. Who in the world is calling this early in the morning?"

Then Maggie replied, "Just try to get back to sleep Fred. I asked myself the same question. But I got this."

Maggie walked the short distance to where the house phone was situated on a nightstand next to a huge portrait. The phone kept ringing until she answered it.

"Hello," Maggie whispered, trying not to disturb her husband any further. A voice on the other end answered with much more excitement.

"Maggie! Maggie! First off, I'm sorry to get you up so early in the morning."

And before the woman on the other end could say another word, Maggie, who recognized the voice, blurted out, slightly more than a whisper, "Sandra, what in the world are you doing calling so early in the morning, girl? Is there something wrong?" Maggie asked with much concern.

"No, Maggie. Nothing is wrong. I'm calling to let you know that I got another job, and, and… I'm coming to Chicago!" Sandra said.

"What?" Maggie replied. "Why, you got a job here in Chicago? Well, congratulations! I'm so happy for you. I can't wait to tell Fred. You know he's fast asleep. But no, Sandra, don't worry about calling so early. I had planned to get up early to fix Fred a nice hot breakfast anyway. So I might as well stay up."

Then Sandra responded, "Maggie, I'm so sorry to call you at such an early hour, but you might want to put that breakfast on hold, because the new job is with an accounting firm right in the middle of downtown near the lake, and they invited me as well as other new hires to brunch later this morning.

"Now here's the kicker, Maggie; they said we could invite another couple too. When they said that, I immediately thought of you and Fred. I just wanted to make sure you two could come. And I sure hope you can. I hope the both of you can make it. I can give you the specific address. Of course, I'll have to leave early from here in Detroit to get there in time for the ceremony. Anyway, the address is simple enough to remember. It's 430 Lane Blvd."

Sandra continued with much emotion, "You know, Maggie, you mean so much to me and so does Fred; I just couldn't let you two not be a part of my success. I mean, you're the one responsible for me going on that cruise to Bermuda the other week."

"Maggie blurted out in an even louder voice, repeatedly, "Cruise? Cruise? Cruise?"

At that point, Fred, who was fast asleep, woke up because of Maggie's noise and movements. Maggie had not gotten up at all. She was still lying there beside him, dreaming. Fred had been undisturbed until she began excitedly talking in her sleep. The both of them were deep in slumber when suddenly she uttered that word over and over again. Finally, she woke herself up as well as her husband.

Fred gave her his urgent attention, saying "Mag! Mag! You're having a nightmare! You must have that cruise you were telling me about last night still on your mind. You just said the word, cruise, over and over again."

--------ANALYSIS OF A DREAM--------

In response to her waking him up, Maggie said, "I'm so sorry, honey, but I guess I haven't gotten over that dream I told you I had last night—about the cruise that we all were on." She continued, "When I went back to sleep, I dreamed that the phone rang and, while not trying to disturb you, I got up to answer it. But I wasn't successful, because in the dream you woke up and you said to me, 'Who in the world is calling at such an early time in the morning?' And when I answered the phone, Sandra was on the other end telling me that she got a new job and was moving to Chicago."

Maggie gave Fred a prolonged analysis of the significance of her dream. "Fred, the strangest thing about the dream is that Sandra told me how happy she was that I took her on the cruise to Bermuda, and that's what I dreamed about earlier last night. What a coincidence? Don't you think, Fred? And can you imagine, in that second dream I had, she told me something that happened in the first dream I had last night? Do you hear me?

"Okay! Okay, Mag! I *do* hear you," Fred replied.

Maggie continued, "Now ain't that something, Fred? I have never mentioned to Sandra about going on a cruise before, and we certainly haven't been on one."

Maggie gathered her senses and saw an opportunity to promote their next vacation. She said, "Well, let me calm down, Fred. Maybe *we should* go on a cruise. Yeah, maybe you'll take me on one sometime, Fred."

Before Fred could respond, Maggie assured her husband, "Don't worry, honey. I'm just kidding about that—about going on a cruise. But I'm sure it would be a lot of fun. That is, if you decide to take me on one!" Then she gave him a wink, telling him that she was more serious than she was pretending to be about the idea.

In an attempt to change the nature of the conversation, Maggie said, "But let me tell you this: Sandra did talk about her trip to Bermuda. But she went there on a plane, and it was only an hour and a half flight. The cruise that I dreamed about last night took over seven days for everything to happen—at least everything that happened in the dream that I can remember. Dreaming about going on a cruise is one thing and actually going on one is another. But you know, Fred, I wouldn't mind going on one despite being around all that water.

"Yeah, that was a detailed dream I had last night, Fred," Maggie continued. "But, you know, the more I think about it—no! It wasn't a coincidence. Maybe I'll have a clearer understanding of what the dream meant later."

Maggie continued, "But then later in the night… Well, really it was much later, something like early this morning, is when I had this other dream just now before I woke up. I hate to repeat myself, but I think it was really weird that I would dream about how our friend Sandra thanked me for taking her on a cruise—a cruise I didn't have except in my dreams. Now, that's something else. Like I said, something that I don't think is a coincidence."

Fred responded, "Yeah, Mag. You just told me. I mean, how many times are you going to tell me about that dream?"

Maggie tried to ease the guilt she felt about talking about both her dreams so much. She said, "I know you're tired of listening to me, Fred. At this point you're probably only interested in that hot breakfast I said I would make for you before we went to sleep last night. So, enough of dreams. I'm going in there and prepare that breakfast."

--------THE MEANING OF DREAMS--------

After Fred patiently listened to what Maggie had to say, he surprised her when he expressed an interest in knowing even more about the dream she had. He said, "Now, wait a minute, Mag, breakfast can wait a while longer. Since you've gotten me up this early in the morning talking about your dreams, I want to give my input on the matter. Let me just say that your dream, the way you described it, is very interesting, Mag."

Fred continued, "You know how I feel about coincidences: I don't believe in them. Yeah, I agree with you. I don't think the dreams you had were coincidences. And I feel this way because I think that God has a reason for doing what He does and that includes His involvement in our own thinking and actions, including our subconscious actions like our dreams."

Fred added, "You know, Mag, the subject of dreams appears many times in the Bible in both the Old and New Testaments. If you remember in Bible study at the church a few weeks ago, the pastor talked about the dream King Nebuchadnezzar had and how Daniel the prophet interpreted it for him. He even mentioned it in a sermon we heard a few weeks ago. Just ask the Manleys; they were there."

Then Maggie said, "I remember that sermon, Fred, the theme of the message that day wasn't dreams though; it was a series of passages that came out of Matthew 7:15-20 when the topic was the Fruits of the Spirit, how we'll be known by the good fruit that we bear."

"Okay, I remember that sermon, Mag, but the pastor did touch on dreams and what they mean. And he mentioned that, even in the New Testament, Pilot's wife told him she had a dream about Jesus that troubled her much and because of it begged her husband to let Jesus go free. But you know the story; the crowd influenced Pilot more than his wife did, and, as a result, he fell for the crowd's demand to have Jesus crucified. When Pilot realized they were so fervent about it, he caved in to the people's wishes and let the criminal, Barabbas, go free, and the rest is history— Christ's crucifixion."

"Pilot tried to dismiss what his wife told him she had dreamed, and he allowed Jesus to be crucified by washing his hands of the matter. But putting issues under the rug, you might say, never works for anybody, not then and not today."

By now Fred was so intrigued with Maggie's dreams, he continued, "Yeah, dreams are important. And who knows. Maybe there's something to the dream you had earlier last night when you envisioned going on a cruise. And the same is true regarding the other dream you had later this morning about Sandra calling you— when you woke me up."

------------ANTICIPATING THE TRIP----------

Then Fred raised a question that brought a drastic change to the conversation they were having. "My goodness, how in the world did we get into this heavy discussion about the scriptures this early in the morning?"

Maggie responded, "Yeah, Fred. You're right. I need to go in there and start breakfast."

"Okay, Mag," Fred replied. He continued, "Mag, you've really gotten me interested in the dream you had last night. Excuse me, I mean dreams!" Fred corrected himself.

Totally changing the subject, Fred said, "I've really wanted to do more for your birthday than to just have dinner at that restaurant we went to the other night. So maybe I can make up for it by really doing something special."

Maggie interjected before Fred could finish what he was saying. "What? Do you mean you're going to take me on a cruise?" And before Fred could answer, she added, "Oh, Fred, I knew you would do something special on my birthday—something other than just going to a restaurant for dinner. But I won't complain."

"No, no, no! Maybe not a cruise," Fred quickly responded. "But I'll tell you what. Why don't we take a trip to somewhere where it's warmer, especially at this time of year? Maybe Florida? It'd be a lot better than dealing with all the cold weather we have here in Chicago—if only for a few days. I know it wouldn't be like a cruise, but I think it could be just as much fun."

"Oh, Fred, that would be great!" Maggie responded. Then she added, "I've never told you this before, but I wouldn't mind relocating to more of a tropical place like south Florida. I don't think anybody ever gets used to all this cold weather up here—even people like us who are from Chicago and Detroit!"

Fred responded with a smile, "Now don't you claim Detroit as your hometown. You know you're actually from Flint!"

When Maggie didn't respond to that last comment, Fred said, "Okay, Mag. Who knows? The idea of us moving to south Florida might come true for us one day. But for this day, why don't you go ahead and fix that breakfast, and I'll go back and try to get a little more sleep—one more time. And promise me this. Just don't have any more dreams, will ya?" Then he added, "Just kidding! Love you, hon!"

He then reminded Maggie, "Just tell me when breakfast is ready, and I'll get up and get dressed."

Before going to the kitchen, Maggie thought about what her husband just said about getting *back* to sleep. She remembered Fred had told her he wanted to go back to sleep "one more time." *Just one more time?* Maggie thought seriously about what Fred had said. *Now I wonder, did he really wake up the first time, or did I really hear him only in that dream?* Then she stopped her contemplation on the matter and finally said to herself, "Oh, well, let me stop messing around and go in there and fix this breakfast."

--------VYING FOR ATTENTION--------

After a little while in the kitchen, Maggie finally finished preparing breakfast. Then she went back to where Fred was sleeping, and hollered, "Fred, breakfast is ready. She yelled so that her husband would hear her without giving him a shove while he was still asleep; Maggie wanted him to come in to eat while the food was still hot. That was what Fred had said he wanted before he went to sleep the night before—before she had that dream of taking a cruise.

Maggie never had been thrilled about cooking, but she considered it as a means to an end, the result being an chance to communicate with people over a hot meal. And in this case, she saw it as one of the few opportunities she would have to talk with Fred and keep his attention on her. So many times, she thought his mind seemed to be somewhere else because of his writing.

While Mensie, her mother, was still alive, Maggie was not fully conscious of her need to draw her mother's attention. Maggie now realized that she did the same thing with her mother that she did with Fred, which was trying to get and keep the attention focused on her. She really wanted to be "mama's girl" even before she left home for college.

During those early years at home, Maggie seemed to be always in the kitchen with Mensie, talking about everything from Sunday's sermon to her life with boys in school. Certainly, that was the case later when she would come home during the breaks after she had enrolled at MCCU. Of course, it continued even after she married John and later Fred. But Maggie always was close to her mother.

Mensie had managed to frustrate her daughter at times, especially when she tried to get Maggie together with her childhood friend John. But Maggie's focus had been on the man of her dreams, Fred, after they met in college.

Through deep meditation and reflection, Maggie had prepared a nice hot meal for her husband. After all, she had promised Fred that earlier in the morning and even the night before.

--------ANOTHER PHONE CONVERSATION--------

As Maggie and Fred sat at the dining table and had their breakfast, the phone began to ring as it had in Maggie's dream earlier that morning. Just before walking over to answer it, Maggie motioned to Fred and said, not being serious, "Now, Fred, pick up the phone in the other room to listen in. I don't want you to think this is a dream!" She laughed as though not believing he would do as she had told him.

Maggie was only joking with Fred. She *did* want Fred to know that this was not a dream, but she never really wanted him to listen in on her phone conversations—not ever! And Fred knew that. Just as Maggie picked up the phone, out of the corner of her eye she saw that Fred was about to pick up the other phone near him, doing what she had told him. Just before answering, she thought, *Now I know he's not really going to listen in on our conversation.*

That is exactly what Fred was about to do. Not being able to do anything about it at this point, she quickly went ahead and addressed the caller, "Hello. Who am I speaking with?" Maggie asked.

"Maggie, it's me, Sandra. How are you this morning?" Maggie's friend Sandra answered and identified herself immediately.

Then Maggie answered, "I'm fine, Sandra. And how are you doing? It seems as though I was talking with you only short time ago earlier this morning."

Then Sandra replied, "I'm fine, Maggie. But it's been a few days since we last talked. And that's because I've been away in Canada for the last three days and just returned to my apartment earlier this morning. I'm pretty tired because it was a surprising amount of traffic on the road to be so early in the morning.

"I guess it was around 2:00 when most patrons at the casino started to head home. Many of them live across the river in Detroit like I do. Anyway, when I got home early this morning, I went straight to bed and fell asleep almost immediately. But I'm fresh now. And, Maggie, I wanted to get up early after sunrise and give you a call. So, it wasn't me that you talked too."

Sandra explained in more detail what she was doing in Canada. "I went across the border into Winsor to gamble a little, and I just made it a weekend trip."

Maggie replied, "Now, Sandra, I thought you had given up all that gambling, being spiritually transformed and all."

Sandra responded, "Well, Maggie, my spirit was certainly in that casino last night, and I was probably there later than I should have been. And, listen, there's nothing wrong with gambling a little to have a little fun. Now, you can't go overboard with it and become addicted. And I'm not addicted, Maggie. I just wanted to get away a little bit."

"Anyway, that's not what I called you about," Sandra said to Maggie as she finally started to address the reason for her call. "I want to talk to you because I have a new job!"

"You have a new job?" Maggie interrupted.

Sandra was ready to give details about her new position, but Maggie couldn't wait to tell her about the dream she had.

"Before you say anything else, Sandra, let me tell you what happened last night. I had a dream that you called me and said you had a new job and that you were coming to Chicago to work."

Before Maggie could continue, Sandra interjected, "Wow, Maggie. Now it's very interesting that you would dream about something that was a reality for me and not know anything about it. But you know what? I love Detroit, and it would be too much for me to get a job in Chicago and commute between the two cities every day. I mean, it would really have to be a great position—with salary and benefits—for me to make a move like that, to relocate from where I am in Detroit to Chicago. So, from that standpoint your dream was not about what actually did happen to me over the last several days in regard to my job prospects, because the new job I got is right here in Detroit, practically around the corner from where I live."

Sandra continued, "But let me say this, Maggie, I really want to thank you for your help in getting me the job at Faith Methodist. That was the only job I've had of any significance before my present job came about. Your last husband's father, Pastor John Sr., knew your mother and your whole family well, and I think that went a long way in him considering me for that position back at Mark Methodist in Flint."

"And I'm thankful to your late husband, Pastor John Jr., too, who was with you at Faith Methodist when he moved on to that church in Detroit. So, I'm indebted to you Maggie, given your connection to Pastor John Sr. and his son John Jr., whose accident was such a tragedy. I still can hardly believe that he's gone," Sandra said with some emotion.

Sandra soon gathered herself and continued, "But don't let me do all the talking. You know I can be quite talkative sometimes. So, go ahead, Maggie, and finish telling me about the dream you had, girl."

Maggie replied, "Well, that's about it, Sandra. I don't have too much else to tell. I just think it wasn't a coincidence that I would dream something as detailed as you getting a job and then, after waking up, getting a call from you and you telling me about the new job you got. It's more than interesting; it's kind of creepy if you ask me. But anyway you've got to tell me more about this new job."

"Well, girl, let me go ahead and tell you about it, but it's not official yet. I do have some papers to fill out and meet with some administrators before I get the job. But believe it or not, you are connected to the position I'm supposed to get. At least you used to be."

Surprised at that statement by her friend, Maggie asked, "I'm connected to it or used to be? In what way, Sandra? Now I'm very curious."

"Well, let me tell you, Maggie, but first you'll probably have to sit down, that is, unless you're already sitting."

Maggie said, "Never mind that, girl; just go ahead and tell me, Sandra. It can't be so bad because I love the fact that you're advancing in your career."

Sandra said, "Well then, Maggie, I got the position that you used to have at the law office of Johns, Jarred, and Jones, as the lead administrative assistant."

After Sandra spoke, there was a brief pause over the phone, a second or two of complete silence.

"Are you still there, Maggie? Are you all right?"

After Maggie recovered from the initial shock of what Sandra had told her, she said, "Well, Sandra, that's great! Let me ask you, how did you get connected to the law office?"

Sandra replied, "Well, that's a long story in itself. But I can tell you more about it tonight. I can only tell you now that I was invited to a banquet introducing new hires to the agency, and I was told that I could invite my significant other. Well, Maggie, as you know, I don't have a significant other, but I do have you two—you and Fred. The both of you have done so much for me. The other thing I wanted to talk to you about, or really wanted to ask, is would you accompany me to that banquet tonight? It would mean so much to me, Maggie. And I hope you two can make it."

Like moments earlier, again there was a period of silence over the phone. But this time Maggie answered Sandra more promptly and said, "Sure, Sandra, we'd be honored to be there with you. I believe that Fred is free tonight too."

Sandra informed Maggie of the time and location of the event as well as some other details. After a little more chitchat between Maggie and Sandra, they ended their early morning conversation.

Maggie was intrigued about two things concerning her talk with Sandra. First, she was amazed that Sandra was on her way to employment at her former workplace at the law office. And second, what stuck in Maggie's mind the most was that Sandra's invitation to attend an event that signaled her new place of work was a repeat of what she had dreamed about the previous night.

She explained all of this to Fred in a fair amount of detail, describing how amazingly the dream and real life had coincided. But now Maggie was back to reality, and the job Sandra told her about was not in Chicago as she had dreamed. It was in Detroit at her old law office no less.

-------A HUSBAND AND WIFE TALK---------

After her conversation with Sandra, Maggie went back to bed where Fred had returned after listening in on their conversation. She began to converse with, even confront, her husband about listening in on her conversation.

"Well now, Fred, what do you think—since you were intent on eavesdropping on what me and Sandra had to say?" she asked sarcastically.

Fred replied, "Well, Mag, you do know you told me to pick up the phone, don't you?"

Maggie retorted, "Now, Fred, do you do *everything* I tell you to do?"

Fred thought about the question, then said, "Well, you know, Mag, I always listen to you, but I will admit I might not *do* everything you want me to."

Maggie's response was, "Fred! I can't believe you said that! Then she paused for a second, and continued to say, "Well, at least you're honest about it. Now as for me, Fred, I try to do everything you wish for me to do, that is, at least I try if it's reasonable."

Fred agreed with his wife when he replied by simply saying, "You do, Mag!"

Maggie then tried to divert the conversation away from them to their friend, so she asked, still in a somewhat derisive manner, "Anyway, Fred, what you think about what Sandra said, since you were intent on listening in?"

Fred replied, "I think she should be congratulated based on where that woman has come from. I mean, when your pastor back at Mark Methodist hired her, what was she doing? Dancing around poles and earning money in what has been recognized as the world's oldest profession?"

Maggie replied, "Now, Fred, do you really have to go there? I remember her telling Mama one time when she visited my parents that her mother left her at an early age, and after that she got taken in by foster parents who she did not like. Then she ran away and ended up on the streets."

Fred asked, "So, Mag, are you giving her a pass for what she was responsible for?"

Maggie replied, "No! But, Fred, that woman has been through a lot. Anyway, I just look at how far she's come. Now, you'll have to admit that, Fred."

Fred then brought up more incriminating thoughts that he had about Sandra. He said, "I guess you're right, but I can never forget what happened when she came to Minnesota that time, claiming to have a sister up there, but I really believe she was there to see me. That's right, Mag, to carry on some kind of romantic relationship with me."

Maggie started to laugh and said, "Hey, Fred, I can't believe that! You and Sandra? Now what do you two have in common other than we're all just friends to one another?"

Fred responded, "What are you saying, Mag, that another woman can't be attracted to me?"

"Oh, Fred, get a hold of yourself," Maggie replied. "We both know that we were made for each other. Why, you're the man of my dreams for heaven's sake."

After those words, Fred responded to his wife by saying, "Well, honey, I have plenty of sense; I'm not gonna argue with that. Yeah, I have to admit, I fell for you the first time I saw you at that social in Maxwell Gym back on campus."

"Yeah Fred, I can't forget *that* night. So you see, Sandra knows that we have a strong relationship. And I know this because Mama told me that she let Sandra in on everything about us before she passed. Yeah, Sandra doesn't have an interest in you. It's all a part of your imagination. And one more thing, Fred, you shouldn't assume a romantic involvement just because two people are friends."

Maggie continued, "And another thing, Fred. Sandra is a new person ever since that visit to Bermuda. And remember, she's the reason my father was so uplifted during times when I didn't see my parents as often as I should have. Why, Sandra is like a sister to me, especially since Mama's been gone."

In an effort to change the conversation, Maggie said, "Anyway, enough about Sandra. I believe she wanted us to be at the Marriott Hotel by 7:00 this evening, which means we have to leave here not later than 3:00. Will you be ready to drive over to Detroit by then?"

"No problem. I'll be ready by then," Fred answered.

Then Maggie responded, "Good! We should have enough time to get there. It's a nice drive," she said. Maggie continued, "Sandra told me the name of the hotel, but there are several Marriotts in Detroit. I'll call her back to get more detailed information about which one we need to go to."

Fred responded, "All right, Mag, I'm going to the library this morning to read up on some things, but I'll be back by 2:00. That should give me enough time to dress, and we should be on the road by 3:00. That should give us enough time to make the drive and get to the hotel in time for the banquet."

Maggie said, "Okay, I need to do some housework while you're gone anyway and may even take a nap early this afternoon. I guess those dreams last night took away from a solid rest that I otherwise would have had."

So, both Maggie and Fred's day was planned before the big event that they would attend later that evening. Before leaving the house, Fred reminded Maggie, "You know, Mag, getting back to what we were talking about earlier, it's possible for Sandra to have an interest in me, not that I would return the favor."

Maggie responded by simply saying, "Oh, sure."

CHAPTER TWO
LET'S DANCE

---------PREPARING FOR AN EVENT--------

"Fred, Fred, are you ready to go? I'm really ready to attend this event. We've got a four-hour drive ahead of us," Maggie said, making a strong appeal to her husband to get going.

Maggie had taken that nap she had talked about and Fred had attended to his business at the library. He returned home at 2:00 as he told Maggie he would. Now, she was dressed and ready to make the drive to Detroit to attend Sandra's event and was in the process of heading out the door. Meanwhile, Fred had not yet left their bedroom.

Maggie looked forward so much to going back to her old workplace, at least to the hotel where her former colleagues would assemble for the event. She especially anticipated a special treat that Sandra had mentioned to her: there would be a lot of dancing after the banquet.

"Come on, Fred. It's already 3:00 and we need to be leaving now," she said. The volume of her voice was a little less than a yell because they were in separate rooms of the house. Fred was still in their bedroom getting dressed for the evening while Maggie was in the adjacent living room.

"All right, Mag. I just have to slip on my shoes, and I'll be ready to go," Fred answered.

Soon he emerged from their bedroom wearing black slacks and a tan blazer with a dark brown turtleneck underneath, a combination that Maggie had gotten him for Christmas. When she saw him, Maggie commented, "I see you're finally ready, handsome. You really look good, honey. Maybe I should have something to worry about—you hooking up with Sandra I mean." Before Fred had a chance to respond, Maggie quickly added, "Just kiddin'!"

Maggie *did* find a way to offer something positive when she added, "It reminds me of the way you looked when we were back at MCCU at that social where we first met. But you have to admit, your dress now is much improved over what it was then. I might have to rethink how Sandra might look at you tonight, Fred," she said with a smile, remembering that she had dismissed his claim that Sandra had romantic desires for him.

Fred replied, "Aw, Mag, you don't have to worry about me and Sandra tonight. You should know my eyes are only for you. And, besides, you look good yourself," Fred offered, complimenting his wife.

"Well, thank you, Fred. But what ya mean, 'not worry about you and Sandra *tonight*?' Is there some other time when I *should* be concerned?" Maggie inquired of her husband.

Fred replied, "No, Mag! I didn't mean it like that! Stop kidding around and let's make sure the blinds are closed and all the lights are out. We probably won't return until much later tonight."

"Why, thank you, Fred, for that answer, but I'm not kidding!" she replied with another smile.

Deep inside, however, there was a seriousness about Maggie's response concerning what Fred had said about Sandra—about how possible it was for Sandra to have romantic feelings for him though he stressed that he only had eyes for her, as he put it.

Maggie *was* concerned about what Fred said about returning home later that night. "Now you said we'll be returning tonight?"

Then without giving him a chance to answer, she repeated the question, "Return tonight?" She added, "No! No! I made reservations to stay overnight when I called the hotel earlier today. Yeah, we'll be returning home tomorrow late in the morning after breakfast."

"Okay, Mag. Let me go back and get my night clothes for our stay overnight then and get a change for tomorrow. Then we can get going."

"Okay, Fred, but don't take long. I'll be out in the car," Maggie said.

--------ON THE ROAD-------

The drive from Chicago to Detroit was uneventful, especially considering that normal conditions at rush hour were bumper-to-bumper. But it was Saturday, so it was smooth sailing. Fred simply put the address of the hotel into the vehicle's GPS, and they were guided along Interstate 94, the main thoroughfare between the two cities.

After about three hours on the road, they entered the outskirts of the Detroit metro area and, after another thirty to forty minutes, they had arrived at the Marriott Plus, one of the larger hotels in the chain in the Detroit area.

"My, my! This hotel is very impressive," Fred said to Maggie as they approached the building. They soon found a parking space available near the front entrance.

They got out with their belongings and fought the brisk cool air before they entered the building. The hotel bellman greeted them and guided them to a desk with personnel from the law firm where Maggie had worked. Some of the people were familiar with Maggie as a former employee. She had worked at this firm after graduation from college. Eventually, Maggie left the position to start her day care business.

--------MAGGIE MEETS JACKIE--------

Maggie finally arrived to where she once would have sat to welcome visitors and communicate with all kinds of people. As she approached the table, she saw Jackie, the assistant to one of the lawyers in the firm.

"Hello, Maggie," Jackie greeted her. "What brings you here today? I thought you was all tied up in your childcare business down there in Chicago."

Maggie responded, "Hello, Jackie. To answer your question, I do find time to get away occasionally. Actually, I'm here because of an invitation I received from a friend of mine who is being honored tonight as a new hire," Maggie told her.

"Oh really?" Jackie replied. "You mean you're here as a guest of Sandra?" Jackie asked.

"Yeah!" Maggie replied. "Sandra and me go way back. She used to work with me at the church I attended when I was living in Detroit. And even before then, I knew her when she worked at my home church back in Flint."

Maggie added, "Are you familiar with Faith Methodist Church?"

Jackie replied, "Oh, yes! What a dynamic minister you had over there. I was really saddened when he died." Not knowing Maggie and her relationship with her previous husband John, Jackie uttered, "I remember people saying that his wife was really a bitch. You know what I mean?"

Shocked at Jackie's words, Maggie said, "No, I really don't know what you mean. And by the way, he was my husband."

Momentarily stunned at Maggie's response, Jackie simply said, "Oh! I wasn't aware that *you* were his wife."

Jackie looked down at the desk in front of her, obviously mortified now by her communication with Maggie and sharing such personal information based on hearsay.

Without intervening and giving Jackie a chance to recover, Maggie just stood there, waiting to hear more.

Finally, Jackie said, "Well, I'm so sorry about your husband's death." Then she asked, "That hasn't been long ago, has it—I mean since your husband died?"

"No, not very long ago," Maggie answered.

Jackie replied, "Well, that's interesting." Then she added, "Now, who is this handsome fellow you have here?"

"Sorry I didn't introduce my husband to you. This is Fred," she replied.

"Hello, Jackie," Fred greeted her.

Jackie spoke directly to Maggie, saying, "My Lord, it didn't take you much time to get hooked up again, did it?"

Before Maggie could respond, Jackie remembered she hadn't returned his greeting. "Oh, hello Fred," she added almost as an afterthought.

Maggie considered that last comment by Jackie—about her getting married so soon after the death of her last husband—crude and distasteful.

Meanwhile, Jackie kept her attention on Maggie's husband. "It's nice meeting you," she said while looking at him up and down.

Fred seemed a little embarrassed, but he kept his composure.

Jackie said, "You have a good woman here, Fred. But I'm sure you know that."

Fred continued to look at Maggie as he replied, "Yes, she's very special."

Then Jackie said, "I have to tell ya, Maggie, I was going to say that Fred looks a lot different from your companion the last time I saw you back at the office. But I wasn't able to get a good look because I was so far away. It was some function but I don't remember what it was."

Then Maggie decided to help Jackie out a little. "Well, Jackie, that probably was my *last* husband, John. As I said, he died as a result of injuries from an automobile accident shortly after I left my position here," Maggie continued.

"Oh, yeah, you did say he was your husband, didn't you?"

Maggie responded rather tersely, "That's right, Jackie; I was married to 'em." Maggie then looked at Fred, seeming to be more than eager to leave the front desk and particularly to end the conversation with Jackie.

Before Maggie and Fred could get a way, Jackie responded, "Oh, yeah. Of course!" As if she suddenly recognized Maggie's displeasure, she added, "Like I said, I'm so sorry talking about you like I did. You know how people talk. A lot of the information that goes around is not true anyway. I did hear that he got a lot of things done at Faith Methodist, and I'm sure you were a fine first lady. And I hate to repeat myself, but I was so sorry to hear of his passing, Maggie."

Trying to dismiss the communication, Maggie responded, "Don't worry about it, Jackie."

"Well, listen," Jackie said. "Let me get you two signed in, then you can venture right over there near the side door and partake of all the food. And again, it was nice meeting you, Fred."

"Yeah, the same pleasure was mine," replied Fred.

Before leaving, Maggie said, "Hey, Jackie, as I remember, your husband used to come by the front desk often to ask about you. Well, how is he doing?"

"Sad to say, we're divorced," Jackie replied.

"Oh! I'm so sorry I asked," Maggie said.

Then Jackie replied, "No, no! That's okay…. The bastard actually was a problem to live with. He hardly wanted to go anywhere, just wanted to hang around me all the time at the house. Well, he did go to church a lot; in fact, I think he cared more about church than he did me! And as far as him coming by the office a lot, I guess he thought I was making out with someone over there at the firm. And besides, the man, like I said, the man was always in church.

"By the way, we were members of Tenth Street Baptist on the south side of town. They were just too loud over there for me, running and jumping all over the place. Anyway, I don't have to deal with that now."

Then Jackie changed the tone of the conversation, adding, "Hey, Maggie, I don't mean to drop all my problems on you. Anyway, nice seeing you. Why don't you two go over there and help yourself to some hors d'oeuvres. I see someone now who could sit here and sub for me for a while."

Jackie then said to a younger lady who just walked up to the table, "Messy, why don't you sit here while I go over there and grab something to eat and meet some people?"

"Okay, Miss Jackie; stay away as long as you want to," Messy replied.

"Thank you, Messy," Jackie replied to the young lady. Then she turned back to Maggie and said, "Maggie, Messy was just hired at the firm a few days ago as an intern."

"Well, hello, Messy," Maggie said.

"Hello," Messy returned the greeting. Then she took her seat at the desk to replace Jackie for a while.

"Well, Maggie, I'm gonna go over here and greet some of the other guests," Jackie said.

"You go ahead and do that, Jackie. Me and Fred are going over where the food is and grab some bites like you suggested," Maggie replied.

Fred and Maggie parted ways with Jackie at that point and made their way over to where the food was. Maggie then saw several former co-workers she had not seen since she left the firm. She made conversation with some of them for a while as they partook of some of the delicacies.

After consuming some of the items in front of them, Maggie and Fred walked over to their designated table, the one reserved for them by Sandra, who had yet to make her entrance into the venue. But that would soon change.

--------PREPARING FOR THE OCCASION --------

The event space, identified as Phillips Hall, was large enough to seat well over a hundred people, although about half the room was filled by the time all invited guests had arrived. Reserved tables were filled with the special invited guests and firm personnel. Sandra and her guests were among those.

Other invited guests were seated in several rows of chairs away from the reserved tables for administrators of the firm, a few lawyers, and the new hires and their guests. Each table sat six and was eloquently adorned for the occasion with cloth table linens and lit candles in the center. A small band was on a stage playing soft jazz.

There was a buzz in the air as the festivities were about to begin. Just before the master of ceremonies appeared on the stage, Sandra walked in and took her seat beside Maggie, who was sitting next to Fred.

"Hello, you two. I'm so glad you could make it," she whispered as the MC was about to start the program.

Sandra continued, "Let me get myself together." She took a small mirror from her purse and touched up her lips and then added, "There, I'm ready to give my little talk." Sandra whispered, "After talking to you this afternoon, Maggie, I went back to sleep and almost overslept and missed my own event. Can you imagine that? I didn't even have time to fully make myself up. But I'm here now," she said as she puckered her lips.

Soon, the MC approached the podium. He adjusted the microphone and began to speak. "Ladies and gentlemen, my name is Shaun Lockhart, your master of ceremonies for the evening. We're here to recognize new employees of the firm. There are two ladies I would like to introduce to you now. At the table to my right is Ms. Charlotte Lowe with her friend Cedric and her parents Cassy and Woodrow. At the table to my left, we have Ms. Sandra Hughes with her friends, Mr. and Mrs. Fred Mints."

Lockhart continued, "Ms. Lowe will be joining us in the public safety division as a computer programmer. Ms. Hughes will be with us now as our lead administrative assistant in the administrative division of our firm. By the way, Ms. Mints whom she invited to this event, is a past employee in that division, and I'm sure you all know her. She's sitting right there at the table with her husband. Maggie was with us for several years and provided invaluable service to our firm. I'm confident that Ms. Hughes will do the same.

"Ms. Hughes will replace Ms. Brown, who could not be here tonight to represent that administrative position. But we look forward to both new hires invited to this celebration having a long career with us. Ms. Hughes' position is especially important because, by being near the front entrance at our home office, she will greet those who enter the facility. As I said, I'm sure she'll do a fabulous job as will Ms. Lowe in the computer department.

"Now, after this scrumptious meal that we're about to partake, each of these individuals will come before you and tell what they anticipate by working here. These tributes will happen after we have a fabulous meal that has been prepared for us. So, now, we have Chaplain Perry coming to us to offer the blessing," Shaun said in conclusion. After their meal, everyone looked forward to hearing what the new hires had to say.

Thanks *be* to God for His indescribable gift!
- 2 Corinthians 9:15

--------SANDRA'S REMARKS-------

Sandra had the more prestigious of the two positions that were filled by the new hires. So, when she got up to give her remarks after a rather short speech given by the other new hire, Charlotte, Sandra took center stage. Sandra got up from her seat and walked confidently to the podium.

Sandra began her remarks by thanking the firm's administrative personnel for considering, then hiring her in the position. She said, "I would like to thank everyone for this opportunity. But I realize the ultimate thanks goes to God."

Not long after that she began to sing the praises of her two guests, Fred and Maggie.

"I want to say that I wouldn't be where I am now without the help of my friends Fred and Maggie Mints."

Then she addressed her comments to Maggie directly, looking squarely at her, "Maggie, you know how I feel about you. You've been like a sister to me, and I'm dearly indebted to you for all that you've done."

Then she returned her attention to the audience, saying, "I'd like to tell everyone that it's not only Maggie that I'm grateful for, but I'm particularly thankful for her late mother, Mensie, who was more like a mother to me than she ever knew." Emotion overwhelmed Sandra, and tears spilled down her cheeks to such an extent that the moderator, Lockhart, came to the podium to hand her some tissue.

"Thank you, Shaun," Sandra said, then continued to honor another friend, who was not present at the event. She said, "While I'm grateful for the Mints being here, I'm just sorry that another friend of mine, Erin Pearson, who was the reason my life dramatically changed after visiting her in Bermuda, is not here tonight. She's probably back at home at her island resort where I visited almost two years ago. Oh, how I wish Erin were here now.

"My wish is that someday we will meet again and, more than that, that she will receive the kind of blessing that I got when I visited her at her resort at that time." Sandra began to tear up again as she continued to talk, at times barely audible. Then she continued, "It's such a beautiful evening, and I'm sure the stars will be out tonight— just like they were on my last day there in Bermuda. It was a spiritual experience that I will never forget."

Soon Sandra finished her remarks and received a standing ovation, something her new co-worker Charlotte did not get after her brief remarks. Charlotte's face revealed a small sense of embarrassment over the accolades given to Sandra.

Sandra's remarks affected Maggie so much that she felt she needed to give a response right then and there.

While Sandra was still standing at the podium, taking in all the adulation being thrust upon her from those in attendance at the event, Maggie stood up and began her own unscripted, unsolicited remarks. She said, "Sandra, I can' t help but stand up and offer my congratulations on your new position."

Then Maggie turned toward the other reserved table and said, "And that goes for Charlotte as well. I wish you nothing but the best in your position too. Then she returned her attention to her friend. "But, Sandra, you're special. And you mean more to me than you will ever know.

"Something else that we all can't dismiss. You mention your friend Erin. Well, she's my friend too because of you. And I'm going to call her tonight and let her know what you said about her."

After those comments, Maggie turned her attention from Sandra to the rest of the audience assembled and said, "I want all of you to know that you're getting a quality individual here. And I don't mean to disregard protocol, but it's something that I felt I needed to say." Then Maggie turned toward the other reserved table again and said, "Forgive me, Charlotte, for taking so much time talking about Sandra. But you're starting this job with just a wonderful person who's coming in with you."

Maggie tried to continue but she could no longer hold back the tears. Fred did his best to console her by holding her hand and squeezing it a little as she stood there beside him. It took a few seconds for Maggie to regain her composure.

After Maggie finished making her remarks, the band started playing again, this time a tune in honor of both the new hires as Sandra continued to stand at the podium. All the emotion in that place was just too much for Maggie, so she had to excuse herself and make a brief visit to the ladies' room.

--------GETTING ACQUAINTED--------

After the band had played a tribute to the new hires, Sandra began to walk away from the podium and towards her reserved table, but, being overwhelmed with emotion, she was barely able to walk that short distance. The conductor, who was situated directly behind her, saw Sandra's uneasiness and began to lead the band in playing some smooth jazz.

Fred started to get up to give Sandra some assistance, but then he saw someone approaching her to help. He later learned that it was an off-duty security guard and an employee of the firm. The man who assisted Sandra was standing by a door behind the stage. When he saw that Sandra needed help, he motioned to another employee standing nearby to take his place.

"Hey Joe, come over here for a minute. I'm going to step away for a while so you can stand here by the door until I get back," he said to the coworker.

Then the guard promptly came over to assist Sandra to her seat. When he arrived to where she was, he asked, "Are you all right, ma'am?"

"Yes. I'm fine," Sandra replied to the man, overwhelmed by all that had taken place.

"Now who are you?" Sandra asked him. Then the fellow responded, "My name is Freddie, and I've worked in the security department in this firm for some time now, but I just arrived as the band had finished playing a tribute to the new hires."

At the time Sandra was clearly distracted and overcome with feelings.

Freddie said, "Come on. I'll help you get to your seat."

As Freddie escorted Sandra to her seat, the band increased the volume of their play that had started moments earlier.

He said, "I saw you standing at the podium and must have just missed your talk. I can tell from the expression on everyone's faces that it was quite moving. And I could tell you needed some help going back to your seat. So, I said to myself, 'Let me go help this lady.' So here I am."

Trying to clear her head, Sandra responded, "Well, thank you, sir."

As they moved to the steps exiting the stage, Freddie added, "Watch your step."

Sandra appreciated the man's assistance. As they walked the short distance to her seat, she said, "Thanks again for helping me."

Freddie steadied her. Just before getting back to her seat, Freddie said, "The firm called me to take the place of a security officer who couldn't be here."

After assisting Sandra to her seat, Freddie greeted Fred and said, "Sir, I assume you are with this beautiful lady."

Sandra blushed at those comments.

Fred replied, "No! I'm with my wife, who had to step out for a moment. We're here as guests of Sandra at this event."

Then Freddie added, "Oh! So, your name is Sandra?"

"Why, yes, and I'm sorry I didn't identify myself."

"No worries," Freddie replied.

Sandra affirmed Fred's response, saying, "But, yeah, my best friend is with me along with her husband, this man right here," She placed her hand on Fred's shoulder. Then Sandra asked Fred, "is Maggie all right?"

With his eyes still planted on Freddie, Fred answered, "Yeah, she's fine. She just had to step away for a minute."

As Fred uttered those words, he thought, *I wonder what this guy is up too?*

Meanwhile Freddie had his own thoughts churning after Sandra mentioned Fred's wife Maggie. *I wonder is this the Maggie I know.* Freddie did not pursue the matter further in his mind.

Sandra made a comment to Freddie, who stood at the table. "You sure aren't dressed like a security officer."

"Well, as I said, I'm only a replacement for a security officer who couldn't be here, so I'm not properly dressed for what I'm supposed to be doing. I had to throw something on quickly because I was called just before the start of this event. The person who was scheduled to work tonight on the evening shift called in sick, so administration called me to work some overtime. Listen, I'm not gonna give up working overtime. Now, I really don't mind though, because it gets kind of lonely around the house."

"Oh, I see," Sandra said.

After a pause to see what he would do next, Sandra finally got the nerve to say to Freddie, "Well, just don't stand there; have one of these empty seats.

Fred interjected, "Sandra, the man is on the clock."

Freddie said, "You're right, sir, but there's someone at the door where I came from, and he can be there for a while."

Then he turned back toward Sandra and said, "So, yeah, I can stay for a little bit." After that brief but tactful interaction, Freddie went ahead and accepted Sandra's offer and sat down beside her. At that point, Fred simply looked away.

---------LET'S DANCE---------

Soon the MC returned to the mike and said, "Well, everybody, after that nice meal, I know you all are ready for dessert. An attendant will be by your table soon to offer you a selection of four items. In a little while, the band will start playing tunes that will send you all out onto the dance floor. None of this smooth jazz like they've been playing. Now that music is fine; it has its place, but I need for all of you to get up, to *get down*, to use an old expression, out there on the dance floor."

Then he used his finger to point to that area of the room. "I'm hopeful that the area over there will be crowded with dancers soon," he said. "So get yourselves ready. But first, we'll have our guests of honor grace the floor, which means Sandra and Charlotte. Are you two ready?" He urged them to get up and start things off.

Charlotte was eager to dance with her friend Cedric, so they immediately took to the floor. It was an awkward position for Fred, who in the back of his mind wanted to escort Sandra out to dance, knowing that she had no one to accompany her at that time, although the replacement security officer was sitting next to her.

It appeared to Fred that Freddie was beating him to the punch, making a strong move on his friend Sandra. Not only that, but he realized that only moments earlier he had imagined himself dancing with Sandra. Fred quickly gathered his emotions and recognized that would not be a good idea because Maggie would soon return from the ladies' room. It would not look good for him to be dancing with Sandra after hearing Maggie's thoughts earlier about being with her. In any event, Freddie would take care of partnering with her on the dance floor.

Sitting next to Sandra, Freddie asked, "Is anyone with you?"

Without allowing Sandra to answer the question, Fred spoke up and said, "Yes, as I said before, she's with me and my wife."

Freddie replied, "Oh, I see."

As the band started to play, Freddie disregarded Fred's statement and offered a solution to Sandra's issue of not having a dance partner. He thought, *I could be her escort, at least for this moment!* So, he said abruptly, "Let's dance!" He thought, *Before she has time to say no, let me justify what I'm saying.*

Then Freddie added, "Yeah, let's dance to this first song of the evening. I see you don't have a partner, and the administration is expecting the new hires to at least dance on the first song. You see the other new hire and her partner have gone out already. They're out there now! So, I'll be your escort at least on the first song. Is that okay with you? And you *don't* have an escort, right?"

"Yes!" Sandra replied enthusiastically. "I mean no. No, I don't have an escort. As I said earlier, I'm only here with Fred and his wife."

"Well, then, you don't have an escort! That settles it!" he said as Fred continued to look on in bewilderment.

Freddie reached out his hand towards her hand and said again, " Let's dance!"

Fred had momentarily forgotten about Maggie having gone to the ladies' room. His mind was on what Freddie was saying and on Sandra's acceptance of his invitation to dance. And Fred's concerns came to reality when she finally relented to Freddie, saying, "Yes, I think I will. And you're so kind, sir."

Sandra accepted his hand to guide her onto the dance floor.

"Sir? Oh, just call me Freddie. Remember, I told you my name when I helped you from the podium up there! Remember?"

"Oh yeah. I do remember now...Freddie. Anyway, you're so kind."

As Fred listened to their conversation, in his mind he rephrased Sandra's statement of gratitude towards Freddie posing it as a question: *You're so kind?* Then he continued to think, *this guy just wants to hit on you. Can't you see that?*

Despite Fred's obvious concerns, Freddie continued his dialogue with Sandra. She took his extended hand and rose. They then slowly strolled the short distance to the center of the dance floor, where Charlotte and Cedric had gone already.

Freddie, who happened to have been romantically involved with Maggie during her time at the law firm, was still unaware that she was the wife of the fellow he had greeted and whom he perceived was looking at him in contempt. Freddie had no knowledge of Maggie's presence at this event. He had yet to know the identity of Maggie, who had excused herself before he had a chance to see her.

Freddie had arrived at the event too late to see Maggie prior to her going to the ladies' room as she was overcome with emotion because of Sandra's speech. He had entered the event just as Sandra was finishing her remarks, statements that affected Maggie so much that she had to excuse herself. Freddie never saw her leave.

Meanwhile, Fred had no knowledge of Maggie's past relationship *with* Freddie.

There they were, Freddie and Sandra, along with Charlotte and friend Cedric, dancing to the tune played by the band.

Fred began to worry about Maggie, who had not yet returned from the ladies' room. He thought about asking a woman sitting nearby to check on his wife. Competing for his inner focus was Sandra dancing with this stranger.

Despite Fred's renewed dedication to Maggie, a part of him, the flesh part, still had somewhat of a sensual feeling towards Sandra, and it showed in his demeanor as he watched her dance with Freddie.

A wayward spirit rose within Fred as he saw Sandra dancing with a person she felt appreciative after he assisted her in leaving the podium and stage.

--------MAGGIE'S RETURN--------

Fred finally saw Maggie heading back to the table. When she sat down, Fred asked her why it took her so long to return.

Maggie replied, "Forgive me, Fred, for being away from the table so long. But I had finished freshening myself up and recuperating from that emotional speech that Sandra gave when my daycare worker, Mary, called to talk to me. I just couldn't get away. She ended up telling me some personal issue that she has and that she could not come to work on Monday. She tried to explain to me what the situation was, and, as I said, I just could not get away. Anyway, I'm back now. I'm just sorry I didn't get back in time to go out on that dance floor."

After giving Fred that explanation, Maggie asked, "Where is Sandra?"

Without him having to answer, Maggie noticed the open area filled with dancers and saw that Sandra was one of them.

Fred replied, "She felt obligated to go out there, I guess. Anyway, yeah, she's out there dancing."

Maggie couldn't figure out who she was dancing with. "Hey, Fred, who is that guy dancing with Sandra? With all the people out there, and with his face turned away from us for the moment, I can't tell who it is."

Fred replied, "Well, he described himself as an employee here at the firm. He helped her back to her seat when she finished talking. That happened just after you left to get refreshed."

Maggie asked, with a degree of bewilderment, "Well, why didn't *you* help her back? I mean, couldn't she walk that short distance back to her seat?

"Well, Mag, Sandra appeared to be unstable when she finished her speech, and I guess the fellow saw her and tried to help."

Maggie said, "But why didn't *you* go up there to help her?"

"Like I said, Mag, the guy was practically on top of her by the time I was about to get up, so I just let him help her back."

"Oh, well," she replied.

Maggie continued to try to identify the man who was dancing with Sandra. The thought didn't come into her mind that it could be her old flame, Freddie, because she couldn't see his face.

"Mag," said Fred, "you spoke of Sandra having an emotional effect on you. Well, she must have had a similar effect on herself because she was barely able to make it back here to where she was sitting. That's when this guy helped her back to her seat because she got too emotional to return to the table by herself."

Maggie said, "Yeah, it was emotional for me too. That's why I just had to step out for a while. But like I said, while I was away, I got tied up with Mary."

"Well, this place *is* well lit, and he was right here at the table, so I got a good look at this guy. I've never seen him before," Fred said.

The dance floor became so crowded that it was even more difficult for Maggie to get the look she wanted in order to identify him. She became more curious about who he was. To satisfy her curiosity, Maggie asked, "Fred, what does he do? What is his position here at the firm?"

Fred was ready to at least give Maggie his name when she got a better look at him while he was dancing with Sandra.

Fred began, "The guy's name is Fred…"

But before he could complete saying all his name, Maggie shouted, "Oh, for heaven's sake, it's Fred…" And, like her husband just a few seconds earlier, Maggie failed to complete saying his full name. Instead, she said softly to herself, and Fred heard her, "It's the person I used to work with here at the firm."

As best she could, Maggie tried to keep Fred from knowing that she knew him as a past acquaintance. But Fred heard her mumbled words and asked, "Do you know this guy?"

Knowing that she could no longer deny knowing him, she replied, "Yeah, I've seen him around at the firm."

Maggie tried to recover from her initial shock at seeing her old coworker with whom she had romantic experiences.

Fred looked on in bewilderment before asking her about him again, this time for some clarification. "Mag, how well do you know this guy?"

Maggie answered, "Yeah, he was an employee at the firm when I was there, and we've seen each other at social events."

She tried her best not to reveal any more personal information about their involvement together. And Fred soon gave up trying to become more informed about the guy—*from her.*

--------FREDDIE'S CONVERSATION WITH SANDRA--------

As Sandra continued to dance with Freddie, Maggie just sat there, thinking about the times she had with him. While Fred continued in his state of bewilderment, Sandra remained in the moment, dancing to the music that continued to play. Sandra and Freddie had begun to converse with one another, and the band played a rendition of "Midnight Train to Georgia."

The song immediately conjured up thoughts in Fred's mind of the time when he first met Maggie back on the campus of MCCU. That night long ago the band had played "Georgia On My Mind" as he and Maggie fell in love. He only wondered whether this song tonight was having the same effect on Sandra and on this guy as another tune about Georgia had on Maggie and himself years earlier when they too were serenaded by music on a dance floor at Maxwell Gym.

Back on the current dance floor, Sandra began to ask Freddie about his personal life, but only after a personal compliment. She said, "You do know you're a good dancer, don't you?"

Freddie replied, "No, I don't. Then again, I don't like to give myself compliments."

"I understand," Sandra replied.

She added, "Anyway, I'd like to know if you replace your co-workers here at the firm often when they call in sick?"

Freddie responded, "No, not at all. In fact, this is the first time I've had to fill in for someone. But, believe me, I've had enough work to do on my regular shift."

Freddie continued, "So tell me more about your guests. You introduced me to Fred, but he said his wife had stepped out.

Sandra replied, "Yes, they're my best friends. And Maggie, Fred's wife, is such a wonderful woman. I'm envious of her because she's so faithful to her husband, and I tell her constantly that I want to grow to be just like her."

After telling Freddie that piece of information, there was a pause before he replied. Sandra's head rose only to his shoulders, and she was practically breathing on his neck as they looked in opposite directions.

"Freddie, are you still there?" she whispered. "You've gone silent on me."

Freddie finally responded, "Oh, yeah, Maggie, your best friend, huh?"

Sandra said, "Yes, Freddie, she's one of the reasons I ended up getting this job. I owe a lot to her. I've had a lot of opportunity to hurt her, but I've learned my errant ways are not what God wants for me."

They continued to dance as the music was about to end. That's when Sandra said, "I can't wait for you to meet her. You'll see how wonderful a woman she is."

Freddie had an extended inner dialogue concerning Sandra's reference to God as their dance neared completion. *Oh, no. I hope this is not another one of those religious fanatics. But I can't believe it's Maggie she's talking about. Maybe it's another Maggie, one that I don't know, because the Maggie that I know definitely wasn't faithful to her husband.*

Freddie's thoughts were fleeting, but his momentary silence prompted Sandra to ask, "Now what are you thinking about?"

"Oh, nothing important." Absentmindedly, he added, not realizing he was divulging his knowledge of Maggie, "Yeah, she's pretty wonderful." He only intended to respond to her earlier comments.

Sandra was so caught up in the moment, she had no idea what Freddie was thinking much less the fact that his comment suggested he knew Maggie. The number ended and they began to walk back to the table reserved for the new hires and their guests.

------- FREDDIE MEETING MAGGIE, AGAIN-------

The band finished the music they were playing for the honorees; Sandra and Charlotte, and their dance partners went back to their tables. The dance floor cleared, and everyone returned to their seats.

While Charlotte and Cedric were on the dance floor, her parents had come over to introduce themselves to the Mints.

Sandra and Freddie walked casually back to the table where they were sitting. Meanwhile, Charlotte's parents returned to the table that was reserved for them.

As Sandra and Freddie approached her seat, the eyes of both Fred and Maggie were on Freddie. When Maggie first recognized him moments earlier as he danced with Sandra, she was stunned to see who it was. As Sandra arrived back at her reserved table with Freddie, Maggie's shock of seeing him there had subsided *somewhat*.

Sandra spoke up and said, "Maggie, I saw that you had stepped away from the table, but I'm glad you're back. I'd like for you to meet Freddie. He escorted me back to the table after I gave my talk, but Fred said you had just gone to the ladies' room to freshen up. And you had not returned from there when we left the table to go on the dance floor. Of course, Freddie, you've met Mr. Mints."

Then Fred said, "Hello again. Meet my wife, Mag, I mean Maggie. Never mind me, I just call her Mag."

Freddie replied, "I understand." Then he extended his hand gingerly towards Maggie's for a handshake.

As Freddie formerly greeted Maggie, Fred then implored him and said, "Now, Freddie, you can do better than that! Just a handshake? Go ahead and give her a hug. You know, we're huggers around here."

Hesitantly, Freddie moved towards Maggie to do just that—to give her a hug. As Maggie remained seated, Freddie stooped down and gently held her, and whispered in her ear, "Hello, Maggie. I mean, Mrs. Mints."

Freddie greeted her as though it was earlier during their relationship by calling her by her first name. But he quickly corrected himself as Fred had done when *he* called her Mag instead of using her full name.

Maggie extended her arms towards Freddie to reciprocate his embrace—if only at the request of her husband. She cringed as she was reminded of the aroma from when they were last together, so close together, back at his apartment when she decided to pick up that parking ticket he had given her. At that moment as she entered his place, taking shelter from the storm raging outside, Maggie recalled the embrace she had hoped would lead to something more intimate than it turned out to be. With those thoughts in her mind, Freddie released the embrace and rose back from his stooped position.

Freddie then apologized to everyone for having to leave. "I'm glad to have met everyone, but I have to go now and return to where I'm supposed to be working tonight." Freddie gave Sandra his hand to shake again, but this time leaving a note in her palm with his phone number on it as she released his grip.

As Freddie returned to the door where he arrived just after Sandra's speech, everyone at the table began to consume their choice of dessert that had now been delivered.

The rest of the evening was a festive affair with the band playing an assortment of songs with the dance floor again now filled with the event's participants dancing the night away. Maggie and Fred as well as Charlotte and her partner and her parents also danced to the music being played.

Fred did get to dance one time with Sandra—in the presence of Maggie—but she had persuaded him to do it because Sandra did not have a partner after Freddie returned to his station at the door behind the band.

When Sandra returned to the table with Fred accompanying her, she just sat there, taking in all that was before her. Her former dance partner, Freddie, was now on duty at the door. All the while he was gazing at Sandra and wanting to be with her.

As the MC had hoped, the floor was crowded with dancers.

CHAPTER THREE
A SERVANT'S REWARD

It was 9:00 and almost everyone had left the event except the honorees and their guests. Sandra, Maggie, and Fred remained seated at their table while Charlotte, her friend Cedric, and her parents, lingered at the other reserved table. Both tables had been moved closer together so that the featured guests could more freely converse with each other.

Freddie, who had been working at the door behind the stage, wanted to join them. But he had a trip coming up the next day, so he decided to go home. Besides, Freddie had sensed that the man sitting next to Sandra, her old friend Fred, had been cool towards him as he conversed with her. Freddie knew that Maggie had been mystified not only by his presence at the event but also by his closeness to Sandra while they danced. Sandra had no knowledge about his prior relationship with Maggie. With all this clutter going on in his mind, Freddie gave Sandra one last glimpse, then headed out the back door where he had entered several hours earlier.

The honorees and their guests were finishing their conversation and talked finally of retiring for the evening. Before their departure, the event's MC, hotel manager, and a former administrator at the firm, Shaun Lockhart, came to their tables and chatted a little with them.

"Hello, good people. I hope you enjoyed tonight's festivities. I think it was a grand event. And again, Sandra and Charlotte, it's so nice that you two are coming on board at the firm. I'm just sorry I won't be there to help welcome you, since I'm now here at the hotel. And it was a pleasure to have met your guests."

Mr. Lockhart continued, "And, Maggie, maybe you need to rethink your retirement from the firm and consider coming back in some capacity. I'm sure they can still use your services. You *do* know that your contact information is still on the company website."

Maggie replied, "Mr. Lockhart, I thank you for the suggestion, but I'm having so much fun in retirement; I can't see myself working anywhere fulltime again. Besides, I have a fulltime job at home working in my daycare operation. But the key there is that my niece is helping me out, so I have a lot of free time. It gives me so much flexibility."

Maggie went on to tell Mr. Lockhart, "As you probably know, while I had a good position here, I was pretty much stuck at the front desk all day."

After thinking about what she just said, Maggie turned from the manager and looked at Sandra, saying, "But, Sandra, don't take that as a negative, because the firm is such a great work environment. And the pay is not bad either."

Mr. Lockhart confirmed what Maggie's statement, adding, "Yeah, Maggie, I'm sure the firm will take care of both Charlotte and Sandra financially. I think they'll be well pleased with the contracts they'll get.

"Well, it's getting pretty late and past my bedtime, so I'll say goodnight to all of you," he added.

Before he left, Mr. Lockhart added, "By the way, I notice that you, Sandra, were the only one of all of you without a reservation at the hotel for the night. What are your plans?" he asked.

"Mr. Lockhart, I'll be driving back to my apartment tonight. It's pretty late but at least the traffic won't be too bad," she told him.

"No! You won't drive yourself home tonight," he said to her emphatically. You're staying right here at the hotel until tomorrow. Just check in with the clerk at the front desk, and there'll be a room for you—all expenses paid."

"Oh, thank you, Mr. Lockhart. I guess I'll have to sleep in what I'm wearing now tonight, because I didn't bring any extra clothing," she said.

"Well, I can't help you with that—your night clothes and all. But I'll tell you what, the gift shop is open 'til 11:00 and you still have time to stop there and get some items you may need 'til morning. You should be able to at least get the toiletries you need as well as some nighties. Just go by there and let the attendant know that anything you need can be placed on the hotel's account, and be sure to tell her that the hotel manager—that would be me—told you to come by and get whatever it is that you need. I'll stop by there on my way out to let the attendant know you'll be coming by."

"Oh, thank you again, Mr. Lockhart," Sandra said.

He nodded politely. Then he said to everyone assembled, "I'm outta here, you good people. Goodnight, everyone."

Then Mr. Lockhart mumbled to himself, "Um, I have to go to my car and get some luggage." In a louder voice, he said, "I gotta go to my car and get some things. But I may see some of you in the morning at breakfast, because I'm staying here at the hotel tonight too. I saw the weather forecast, and the temperature is supposed to be dropping rapidly tonight. But I gather no one in this group has to go back out, so everyone should be snug and warm for the remainder of the evening. So again, have a good night, and I may see some of you at breakfast in the morning."

"Goodnight, Mr. Lockhart," everyone said in unison.

After that almost all the remaining guests in attendance said their goodbyes to each other and began to go their separate ways. Most went to their living quarters, but Sandra stayed and had begun to chat with Maggie and Fred and remained in the lobby for a while.

‑‑‑‑‑‑‑‑A LONG DAY FOR SANDRA‑‑‑‑‑‑‑‑‑‑‑

Throughout her discussion with Maggie and Fred, Sandra grew more and more fatigued and longed to get to her room and get some rest. It had been a long day for her, having gotten up early in the morning when she made that phone call to Maggie to inform her about the event. And she had so little sleep the previous night because of her return from the casino so early the previous morning. Then she said softly to herself, "Thank goodness for Mr. Lockhart. What was I thinking? Driving home on a night like this."

Sandra was thankful for having been given a room at the hotel for the evening by Mr. Lockhart. Sandra had concluded a successful but busy day participating in her event. Meanwhile, Maggie and Fred had decided to stay up a little later and sit in the lobby.

As they left the event room, Maggie said, "Sandra, I know you're very tired from the day's activities, so we'll see you in the morning at breakfast. Me and Fred will sit in the lobby for a while."

"Okay, you two, I'm heading in, and I'll see you at breakfast," Sandra replied.

As Sandra made her way to eventually get to her room, she passed her new coworker Charlotte and her guests and said her goodnights to them. Her focus turned to getting the toiletries she needed to make the remainder of the evening and night as pleasant as possible.

She chatted with her friends a little more while walking through the lobby towards the front desk. Her plan was to ask an attendant for directions to the gift shop.

Not long after her chat with the Mints, Sandra arrived at the front desk. While there she received lodging information from the hotel clerk, then got directions to her room. She also was given directions to the gift shop. Soon Sandra started on her way to her room, knowing that she would pass the gift shop on the way.

As Sandra began the journey to her room, it was evident that the ambiance of the hotel environment had changed dramatically. The activity and crowds that Sandra encountered when she first arrived early in the evening had ceased and now the hotel had become quiet. In the lobby only a few individuals lingered, apparently making their way to accommodations for the night.

-------SANDRA'S WALK TO HER HOTEL ROOM------

Sandra walked along a hallway where several small shops on either side had closed for the evening. Many of them had a showcase of items for purchase in large, well-lit display windows. Soft, classical background music had replaced the hustle and bustle of the crowded hotel earlier in the evening.

One establishment she passed displayed manikins neatly dressed in light clothing that she wished she could purchase, but the store had already closed. Sandra especially wanted overnight garb such as pajamas. She also saw clothes she could use as a change when she dressed for breakfast the next morning. But all these items could only be viewed through a large display window.

After passing the clothes store's window, she came to an equally well-illuminated showcase of a jewelry store. The items displayed there sparkled like the expensive jewels they were, and Sandra knew that she could not afford anything there. Before too long, Sandra finally arrived at the gift shop that had not yet closed. A sign next to the entrance indicated that closing time would be at 11:00. She reached the store's entrance only a few minutes before that time, so she had just made it and was the only patron in the place.

Sandra met an older lady who was obviously the caretaker and who seemed to be preparing for closing. But the lady saw Sandra approaching and remembered that the manager had been by earlier to let her know she would be there.

"Hello, madam," she said to Sandra as she entered the store.

"Hello. I'd like to see what you have," Sandra replied. "I can make my decision on a purchase in just a few minutes. I won't keep you from going home," Sandra reassured her.

The attendant replied, "Just go ahead and feel free to get what you need. The manager came by earlier and said you'd be here. You're Ms. Hughes, right?" she asked.

"That's right, Miss. I'm Sandra Hughes, and, like I said, I'll be only a few minutes."

Sandra picked up the toiletries that she needed, including some pajamas and a top to sleep in. She was about to pay for the items when the attendant said, "Don't worry about that, honey. The manager has put everything on the hotel's bill."

"Oh, yeah, I remember he did say that," Sandra replied. Then she wished the attendant a good evening before she left.

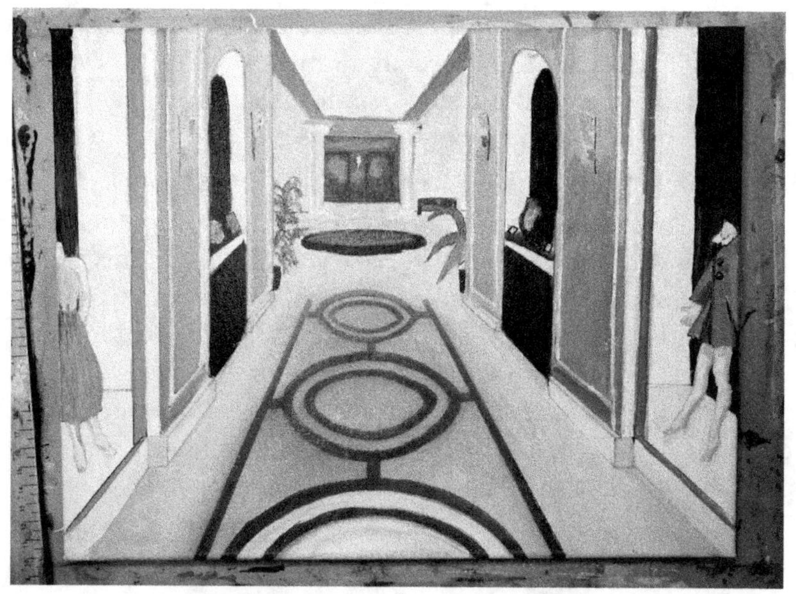

FIGURE 2: DARK HALLWAY

You will show me the path of life; In Your presence is fullness of joy; At Your right handare pleasures forevermore.

-
                              Psalm 16:11

--------A CALL FROM FREDDIE--------

Sandra started the walk to her room down a long, darkened hallway with only wall lamps beside each living quarter to illuminate her path. The stroll reflected her life at the time—she was in a dark place looking for the pleasures of love—not knowing that what she really needed resided deep down within her spirit. Nonetheless, she was confident that God would provide the right path for her. Freddie, whom she had just met, just might be the answer to her prayers – she thought.

Prior to Sandra arriving at her living quarters, she witnessed a hallway complete with artificial plants of all sorts and streams of flowing water—the essence of an interior water park.

As she continued to her room, she came upon several benches and decided to sit on one of them for a minute to examine what she had gotten from the gift shop. Her cell phone then rang, and, when she retrieved it from her purse, she was surprised to see that caller ID revealed that it was Freddie.

"Hello, Freddie. I'm surprised to hear from you," she said.

"Hello, Sandra. Sorry to be calling you so late at night. I guess you're wondering, why is this guy calling me so soon after we first met?"

"Yeah, that's right, Freddie. It's late. And we did just meet. But what I really want to know is how did you get my phone number? I know you gave me yours when you shook my hand and we said our goodbyes earlier this evening at the event, but I'm certain I never gave you mine."

Freddie responded to her concern, "Yes, I know, Sandra, but I just had to give you a call tonight since I'm leaving town early in the morning. So, I checked on the company website and found that all your contact information is there."

"You know what, Freddie? Since you mentioned it, I do remember now that one of the firm's previous administrators, Mr. Lockhart, stopped by our table after almost everyone had left, and, among other things, mentioned that the new hires' contact information usually is placed on the website. You had already left the table by then."

They continued their conversation for a while.

"It's good you called now," Sandra said, "because I'm almost in my room and I'm sure that I will go right to sleep once I get there. I've been up since early in the morning and didn't get much sleep the previous night because I had just come home from out of town."

Sandra said something else to Freddie that she was curious about. She asked, "speaking of being out of town, you said you're taking a trip tomorrow morning?"

Freddie replied, "Yeah, I have a cousin who owns a resort in Miami who invited me down to plan for a grand opening, so I wanted to take advantage of the time that I have off. You know, when I was called in earlier tonight to take the place of a coworker, I was packing for the trip. But I had to quickly switch gears and take the place of this other employee. I really didn't want to, but now I'm glad I did because otherwise I wouldn't have met you."

Sandra was exhausted when Freddie called and found it challenging to focus on what he had to say. But that last statement really perked her up. At first, Sandra did not know what to say after those kind remarks, then she finally thought of something.

"Well, that's sweet of you to say," she said. Then she talked about the coincidental circumstances of their meeting.

"You know, Freddie, it's rather interesting how we met, and not only that but the connections we have to each other through people we know. I mean, you know some of the same people that I do. I had no idea that you were acquainted with Maggie. She's never mentioned your name to me. And I think of her and me as being very close."

Sandra continued, "Anyway, you know how women are. We talk about a lot of things, and sometimes we let secrets out of the bag, you might say. We just have to be careful sometimes of what we say and who we say it to. You know what I mean?"

Boy, did Freddie know what she meant. He had to be careful not to reveal his rather personal association with Sandra's friend Maggie. With those thoughts in mind, he said, "Well, I do know. But sometimes it's best just to stay quiet and not talk a lot about the past, especially if that past hasn't been a good one."

Sandra responded, "I'm not sure if I understand what you're saying on that point. I mean, it's good to know some things about a new person that you've been introduced to, including the not so pleasant things. Now, let me ask you, do you know what *I* mean?" Sandra asked, in a cordial manner trying to turn the tables on Freddie.

"I believe I do, Sandra," Fred replied.

Then Sandra said, "Okay then Freddie. But as far as Maggie is concerned, I *do* know that she's a wonderful woman, a faithful wife to Fred. I mean, I don't think she would ever do anything to hurt him. You don't find those kinds of women often. Yeah, I think Fred is really fortunate to have her as his wife."

That last point was intriguing to Freddie, who knew all too well his romantic involvement with Maggie. But he played it safe without saying any more about the topic.

"Well, Freddie, this discussion is what a lot of women talk about all the time, you know, different things that women talk about. But I do know that Fred brags about Maggie every chance he gets, saying how faithful she is to him, and I believe he's faithful to her too. And the reason I say that is because there was a time when I actually was attracted to him."

Freddie interjected, "You're kidding. You had romantic feelings toward Fred?"

"Why, yes, Freddie. Why is that so hard to believe? Let me tell you, in my discussions with Maggie, she told me about how good he looked even on the basketball court. Yeah, that's right, he played a little basketball at the school they both attended when they first met—before he went to Hawaii when he graduated early. It's a long story, Freddie, but almost everyone believes that he was a good catch."

Freddie responded to what Sandra told him, "Well, well! A basketball star, huh?"

Sandra replied, "Yeah, that's right! He was very popular on campus, according to Maggie. Anyway, I guess it was just my flesh overwhelming my sense of judgment when I wanted to be with him. To be with Fred, I mean.

"But you know what, Freddie? He never took the bait. He remained true to Maggie because he knew she was true to him. They're just a wonderful couple. I'd be so upset with anyone who would try to break up such a happy marriage. I can only thank God that somehow I came to my senses."

Sandra's comments continued to echo in Freddie's mind, given his past with Maggie. But that relationship was over in his estimation ever since the dream he had about his wife and son being killed in an automobile accident. He was just now trying to get his life back together because they ended up being separated from each other. He hoped that Sandra might become a big part in his moving forward in life after that loss.

--------THE MIAMI / BERMUDA CONNECTION--------

Sandra continued, "My transformation, Freddie, really started when I made this trip to Bermuda and met a person who was the owner of a resort there. Her name is Erin, and she helped me change my life. It's interesting that your cousin also is an owner of a resort—in Miami."

Freddie replied, "Yeah, it's interesting that your friend is the owner of a resort. You know, my wife used to say that there are no coincidences in life, that God orchestrates everything, as she put it.

"You know, Sandra, I really do miss her. Oh, I forgot to tell you that I was married for a while, but I'm divorced now. And I have to tell you it's all my fault. I tried to explain to her a relationship that I had with another woman. But I guess she didn't want to hear it, so she packed up her things and moved out and took our little boy."

"I'm so sorry to hear about that, Freddie. If only the woman you were with knew how much pain she caused, I believe she should have had the courage to somehow make amends both to you and your wife. And I'm not letting you off the hook either, Freddie. I really think that you should have remained faithful to your wife. But I guess that's spilled milk as they say."

Freddie thought, *If only she knew that the woman I was seeing was Maggie.*

"Well, Sandra, you're right. I did something that I'm not proud of. I should have known better. But like you said, it's spilled milk, and there's nothing I can do about it now but to try to do better."

"Well, Sandra, I guess I need to go. No need to have a pity party. Besides, I only have a few hours left before I leave for the airport tomorrow morning to make my flight."

Before Freddie got off the phone, Sandra added, "Freddie, my friend Maggie said that she would be calling this friend of mine I was telling you about that I saw in Bermuda to tell her about the event earlier this evening. I'm sure she'll probably mention how far I've come since I was down there at her resort. Maybe I'll get her to tell you my story at some point. It's definitely a story you won't forget.

"Oh, well, anyway, I'm glad you called, Freddie, and I'm sure we'll be in touch."

Freddie said, "Okay, Sandra. Again, it was nice meeting you, and I would love hearing your story from her. But you know what? I would much rather hear it from you!

"And one more thing, I'd like for our friendship to continue. Who knows where it might lead!"

Sandra responded, "Freddie, you're really funny! Goodnight."

With that they ended their conversation.

-------ANOTHER PHONE CONVERSATION-------

After talking with Freddie, Sandra left the bench and headed to her room. After her long day and lengthy conversation with Freddie, she was ready for bed. But her rest would have to wait because of another phone conversation. The phone in her room rang before she could change for bed. After hesitating to answer it, Sandra gave in to see who was calling.

"Hey, Sandra," Maggie said as soon as she picked up the phone.

"Oh, hello, Maggie. I didn't expect to hear from you so soon." Then Maggie responded, "Well, me and Fred are still in the lobby. But I just wanted to tell you before you went to sleep that the event tonight was very nice. It was just a nice celebration of you and Charlotte becoming employed with the firm."

"Thanks, Maggie. I'm so glad you and Fred could come. And I was fortunate enough to have met someone too! I met Freddie and even got to know him a little bit. Anyway, Maggie, I guess I won't be seeing much of Freddie within the foreseeable future because he's going down to south Florida to visit a cousin of his who is starting a resort down there."

Maggie asked, "Sandra, didn't your friend Erin in Bermuda tell you she had a desire to relocate to south Florida?"

Sandra answered, "Yeah, Maggie, she did say that once, but I don't know how serious she was about it. I mean, she really loves what's she's doing there in Bermuda."

"Well, that's interesting," Maggie replied.

Sandra continued, "Like I said, Maggie, I got to know a little of his history – this guy Freddie I mean. And, believe me, he's had some issues, but he seems to be a nice person."

Maggie's eyes squinched when Sandra made that last statement, knowing that once she had the same feeling towards him. In fact, he was more than nice—she had a close romantic relationship with him.

Sandra continued, "You know he called me when I was walking to my room, and we had a deep conversation. It was only a few minutes ago. He told me about his wife and how she walked out on him because she felt that he was being unfaithful. Then I asked him if it was true. And he said it was, and he's had terrible feelings about it. And you know what I told him, Maggie? I said that he shouldn't have allowed that woman to mess up his marriage. I also told him that if I were his wife, I would have found that hussy and given her a piece of my mind.

"But you know what, Maggie? I also told him that he shouldered some of the blame. You know how that goes; it takes two to tangle as they say."

Maggie thought that was a lot of information to absorb, knowing that *she* was that woman Sandra was talking about. Maggie decided to abruptly end the call. She said, "Well, that's interesting. But I gotta go now, Sandra. I'll see you tomorrow."

"Okay, Maggie. I can't wait to get in that bed," Sandra said and ended the conversation.

After that, all Sandra could do was to flop on the bed—clothes on and all. She didn't even bother to turn the TV on or to put on the pajamas and top she got from the gift shop. She just brushed her teeth, lay across the bed, and went to sleep.

--------JENSEN'S PUB--------

After her phone conversation with Sandra, Maggie and Fred had ventured over to a comfy couch in the lobby to sit a while.

Fred said, "Hey, Mag, had Sandra gotten to her room when you called her?"

Maggie answered, "Yeah, Fred; she had just gotten there."

Fred said, "While you were arranging for our room earlier, I was talking with the concierge about interesting places to visit around the hotel, and he mentioned that right next door is a place called Jensen's Pub, a spot he said is perfect for casual dining with an assortment of mixed drinks. It's only a short walk from here."

Fred continued, "You know, Mag, we've had a great dinner at the event, and based on what the concierge was saying, this place would be perfect just to go and chill out for a few minutes—maybe for a half hour or so. What do ya think?"

"Sounds good to me, Fred," Maggie replied.

Fred was a social drinker; he loved an occasional rum with Coke over ice or orange juice and vodka. He found that these drinks stimulated him, assisting his mind to relax, which was certainly what he needed after the event of the evening. He still could not get over Sandra's fascination with Freddie and saw an opportunity to express those feelings to Maggie. Jensen's Pub would be a perfect place to do that in his estimation.

Although Maggie was not a drinker of alcoholic beverages, she remembered the time when Fred proposed to her at the Lamour near Fred's condo in downtown Chicago. The champagne they consumed at that restaurant made her tipsy, and it took her a while to become level-headed again. At any rate, Maggie decided to go with Fred to the pub and consider her own feelings about seeing Freddie again—with another woman, her friend Sandra.

"Fred, let me run to the room and get a jacket, and I'll get one for you too. I know you said it's not a long distance away, but *it is* outside and it's pretty cool out there," Maggie said.

"Okay, Mag. Like I said, it's only a short walk, but that's a good idea to get a jacket."

Maggie quickly got their jackets, and soon they were on their way to the pub as Fred had been directed to go by the concierge. As they had figured, the walk was short, but the air was brisk, typical of an evening in Detroit during the early fall.

Soon Maggie and Fred entered the pub, where they were met by several TV screens mounted on the walls—some larger than others. Regardless of where customers were sitting, a set was in clear view. Programs were being shown from sporting events to talk shows. They were two of the few patrons in the establishment at that late hour and were guided by an attendant to a booth where a miniature TV was on the wall between them in a cozy and intimate spot.

Once comfortably seated, they were offered a menu, and Fred said to a server, "Young lady, things are really slowing down around here, huh?"

"Yes sir. It was really crowded in here only a little while ago, but as you said things are slowing down now. But we'll be open for another hour."

Fred said, "Well, we don't need a regular menu because we're not getting any food. Do you have a beverage menu?"

"Yes, we do," the server responded handing Fred the drink menu. "Here it is. You can look over it and I'll be back in a minute to take your order."

Fred reviewed it and, by the time the server had returned, he was ready to order. Maggie looked at the menu as well, but she decided not to order anything. After Fred placed his order, it was not long before the server returned and delivered Fred's drink, plus an iced tea for Maggie along with some chips. The server didn't want her to be excluded from having refreshments.

She said, "I decided to bring you a little something too, Miss. I didn't want you to be sitting here and just watching your friend sip on his drink. It's on the house!"

"Thank you," Maggie responded.

Now, Fred and Maggie were ready to discuss the night's festivities and, more specifically, Sandra's involvement with Freddie. As for Maggie herself, thoughts about that connection were more personal. There was a constant battle between her flesh, still wanting to be with Freddie, and her spirit, which led her to avoid such a relationship.

Maggie really wanted to know more about Freddie's current personal life, which he apparently felt comfortable telling Sandra about. Maggie planned to get more information about his life one way or the other—most likely from Sandra. As she sat there with Fred, she experienced an ongoing conflict between her worldly thoughts about a past relationship with her former workmate and her genuine interest in what her husband had to say about him.

FIGURE 3: JENSEN'S PUB

Elijah came near to all the people and said, "How long will you hesitate between two opinions? If the Lord is God, follow Him; but if Baal, follow him." But the people did not answer a word.

- 1 Kings 18:21

--------MAGGIE ON THE PHONE-------

As Fred and Maggie waited for their refreshments, an interesting story that was advertised only moments earlier appeared on the TV where they were sitting and immediately captured even more of Fred's attention. It was a talk show with one of the leading authors in the country discussing the secrets of his success in self-publishing and the various methods of book publishing. Given his interest in writing, Fred was glued to the TV screen.

Maggie had no interest at all in the topic. One of her secret peeves with Fred was that he often paid more attention to his writing endeavors than he did to her. At that moment, Fred halted between two decisions: to converse with his wife as planned or be diverted to an outside interest of his – that of being an author. He chose the latter.

With Fred tied to the TV, Maggie saw this lull in the conversation as an opportunity to go into the lounge to make the phone call to Erin that she had planned to do. She looked forward to discussing the events involving Sandra earlier in the evening.

"Excuse me, Fred. I see that you're glued to this TV program, so I'm going into the lounge to make a phone call to Sandra's friend Erin in Bermuda," Maggie said.

While still staring at the TV, Fred said, "Okay, Mag. I'll be here when you get back."

A unique feature of this pub was that in the front lobby there were small booths on the side with a chair in them for people to have a degree of privacy while comfortably making phone calls. What made it so special this time was that no one else was around in the lobby, so Maggie had the whole area to herself and could speak as loudly as she wanted.

As Maggie sat in a booth near the front entrance, she began to dial Erin's number. Immediately Erin received the call and answered, "Hello."

"Hello, Erin."

"Oh, Maggie, I'm so glad that you called," Erin said, immediately recognizing Maggie's voice.

Erin was so glad to hear from her friend and said with a bit of emotion, "Maggie, I'm really happy to hear from you. How have you been doing?"

Maggie answered, "Oh, I've been fine, Erin."

"And I'm so sorry for calling you late like this – I know it's after midnight there in Bermuda where you are. "But I believe you'd like to know what's happening with your girl, Sandra." "No worries about the time Maggie – I'm usually up late at night anyway.

"So how is she doing these days? I haven't heard from her much since she left Bermuda."

"Well, she's been doing well. As a matter of fact, she's gotten a new job, one with higher pay and more benefits," Maggie told her.

"Well, praise the Lord! I'm glad to hear that," Erin said.

"Yeah, Erin, she's doing really well."

Erin continued, "You know, Maggie, I can tell that God is continuing to work in Sandra's life."

"You're right, Erin. God has been very good to Sandra. And let me give you an example of something that happened to her just over the past day. And it involved a dream I had about Sandra earlier this morning. But let me tell you how it all started, Erin. It seems like a long time ago, but it was just last night when I had another dream—before the one I just told you I had earlier this morning.

"Well, the dream I had before that one, last night after I went to sleep, was a wonderful dream with a lot of detail. It was about me going on a cruise with some friends of mine, including Sandra, to see you there in Bermuda. It was such an exciting trip. It seemed so real. And one of the things I clearly recalled was you saying that one day you'd like to move from there to a place that's similar here in the U.S."

Maggie continued, "In the dream I remember you telling Sandra that you had a desire to go to south Florida. Now, Erin, that's a miracle in itself because of me having a dream where you expressed a desire that you actually told Sandra about months before at your resort in Bermuda. I know because she told me so. Now that's amazing."

Erin replied, "Yeah, Maggie, you're right. I do remember talking to Sandra briefly about that when she was here. And, yeah, that *is* amazing—the fact that you had a dream about something me and Sandra had talked about months earlier. I guess you kept that in your subconscious until it came out in the dream you had."

Maggie went on to tell Erin, "But, yeah, Erin, Sandra told me some of the things you two talked about and what she experienced when she visited you at your resort. She told me about the three signs and all, the signs she said you encouraged her to look for, and the both of you ended up seeing those signs before she left and flew back to Detroit. As you know those signs were about seeing stars in the sky and sand on the beach. Sandra declares that seeing those signs was the key to her healing. But more than that, she said that you stressed the importance of simply believing what the scripture says *about* your healing—that we're already healed if we believe!"

"You're exactly right, Maggie. And now I have to believe the same thing for my desires in the same manner that she believed for her physical as well as for her spiritual healing. I think I told her I would be doing that before she left, believing that my desires will somehow materialize. I guess that's how she knew I had a desire to relocate to south Florida."

Then Maggie said, "Erin, that's what I want to get to, and that's about your desires being met."

"Well, go ahead; please tell me about it. I do want my desires met, girl!"

"Well," Maggie said, "like I said I had a dream about Sandra earlier this morning. In the dream she called me when I was getting up to make Fred some breakfast, and in the process I woke my husband up.

"The amazing thing, Erin, after I *did* wake up moments later, like in the dream I had earlier, I was going to make Fred some breakfast. And a short time later when me and Fred were having that breakfast, the phone rang for real and when I answered it, I found it was Sandra.

"That's right, Erin! Sandra called for real after I dreamed about her calling minutes earlier! Anyway, during the actual call, she told me she was inviting me and Fred to this special event for new hires that ended up happening earlier this evening. Yeah, all of this happened in just one day when I had a dream of Sandra calling me and telling me she had found a job, and, later after I woke up, she actually called me to tell me the same thing. Now that's incredible, Erin!"

After Maggie's description of what she dreamed, Erin said, "That *is* amazing Maggie. It's amazing how God can show us things through dreams. And your dream was so synchronized; everything seemed to fit together. I mean, how you dreamed about her calling and telling you about a job she had gotten, and then, after you woke up, she actually *did* call and told you the same thing. My, my, my! Now, Maggie, you know God works in mysterious ways His wonders to perform, I think it says somewhere in the scriptures."

Then Erin continued, "Yeah, that was a miraculous thing you experienced, Maggie, that involved Sandra, although a part of it was only in a dream. But what makes it so eerie is that the other part of this experience went beyond what you dreamed about. It became reality when you woke up. Awesome!

"But, Maggie, while your dream experience is all very interesting, I still don't see how that relates to my situation," Erin said.

"Well, hang on, Erin; let me tell you. When Sandra called and told me about her new job, she invited me and Fred to this event that honored her and another new hire the company made. I won't get into all of the details, but we ended up going to the event, and that's when Sandra met an old friend of mine that I used to work with.

"And by the way, that's another story that I won't get into right now. But, anyway, when the event was over, which was only earlier tonight, I talked with Sandra on the phone, and she told me about how my old friend mentioned to her an upcoming trip he had to visit a cousin of his in Miami who is starting a new resort in that area. That's when I thought of you.

"So, there you have it, Erin. You now have a contact in southern Florida in the Miami area. Well, let me rephrase that. You don't have the contact yet, but I'll talk with Freddie—that's his name—who is an acquaintance of Sandra and see if I can get you together with the contact he knows in south Florida, who happens to be his cousin. And that's where you come in. His cousin is starting this new resort in that area. And that's the main contact I'm talking about, Freddie's cousin who's starting a new resort in south Florida."

---------**WOW!**---------

After hearing what Maggie had to say, Erin could only say, "Wow!"

"Yeah, Erin, that was my reaction when I first heard it—at least in my spirit at the time—and I can sense that same excitement in you," Maggie said. "Listen, Erin, this is what I'll do. I'll try to get Freddie's cousin's number in south Florida. Then I can give it to you, but I can also give *your* number to Freddie so that he can in turn give it to his cousin. Do you see what I'm saying? Then hopefully, his cousin will be interested enough to give you a call. But don't worry: I'll also enlighten Freddie about your professional background as a resort manager. I'm sure he'll tell his cousin about that. So with all that information about your credentials as well as your number, the odds are that he'll give you a call, Freddie's cousin, I mean."

Erin replied, "Yeah, Maggie, I do see what you're saying. And I think that's great. Yeah. I hope you do get his contact information because I'd love to talk to him about possibilities."

Maggie responded, "Okay, so I'll do that. And by the way, in addition to me giving Freddie your number, I'll give you his number, so you can call him if you'd like. In that way, you'll increase the chances of making contact with his cousin down in south Florida. If you can reach him, who knows what might happen."

"Thanks so much, Maggie, for your help in making this contact," Erin said. "Yes, I remember telling Sandra that I had a desire to go to south Florida. Of course, the main thing we were talking about at the time was her desire to get well; in seeking that, she drew closer to God while she was here."

"Yeah, Erin. Sandra told me all about her experience with you in Bermuda, and it was quite a testimony," Maggie said. "To be honest about it, my mother told me a lot about the experience Sandra had because Sandra gave her a lot of the details, and my mother just transmitted some of that information to me. I'm sure you're aware that Sandra and my mother as well as my father were very close."

--------MAGGIE'S INDISCRETIONS--------

Erin digressed for a moment and asked, "Now where were you while Sandra was spending so much time with your parents, Maggie?"

Instead of answering the question, Maggie wanted to quickly return to the good news she had for Erin and her prospects of relocating to south Florida. She wanted to avoid any thought of where she was much of the time when she was not at her parents' house when Sandra was there; she was well aware that she was with Freddie during much of that time.

Maggie said to Erin, "When I used to come up from Chicago, I spent a lot of time shopping in Detroit instead of going to Flint where my parents lived. And I'm so grateful for Sandra helping me during that time."

Maggie tried to redirect Erin's focus in their discussion, saying, "Getting back to your desire to be in south Florida, though, I think that contact I've been talking about is for real—genuine. You two only have to get together at some point."

Erin replied, "That's great, Maggie. I'm looking forward to communicating with that contact."

After giving Erin the information on the contact in south Florida and managing to avoid mentioning her personal relationship with Freddie, Maggie concluded the conversation by saying, "Well, I think I'll be going now. It was so nice talking to you again, Erin. I'm actually sitting with my husband at this small food place not very far from the hotel where we're staying. We're just chilling out for a few minutes, but we'll be returning to our hotel room soon. And I'll get back to you in a day or so to give you Freddie's phone number. Like I said, hopefully you'll be able to contact his cousin in Miami."

"I'm so glad that you called, Maggie," Erin said. "I'll always appreciate the help you're giving me."

"Well, let me go. Nice talking to you and we'll talk later," Maggie concluded.

"Okay, Maggie. Bye now and thanks again for everything that you're doing. Bye," Erin said.

With those last words, the two ended their conversation. Maggie hoped that would put an end to her thoughts about what happened so many weekends when she was not at her parents' house but rather having indiscretions with Freddie.

Maggie soon returned to Fred and hoped the program he was watching when she left him minutes earlier had ended.

--------RETURN TO THE ROOM--------

When Maggie returned to the booth where Fred sat, she *did* find that the program had ended. And she thanked God for that! When she arrived, Fred was sitting in his seat with eyes closed, probably somewhere between sleep and wakefulness.

"Fred, Fred," Maggie called hoping to stir him. She quickly got his attention.

Groggily, Fred said, "Oh, Mag. I guess I dozed off."

"I've finished my little talk with Erin. Now let's go to the room and get some sleep," Maggie said.

They left the pub with the iced tea and chips the waiter had brought for her still untouched. Soon they were back in their room, and they both got a well-deserved, good night's sleep.

--------THE NEXT MORNING--------

Morning finally came for all those involved with the event the previous night. For Sandra had gotten a sound sleep still wearing the gown she had donned for the event. She awakened early in the morning, which gave her time enough to catch some of the news. She decided to wait until 8:00 a.m. to leave the room since the shop where she saw the clothes displayed in the large window was due to open then.

A few minutes after that time, Sandra made a quick run to the shop to get something to wear for the day. When she returned to the room, she showered, put on her new clothing, and then headed to breakfast. Sandra planned to return to her apartment later in the day. But first she would meet Maggie and Fred once more.

Maggie and Fred slept until just past 9:00 that morning when Maggie was awakened by a phone call. As had happened the previous morning, Sandra called her while she still was in bed.

"Hey, Maggie. I hope you and Fred had a good night's sleep."

"Thanks, Sandra," Maggie replied. "I hope you slept well yourself."

"Yes, Maggie. I slept well," she said. "I've been up for a while. I read the paper and am now getting myself ready to go over to have breakfast. Will you be ready to eat in about an hour? At around 10:00?"

Maggie responded, "Sandra, it may take us that long to get out of bed, then another hour to get dressed. How about we meet you at 11:00?"

"That's fine, Maggie. I'll see you then," Sandra said.

Maggie and Fred stayed in bed a little while longer, then took turns getting up and dressed for the day. They soon were ready to make their way to the dining area for breakfast.

--------MAGGIE, FRED, AND SANDRA--------

When Maggie and Fred arrived in the dining room, they saw Sandra sipping a cup of coffee.

"Good morning, Sandra," Maggie said as she and Fred approached her table.

"Hello, Maggie. Hello, Fred," she greeted them.

"Sandra, let me run over here and get my coffee," Maggie told her.

Maggie went away and left Fred and Sandra alone to talk for a while.

"How do you feel the morning after your big event last evening?" Fred asked.

Sandra answered, "Everything was great, Fred. And Maggie's comments about me were very touching.

"You know, Fred, you two have meant so much to me that I can't even measure it. Anything I can do for you, just let me know."

Fred interjected, "I'm glad you feel that way, because I want to talk to you about something that's going to be really special, and it involves Maggie. I'll just get with you a little later here in the lobby and tell you about it—to fill you in on the details."

Sandra replied, "Oh sure, Fred. Like I said, anything for you two." Sandra then got more personal with Fred, adding, "And, Fred, you know how special *you* are. I'd like to think that we have a special relationship. I'll give you a little signal—with the wink of an eye—when I think it'll be the best time to get together or if there's something I think we need to talk about."

Maggie returned from getting her coffee and said, "Did I hear something about a relationship?"

"Oh, yeah, Mag, I was telling Sandra that you have to be careful that you develop healthy relationships and be aware of who you are involved with," Fred said.

Maggie said, "I'm sorry, Fred, but I thought I heard Sandra talking."

Fred replied, "Well, Mag, we both were talking about the subject."

Not being entirely truthful about the nature of their conversation, in an indirect way Fred was trying to divert attention away from any notion of a special relationship he may have had with Sandra. At the same time, he wanted to suggest an uneasiness he had about her involvement with Freddie and to let her know about being aware, as he put it, of the people she might be being involved with at any given time.

Maggie responded to Fred's description of their conversation by saying, "Okay, Fred. I'll accept that, honey."

Sandra, being perceptive about that last comment Fred had made to Maggie, said, "Yeah, Fred, I realize that you have to be careful. But sometimes I think God brings people into our lives, and I think that's what happened when I met Freddie last night."

Looking for confirmation, Sandra added, "Maggie, don't you agree that God sometimes brings people into our lives for our own benefit?"

Maggie replied, "Yeah, you're right, Sandra. But Fred has a point too. At the same time, you need to be careful who you develop a relationship with these days. You need to make sure you know their history. Because men—sometimes they can be deceptive because they're so eager to get what they want."

Fred interjected, "You know, Mag, that works for women too!"

"Of course, it does, honey," Maggie said.

--------FREDDIE ON THEIR MINDS--------

In some way, the whole discussion centered around Freddie even though none of them mentioned his name. After they placed their breakfast order, Sandra asked a more direct question, sensing that Freddie was among their thoughts.

"Is this discussion about Freddie, the fellow I met last night?"

Maggie and Fred looked at one another, not really wanting to answer. Seeing their hesitation, Sandra took the initiative and said, "I think he's a nice fellow. And, Maggie, you said you used to work with him at the firm?"

Maggie replied, "Yeah, we've seen each other." She chose her words carefully to avoid giving any information about their intimate association in the presence of Fred. Nonetheless, the discussion immediately brought to Fred's memory the time Maggie called that name, Freddie, in her sleep. At the time it happened, he had dismissed the incident, assuming she simply extended his own name while not conscious of it.

At that point Fred said, "Let me go and get some coffee too. I could use some right about now, and I'll go to the smoking area to light up my cigar for a little bit before I come back." So that's what he did, leaving Maggie and Sandra at the table to continue their conversation about Freddie.

As they sat alone together for a little while, Maggie felt this was an opportunity to give Sandra more detailed information about Freddie than she was willing to do in the presence of Fred.

"Sandra, I was really touched by those comments you made about me and Fred at last evening's event. I was so proud of you."

"Well, Maggie, you deserved every one of those accolades."

Maggie continued, "You know, Sandra, Erin had just as much to do with your success as I have. She really did a lot to renew your mind and your spirit when you went to Bermuda."

"I certainly know that, Maggie; she practically saved my life," Sandra confirmed. "But it was your parents, Mensie and Matthew, who took me in like I was their own child—and you accepted that, Maggie."

Maggie finally got to what she really wanted to talk to her friend about in the absence of Fred. And the topic of discussion would be Freddie.

"Okay, Sandra, let me talk about what I really want you to digest. Let me start by telling you something that's been bothering me for a while. And it concerns Freddie. You know, he was a friend of mine at the firm when I was working there and a very good friend at that."

Sandra replied, "So you knew him well?"

"Yes, Sandra, I knew him quite well," Maggie replied, stopping short of implying a romantic relationship.

"I'm telling you this because I want the best for you and, at the same time, I want to keep my peace about the situation," Maggie said. She went on to say, "I won't go into that any further, but I've grown to appreciate what Erin did for you as well as for my mother indirectly through you. I mean, my mother knew a lot more about your relationship with Erin than I will ever now, like what you were talking about a minute ago," Maggie said. She was referring to the details that her mother Mensie gave her about Sandra's time in Bermuda, information Mensie received from Sandra herself.

Not being totally clear about what Maggie was trying to say, Sandra asked her more directly, "So what are you saying, Maggie?" Sandra was totally confused.

Then Maggie said, "Let me get to the point then. Because of the change I've seen in you, I've been much more appreciative of Erin and what she did for you when you were in Bermuda. Sandra, you've said often that Erin is the most faithful person that you've met. And that's the main reason why she was able to connect with you on a spiritual level and be an important part of your recovery when you were sick. And I can tell, you've changed a lot as far as the whole person is concerned, and you owe a lot to Erin for that," Maggie stressed.

"Well, Sandra, Erin has said she had a hidden desire of going to south Florida, not to visit but to actually relocate. To be frank about it, I wouldn't mind relocating there myself one day. Anyway, the thought came to mind that Freddie's cousin would be a good person for Erin to connect with, to see what possibilities there might be in her hooking up with him—since she's in the resort business herself."

"I see what you mean, Maggie. Say no more. I told Freddie that I'd be getting back with him later this week. But this idea gives me even more reason to get in touch with him sooner," she said to Maggie.

At that point Fred returned from smoking his cigar. With assurance that Sandra would talk to Freddie about Erin, connecting her with his cousin, Maggie soon ate a hefty breakfast with Fred and Sandra. After continuing to chat while eating, they eventually headed back to their rooms to pack their belongings and check out of the hotel.

--------SANDRA CALLS FREDDIE--------

It didn't take long for Sandra to give Freddie a call. He had encouraged her the night before to give him a call after he arrived in Miami, and his plane landed shortly before noon Eastern Time. Sandra returned to her apartment in the early afternoon and called him.

After only a couple of rings, Freddie, who was on his way to the resort, answered, "Hello!"

"Hello, Freddie! Just calling as we had talked about."

"Oh, Sandra, I sure was hoping you would call. You've been on my mind ever since I left you last night," he told her.

"Well, I hope you're doing well. You know, last evening I really had a good time. So, where are you now? Have you arrived at the hotel yet?" she asked.

"I'm almost there," he said. "I got an Uber and it's some distance from the airport."

After about a minute or two, Freddie added, "Sandra, I've just arrived and am about to get out and take my luggage to the room. Could you call back in a few minutes?"

"Sure, Freddie," she said.

After they ended their brief conversation, she went about doing some chores before calling him again.

About an hour later, Sandra called Freddie again.

"Hello, Sandra," he said. "I expected you to call back sooner."

"Well, I got tied up doing chores. Sorry for the delay.

"No, that's fine. I've been here for a while now just trying to get adapted to new surroundings."

"You know it's so much warmer down here than it is in Detroit, but I guess that's what you'd expect."

"Yeah, I kinda wish I were there now. I really do like warm weather."

Freddie replied, "Well then, why don't you come on down?"

"Now, Freddie, you know that's not possible, not right now anyway."

"I was just kidding, Sandra, even though it would be nice for you to be here with me," Freddie said.

"You're moving a little fast aren't you, Freddie?"

"Sorry, I guess you're right," he said. "Listen, what about this idea that your friend—Erin I believe you said her name is—might want to visit the area. And she's the owner of a resort in Bermuda?"

Sandra answered, "Yeah, Freddie; she mentioned to me that at some point she would like to move to south Florida. She said she just didn't have any connections down there."

Sandra continued, "You know, you just mentioned something that I had planned to talk to you about. Since your cousin's resort will be there in Miami, Maggie wanted me to mention to you about getting your cousin and our friend Erin together some time."

Freddie replied, "Well, I certainly can ask him about it. I know he's the owner, but I don't think he wants to be in charge of the day-to-day operations of it. But let me find out," he assured Sandra.

"Oh, that would be great, Freddie. I'll be looking to hear from you tonight after you talk to him, and then I'll be able to give Erin some news on it. I'm sure Maggie will be excited about it too."

Freddie responded, "Okay, I'll call you later tonight once I finish talking to him."

Sandra asked, "So what's your schedule like now that you've arrived in south Florida?"

"Well, now that I'm in my room on the premises of my cousin's resort, I'll relax a little and then see my cousin later this afternoon. We'll probably have dinner, and then he'll show me as much of the resort as possible later tonight. After we do that, I'll call you and give some positive news, I hope, and then go to bed."

"I'm really looking forward to him telling me what kind of arrangements he plans to make in running the place down here. After all, it's one of the reasons I'm here. I guess I'm mixing business with pleasure."

That last bit of information coming from Freddie meant a lot to Sandra because it would give her an opportunity to bring her friend

Erin into the conversation again and further discuss her desires to move to the area as well as her experience in running a resort.

Freddie continued, "Yeah, Sandra, as far as your friend Erin connecting with my cousin, I'm not sure how the two might connect, but I'll find out a lot more on that when I talk to him later. Like I said, I'll give you a call—I'd say around 10:00 tonight before I go to bed. I'm pretty sure by then I'll have some information for you," he told Sandra.

"That's great, Freddie," Sandra replied. "Well, I know you have lots to do, so I'll be looking to hear from you later tonight. Bye."

"Bye," Freddie replied to end the conversation.

--------AN EXPECTED CALL--------

As the evening grew later, Sandra waited patiently for Freddie to return her call with some good news regarding his cousin's interest in having Erin with him in Miami to help in starting his new resort.

Freddie expected to talk with his cousin Sinbad and get information about his resort that he later would give to Sandra. He did not have a lot of interest in it himself except for helping his cousin and enjoying a few days away from the wintry conditions back in Detroit. His focus was on making Sandra happy, because he was really interested in her becoming a friend—perhaps more than just a friend.

Freddie met his cousin Sinbad in the lobby of the hotel. After some casual conversation, Freddie finally mentioned Sandra and her friend's desire to come to south Florida.

"Sinbad, like I said at first, I'm really looking forward to seeing your resort down here, but a friend of mine back in Detroit referred me to a friend of hers who would like to relocate down here in south Florida."

Sinbad responded before he could finish, saying, "That's good, Freddie, but how does that involve me?"

"Well, according to my friend in Detroit, her friend, who lives in Bermuda, has a resort there. That is, she's the manager of a resort, and she would like to move down here."

"That's interesting," Sinbad replied. "I've been looking for someone to head up this place. So, yeah, give me your friend's contact information and maybe I can call her. Better still, maybe I can call this friend of hers who is a resort manager in Bermuda."

"That's great, Sinbad! I'll let my friend know. I'll give her a call when I get back to the room," Freddie told his cousin.

-------BREARER OF GOOD NEWS-------

Before long after Freddie's talk with his cousin Sinbad, the 10:00 hour had arrived, the time he said he would call Sandra. Most importantly, he had gotten all the information he felt he needed to give her some news about his cousin's willingness to meet her friend Erin and to consider her to be a partner with him in running his new resort.

In his short talk with his cousin, Freddie learned a lot about the resort for his own purpose, which was to take advantage of everything that it had to offer during his short stay there. He only wished Sandra was there to enjoy it with him. But Sinbad also gave him the indication that he would consider Maggie's friend, Erin, to help him in managing his new resort. Freddie was eager to give that information to Sandra.

-------FREDDIE CALLS SANDRA-------

Freddie called Sandra just after 10:00 p.m.

"Hello, Sandra," he said. "How was your afternoon?"

Sandra replied, "It was fine, Freddie, but I have to admit I've been on pins and needles, waiting for you to return my call. I'll be phoning Maggie when I finish talking with you, and hopefully I'll have some good news for her to transmit to Erin."

Freddie began to wonder about the relationship both Sandra and Maggie had with Erin. That thought prompted him to ask, "While I'm talking with you, Sandra, let me ask you something. I'm confused. Over the last day or so I've heard you talk about your friend Erin a lot. It's obvious you two had a great relationship while you were in Bermuda. Well, I was just wondering, why do you have to get Maggie to call her? Why don't you call her yourself and give her the good news?"

Sandra responded to Freddie's concerns by saying, "Well, Freddie, you really don't understand the relationship among us three. Erin is important to me, again, because she was the key to my regaining my physical strength. Through her encouragement, I was able to gain the faith that I think led to my healing both physically and spiritually.

"But the truth of the matter is that Maggie, in a certain way, is just as important. And I say that because Maggie took me in as her sister when I was being contrary in a lot of ways even with her. And what I mean by that is, like I said earlier to you, Freddie, I did have romantic feelings towards her husband Fred at one time. But because of my experience in Bermuda with Erin, I was able to overcome those feelings—with the help and guidance of God, of course.

"So, I owe Maggie—not to mention her late mother and father—a lot of gratitude. I wouldn't dare take away the enjoyment she would feel by telling Erin myself the good news that I hope you will tell me after I stop talking," Sandra said in conclusion.

"Well, I must say that's interesting, Sandra. I really respect you for that."

She was anxious to hear what Freddie had to say about his cousin's willingness to meet and, more importantly, to work professionally with Erin in south Florida at his resort. Freddie finally gave her the information she was hoping to hear.

"Well," Freddie continued, "let me tell you about the conversation I had with my cousin Sinbad. I did talk to him about Erin—about the things you told me about her and her desire to move to south Florida. And I also mentioned her qualifications in resort management. Sinbad said he would be happy to talk to her. And not only that, if things go well, he said he'd be able to assist her in moving from Bermuda to here, to the resort."

Sandra replied excitedly, "Oh, that's great, Freddie! I could just kiss you right now!"

"Well then, just go ahead," he encouraged her in jest since their conversation over the phone would not allow that.

Sandra said, "Now Freddie, you know that's not possible."

Nevertheless, Sandra imagined his embrace and perhaps a kiss on the cheek. For now, however, because of their physical distance from each other, she had to be content with her imagination and hope that at least a casual relationship would ensue with Freddie.

--------A SERVENT'S REWARD--------

After her phone conversation with Freddie, Sandra knew that God had rewarded His servant Erin for her dedication in transforming her life.

The good news being transmitted to Erin had not manifested itself—yet. But it would. It would be a servant's reward.

Sandra knew that the good news Erin was looking for would soon be delivered. She only had to call Maggie to let her know what Sinbad said to Freddie regarding the prospects of Erin joining him in south Florida. She assumed that Maggie would call Erin as she said she would to let her know of the good news. At this point, it seemed as though everything was done with the expectation that Erin's desire to be in south Florida would soon materialize.

CHAPTER FOUR
GOD'S DEMANDS

Maggie was relieved at the good news she had been told by Sandra and felt thankful that Sinbad was considering Erin to work for him at his resort. Given Freddie's optimistic report to Sandra, Maggie wanted to call Erin right away to share this news.

--------MAGGIE CALLS ERIN--------

After several rings, Maggie started to become apprehensive about phoning her so late in the night. She was about to hang up when a groggy voice answered, "Hello."

"Hello, Erin," Maggie said with excitement in her voice.

Upon hearing that it was Maggie, Erin perked up and said, "Oh, hello, Maggie. Sorry if I'm not levelheaded right now; I just woke up from a deep sleep. How are you doing tonight?" she asked.

"I'm find, Erin," Maggie replied. "Listen, I know you're sleepy, so I don't want to keep you up long. I just wanted to tell you that Sandra talked to the fellow she met at the event I was telling you about—Freddie—and he said that his cousin, who is starting a resort in Miami, was willing to talk to you about possibly running his resort."

Erin quickly became fully awake and said, "Am I hearing you right, Maggie? You found a connection for me in south Florida?"

"Yes, Erin," Maggie replied. "And I'll tell you what, based on what your friend and mine, Sandra, told me about him, as told to her by her friend Freddie, this cousin of his seems to be a fine fellow who is definitely looking for someone to run his resort. Erin, it seems to be a perfect fit for you."

Erin replied, "Maggie, Lord knows how I've prayed for something like this to happen. Don't get me wrong; I have enjoyed being here in Bermuda. It's a special place for me. And it's extremely special because of my experience with Sandra when she was here. I'm just on an emotional high right now, Maggie."

"I know you are quite emotional about it, Erin. That's why I wanted to tell you—so I could feel some of that excitement I knew you would have. Well, listen, Erin, I just wanted to call and tell you that. I know the Lord will direct your actions from this point, just like He's done in the past. But what I want you to do is to call Freddie's cousin. Freddie wanted to make sure I tell you that it's fine to bypass him and talk directly to his cousin. Freddie seems to believe that things can move along a lot faster that way."

Maggie gave Freddie's cousin's phone number to Erin and then ended their conversation.

Erin couldn't go back to sleep because the good news made her feel excited about the future. She tossed and turned for the remainder of the night and couldn't wait for the morning to come when she would give Freddie's cousin Sinbad a call.

--------ERIN AND SINBAD ON THE PHONE--------

Usually when Erin would wake up in the morning, she would get a cup of strongly brewed coffee. On this day, however, she avoided her morning pleasure to make sure she called Freddie's cousin about coming to Miami to help run his resort. Erin called Sinbad using the number Maggie had given her. The phone rang once; then on the second ring someone answered, and she heard a voice say, "Hello. Who am I speaking with?"

Erin replied, "My name is Erin and I was referred to you by your cousin in Detroit, Freddie. I assume this is Sinbad, a cousin of Freddie. Is that you?"

"Oh, yes, I'm Sinbad, Freddie's cousin, and he told me about you. And I've been expecting your call," he said.

"Well then, I guess you know what I'm calling about," Erin said. "I was talking to a friend of mine and she said that your cousin told a friend of hers that I might be of some help to you and the start of your resort there in Miami."

Sinbad replied, "Why, yes, my cousin Freddie told me about you, and I was impressed with your work in managing your resort there in Bermuda."

"Well, listen, we're having a big event here in three weeks, and I'm going to connect everyone who might be involved in this venture and that certainly would include you. I could make hotel reservations for you here at the resort if you like. Just let me go over some things, and I'll get back to you with the specifics."

Erin said, "That sounds great. The next week will give me enough time to prepare things here in Bermuda for the few days that I'll be away."

Sinbad replied, "Good; I'll get back in a few days. And, again, it was good talking with you, and I hope things will work out."

"Thank you, sir, and I will look forward to your call," Erin responded. And with that, the conversation ended.

By the end of the week, Sinbad *did* call Erin again and gave her the specifics as he had promised.

Erin responded to his ideas, saying, "That's great, sir,"

Sinbad interjected, "Just call me Sinbad."

"Okay, Sinbad. I'll book a flight for the day before the event, and I should arrive by that afternoon

"That's good. I'll have a friend of mine, Casey, come to pick you up at the airport. Just make sure you confirm the time that you will arrive. Again, with the event being on Saturday, if you arrive that Friday, we can have dinner that evening and go over some of the details. We can meet in the hotel's dining area at 9:00. It will need to be brief, because I will have an important business meeting out of town the next morning. But anyway, you'll have more than enough time to relax before joining me there. And by the way, we call this place a hotel but it's actually a condo. The suites are very nice, and I think you'll enjoy your stay here over the next three days."

"Anyway, at that time, I can also go through a vetting process, to make sure that you are a good fit for our team, which I'm sure you will be. Then, if you pass that vetting process, at the event on Saturday we can make a big announcement of your involvement with the resort."

"That sounds great, and fair enough—Sinbad." Erin replied.

--------ERIN TO SOUTH FLORIDA--------

After two weeks of planning, the day finally arrived when Erin was scheduled to board her flight to south Florida. She had planned everything from selecting formal wear and informal clothing for the three-day stay to hiring a replacement for her at the Bermuda resort.

The flight from Bermuda was a smooth one. Erin was able to catch an earlier flight that would have her arrive in Miami much earlier than the original 4:00 arrival time. So she called Sinbad to let him know of the change—Sinbad then told Casey, her pickup person, about the change. Sinbad's friend Casey would now pick Erin up from the airport when she arrived at 1:00, some three hours earlier than originally planned. He would then take Erin to where she would lodge for the next three days.

Little did she know that the event scheduled for the coming Saturday was only preliminary to a much larger event scheduled for the fall. But for now, she only had in mind what position Freddie's cousin would have for her. Would she be required to oversee the entire operation as she was doing at her resort in Bermuda? Or would it be more of a shared arrangement with Sinbad? The answers to these questions and more would come later that night.

--------ERIN MEETS CASEY--------

Erin looked forward to seeing Casey after she arrived at the airport and retrieved her luggage. Erin assumed that Casey was female and was surprised that a woman would come to pick her up. Because of this, she figured Sinbad must be an equal opportunity employer, which suited her just fine.

Having retrieved her luggage, Erin stood in the pick-up area near a curb outside the terminal. In the distance, she saw a vehicle coming towards her. As it arrived at her location, Erin's head was down positioning her luggage. When she looked up, the vehicle was right in front of her, and she saw what looked to be a middle-aged gentleman get out of the SUV with a bellman's uniform on. He wore a sign around his neck saying, "CASEY: FOR ERIN PICKUP."

Erin knew this was her transport to the resort. But she had mistakenly assumed that Casey would be a female, and clearly saw, in her judgment, a handsome gentleman who would assist her. *Well now*, Erin thought with eager anticipation. How nice to have this gentleman take her to where she would lodge for the next three days.

As the bellman approached Erin, he said, "Ms. Pearson, I presume?"

"Yes, I'm her," she answered.

While Erin could not wait to get to the resort, she also believed that God, perhaps, finally had answered another prayer that she had all these years, which was to find the right man to be in her life. Casey certainly fit all the qualifications at least on the surface.

Erin had a genuine interest in the man and wanted to find out more about him. Yes, she would get a lot of information during her first visit to the area. She could not wait until it all began!

The bellman said, "I'm here to take you to Sinbad's resort. And he told me about the earlier pick-up time. I'll take your luggage. But first let me assist you into the vehicle." In seconds, Erin was safely in the seat behind the driver.

As they drove off, she said to Casey, "It's funny; I thought you would be a female. I don't know of any males named Casey."

He replied, "Don't feel bad, lady. It happens all the time—people mistaking me for a female until they see me. I guess my mother wasn't thinking when she named me. But I'm all man," he added with a smile as he looked at her in the rearview mirror.

As Casey continued to drive, he said, "And I work out a lot too. Don't you see these muscles? Come on, touch my arm," he said to her with one hand steering and the other resting on back of the empty passenger seat beside him.

To Erin, it did appear that he would pop out of the firmly fitted jacket that he had on. In response, Erin just giggled at what Casey had proposed—touching a stranger like that.

Casey continued, now realizing she wasn't going to touch him, "You know, physical activity keeps me in shape. And although I'm not a great swimmer, I'm in the water a lot. Yeah, I stay in shape any way I can. And if you want to know the truth, I have to with all the driving that I do."

When Casey stopped talking, Erin finally said trying to defend her earlier statement, "Oh, no, I wasn't trying to make light of your name, Casey." Then he said, "I know, Miss. Don't worry about it."

As Casey continued his drive to the resort, he attempted to change the tone of the conversation. He asked, "Listen, how long will you be in town?"

"I'll be here until Monday morning. That's when my flight takes off going back to Bermuda."

Casey said, "Yeah, my friend Sinbad said you were from Bermuda."

Erin corrected him by saying, "Now, I'm not *from* Bermuda. I'm originally from New York, but I went to Bermuda when my marriage failed. At least it was about a year or so after that bad experience."

Casey replied, "Sorry to hear about that."

"I think I've gotten over that now," Erin added. "Anyway, right after my divorce, I took to the streets and got into some of everything, but I saw a preacher one Friday night in a crusade that came to town, and I was convicted about all the stuff I was doing. And you know, Casey, I haven't been the same since. All the things I was doing then, being promiscuous, using drugs and anything else I could get myself into, are in the past now. Even my friends were shady back then. I had one friend who was a crossdresser. I mean, he was all man, like you said you are, but somehow he had a thing about wearing women's clothing. Yeah, he was a strange one all right. But those homosexuals, they're all kinda strange anyway.

"Well, enough about me, what about yourself? And keep your eyes on the road," Erin admonished him. "Are you a Christian?"

"Sure am," Casey replied. "I read my Bible every day." Casey replied. "So you think homosexuals are bad?" he added.

"Well, not necessarily bad, just strange. And that's a judgment I have because I'm not familiar with that lifestyle," she answered.

Then Casey turned the tables on Erin, saying, "Let me ask you another question. Are *you* a Christian?"

"I sure am—washed in the blood!" she said adamantly.

"Then don't the scripture talk against judging those you don't understand?" he asked.

Erin replied, "Well, Casey, it's not so much a judgment as it is believing what the scripture says about certain lifestyles." Then Erin felt a need to explain further and said, "Let me just say this, Casey. What I mean by being a Christian is that I'm a believer, and, believe me, my life hasn't been the same since I've come to know the Lord…. But I do get lonely sometimes.

Casey said, "Well, we can take care of that! I've been here in Miami all my life, and I can show you the ins and outs of the place. And as I said, I'm a Christian too, so we have a lot in common. Although I must say, sometimes people don't understand me. But that's life, I guess."

Erin responded, "You don't find too many what I'd like to call *hardcore believers* anymore. And even among Christians, there are so many different beliefs going on out there. It can be very confusing. That's one reason why you have so many different dominations with people claiming to believe in the same God, but their manner of worship is often totally different.

"But the way I think about it is that we're all individuals, and the Lord works with each one of us based our uniqueness, which is hard for some to take. And that's because, as humans, we tend to look at the exterior of a person—how that person might appear, their personality, looks, mannerisms, what they like and don't like, those kinds of things. And since we don't have extrasensory perception, there's no way of knowing what anyone really thinks and believes inside.

"But thank God he doesn't look at all that. He just looks at us the way we really are internally—what our spirit is like, if we genuinely have a love for Him and are willing to do what He tells us. But God is a spirit, and that's something that we as humans can't see," Erin explained to Casey.

But Erin wasn't finished. "So, don't feel bad, Casey, if there are those who don't understand you," Erin concluded. Then she added, "And when you meet somebody you can identify with, internally as well as externally, it's very refreshing."

Erin enjoyed what Casey was saying about being a fellow believer—long after she had appreciated his good looks. She took what little time she had remaining on the drive from the airport to the resort to survey the south Florida landscape. But while viewing her new surroundings, Erin thought only about getting to know Casey better, because she was attracted to him physically.

--------ERIN'S DECISION ON HER LIVING QUARTERS--------

"We're now at the Monica Bay Resort," Casey told Erin as they arrived at the front entrance. "And don't worry about your luggage. You just go ahead and get checked in, and I'll take everything to your room. It might be a few minutes because I have committed to someone else to transport their luggage to an Uber so they can make their flight later."

Erin assured him, "No worries, Casey. I'll see you when you get there with my luggage."

After that, Erin went to the front desk to complete her registration. When that was finished, she was directed to an elevator nearby where she was taken to the second floor and then walked a short distance to her room.

When Erin reached her place of lodging for the next few days, she was surprised that it was more than just a room; it was a suite! Casey had not arrived yet with her luggage.

Erin was amazed at the size of the place—larger even than the suites she was accustomed to back at her Bermuda resort. There was a small kitchenette and living area with a large couch and recliner. Just beyond the couch was a unique piece of furniture—a nightstand with a large portrait of the beach and ocean beyond positioned on it. Just beyond that was the bedroom with a wide window showing the expanse of the Atlantic Ocean with an extensive beach in the foreground. And it had a nice balcony with two chairs and a table as well. Erin knew that the next three days would be spent in extreme luxury.

Despite the quality of the room, Erin thought it would be even better to be lodged on the first floor where she would have direct access to the beach. She knew that Casey might be delayed because of another commitment, so she decided to call the front desk to see if she could get another room on the first floor.

After receiving Erin's call and listening to her request, the receptionist said that she could have a room on the first floor, but first she had to do some checking and asked her to call back in ten minutes.

When Erin later called the receptionist, she answered and said, "Ms. Pearson, it's really busy right now, so give me a minute or two more, and I'll have an answer for you. Stay by the phone, and I'll give you a call right back."

Only a minute went by and the phone rang. "Hello," Erin answered.

The receptionist on the other end said, "Ms. Pearson, I have some good news for you. I found a suite right beneath where you are now, and it's a duplicate with the same layout as the suite that you're in now, including a stone patio instead of a balcony! All of our suites have similar floor plans."

Erin happily replied, "That's great!" Then she was given directions to the room.

After a few minutes, she ventured downstairs to take a look at the room that was available. The cleaning people had left the door to the suite open, so she was able to enter and get a good look at it. After Erin walked in, she said to herself, "Now this is nice, just like the one upstairs. But wow! Now I'm right on the beach!" She only had to get the luggage that Casey would soon bring to her.

After she returned to the room that was first assigned to her, only five minutes had passed when Erin heard some noise in front of the door. She suspected it was Casey with her luggage. Soon the doorbell rang, and, when she opened the door, there he stood with all her luggage.

"Oh my, Casey, I see you made it." She did not want to mention that he had made a wasted trip because she had decided to move downstairs to another available room. But it was too late to do anything about that.

With the door now open, Casey said to Erin, "Sorry I'm a little late, but, as I said earlier, it's been really busy around here."

Then he asked her if she had some water so he could cool himself down a little. He casually said, "A glass of water sure would feel good right about now."

Not wanting him to continue standing in the door, Erin said, "Come on in and, sure, I'll get you some water."

Erin did not realize at the time he was bringing the luggage into the room with him. She had gone to get him a glass of water, and, when she returned, she saw that he had brought everything in and was in the process of placing parts of her luggage on the floor. Erin thought, *How in the world can I tell him this is the wrong room?*

While harboring those thoughts, Erin gave him the water she had gotten from the sink.

He then told her, "You know, Miss, I sure am glad this is the last job I have today. Not having to take any more luggage around."

Erin simply said, "Oh!"

Then Casey continued, "I've taken so much luggage upstairs then downstairs and all around this place. It can be so tiring. Now I can relax a little. But I know you're eager to open your bags and place things the way you want them. I guess you just want to relax yourself, huh?" Before she could answer, he added, "I'm sure glad my work is over for the day. And do you know what I plan to do, Miss?" He asked her with no intention of her returning an answer. "Yeah, I plan to spend the rest of the day just relaxing. Yeah, that's what I'm going to do."

At that moment Erin knew she had to tell Casey to take all that luggage, place it back on the pushcart, and take it back downstairs for her. Reluctantly, she said, "I hate to tell you this, Casey, but I changed my room before you brought my luggage in. I wanted to tell you, but, while I was getting your water, you had already brought it in. Would you be angry with me if I asked you to place my luggage back on the pushcart and take it downstairs to the first floor, to room 112, just below this room?"

Casey just stood there in bewilderment, disappointed that his work was not really over for the day. Then, in a rather subdued tone, he said to Erin, "Don't worry about it, lady. I'll put all of this back on the pushcart and take it down for you."

Casey continued, "I have only one requirement at this point," as he wiped sweat from his forehead.

"And what is that?" Erin asked him with great curiosity.

Casey answered, "Well, I'd like for you to have lunch with me, not here but at a tavern right on the beach. It's only about a five-minute walk from here. It will be so much cooler there, and the view is magnificent."

"Well, after all the trouble I've caused you, how can I say no?" she said trying to hide her excitement about him asking her out to lunch. Then she added, "Oh, by the way, you can call me Erin."

"Okay then, Erin, everything is all set. Let me go change and I'll see you in about ten minutes in the lobby, that is, after I take your luggage downstairs. Yeah, someone is making me work so much harder today," Casey facetiously told her.

Embarrassed by what she had required Casey to do, Erin simply looked downward but glanced up at him in hopes that in some way he would feel sorry for her.

Casey took Erin's luggage to her new accommodation downstairs. Just prior to their walk to the tavern, he went to the employees' dressing room to change from business to casual attire, and Erin was left in the front room of her new suite to sort out her luggage. This would be her haven, she felt, for the balance of her three-day stay in Miami. But for now, she was mainly concerned with that afternoon lunch date.

After Erin's luggage had been brought to her new suite she arranged some items, then went to the lobby where she would soon meet Casey. As Erin waited for him, she surveyed the area and was impressed with the décor. She was fascinated with the huge fireplace with several seating choices around it. She thought, *Interesting, a fireplace in Miami.* Without giving any further thought about that, Casey soon arrived, and then they were off to lunch.

--------A WALK TO SEASHORE TAVERN--------

It was a warm but not hot afternoon. As Casey and Erin walked from the resort towards Seashore Tavern, a brisk sea breeze coming in from the Atlantic met them. Erin was wearing a light top, shorts, and sandals; she was tempted to remove her sandals and to step away from the narrow, slightly elevated walkway to sift her feet through the warm sands. But she resisted that temptation, knowing she would have that opportunity later.

Erin's stroll along the seashore reminded her so much of her life in Bermuda. Walking along a sandy beach in a tropical paradise was familiar and comforting. The two of them were tempted to challenge the roaring oceans waves not far away by taking a dip. But they refrained and stayed focused on going to the tavern and on each other.

Shortly they arrived and Casey said, "Well, here we are."

"This is really nice," Erin said back to Casey.

A linear bar was situated closer to the back of the establishment near one of several oceanfront resorts. Here patrons could order all kinds of alcoholic beverages that were positioned on elevated shelves on a back wall. And just above the bar was an assortment of drinking glasses—all shapes and sizes—that glistened and held together by holding fixtures suspended from the ceiling. The ceiling lighting seemed to give a rather shiny glow in what was otherwise a dimly lit, shaded area, a stark contrast to a sunny afternoon.

There were already four people sitting at the bar, far fewer than the crowd that usually prevailed later at night during hours of business operation. Erin and Casey would not join those at the bar; they went to a part of the tavern that was more like a restaurant where straw-covered dining tables were located.

It was in this area, near the front of the tavern, where there was a row of tables that had straw umbrellas covering them, secured by a narrow steel beam extending from the middle of each table.

They were fortunate to find one of the tables was situated separately from the other three. It provided some degree of privacy where they could have a clear view of the beach and the ocean beyond, and where they could receive the maximum effect of the incoming ocean breezes – it was almost intoxicating and so relaxing.

So they ended up just sitting there, having an honest discussion.

FIGURE 4: A WALK TO SEASHORE TAVERN

And Jesus answered and said to them: Take heed that no one deceives you. For many will come in my name, saying I am the Christ, and will deceive many.

- Matthew 24:4,5

--------MORE DISCUSSION--------

Erin had a particular interest in learning more about the resort, Miami as a city, and the entire region of south Florida. She also looked forward to becoming more familiar with her new friend, Casey, as a person. Beyond that, Erin was looking forward to learning more about what soon would become a place she would call home.

After taking a seat at the table, an attendant came to greet them.

"Would you two like a drink?" the server, a neatly adorned young lady, casually asked.

Before Erin could answer, Casey asked, "Do you drink alcoholic beverages?"

"No, I gave that up a long time ago."

"Good," Casey replied. "I think drinking alcoholic beverages is the work of the devil, trying to deceive people in their minds. I just can't stand the smell of the stuff."

Erin said, "Yeah, alcohol consumption is a big problem in some circles, but I know people who casually drink, and I don't think they're possessed or anything."

To keep the server from waiting, without responding to Erin's last statement, Casey made his order. "I think I'll have some iced tea. What are you going to get?"

Erin answered him by telling the attendant, "Just bring me a glass of water for now."

The attendant said, "Okay. Your refreshments are coming right up. Here's a menu and, by the time I come back, I'll take your food order."

Soon after that the attendant brought them their refreshments.

As they sipped their beverages, having reviewed a menu and ordered their food, Erin was eager to find out more about Casey. She asked, "So you don't drink?" Then she quickly added, "Alcoholic beverages, I mean."

Casey answered, "No. As I said, I hate the smell of wine, liquor, or any stuff like that. Besides, it would certainly get in the way of my driving. You know I have to be very responsible. The people I take different places have put their lives in my hands."

Erin responded, "You seem to be passionate about your job. You've been doing it for a while?"

"Yeah, ever since my friend Sin hired me some years ago."

Erin reacted to the name Casey called Freddie's cousin. She asked, "Sin?"

"Yeah, that's what I call him, Freddie's cousin Sinbad. I guess you know that his cousin and me are friends, don't you?"

Then Erin tried to give him an answer, hoping that it would be sufficient. She said to him, "No! Freddie never got that much into detail about his cousin's friends. At least I don't remember my close friend Sandra telling me that Freddie had mentioned that to her. But I may be mistaken – so much has been going on lately."

"Now, who is Sandra?" Casey asked.

"Oh, Sandra is a friend that I met when she visited me in Bermuda."

The discussion at that point was getting rather complicated just in time for the attendant to return and for them to receive their meal.

At that point Erin was more curious than ever about the relationship between Casey and his friend Sinbad, Freddie's cousin. But her curiosity had to wait.

She said, "Wow! The food looks good, doesn't it?"

Casey replied, "Yeah, the food down here is very good. But what about Sandra, you were getting ready to say?"

"Casey, we can talk about Sandra later. The food looks so good. Let's eat!" Then she said to the waitress, "Hey, ma'am, I'll take a Sprite now."

Sandra was eager to eat her grilled salmon and brown rice with veggies on the side. They partook of the meal they had received, and at least temporally enjoyed the ambiance of the tavern with the white sands and crystal blues waters of the nearby beach.

Once they had finished their meal, Erin was eager to continue the discussion she had with Casey earlier. She said, "I guess you know that Sinbad's cousin Freddie is friends with the person who visited me in

Bermuda—Sandra. And it was *her* friend Maggie who introduced me to *your* friend, Freddie's cousin Sinbad."

"Well, to be honest, I haven't asked Sin about all that. You know relationships can be complicated. And as far as me calling Freddie's cousin Sin, let me say that's Freddie's cousin's nickname and what I call him. The strange thing about it is that I'm the only one who calls him that. And Freddie—when I see him—gets a little irritated when I call his cousin Sin. I guess he would be more of a problem for me, but he lives up there in Detroit. But my brother Bernie lives down here, and he feels the same way. I don't think Bernie likes me very much, so I have to be careful and not say Sin when I'm talking to or referring to him when either Freddie or Bernie is around."

"Um, that's interesting," Erin replied.

Erin then asked about Bernie. "I don't know Bernie. And let me ask …."

Casey interjected before Erin had a chance to ask her question, saying, "And you don't want to know him."

Erin replied, "Well, I certainly don't want to get into any family feuds."

But she really didn't mean it because she was about to continue asking Casey about his brother, but, just as she was about to inquire, the attendant returned and offered them an array of dessert choices.

"We have a nice assortment of desserts from which to choose," the attendant said. After showing them the selection, she continued, "I personally would recommend devil's chocolate fudge cake."

Erin and Casey considered that as well as the other options presented. They made their decision, and both decided to go with the attendant's recommendation.

As they ate, Erin said, "Casey, I was gonna ask you about Bernie, but tell me this. What do you expect from this event that your friend will be putting on tomorrow?"

Casey replied, "Well, that's a good question. Sin doesn't let me in on things—what his business dealings are. But Bernie seems to be up on all that."

"Oh, by the way, I'll introduce you to my brother if I get the chance tomorrow. He usually comes over to eat breakfast, and I know I'll be working all day tomorrow. So, if you see me at breakfast tomorrow morning, I'll point him out to you and get you two together. I'm sure he'd want to meet you."

Erin seemed to be mystified at Casey's interest in getting his brother together with her because she was really interested in *him* and less interested in his brother whom she had not met. She believed it was strange that Casey would not come on stronger to her.

She thought, *Oh, well, I need to get to meet as many people as possible, and I can imagine the number of people Casey knows with his job, not to mention family ties.*

--------BACK TO THE RESORT--------

Erin knew she needed to get back to her suite to settle her belongings for her weekend stay, so she and Casey agreed to end their lunch date and began walking the short distance back to the resort. It was early afternoon and Erin still wanted to get to the beach; but it seemed that Casey was less interested in going there than she was. Then Erin thought, *Wait a minute! I do need to get back and get some rest before my meeting with Sinbad tonight. After that I need to get some rest for the long day tomorrow. Going to the beach will have to wait.*

Erin did look forward to meeting with Sinbad later that evening for dinner. He would go over many of the specifics of her job at that time. Erin understood that the success of her venture into south Florida would depend on that vetting process she would have with Sinbad.

After her meeting with Sinbad, Erin had planned to return to her suite and prepare for the events the next day, which would include not only the main event Saturday evening, but also a trip to the beach prior to that time during the day where she would just relax.

After her time with Casey at the tavern, tiredness had overcome Erin by the time she got to her suite. She managed to muster enough strength take her clothes out of the luggage and put them away for her weekend stay. After that, Erin was content to grab a soda and some popcorn to munch while sitting on the patio enjoying the wonderful sunset beyond the beach and ocean. Having changed into more comfortable attire, she said to herself while sitting there, "What a serene sight! It's so peaceful out here, and this view is magnificent!" Then she said, "I'm glad Sinbad scheduled our meeting at 9:00 tonight – that will give me more than enough time to rest and prepare for it."

The calm breeze from the ocean seemed hypnotic. Watching the orange sun set against the blue sky and the feeling the gentle breeze wash over her made Erin wish for that special someone to share all of this beauty with her. Erin had thought that person might be Casey, but she already had begun to sense that likely would not be the case.

As twilight turned into early evening and eventually into nighttime, Erin could not help but remember what Sandra saw on her last night on the beach in Bermuda. The stars were just beginning to come out but were far from the magnificent array they had provided Sandra on that night back in Bermuda. That canopy of stars had turned out to be a sign that Sandra would not only receive her physical healing but in a sense her spiritual essence as well.

As Erin sat on the patio, she began to doze off. After a brief nap that she desired, she returned inside the suite to freshen up and prepare for her dinner meeting with Sinbad.

--------ERIN MEETS SINBAD--------

Soon after her relaxing time on the patio, Erin did meet with Sinbad at the hotel restaurant. Being refreshed after her nap on the patio, Erin took a short walk to the restaurant inside the building.

During her stroll Erin's thoughts turned to what she was about to experience with the owner of this resort. She thought, *Will I be required to oversee the entire operation as I've done at my resort back in Bermuda? Or will it be more of a shared arrangement with me working directly with Sinbad?* The answers to these questions in her mind would come in a few minutes.

When she arrived there, she found Sinbad sitting in a booth near the back with a sign having his name on it. She went over to introduce herself. "Hello Mr. Sinbad." "Hello Erin, nice finally meeting you in person. And as I said earlier on the phone, you can just call me Sinbad."

"Well, okay – Sinbad. You know it's a lot different talking to you in person than when we talked over the phone," Erin said.

The deep voice that greeted her defied what she perceived during their phone conversation earlier.

Sinbad said, "Yeah, it's a lot different talking to someone in person than on the phone. Anyway, I'm happy to finally get to see you."

From that point on they had casual conversation where Erin did learn much more about the position she sought. After a nice meal Sinbad started that vetting process. He asked her questions about the resort she has operated back in Bermuda, as well as what she expected of her overseeing his resort in south Florida. Soon the dinner meeting would be over.

Maggie felt well about the vetting that Sinbad had with her. After that she went back to her suite to retire for the evening. Erin looked forward to a good night's sleep and could not wait for the main event to occur on tomorrow.

As Erin contemplated the events of the next day, little did she know that the activities scheduled for Saturday evening would be only preliminary to a much larger event scheduled for the fall.

Erin finally returned to the bedroom of the suite and retired for the night. She wouldn't sleep late into the morning, however, because she remembered her friend Casey saying that his brother would likely be at breakfast. He might be able to shed more information on the upcoming event later that evening headed by Freddie's cousin Sinbad. She also hoped to get some inside details from Casey's brother Bernie about the position she would have at the resort, which was something Casey told her he could not provide.

Her contemplation of things to come would not last long as she finally went to sleep.

--------BREAKFAST AMBIENCE--------

Finally, the day had come when the major players in Sinbad's resort would be on hand for an opening reception at 6:00 in the grand lobby of the resort., two hours before the big event scheduled for 8:00. Until then Erin anticipated a day of relaxation, and maybe a trip out to the beach.

Erin remembered that Casey said his brother would likely be at breakfast, so she anticipated meeting him. As she continued to lie in bed, she thought, *Casey's brother might be able to shed more information on the upcoming event later tonight, since Casey was not able to tell me anything.*

Erin soon did her routine of grabbing a cup of coffee and reading a portion of a chapter of the Bible before getting in her morning walk at the resort's exercise facility not far from her suite. After about 30 minutes, she would be invigorated and ready to shower, get dressed, and start her day.

She thought seriously about going out to the beach, but more than that she just wanted to relax and prepare for the event later in the evening.Erin's first order of business was to have a nice breakfast and hopefully meet Casey's brother so she could get more inside information about the upcoming event. After getting refreshed with a shower and dressing for the day, Erin left her suite and made the short walk to the dining area. She resisted getting a second cup of coffee and instead requested some orange juice and proceeded to order her breakfast from an attendant who provided service.

"So, this is south Florida?" Erin said to herself in great wonderment. A large window provided a view of the beach and the ocean beyond. The bright sun had just begun to rise over the eastern horizon. She saw a few cleaning personnel setting up a line of beach umbrellas not far from the incoming waves for the purpose of accommodating hundreds of beachgoers later in the day. At this early hour, only a few tourists strolled along the sand where the water rolled onto the beach.

Seagulls were already flying in search of discarded food fragments. Closer to the facility, birds could be heard chirping away, and the sound added to the ambiance of the environment. The few people Erin saw at that time would soon transition into larger crowds later in the morning and especially by mid-afternoon.

Meanwhile, the dining area itself had begun to receive guests of the resort, with a scattering of patrons throughout the dining hall. After enjoying the magnificent view of the beach, Erin turned her attention to the few patrons that were scattered throughout the dining room. She noticed a gentleman sitting with a young boy at a table in the distance along a back wall.

She could not believe it! She said to herself, "Hey, that's Casey sitting over there. Now, I know he sees me. I wonder why he hasn't spoken. And I wonder who is that boy with him? Could it be his son?" Erin continued to ponder.

She kept looking in his direction to try and get his attention. Finally, the guy did look towards her, and she gingerly waved her hand at him. He waved back, appearing to wonder why this woman was signaling him.

Erin turned around to take another bite of her food when she saw who looked to be a bellman walking through the dining hall entrance and immediately recognized him as Casey. She did a double take, trying to figure out who the person was she waved at that looked so much like him.

Before Erin could finish the thought, Casey walked up to her and said, "Hello, Erin."

Without speaking, she turned her head around and eyed the fellow with the boy who appeared to be a carbon copy of Casey. To avoid being rude, she twirled back around and finally greeted Casey by saying, "Oh, hello, Casey."

Perceiving her confusion, Casey said, "I understand why you're confused, Erin. I didn't tell you that I have a twin brother, and that's him sitting over there with his son."

"Whew! Well, that explains it. Yeah, Casey. I was very confused there for a minute. You didn't tell me that your brother was a twin. I thought that was you sitting over there and believed that you just didn't have the courtesy to speak to me."

Casey smiled and continued, "No, no, Erin! I'm not rude like that. Anyway, as I said yesterday, I want to introduce you to my brother Bernie. I told him a little about you—why you're down here. So, stay right here, and I'll go and get him."

Casey went over to get his brother, and they both returned to Erin's table. Then Casey introduced them to each other.

"Bernie, I met this young lady yesterday, and her name is Erin. Erin, this is my brother Bernie, and his son Jacob is still sitting over there. I'll leave you two together now because I have work to do."

Then Bernie said to his brother, "Thanks Case," referring to him by his one-syllable nickname.

--------ERIN MEETING BERNIE--------

As Casey left, Erin invited Bernie to take a seat. After he sat down, she asked, "Can I call you Bernie?"

"Sure! I've been called that all my life," he said with a smile. "And can I call you Erin?"

"Of course."

"Well, it's nice meeting you, Erin," he said.

"Likewise. And, Bernie, your son can come over here too."

But Bernie rejected that idea. "No, no, my son kinda likes being by himself. I'm trying to get him to be more sociable. Well, I guess because of that, maybe I *should* bring him over. But I want to focus on you right now. He'll be fine."

"Now, I understand that you want to get on the payroll here—to work for Sinbad?" Bernie asked.

Erin replied, "Yeah, that's about right. But I have to tell you, I was…I mean, I am my own person where I work back at my resort in Bermuda. I don't know how it's going to be working directly under someone else like I guess I would be doing here."

Bernie then began to share some of the "inside information" she desired to have about the job she was applying for and the day-to-day duties. He said, "Well, you really wouldn't be working directly under him like on a day-to-day basis. In other words, he wouldn't be breathing down your neck every day. That's not how Sinbad operates. Besides, he's not even here most of the time. He's given the day-to-day duties to me. And so far, I've been able to handle it.

"Anyway, he really wants someone like you to be the hands-on person around here. Case gave me a little information about you and why you're here, so you being around would help me out a lot. And I have to tell you, I've talked to Sinbad a little about the possibilities of you working here. He's examined your work history, and he really likes your experience. I guess he feels that you can run the resort independent of anyone else's help.

"Now, don't get me wrong," Bernie continued, "I'll be here to help you if you need it. But you won't be under anyone's direct supervision. How would you like that?"

Erin replied, "Well, I have to admit, that's sounds great. I mean, it'd be perfect for what I want to do. You might say I kinda like calling the shots. Don't get me wrong; I'm not against being supervised. But let me ask you a question, Bernie. If *you* are handling the day-to-day functioning of the resort, why does Sinbad need someone like me?"

"That's easy to answer. I don't have that much experience as a manager, and Sinbad wants to bring in a professional who knows what the hell they're doing! Someone like you!"

"Oh, I see," Erin responded.

"Yeah, it seems to me that you would be a perfect fit to work for someone like Sinbad," Bernie confirmed. He seemed supportive of her taking the position.

--------REFLECTIONS--------

Erin really liked what Bernie was saying, but she didn't want to give herself away and make him believe that she was eager to be accepted by Sinbad as one of his employees under any kind of conditions. She really wanted to come to south Florida, especially to work in the same position as her current job in Bermuda as the director of a resort.

So far everything seemed perfect except for the fact that Casey seemed not to have a particular interest in her. From her point of view, he was definitely attractive enough, polite, and, most importantly, he talked about Christian values that were dear to her heart. But she certainly didn't want to put any pressure on him or anyone else for that matter to form a strong, even romantic relationship with her.

Erin was intent on remaining focused on the acquisition of a job that she really wanted. After all, she was there to obtain a position, the perfect position in her estimation, based on what she had heard so far, so she just tried to concentrate on the job as Bernie described it. It appeared to be an ideal situation for her.

--------FAMILY LIFE--------

While talking with Erin, Bernie kept an eye on his son still sitting across the dining hall. He tried to explain his divided attention, saying, "You know, Erin, it's challenging raising a kid by yourself especially as a father. I guess you can't relate to that."

"No, as a woman, I can't relate to a man raising a child. I know it's different for a man to be raising a kid. But I *can* relate to what you are saying as a parent regardless of gender. I mean, what I'm saying is that I understand, because I too have a young son that I'm raising by myself—well, sort of. Anyway, he's actually about the same age as your boy. And yeah, even coming here I had to get a sitter for him before I left."

Bernie interjected, "Wait a minute! What da mean you're sort of raising your child? You're either raising the kid or you're not! Come on now! Let me in on what you're saying," he asked her defiantly.

"Well, it seems you really want to know. But I'd rather not talk about that right now."

"Well okay," Bernie said. "I won't pressure you."

"Anyway, Jacob is 10 years old, so he's getting to the age where it's really challenging to raise him alone," Bernie said. Before Bernie could finish that line of thought, he saw Erin's facial expression change suddenly, which prompted him to ask, "You seem to be mystified by that information—my son's age, I mean. And by the way, how old is your son?"

"I was just thinking when you mentioned your son's age. Well, my son is 10 too, so we have something in common."

Bernie responded, "Well, how about that! The same age." He continued, "Anyway, getting back to what you were saying about you 'sort of' raising you kid. What about your husband? Did he pass on and leave you a widow or something?"

"Well, Bernie…."

Erin started to answer, but before she could finish Bernie interrupted her and said, "Pardon me, Erin. Let me get this off my chest. My wife Quansie died unexpectedly last year." He began to get emotional but continued, "So, over the past year, I guess I've been like a 'Mr. Mom' around the house."

In an attempt to console him, Erin said, "I'm so sorry to hear about that."

"No, no, do not feel sorry for me because she lived a good life while she was here. And you know what they say, you only live once. You just have to make the most of the time you are alive."

--------SPIRITUAL INSIGHTS--------

While sorry for learning of Bernie's wife, Erin objected to his idea that you only live once. She told him, "Well, Bernie, you do know that's a false statement you just made, don't you?"

Before she had a chance to continue with her point, because he did not understand what she was saying, Bernie interrupted, "Incorrect statement? What did I say that was so wrong?"

"Bernie, I'm a Christian woman and I've been taught that, no, you don't live once. We all have a spirit and because of it we have an opportunity to live beyond this present physical life in a spiritual dimension."

With a bit of derision and disgust, Bernie said, "Are you one of those 'holier than thou' people trying to impose their religion on others, talking about God all the time?"

Defending herself, Erin said, "Well, Bernie, I see now that you're nothing like your twin brother Casey. We had a deep conversation yesterday about spiritual kinds of things, and he's a strong Christian and espoused many of the beliefs I have."

"Well, I really don't know what 'espouse' means, but, anyway, let me tell you this, lady. I see it every day how some people supposed to have all this faith—I suppose a faith in God—and many of these same people are doing everything that the so-called sinners are doing. I just don't understand it.

"Listen, Erin, I don't mean to get on your bad side. I really would like to get to know you more, and obviously I hope you get the job you're applying for."

"Okay, Bernie, I guess we got off on a tangent there. But I think we may be more alike than different. And one reason is because of our marital past. You mentioned that your wife passed last year. Well, some time ago it seemed as though my husband died as well. That's what I was gonna to tell you, before you interrupted me by talking about your deceased wife. Anyway, we got a divorce, and I've been raising my child alone too."

--------BAD MEMORIES--------

As they continued to talk, Bernie wanted to know more about why Erin and her husband got a divorce. He asked, "Erin, sorry I interrupted you earlier. You seem so easy to live with. I mean, I know you have your faith, but I can tell, you don't find too many people that are as well-grounded as you are. And I can really appreciate that. So, what made you and your husband want to leave each other?"

Erin did not want to bring back bad memories, but she felt some obligation to tell Bernie the truth about her marriage.

"Well, Bernie," she said, "it's a long story, but what choice did I have when I found that my husband was cheating on me? I mean, I caught him in the very act of having sex with someone else when I came home early one day.

Bernie replied, "Yeah, that would be enough to leave. As a matter of fact, I probably would have shot the both of them right then and there! I don't have much patience for some things, and that's one of 'em. I mean being unfaithful to someone that you're committed to for life—like in a marriage—is a reason to cut ties. Hell, and to cut him too!"

Erin then said, "My, my! Your language, Bernie. I'm telling you, you're nothing like your brother even though you're twins."

"Hey, hey! Whatcha doin' condemning the way I speak?"

"No, Bernie," Erin replied, "I'm just not use to that kind of talk. I mean, it's been a while since I've been on the streets when I used to hear people say everything under the sun. But, Bernie, gettin' back to what you said about not having the patience of dealing with an unfaithful spouse. Well, I'm glad you feel that way. I feel that way because I feel a lot of men just want to play the field, you might say, without regards to the feelings of their mate. Anyway, that wasn't the only thing that was so hurtful."

Bernie interjected, "What? I mean, what could be more hurtful than finding your husband in bed with another woman?"

Erin responded, "The answer to that question, Bernie, was that it wasn't a woman that my husband was with; it was another man!"

"What?" Bernie responded, then continued to ask a question for clarity, "Another man?" A bit confused he continued to say, "That's something I can't relate to. I can't even imagine something like that. Yeah, you needed to get out of that situation. That was a natural hell hole."

--------REVELATIONS--------

Trying to change the conversation, Erin said, "I don't want to get stuck talking about my past. I have my own thoughts about homosexuality. But I won't reveal those thoughts now. I'm here in south Florida to hopefully move forward with my life professionally.

And your partner, Sinbad, will have a lot to do with that. So where is he now?" she asked. Before he could provide an answer, she commented, "I know you said he has been away for a few days but that he'll return in time for the event later today."

Bernie finally got the chance to answer Erin. He said, "Sinbad's in Jamaica. He goes there a lot just to get away. But he's away a lot and half of the time I don't know *where* he is."

Bernie continued to be intrigued with Erin's reply about her husband's relationship with another man. He mentioned, "I know what you must have felt when you found your husband in the situation you talked about. Like I said earlier, my brother Case and Sinbad are *good friends*."

Erin replied, "So? They are friends. What's so special about that? I know a lot of guys who are good friends with other guys. You make it seem like he's a homo or something."

With a degree of irritation, Bernie replied, "Please don't use that term. It's degrading. I mean, we're all God's children, and everyone should be treated with respect."

"Well, why are you becoming so defensive, Bernie? I mean, some things are stated in the Bible as being an abomination to God, and that's one of them. And I'll tell you another thing. That's one of the main reasons I left my husband—his lifestyle. I just didn't think I could deal with that."

Bernie responded, "Well, Erin, everyone has their opinion. And, by the way, the Bible also says not to judge someone else's behavior. I mean, don't get me wrong. We should be aware of what other people are doing, so we can make our own decisions one way or the other based on their actions. But don't judge them; that's up to God to do that.

"And something else, Erin, like you said before, we're probably more alike than different even on an issue like this. But that's neither here nor there, as they say. My brother Case and Sinbad are good friends, and it's something I have to live with and accept every day."

"Bernie, I still don't see how that relates to the genuine relationship between two men."

"Well, that's just it; they are more than just friends. They are *special* friends."

Erin replied, "What are you saying, Bernie? Are you saying that there is something going on between them? That they are ..."

Before she could say the word that commonly describes same-sex relationships, Bernie confirmed her fears when he came right out and said, "Yeah, they're a gay couple!"

Erin remained silent but only for a moment. "Oh, my word!"

Before she could say anything else, Bernie told her, "Now listen, Erin, they don't make a big deal out of it; it's just common knowledge around here that they are in that kind of relationship. I guess it's just accepted." He continued, "Sinbad has so much influence, no one would dare challenge him on his sexuality. And he *is* a nice fellow. I just try to keep my distance—if you know what I mean."

"Well, that certainly sheds a different light on things," Erin replied.

Bernie tried to be more upbeat in his discussion. He added, "Listen, Erin, I'm gonna have to go out to get some work done. I'll see you at 6:00 at the event. It shouldn't take long. Sinbad doesn't like long, drawn out formal events. And after the event I'd like to take you to the tavern, where you went yesterday with Case.

"That sounds fine, Bernie," Erin said. "I'll probably go on the beach, take in some sun today before it gets so late and just think about some things before I come back to the room and rest a little before that event."

"Well, let me bring Jacob over to meet you. I'm sure he's about ready to go."

Bernie went back to his table and soon returned with his son. Erin was amazed how much he was like her own son. She wondered whether they would ever get a chance to meet each other, especially after the revelation she just got from Bernie about his brother and the man who was potentially her future boss.

--------A TRUSTED FRIEND--------

Erin gave Sandra a call after she returned to her suite.

"Hello, Sandra. How are you doing today?" she said after her friend answered the phone.

"Erin!" Sandra returned the greeting loudly, seemingly surprised to hear from her. In a more subdued voice, she asked, "How is everything down there in Florida?"

"Everything is fine here, Sandra. And, Sandra, it's south Florida you know. Florida is a long state, and it's really nice down here where we are. I don't want to make you envious, but I'm going to the beach in a few minutes. Can you imagine?" Erin continued, "Now I'm not trying to make you feel bad, but you don't have this in Detroit—the weather I mean. The breeze feels so good when you're on the beach."

Sandra agreed, "Yeah, you're right, Erin. You know with any breeze here in Detroit, it means you'd better have your coat on!"

"I guess you know I'm trying to get you guys in Michigan to move down here, including Maggie over in Chicago," Erin said. Then she continued, "You and her, along with her husband Fred, are invited to come down here when I get established. This would be a great vacation for you all, including Courtney and Gates as well as our friends in the New York area. But more than that, living down here would be just wonderful."

Sandra responded, "Now, Erin, you're talking about us moving down when *you're* not even there yet? But let me ask you something. Have you met Freddie's cousin? I sure hope he gives you that position."

"Sandra, remember what I told you back in Bermuda? You have to believe that you will receive the blessing that you want. But, more than that, you have to believe that you already have it by faith. So that's what I'm doing, speaking it by faith that I already have the position," Erin said to her.

After hearing those encouraging words, Sandra said, "Okay, Erin. I hear you loud and clear. Yeah, I think it can happen—that you will get the job you desire just like I got my healing back in Bermuda. And, in the same way, I believe that a group of us here in the Detroit and Chicago areas as well as Katie and Sheri's clan over in the New York City area will be coming down soon. We just have to figure out the details, and I'll keep you posted."

Erin wanted to end her talk with Sandra because she was eager to begin to prepare for the evening's festivities.

"Sandra, that would be great—all of you coming down here. Well, it's always good talking with you, and I'll keep you posted on what's going on down here. By the way, please give my regards to Maggie, and I'll talk to you later. Bye."

With those words from Erin, the conversation ended.

--------THOUGHTS OF A SIGN--------

Erin spent only a small amount of time changing into her beach attire. She was excited to get under an umbrella out on the beach near the rolling waves of the ocean. She would take a book given to her by Maggie, which was Fred's most recent published work.

Once on the beach, it was time for Erin to relax and just think about what had transpired thus far in south Florida and to contemplate what would happen at the event a few hours later in the evening.

Erin soon found a beach chair to her liking. While lying there, all she could do was to think back to the time in Bermuda when Sandra had come to visit her. Erin recalled her discussion with Sandra about receiving a sign that would give her confidence that she would receive both the physical as well as the spiritual healing that she needed.

Now, Erin needed her own sign— some assurance that she would have a successful transition into her new life in south Florida.

Erin continued to lie there with her eyes shifting between the ocean before her and the blue sky above. Meditating on a beach chair under an umbrella, she welcomed the cool breezes from the ocean. She was content to watch other tourists brave what seemed to be violent ocean waves unrelentingly rolling again and again onto the beach. She even witnessed a surfer well beyond what she considered a safe distance from solid ground.

After several minutes of enjoying this scene, Erin decided to return to her suite to rest before the evening's festivities. She took a brief nap and afterwards got up and dressed. In a few minutes she was ready to leave her bedroom and go to the main conference hall where the event would be held.

Just prior to her leaving for the event, the phone rang.

"Hello," she said.

"Hello, Erin. This is Sinbad. I've just returned from my out-of-town trip and wanted to make contact with you again since we'll be proposing your part in running our new resort here in Miami. So, are you excited about the prospect of working with us—to see us grow?"

"Yes, Sinbad," she replied. "I've been eager to talk with you mainly about my part in being here at the resort."

Sinbad interjected, "Let me correct you. You simply won't be a part of things around here; you'll be running the place. And from what I've heard from my cousin Freddie, I won't be disappointed."

Erin responded, "Well, I appreciate your confidence in me."

"That's great. Let me go now," Sinbad said, "and I'll see you in a few minutes."

Despite all the positive aspects she had gained from being at Sinbad's resort thus far, Erin's knowledge of his relationship with Casey cast a huge cloud over whether she should even consider accepting the position. Like when Sandra visited her at her resort in Bermuda, Erin felt she needed a sign from God to assure her that she was doing the right thing by joining forces with Sinbad and his resort in south Florida.

In her estimation, the encouragement Sinbad had just given her would not be enough to be the sign that she needed. She wanted more of a confirmation that she was doing the right thing in coming on board to work for Sinbad.

--------THE EVENT--------

Erin left her suite shortly after the conversation with Sinbad and soon entered the conference room. She had expected to find a crowd of people when she arrived, but she was met by only a small group that seemed to be less than 20 folks. The conference room's capacity far exceeded that.

When Erin came in, she was given a name tag and directed to a seat at a table near the front of the room. Four other people were already seated, and the table was marked "reserved" with her name among the place cards. So that was where she sat.

A small podium stood in front of the table, and Erin assumed that Sinbad would be there to address the group, which was what happened. A rather short gentleman walked in and approached the reserved table. After greeting those who were already seated, he took a chair next to Erin and said to her in a low voice, "Hello, Erin, it was only last evening when I first met you, but it seems like I've known you longer that just one day. Anyway, hello again."

"Well, hello, Sinbad; it so nice meeting you in person again," Erin said. Then Sinbad replied, "Thank you Erin. And good evening again to all the rest of you. I want you to know that we anticipate Erin here, will be coming to work with us at the resort."

After having light conversation with the others at the table, Sinbad whispered to Erin, "Like I said last night, Freddie told me a lot about you, and I am impressed with everything he said." Then he raised his voice for everyone present at the table to hear, and said, "Well, things are about to start. And since I'm the ringleader around here, you might say, let me go up and address everybody here tonight. Please excuse me," he said to all those present at the table. Then he got up and walked to the podium to address everyone in the room.

Erin thought to herself, *I know I got a lot of information last night, but hopefully he will give even more of the inside information I've been desiring to get for a long time about all of this.* Erin was about to receive the details from the person who really counted, Sinbad himself – at least in a public forum, because they did meet the previous evening, but only for a short time. While those thoughts raced through Erin's mind, Sinbad had risen and taken the short walk to where he would speak. He briefly surveyed the small group assembled.

As he struggled to see over the podium, he began to give his remarks: "Ladies and gentlemen, I'd like to thank you all for being here this evening. As you know, our resort will be opening September 1, which is on a Friday. I'm looking forward to this being a successful venture. Lord knows I've been working on it long enough. You people who are here in this room will form the foundation of this enterprise. With your efficiency we will provide people from all over south Florida, as well as those from other parts of the country and the world for that matter, with top quality entertainment and leisure. We'll have a unique beach resort like no other in the country. And you'll be the backbone of it, that is, the key personnel of the resort."

"Now, I've selected a person who will guide this ship on a day-to-day basis and she's right here," he said leaving the podium and returning to the table. He placed his hands on Erin's shoulder. Then he said, "Raise your other hand, Erin. I want everyone to see you."

She did as he requested; then he went on to identify her.

"This is Erin Pearson, and she's coming on board—at least I hope that will be case—as our led administrator here at the resort.

As resort personnel you may not see her often, but her influence will be felt all over this place, so don't disappoint her.

"Erin, could you please stand and let the people get a better view of you? And, please, just say a couple of words; then we all can eat the food that was prepared by our kitchen personnel with some of them being right here with us now."

Erin did as he requested. She stood and Sinbad encouraged her by whispering, "Go ahead, Erin, and speak to them."

Erin made a brief statement, saying, "Thank you, Sinbad, for those kind words. And thank all of you for being here and supporting me. Thank you for the opportunity to 'guide this ship,' as Sinbad put it. Just remember, if I decide to come on board, I will be here for all of you. Thank you."

A light applause followed Erin's remarks. Sinbad wiped his mouth and returned to the podium to make his final remarks. He said, "We thank Erin for those words. And I want to thank her for considering us for her future work. Hopefully, she will let us know her final decision sooner rather than later. But I hope she will accept our invitation, and I fully expect that she will. So now, let's eat."

After Sinbad completed his remarks, a meal was served and everyone indulged themselves for the next hour. He returned to the seat next to Erin, but he would not stay there for long. After he ate only a little of his food, Sinbad said, "Well, Erin, I'm going to have to run, but I expect to hear from you soon about your decision on accepting the position."

"Okay, Sinbad. I'll give you a call soon and will let you know," Erin assured him.

Sinbad left the dining area. Several minutes after that, everyone had finished their meals. Erin continued to chat with the resort personnel who sat at her table; then she got up and spoke to a few others who lingered for a while. But she really had her mind set on a more casual meeting with Bernie, which would take place after the event.

-------A CASUAL WALK-------

Erin was eager to get some issues off her chest, things that would help her make a decision on whether to accept Sinbad's invitation to work for him at the resort. Shortly after most of those who had attended the event left, Erin went over to where Bernie sat at another table and interrupted his conversation with a coworker. She reminded him of their meeting at the tavern.

"Excuse me," she said. "I'll let you two get back to what you were talking about in just a moment. I just wanted to know, Bernie, if you remembered our meeting after the event tonight?"

"Of course, I remember, Erin. Let me introduce you to Mike. Mike, this is Erin, who was introduced to all of us formally tonight by Sinbad. Erin, Mike is on our board of directors. He's one of those who makes all the important decisions around here."

Mike and Erin exchanged greetings, and then she returned to her table to gather her belongings.

Shortly after that Bernie finished his discussion with Mike and came over to where Erin was and asked her, "So are you ready now?"

"Yeah, I'm ready, but let me take all this back to my room, and I'll meet you over in the lobby in about five minutes."

Bernie replied, "Okay, I'll be sitting on the couch near the fireplace."

Erin then went to her suite and soon returned to meet Bernie where he said he would be.

"Well, here I am," she said upon her arrival. "I'm ready to go."

With that they left the resort and followed the same path toward the tavern that she had taken with Bernie's brother Casey the previous day.

As Bernie and Erin strolled, everything seemed the same as it had been the day before when she and Casey went there. But three things were different: A starlit night filled the sky overhead rather than the afternoon sun. Also, several more people walked along the narrow boardwalk from the resort to the tavern. A few guests were wandering along the beach, apparently relaxing after a busy day touring the area. The day before, Erin and Casey were practically alone on the boardwalk and few people could be seen on the beach.

The third thing difference was the nature of the conversation. Whereas Casey talked a lot about his religion and more ethical subjects such as his objection to alcohol and smoking, Bernie's discussions were upbeat as he spoke about the beach, the starlit canopy above them, and the roar of the ocean. As they continued on toward the tavern, Erin was eager to learn more of Bernie's ideas about working at the resort and, most importantly, his views on working for someone who did not practice Christian principles, in her estimation, because of his gay lifestyle.

"Bernie," Erin said, "your brother's talk with me yesterday was very inspirational because I could identify with his Christian values. My problem is that he doesn't practice what he preaches, being in a homosexual relationship."

Bernie stopped in the middle of their walk and turned to Erin. Not feeling good about her comment, he said, "You know what, Erin? You need to talk to him about that. But let me tell you this. Casey is a good guy, and I try not to get involved in his personal life."

Erin responded, "Well, okay. I didn't mean to get you upset."

"No worries," he replied. "I guess I'm a little sensitive about certain things."

With that behind them, they continued their walk to the tavern.

FIGURE 5: A CASUAL WALK AT TWILIGHT

Now the purpose of the commandment is to love from
a pure heart, from a good conscience, and from sincere
faith.
From which some, having strayed, have turned aside to
idle talk.

-1 Timothy 1:5,6

-------A WAY WITH WORDS-------

Soon they arrived at the tavern. Unlike the day before, the bar in the back of the establishment was filled with patrons. Some of them seemed to have had a little too much to drink. Bernie and Erin had no interest in going there, but, unlike the previous day, they decided to go to an open area of the establishment. They found a table and sat down with direction from an attendant. Despite the straw umbrella above the table, they had a clear view of the night sky as well as the roaring ocean meeting the beach below it.

After finding what seemed to be the perfect spot in the tavern to view all of what nature had before them, Bernie commented, "I didn't mean to talk rudely to you a minute ago."

"Well, Bernie, I'll tell you what you told me."

"And what is that?" Bernie asked before she could finish what she was saying.

As he had done earlier, she simply said, "No worries!"

As they sat there enjoying the serenity of the beach environment, Bernie said, "It sure is nice and quiet out here tonight, wouldn't you say, Erin?"

She replied, "It sure is—quite serene."

Bernie commented, "I just like it when you use those big words."

Erin replied, "Big words? You mean you don't know what *serene* is?"

"Yeah, I do," he said. "But I try to choose my words carefully, depending on the environment I'm in and who I'm talking to."

"So what kind of words would you use talking to me?" Erin asked.

After pausing to gather his thoughts, Bernie said, "I would choose words that would describe a beautiful woman!"

"Oh, Bernie, you do have a way with words, although some of them are not very wholesome, like the word you used earlier," Erin said.

Bernie replied, "You mean the word 'hell'?"

"Yeah, there are some words that don't belong in a believer's vocabulary."

"You know, Erin, in a lot of ways you're like my wife who passed on. She was particular about a lot of things like you are."

-------INTIMATE CONVERSATIONS------

At that moment, a horn could be heard blowing in the distance.

"Bernie, do you hear that horn blowing?" Erin asked.

"Oh, yeah, that's from a cruise ship that has sailed away from a nearby port.

Squinting to try and see the vessel, she said, "Oh, yeah, I do see it—just barely—way out there in the ocean! It seems to be so far out there you can hardly see it just below the horizon. Look, don't you see it?" Then Bernie pointed in the direction where he saw an image of a moving vessel and said, "You mean right over there?" "Yeah, right there," she replied.

Bernie moved closer to her to get a better view and said to her, "Yeah, now I see what you're seeing. And I'll have to admit, it's far, so very far out there!"

As she gazed into his eyes, Erin continued, "Well, this is what I mean by serene—that is, what's going on around you. It just adds to the ambiance of the environment, as you just mentioned, that you're in."

"Ambiance—there you go again."

"Oh, Bernie, get a hold of yourself!"

"Just kiddin'," he replied.

Then he pointed again to the ship, which was barely visible. He pulled her close to him as he pointed his finger in that direction, saying, "Look a little closer if you can—out there. You can even see some smoke coming from it. What a sight! Yeah, from here the ship only appears as a tiny light glistening in the dark with that grayish-white smoke coming from its top." Then he turned towards her and said, "Who knows? It may be sailing to Bermuda."

Bernie's motive with that statement was to get Erin's attention and more than that to become intimate with her, and he was successful—somewhat.

It prompted her to say, "You know, Bernie, it reminds me a lot of a time back in Bermuda when my friend Sandra visited me. She had a bad health situation at the time, and we ended up talking about signs she would have to assist in the healing of her condition. And one of those signs was a starlit night like what we're looking at now," she added as she pointed to the heavens.

Being mystified by her comments, Bernie said sarcastically, "Oh, great. I'm trying to get close to you, and you're talking about Sandra's healing!"

Erin responded, "Sorry about that, Bernie."

He realized that he would not get close to Erin at this point because of the nature of the conversation.

"Let me ask you something, Erin. What did Sandra's healing have to do with a starlit sky? And how can a starlit sky help in any way to get someone healed?" His tone was derisive, but Erin had an answer.

FIGURE 6: A DISCUSSION AT TWILIGHT

Trust in the Lord with all your heart, and lean not on your own understanding; In all your way acknowledge Him, and He shall direct your paths.

-Proverbs 3:5,6

-----ALL THINGS WORK TOGETHER FOR GOOD-----

Erin gave Bernie a rather lengthy answer to the question he posed.

"Well, Bernie, I know this is not as romantic as you would like, but this scene has a special effect on me. I mean, as I told Sandra at the time, the stars in the sky right now are majestic—just as the sky appeared when my friend looked up that night on the beach back in Bermuda. But, Bernie, at the time she had a very serious health condition, and I told her that it wasn't the starlit sky that would heal her. It would be her belief in the One that made those stars that would do the trick," Erin said as she again pointed skyward to emphasize what she was saying. "Yeah, Bernie, it would be her belief that God could heal her despite how she felt that night.

"And that's all that a sign does," Erin continued. "And I told her that the celestial beauty above might bring us good feelings, but it's not the thing that brings healing. But, oh, when she saw that sign, Bernie, those stars, it made her feel a lot better.

"But again I stressed to her that healing wouldn't materialize because of the way she felt; it would be because of her belief not just *in* God but her belief in God's ability *to* help her.

"So, Bernie, it was Sandra's faith in the word that guaranteed her healing. Yes, it was her belief that God could and would heal her. That's what it says in His word, the Bible."

"The Bible, huh?" Bernie asked continuing to be derisive in his comments. Then he said more blatantly, "Well, what do ya know, I have a prophet on my hands."

Erin replied, "No, Bernie. I'm not a prophet. I'm just repeating what it says in the Bible about what we all have if we believe. And this is what it says in Mark 11:24, and I'm paraphrasing without reading it because I'm so familiar with this scripture. It says that we can have anything we pray for, including our physical healing, but we *do* have to believe—sincerely believe that we have received it.

"The way I look at it is that God wants to heal us of anything that's coming against us. But we have to believe what the scripture is telling us is true. At least we have to sincerely believe it if we want healing to take place. And believe me, Bernie, that's what Sandra needed when she visited me back in Bermuda. She was in that bad a condition, both physically and spiritually."

Bernie did not know what to say after that exposition by Erin. He simply said, "You're some woman, you know that?"

She replied, "Well, Bernie, don't build me up so much. My life hasn't always been one of faith, and it probably was not much different than what your life has been like. You know, sometimes you have to hit rock bottom before you learn some of the things that I've learned. But you know what? Without some of these challenges, it's hard for someone to come to that point in their own lives where they feel they need God. So, maybe you haven't gotten to that point yet," she said.

"Well, Erin, I agree maybe I haven't."

"Well, don't worry about it. In another scripture it says that all things work together for the good to those who love God, and you do love God, don't you?" she asked.

"Sure, I love God, and I try to do what's right."

--------A WORLD OF DOUBTS--------

Bernie tried to change the nature of the conversation by saying to his new friend, "Listen, Erin, let's talk about the reason you're here and your feelings about working for Sinbad."

Erin began to spill out the thoughts that had been weighing on her. "You know, Bernie, I'm not sure if I should follow through with this job. I mean, it may not be right to accept a job just because I want it and not consider the compromising of my values."

"Compromising your values? What in the world are you talking about? What values are you talking about being compromised?" he asked.

Erin tried to give him an answer. "If you want to know the truth, it's about your brother Casey and his relationship with Sinbad. For heaven's sake, Bernie, it's two men sleeping with one another! Now in the scripture that is an abomination in God's sight. And if I capitulate and give in to the temptation of my fleshly desire, that is, my desire to accept this position with Sinbad being my boss, I'll be enabling something that's wrong, something I don't believe in. It would be like me promoting that lifestyle for heaven's sake. Now as a Christian, I feel that might not be what I should do. So, Bernie, I'm debating whether I should even accept the position that Sinbad has offered me."

--------BERNIE'S RESPONSE TO ERIN'S DOUBTS--------

After Erin's lengthy discussion, Bernie shed a little more light on his background. He said, "Erin, I didn't tell you this, but my father was a minister. In fact, he still is in one of those very strict denominations. He's Presbyterian, so I know about growing up in a household where morality was practiced. As an adult, my view is that sometimes parents can be too strict in bringing up their children. I mean, my brother Casey and I as well as our sister Mary Ann were never allowed to go to social events at our school or to parties like other kids. Many of them were our friends and *were* allowed to attend. And I think that it affected us as far as our not being as sociable as we could have been. Heck, that part of me may have been passed down to my son, who like I told you, has trouble socializing with others his age."

"Okay, Bernie," Erin said. Then she asked the question, "But what does all that have to do with me and my sticking to my morals?"

Bernie replied, "Just let me say this. I think you should go ahead and take the job my boss is offering you. And the one reason I say that is because I can tell this is your passion. My belief is that God gives us all something that we really love and usually we are good at doing—whatever talent it might be. Sometimes it's called our God-given talent. And your talent apparently is the ability to run a resort like the one Sinbad has here. And it's your responsibility to further develop that talent. And you have an ideal opportunity to do that here in south Florida with Sinbad providing you with that opportunity.

"To be frank about it, his lifestyle shouldn't be a concern of yours, especially if it somehow is connected to what God has given you. As a matter of fact, I believe God demands it, that is, He demands that all of us fulfill our life's purpose, which is tied to our God-given talent. And if you don't do that, you have only yourself to blame.

"Yeah, you can't blame anyone else if you allow yourself to continue to be unfulfilled by not taking advantage of what God has given you. Look at it this way: this opportunity is a gift that God is providing. But it's up to you to take advantage of it, to take the gift!"

Erin said, "Well, I certainly can relate to that. We have to be willing to receive what God is giving us. The real question though, Bernie, is if it's really from God, or is it just our own selfish desires? Anyway, I didn't know that you knew so much of the practical aspects of the scriptures."

Erin continued, "And let me say this. You mean it was my threat of deciding *not* to come down here at your brother's resort for you to get spiritual all of a sudden? Now, your brother is not like that. He doesn't need something to lead him to talk about his faith. He just goes ahead and does it. Based on what little time I've spent with him, I'd say he just comes out and expresses his faith without anything prompting him to do it."

Bernie replied, "Well, I have my ideas about that. Some people talk a lot of religion just to let the people they're talking to know how spiritual they are. But to me, that's a front; it's not really genuine in my opinion—especially in my brother's case given the relationship he's in. Now, I'm not judging anybody including my brother. He's grown; he can do whatever he wants. And as you can probably tell, I love him and everything; I just keep my distance.

"In other words, Erin, Case doesn't affect any of my actions because of his lifestyle. And you know what? He shouldn't affect your decisions either because of who he's sleeping with. That's his business, and I also learned this growing up in the church. I remember my father saying to all of us 'chillins,' that we must let the tares and wheat come up together, and in the end God will do the separating. Now, I don't know where in the scripture it says that, but that's what he used to say a lot."

Bernie continued, "Don't worry, Erin, like all of us, at some point we have to give an account for our actions in this lifetime, so in my opinion we should let God do the judging, and we're responsible for loving people regardless of what they may be doing in their personal lives that we may or may not agree with. I guess what I'm saying is that you shouldn't let the actions of my brother influence *your* decision to work here—especially if it involves your passion.

"Like I've been saying, if you want to get spiritual, this opportunity has been gift wrapped for you by the Master, not by Sinbad, the one that's actually offering you the position. It's God that's pulling all the strings, making things happen. He's sovereign, remember? We as His children are only instruments called to do His service. And in your case, the service is running this resort for my brother!

"At this point, all I can say is that you've been shown something that's good, Erin, and you can check it out for yourself—God's demands for us all—to live the best life we can with His direction. That's in the Old Testament in two places, Micah 6:8 and Deuteronomy 30:19. Oh, yeah, we have a choice in the matter! And I remember my father quoting these scriptures a lot while growing up listening to him preach."

Erin said to Bernie, "I'll do that; I'll take a look at these scriptures."

In all the things that Bernie told Erin, what stuck out the most was that God demands that we follow our passion. In response, she said, "Now, Bernie, that's interesting. I mean when you say that God demands that we follow our passion. Well, I do know about how Jesus said He came so that we might have life more abundantly. And a life down here in south Florida would certainly be an abundant life for me.

"Well, I certainly will think about what you've said in making my decision. Sinbad asked me to call him tomorrow evening to give him that decision. Until then, you've given me more to think about. I never thought about the fact that God demands that we utilize the talents He has given us. I guess what you're saying is that God demands that we make ourselves happy, because He wants us to have that abundant life I was telling you about.

"And you know, Bernie, I'm beginning to get it. It's only when we utilize the talents God has given *us* that we are best able to help others. And that's a bottom line, the way I see it. We all are placed on this earth to be a light, to help others overcome their issues. I guess we just have to get out of our comfort zone sometimes and do the things that God would have us to do regardless of what obstacles are placed in our path. And I now believe the situation of your brother's relationship with Sinbad *is* that obstacle for me."

Bernie replied, "Well, you got it, I *do* believe. That's what *I'm* talking about! Now, let's refocus and concentrate on this beautiful night we have—with that starlit sky and the roar of the ocean waves on the beach!"

"Okay!" Erin answered softly.

CHAPTER FIVE
THE ABUNDANT LIFE

Later in the evening, Erin and Bernie decided to return to the hotel, so they started to walk along the narrow boardwalk from the tavern.

Erin said, "Let's get out on the sand and walk out there the rest of the way. I'll take off my sandals and you can too. It'd be exhilarating to feel the coolness of the sand on our feet at this late hour. I remember this is how it was one evening on the beach back in Bermuda."

Erin recalled how she walked with Sandra from the beach for the last time that night in Bermuda. As Sandra had then, Erin looked up and saw a starlit sky. But her view of the heavens did not signify a physical healing as in the case of Sandra. For her, it meant a renewal of her life possibly in a new location, a place she had always desired to be.

Now, Erin had gained the opportunity to be where she had long dreamed of living. Despite the contentment she had in running the Bermuda resort, she thought about the joy of being in south Florida. She fantasized about the possibilities she now had in fulfilling her passion of running a resort in a tropical paradise. *I sure hope this is the beginning of the abundant life I've hoped for down here in south Florida,* she thought.

--------"I JUDGE NO ONE"--------

A major stumbling block to her abundant new life in south Florida was Erin's disappointment with Casey and his lifestyle—one that she thought would be a part of her everyday life in the area if she were to relocate here. She would have to make a decision on whether to take the job offered by Casey's *special* friend Sinbad or remain content where she was in Bermuda.

With these thoughts about her future, Erin and Bernie returned to the lobby. Instead of retiring for the evening, they sat on the couch near the large fireplace and chatted a little while longer.

Bernie said, "Erin, I'll be away on a business trip tomorrow, but I want you to call me tomorrow evening to let me know what your decision is. I sure hope you decide to come and work with us."

Erin replied, "Yeah, Bernie, I have a lot to think about. I'll spend most of the day tomorrow packing so that I'll be ready for my flight back to Bermuda late Monday morning."

Before they left each other, Erin was curious about something. She asked Bernie, "You know, I've been curious about this fireplace here. Why in the world would you have a fireplace in Florida – south Florida no less?" Then Bernie gave her an answer, "Well, that's all Sinbad's, idea. You do know that they've just constructed this place, and Sinbad had a hand in it – the fireplace – being a part of building. The idea originally came from his cousin Freddie, who Sinbad used to visit on occasion up in Detroit." "Well, that explains it," Erin replied.

Then Bernie told her something else that Erin was not aware of when he said, "And another thing, this is really not a hotel, but a condominium, at least on the first two floors – the rest of the space in this high rise is reserved for offices, which have not been filled yet." To that, Erin simply said, "Okay."

Soon they departed from one another, and they both wondered if their paths would ever cross again. But they had each other's phone numbers, so they would not be far away in communication. The question remained whether Erin would opt for the more abundant life she desired in south Florida or if she would be content where she was in Bermuda. She agreed with Bernie that it was a once-in-a-lifetime opportunity to follow her passion.

The next day came with Erin preparing for her departure from south Florida as she had planned. It didn't take much for her to make a decision. She somehow rationalized in her mind that even Casey, with his questionable lifestyle based on *her* standards, represented one of the stars that she saw as she looked back at the sky the previous night when she and Bernie left the tavern.

In her mind, the glistening light of those celestial bodies represented God's description of His people who would be as numerous as the stars in the sky as well as the sands of the sea. She imagined a large number of souls diverse in terms of their culture and lifestyle. And she now realized that each one of us is different or unique, but we are all God's children nonetheless. And while some might disagree with that assessment, in her estimation each one of us must be guided by that spirit within, the Holy Spirit. She realized that God does not look so much at our outward differences as He does our sincerity towards Him, a characteristic that comes from within.

Erin concluded that Casey, despite her lack of understanding about him, would be in that number as one of the guiding lights as represented by each of the stars she viewed in the sky. Nevertheless, Erin could not imagine how that could be based on her knowledge of scripture. But she also knew that Bernie's assessment of the scriptures was correct and that, despite the circumstances, our likes and dislikes as well as those who may come against us, we should pursue and utilize what God gave us as a talent.

And that's what Erin decided to concentrate on—the positives that she saw in Casey. She remembered a verse of scripture that her friend Maggie had quoted from a Sunday school lesson back at Mark Methodist when they talked on the phone once. Erin remembered Maggie telling her about a time when Jesus was confronted by the Pharisees, the self-righteous ones who were grounded in the law of Moses. Maggie told her of a scripture, John 8:15, when Jesus responded to his critics by saying, "You judge according to the flesh. I judge no one."

And Erin decided that neither would she act as a judge of Bernie's brother and his relationship with her future boss Sinbad should she accept the positon. This approach, in Erin's view, would help her to focus on her talents of being an effective manager of Sinbad's resort if she decided to relocate.

--------ERIN'S ANNOUNCEMENTS--------

After Erin completed her packing and other preparations to leave south Florida late on Sunday evening, she knew she had several announcements to make. First and foremost, she gave Sinbad a call to let him know of her decision.

"Hello!" Sinbad answered.

"Hello, Sinbad. Erin here calling to inform you of my decision to work at your resort. And I want to tell you that I will be coming on board. I'm looking forward to working with you and the crew down here."

Sinbad responded, "That's great, Erin. I was hoping you'd be giving that answer. We're so glad you'll be a part of our team."

"Well, I need to call some other people to let them know my plans. But I'm sure I'll be talking to you more in the near future," she told him.

"Yes, you will be hearing from me, and again I'm so glad you'll be joining us," he said.

"Bye, Sinbad," Erin replied and then ended the conversation.

Erin knew right then and there that the abundant life she craved was within reach and to be taken advantage of. South Florida would be waiting for her.

After talking with Sinbad, Erin tried to contact Bernie to let him know of her decision as she had promised. But she did not receive an answer.

Erin would not call Sandra or Maggie to let them know until late Monday after her return to Bermuda. She decided to call Bernie again at that time.

After she packed and made ready to leave the resort in south Florida, Erin was taken to the airport and soon had an uneventful flight from Miami to Bermuda. Upon landing at the island's airport, she went through exiting protocol and soon returned to her resort living quarters.

After doing some unpacking, Erin gave Sandra a call, but she did not answer, so she then called Maggie, who did answer.

"Hello, Erin! I saw on my caller ID that you were calling," Maggie said.

"Hello, Maggie. How are you doing?" she asked.

"Erin, I'm fine. Are you back from Miami?"

Erin answered, "Yeah, I returned earlier today, and I just want to say that I've decided to relocate there."

Maggie responded with excitement, "Oooh! I can't believe it! That's great, Erin."

Erin replied, "Yeah, it was an interesting trip, and I had to weigh some things in making my decision. But I'm at peace with how it turned out."

Then Maggie said, "That's great! I can't wait to see you, and I'm sure Sandra will feel the same way when she gets the news. Or have you spoken to here yet?"

"Well, no, Maggie. I was going to ask you if you've talked to her. I tried calling her but didn't get an answer."

Maggie replied, "Well, you know how that girl is. She's constantly on the go, so to answer your question, no, I haven't talked to her."

Maggie then took the opportunity to tell Erin that a number of people from Detroit were planning to come down in October in a big show of support for Sinbad and his resort. She told Erin, "You do know I've being getting information from Sandra, don't you? And, of course, she gets her information from Freddie, who has a direct line of communication to his cousin Sinbad."

"Wow! That's great, Maggie! I can hardly wait until that time when we all will be together again."

With that comment from Erin, Maggie was confused. She thought to herself, *I wonder why she said, 'when we all will be together again,' as if we've all been together with her before. I know we've never been with Erin except in the dream I had of going on that cruise.*

Maggie was left to wonder for a while about the reality of that dream, which had seemed so real.

As Maggie continued her conversation with Erin, her friend said, "Yeah, Maggie, I'm sure I'll get some of the same information that you've gotten when I contact Sandra. I'll call her again—maybe tomorrow morning."

"Well, *okay* then," she said slowly, still being mystified by Erin's comments.

Erin finished the conversation by saying, "Okay, Maggie, I just called to give you the big announcement. And remember to tell Sandra that I'll call her in the morning if you hear from her."

"Okay, Erin, you have a good night," Maggie answered.

"You too, Maggie," Erin replied.

With those last words from Erin, the conversation ended.

--------A PROMISE KEPT--------

Erin kept her promise to call Bernie to let him know of her decision. So, she called him not long after she talked with Maggie. The phone rang only twice before Bernie had picked it up to answer. He saw on the caller ID that it was Erin, so he greeted her, saying, "Hello, Erin. I saw that you called last night, but I was out late on business, so I figured you'd get back with me after your flight to Bermuda."

Erin said, "Hello, Bernie. Yeah, I did call because I wanted to keep my promise of calling you. But you weren't available last night. Anyway, I have a feeling I know what you want to hear."

"You've got that right, Erin. I hope you have some good news for me," Bernie replied.

"I sure do!" she assured him. "I called Sinbad last night and told him that I accept his offer."

Bernie said, "All right then! That certainly *is* good news. Welcome to the family!" he told her with much enthusiasm.

--------A PROPOSAL?--------

After the good news Bernie got from Erin, he said, "And I have some good news for you too."

Erin was startled momentarily, remembering what Maggie had told her about how Fred had proposed—like a marriage proposal. It was a total surprise. Before Bernie could say anything, she thought, *Could this guy be proposing to me?* Based on his actions towards her, she thought, *It seems this guy likes me a lot; at least he acts like he does, so let me brace myself.*

After those few moments of contemplation and anticipation, Erin's thoughts turned to marriage. She perked up and waited for what Bernie was about to say with a smile.

"Like I said Erin, I have something very important to tell you, to ask you."

Erin got even more excited by those words. Smiling from ear to ear, she said, "Oh, yes, Bernie, what is it? What is it?" She repeated for emphasis, anticipating a marriage proposal.

"Well, I want to know… I want to know if… you would go with me to Jamaica in a few weeks?"

Hoping Bernie would ask her something more significant, Erin felt somewhat deflated. But she gathered herself quickly, and responded, "Why, sure, Bernie, I'd be happy to come along."

Bernie replied, "Okay. That's great! I'll be going to Jamaica the second weekend in September, and there's more than enough room in the timeshare that Sinbad has down there for another couple. In fact, he has three other timeshares in the vicinity of one another, and plus there is a large arcade nearby. He designates all of that as his unofficial resort. He never goes there – at least I don't think he does; he just has it for special guests who would like to get away from his other business interests here in Miami. And you know, it would be so lonely with just me being in one of those three huge condos he has down there. So I'm glad you agree to come with me, that is, you as well as your kid."

At that point, Erin was dejected not only because it was not a marriage proposal that she got from Bernie but also because he suggested that her son Tony come along too. *How about that! We even won't be alone down there,* she thought. Nonetheless, she was excited because he thought enough of her—and her son—to offer them an invitation to come along with him on a vacation. At the same time, Erin was mystified that he would ask her son to come along as well.

Erin went on, "It's really nice of you, Bernie, to invite me to come along with you on your vacation and especially to allow my son to come with me. I guess I was assuming you'd be alone—with a lady friend perhaps." But, listen, my son and I won't be any trouble."

Bernie replied, "No, Erin, I don't think you understand. I don't anticipant your son being a problem at all. As a matter of fact, I forgot to tell you that my boy Jacob will be coming along with me, so your son and my boy can get together while we're down there. And by the way I don't have a lady friend other than yourself, of course!"

-------PLANS FOR A VACATION-------

After clearing up the nature of Bernie's proposal, his vacation proposal that is, Erin didn't think long about it when she said, "It really sounds like it's going to be a grand vacation, Bernie."

Bernie interjected, "Well, Erin, it will be. I just want you to commit to going with us."

"Okay, Bernie, I have a question for you. Will Tony and I have our own accommodations?" Erin asked.

"Sure!" Bernie emphasized. "Each one of us will have our own bedroom, and you and your son would be on the opposite side of the condo from where Jacob and I will be. The nice thing about it is that there's a large kitchen and living area that separate the two areas where we would sleep, so it'd be very convenient for the adults as well as for the kids."

"Everything sounds grand, Bernie, as I said before," Erin replied. "I'll talk to Tony when he comes to my resort next weekend and let him know of the arrangement. I'm sure he'll be excited." While only a young boy, Tony's father would allow him to fly over from New York to Bermuda on occasions on weekends to visit his mother.

"Good. That's fair enough," Bernie said.

Before Erin finished her conversation with Bernie, she asked him another question. "One last thing, Bernie. You say that Sinbad has other business interests in south Florida. Do you know what they are?"

Bernie replied, "No, I don't have an idea about what he does outside of real estate. But I do know that he has real estate holdings not only in south Florida but also in other parts of the country and, who knows, maybe even in some foreign countries. He's a real go-getter you might say, so he's doing pretty well financially."

Erin responded, "Well, okay. I was just being curious." Shortly after that they finished their conversation.

When Erin had finished talking with Bernie, she made efforts to contact her former husband to make sure Tony would be available on the weekend that Bernie said they would be going to Jamaica. Since their divorce, Erin had minimal physical contact with her ex, but they had an open communication and were civil about their new relationship especially as it involved their son. In fact, even before she returned to Bermuda, Erin was able to talk with Tony by phone to tell him of her arrangements, and she figured he too would be excited about the trip. So, everything was on go as far as Erin and Tony joining Bernie and his son Jacob on the trip to Jamaica.

Erin was now eager to begin packing in preparation for the trip from Bermuda to Miami. Bernie had told Erin earlier that he could secure the air reservations for all four of them to leave Miami for Jamaica. The plan was that Bernie would make the flight reservations for Tony from New York City to Miami as well as for her flight in from Bermuda. They would meet at the Miami airport, and from there all four of them would fly to Jamaica.

Bernie told Erin that he and his son would meet her and Tony at the airport's boarding gate preferably at least 30 minutes before boarding.

--------A PERFECT GETAWAY!--------

Erin thought the trip would be a perfect getaway before moving permanently to south Florida. At the conclusion of the trip to Jamaica, she still would have two weeks to prepare for the actual relocation to Miami. Meanwhile, Tony would take a return flight to New York to be with his father again.

Bernie had orchestrated all the travel arrangements. Erin and Tony were to meet Bernie and Jacob at the Miami airport in two weeks.

The day finally came when Erin and Tony arrived on separate flights to the Miami airport, met each other, and walked to the gate where Bernie and his son were located. Soon all four individuals would form their little travel group. Bernie had hoped that they would meet at least an hour before boarding time, but that would not be the case.

Bernie and Jacob had already arrived at the terminal gate and were in the process of grabbing a snack before waiting on the boarding call. Erin had called earlier to let Bernie know that she and Tony were running a little late but should be there in a few minutes.

"That's great, Erin," Bernie replied. "Jacob and I will be waiting for you and Tony," Bernie told her.

Despite having heard from Erin, Bernie was still concerned about whether she and her son would arrive in time to board their flight. After having eaten some nuts, Bernie sat next to Jacob and said, "I sure hope Erin and Tony will be here on time. It's still early, but it's always better to be too early than too late." Bernie imparted his wisdom to Jacob, saying, "You remember that, son, whenever you have to travel by yourself by plane."

"Yes, sir," Jacob replied.

As Bernie continued to sit nervously waiting for Erin and her son Tony to arrive, he said, "We'll be boarding in a few minutes, and hopefully they're close to being here."

Jacob said, "Don't worry, Dad. Don't stress yourself out. Anyway, I'm looking forward to meeting Tony. Maybe we can do some things while we're on this trip."

"Now, ain't that something—your kid advising you what to do," he said in jest. He continued, "Yeah, son, I'm sure you two will get along just fine."

--------COMING TOGETHER--------

It wasn't long before Bernie spotted Erin and her son heading toward them with only about 30 minutes before boarding. Erin and her son were walking briskly towards them down a crowded walkway filled with other travelers. Tony was trying as best he could to keep up with his mother.

"Come on, son. Can't you walk any faster?" she scolded.

Bernie had already saved two seats for them in the waiting area. When Erin and Tony finally arrived, the conversations between them began.

Being almost out of breath when she and her son got to where Bernie and his son were, Erin said, "Hello, Bernie, and I take it that this is Jacob."

Bernie replied, "My goodness, I'm glad to see you two, and you're almost out of breath!"

"Yeah, Bernie, both of us are tired, but we're here!"

"Anyway, yes, this is Jacob," Bernie replied. "And, Jacob, I'd like for you to meet my friend Erin."

"Hello, Miss. Erin," Jacob said.

"Well, hello to you, Jacob."

"And I see that this is your son Tony?" Bernie noted.

Erin replied, "Yes, this is Tony. Tony, why don't you greet them?"

"Hi, Mr. Bernie, and hi to you too, Jacob," Tony said.

In response, Jacob simply said, "Hi."

After those initial greetings, Erin apologetically said, "And, Bernie, I'm so sorry we're late. I guess we'll be boarding in just a little while."

"That's okay," he replied. "You two just relax in these two seats here until we board."

After they were comfortably situated, Bernie asked, "Well, how has your planning for the trip been, Erin?"

"It's been rather chaotic, but we've made it work. Tony had a flight delay from New York City. But my flight from Bermuda arrived here in Miami at about the same time as his, so we didn't have a problem meeting each other fairly quickly."

While they were waiting to board, a lady sitting across from Erin initiated a conversation. The lady, who was sitting with a male companion, asked Erin, "Where are you folks going?"

Erin answered, "All of us are going to Jamaica."

"To Jamaica?" she said, adding, "Why, that's where we're going!"

Erin realized that was not unusual because everyone in this gate would be going to that tropical paradise.

The lady said, "We're going to a timeshare as guests of Sinbad Mosley."

Erin, as well as Bernie, who was sitting beside her, were shocked at what they heard.

In response, Erin said, "Sinbad Mosley? That's where we're going! We're staying at one of his timeshares!" The lady responded by saying, "Now that's interesting. What a coincidence, we're staying in one of his time shares too!"

Then Erin asked the lady, "What is your name? Maybe we can get together at our place or yours once we get to the resort."

The woman responded, "My name is Lisa, and this is my friend Gary.

"Okay. My name is Erin, and this is my friend Bernie. These are our kids."

After the introduction, Erin and Lisa exchanged contact information including the phone and room numbers of their timeshares.

Lisa then commented to both Bernie and Erin, "You know, this is our first time flying. And we're so nervous because we don't know what to expect. I can't speak for Gary though because he seems to be so calm about it."

Gary said to their new acquaintances, "Yeah, it'll be an experience. It's something you have to deal with if you want to go anywhere long distance these days." Then he turned toward his friend and said, "But, Lisa, I'm a little nervous too now!"

Erin replied, "Well, let me tell you, Lisa, and you too, Gary, all of *us* have flown a lot, and we'll help calm your nerves as much as possible."

"Oh, thank you. It's so good meeting someone who's going to the same place," Lisa replied.

At about that time, the boarding announcement was made over the loudspeaker. "All boarding now on flight 111 to Jamaica! This is the last boarding call!"

Everyone got their belongings and started walking toward the boarding line.

--------TAKE OFF!--------

After the boarding call, passengers quickly entered the aircraft. Soon after everyone had been seated, the plane taxied across the tarmac and got into takeoff position. Shortly thereafter, the plane raced down the runway, and soon they were airborne.

Erin was sitting next to Tony just in front of Bernie, and his son Jacob was seated beside his father by a window. Meanwhile, Lisa and Gary were located a few rows ahead of Erin's group.

Erin's concern about Lisa's fear of flying was evident when she turned around and said to Bernie, "I sure hope Lisa and Gary are okay, especially Lisa because she seemed so afraid of this flight."

Bernie replied, "Yeah, I remember my first flight. I was pretty much terrified like Lisa. But it's something you just have to deal with if you want the advantage of flying, and that is to get you to where you want to go quickly."

As the plane ascended to a cruising altitude, a flight attendant delivered instructions.

After that, Erin blurted out, "I can't believe we're actually in the air on our way to that tropical paradise I've heard so much about!"

Bernie replied by simply saying enthusiastically, "We are!"

Tony yelled, "Look, Mommy, I can see the city and the ocean too. And what are those white things in the water?" he asked with great curiosity. Then he said, "It seems like it's hundreds of 'em."

Bernie, sitting behind him, leaned forward, then said, "Listen, buddy, they're dolphins, hundreds of 'em probably, like you said."

Tony responded, "Wow!" as his mouth gaped in amazement.

Bernie continued, "You know, Tony, they are really plentiful in the waters around Miami. They really love the warm water."

After sharing that information, Bernie asked Tony as well as Jacob, who was sitting beside his father, "Well, are you boys as excited as Ms. Pearson and me about this trip?"

Tony turned around as much as he could to see Bernie, who was sitting in one of the seats behind him to give an answer.

"Yeah, Mister, uh, uh..." Tony couldn't finish his statement because he did not remember Bernie's name.

Bernie relieved the boy of his frustration and said, "Just call me Bernie."

Now, remembering what he had called him back in the terminal, Tony said, "Yes sir, Mr. Bernie."

Bernie went on to tell the boys, "We hope you two can get together over the next few days." Everyone including Erin smiled in agreement. It was clear that Bernie and Erin were looking forward to spending some time together at the resort—alone.

Because it would be some time before they would have a meal, everyone partook of the snacks being distributed during the early part of the flight.

"Snacks and refreshments coming up," they heard one of the attendants say.

After munching on a few items, a little while later they closed their eyes for some rest.

While the boys seemed friendly to one another, the question remained as to how much they would be together and how well would they get along. But, for now, the grownups were definitely excited about the trip, especially Erin, who had her new job in south Florida clearly in sight.

It was a short and uneventful flight as the plane continued in its cruising altitude. Erin looked over where Tony sat, peaked through the small window, and saw nothing but an ocean of white. The plane was now cruising above the clouds.

Everyone had settled into their seats and begun to relax. Soon the plane began its initial descent towards the Jamaican airport. Over the next few minutes, the plane continued to descend until it made a rather smooth touchdown. After the aircraft taxied to the deboarding gate, post-flight protocol began and soon passengers deplaned and entered the Jamaican airport terminal. Everyone was met with what is commonly known in the area as moonlight dancers, young girls that were adorned with a glittering top and skirts made of what seemed to be leaves of native vegetation.

"What a welcoming committee! Never seen anything like this at an airport." Erin said. Everything was so festive.

After pausing to appreciate the dancers, the four travelers, among others, meandered their way to baggage claim, and the wait was on to retrieve their luggage. Once they had secured their belongings, Bernie and Erin along with their sons took ground transportation, an airport shuttle, to their lodgings for their short stay.

--------TIMESHARING--------

During the process of claiming their luggage, everyone had to endure long lines to satisfy customs requirements and the exit of airport property. When that was completed, a neatly adorned chauffer led the group to his vehicle and loaded their luggage. In a huge limousine, he took them the ten-minute drive from the airport to the timeshare property.

Upon arrival, they traveled along a narrow, pebbled pathway with flowering plants and brush on both sides to the resort's front entrance. Finally, they arrived at their destinations, the timeshare that would be their home for the next three days. Shortly after that, everyone registered at the front desk of the main office of the condo complex to gain access to their separate quarters. Shortly after that, they were ready to enjoy the pleasures that awaited them at the resort.

Bernie and Erin had dinner in the main dining area of the resort while Jacob and Tony had lost themselves somewhere on property grounds, probably at the video arcade that was situated in a side area just prior to entering the headquarters.

After dinner, Bernie and Erin entertained their new friends, Lisa and Gary, at their condo. Lisa gave a slight knock on their door, and Erin answered, "Hello, Lisa and Gary. Come on in. Bernie and me were just sitting in the living area talking. The kids are out having fun someplace, I suppose. I'm so glad you all gave us your contact information."

"It was so nice of you to allow us into your space," Lisa said as Erin ushered her into the condo.

"Speaking of space, you all have a nice condo here – it's so large," Gary said.

Bernie replied, "Yeah, we need it with our two boys with us. I think each condo in this complex is catered to the needs of their guests. Now, you mentioned going to the beach earlier. Do you two want to go out there now and just relax a while?"

Lisa replied, "That would be great. Wouldn't you agree, Gary?"

"Yeah, I'm all for it," he replied.

Lisa continued, "Our timeshare condo is not far away at all, so we can go back and put on something more appropriate for the beach and meet you two at the resort headquarters lobby in say…What—about 10 minutes?"

"That would be great. Wouldn't it, Bernie?" Erin asked.

"Sounds good to me!" he replied.

After that confirmation, the two couples would soon be together again and venture onto the beach nearby. After a while, they all met in the lobby of the main building; they chatted a little there before heading out to the beach. Then, they found some beach chairs and situated themselves overlooking the ocean beneath two huge straw umbrellas.

Once they got themselves settled, Lisa said to everyone, "What a relaxing environment. I just love sitting here in this beach chair and rubbing my hands through the sand. It's so invigorating!" Then she admitted, "You know, guys, after being scared and nervous about that first flight of mine, I now realize was well worth it." Lisa finally found the words to express her feelings about being at the resort, adding, "And I say that because this is almost, well, for heaven's sake, it's almost like heaven itself."

Erin replied, "We're so glad you've gotten over the fear of your first plane flight, Lisa."

"Well, Erin, it's not so much that I've conquered the fear of flying, but I did make it through that first flight of mine. But most of all, being here at the resort has made me forget about the fear of that flight.

"I know you can relate to this, Erin, because I know you remember when you had your son. Well, it was kinda like that. I mean, what woman can't remember that experience of giving birth? The joy of holding your own child when it comes makes you forget about all the pain you had while delivering it."

Then Erin, replied, "Well, I can certainly agree with that. It's been a while, but yeah, I felt the same way when Tony was born."

It had been Gary's first flight as well, but he did not show a concern based on his demeanor. While listening to what the ladies were saying about childbirth and how it related to the fear of flying, he commented, "Well, obviously I can't relate to that, but what I *can* relate to is the wait in those long lines of post-flight protocol. I know everyone was glad to finally leave the airport, and, as far as we're concerned, it's great to be here at the resort and just to relax."

"Amen to that, brother!" Bernie agreed.

While sitting there bathing in the ocean breeze, Lisa said to Bernie and Erin, "You know, this timesharing thing is really nice. I think we should do this more often," she added directing her remark to her friend Gary.

After a while, both couples returned to their living quarters.

--------**REFLECTIONS**--------

Later that night, Lisa and Gary went to their condo, and Erin and Bernie found themselves alone in their living quarters because the boys had not yet returned. They decided to sit in the rather large living area between the bedrooms on either side. A huge fireplace was located on the back wall with a large couch in front of it. The flames flickering out of that contraption defied the warm temperatures outside because of the air conditioning inside the facility. It reminded Erin of the huge fireplace situated in the facility back at the resort. She could not understand the presence of such a contraption, other than to provide an ambiance to the setting – and it certainly did that.

Sitting comfortably near that fireplace, they reflected on everything that had transpired. Bernie said, "Erin, I'm so glad you decided to work with Sinbad. I think you can do a lot of good for the organization. But the beauty of it all is that you'll be following your passion."

Erin replied, "Well, Bernie, it was something you said that helped me make the decision. It made me reflect on my own faith and how it might influence the decisions I make. And you helped me realize that my decisions should be based on the talents God has given to me, and in my case the greatest talent I have professionally is in resort management. So as you suggest, that's what I need to focus on instead of something that's not central to my purpose—to my passion. And that passion involves working in real estate like the resort management position that Sinbad gave me.

"And as far as your brother and Sinbad are concerned, it was just as important for me not to focus on their personal life, that is, their gay lifestyle—at least not to the point of having it influence my decision to work there. It was more of a distraction, driving me away from my passion that you talked about. I understand now that is not for me to judge your brother's lifestyle or his friend's for that matter. I will let the Lord do that. I realize that our job as believers is not to judge but to love people even if we love them from a distance. Yeah, to love people who may not conform to our values. So, I need to thank you for that."

Bernie replied, "Well, I can appreciate all that you say. I'm just glad you're with us."

-------CHATTING SOME MORE--------

Bernie and Erin were still conversing when Tony and Jacob walked through the door. Bernie said, "Hello, boys. Did you two have a good time at the arcade tonight?"

Tony responded, "Yeah, Mr. Bernie. It was a blast. There were so many machines over there I'm sure we didn't get to half of 'em. And we ate some good food there too, like hot dogs and hamburgers.

Erin repeated the same question, "And, Jacob, I guess you had a lot of fun too."

Being more reserved than Tony, he simply said, "Yes, ma'am."

The boys then went to their respective rooms and retired for the night. Bernie and Erin soon did the same.

"Tomorrow we'll spend some time on the beach, Erin, so I guess we need to get some rest too," Bernie said.

Erin agreed and they too went to their living quarters for the night.

--------THE NEXT DAY--------

The next day Tony and Jacob were up early before breakfast was served and off to the arcade again. They planned to stay there the whole day, leaving Bernie and Erin alone together as they had hoped. The father and mother of the two boys got up later in the morning and met each other in the dining area. They had a hefty breakfast or rather brunch by this time. After that, they took off for the beach and had a fun day in the sand, threading through the ocean waves, and napping on beach chairs throughout the afternoon.

The most interesting part of their day together would come later when, after a simple dinner indulgence in the dining area of the condo, they re-established themselves on the couch in front of that huge fireplace. It was there where they would find out much more about each other, which would test the strength of their relationship.

--------A TEST OF THEIR RELATIONSHIP--------

Erin and Bernie drew together on the couch, sitting closer than they had ever been before. A mix of intimacy and inquisitiveness that they could not readily explain lingered in the atmosphere. They certainly felt a desire for one another, but they also had a sense of wanting to know more about each other's values and whether those principles could lead to their coexistence in a long-term, intimate relationship such as marriage. It would be a test of their relationship.

Bernie particularly wanted to get to know more about the lady he had befriended— perhaps as a precaution to developing a relationship that he was afraid could not match the intimacy he had with his late wife before her untimely death. Erin had her own concerns about developing a long-term relationship.

Bernie started a serious conversation by saying, "I have to admit, Erin, I've been checking up on you some. You know my brother Casey obviously is very close to the head macho around here in Sinbad, and Sinbad has close contact with his cousin Freddie, who I understand is a friend of someone who had a close relationship with you a while back—back there in Bermuda."

Then Erin interjected, "Okay. I think I know who you're talking about. That would be Sandra. Yeah, Sandra and I became very close. Like I told you when we were at that tavern back in Miami, she came to my resort when she was really down, both physically and spiritually. But I want you to know that we fixed that. What I mean, Bernie, is that the lady was on death's door! She needed to have a liver transplant and didn't have much time left. And get this, less than two percent of the world's population had a match for her. Do you understand that?" Erin repeated. She continued with emphasis, "Two percent! And she had only a few weeks for them to find a match. Otherwise, she would have been a goner! But by God's grace a match *was* found, and she was healed of her condition. Oh, yeah, the doctors gave her only six months to live! Now what do you think about that?"

Bernie sat there speechless for a few seconds, then said, "That's an impressive story. And, yeah, I remember when you told me some of that when we were at the tavern. But at that time my focus was not on a starlit sky or anything like that; it was on you."

Erin interrupted again, "Well, it's not that I didn't want to get more familiar with you at that time, but my mind was still on Sandra. I mean, I was too overwhelmed thinking about the history I had with her back in Bermuda, especially that final night we were together on the beach. I guess my whole experience with Sandra had about as much effect on me as it had on her at the time.

"But another thing I want to get off my chest about your last comment—about it being an impressive story. No, Bernie, my experience with Sandra is not a story as you put it; these are facts that I'm giving you about what really happened at that time."

As Bernie continued to listen to Erin, she said, with a bit of emotion, "You know, God is very real to me, and most people either don't know that for themselves, or they don't understand the scope of His power. But it comes down to whether we as individuals believe that power and, more importantly, believe that power can work for any of us in our time of need. And I do believe the power of God *can* work for us, for you and for me, Bernie. And Sandra is a living proof of that."

Again, Bernie was speechless at what he heard Erin say. Finally, he said to her, "Okay, I get it. God is able to do all that. But we're talking about Sandra, not you. The real question is how does that power, as you put it, affect you and *your* happiness, our happiness?"

Erin responded, "I don't understand what you're asking, Bernie."

--------MAKING A POINT--------

Bernie tried to elaborate. "Okay, let me break it down like I was going to before you interrupted me."

"Sorry I did that, Bernie," Erin said apologetically.

"That's fine. But listen to this," Bernie continued. After pausing, trying to regain his thoughts, he went on to draw an analogy. "Let me give you an example of what I'm trying to say. You know our new friends, Lisa and Gary? Well, as you know, Lisa was horrified at flying yesterday when we arrived here. But she got on that plane despite her fears. And, if you remember, when we all had that conversation yesterday when we were on the beach, she said she had forgotten all about the fear she had when she saw that ocean and the environment we were in at that time. She even compared it to having a baby.

"Well, do you know why she had forgotten about her fears?" Bernie asked. Before Erin had an opportunity to answer, he gave her an answer of his own. "Well, the answer is this, Erin. The way faith works, in my own understanding, is that there is a certain amount of fear involved in our taking action. In other words, we sometimes act with a certain amount of doubt, but we act anyway, hoping and believing that God will do whatever is needed to make us successful in doing whatever it is we're trying to do. Put another way, we act sometimes trusting that God will be there to see us through any situation we might find ourselves in. That's what it says in the scripture; we walk by faith and not by sight."

Bernie then was more direct in explaining why Lisa and Gary had forgotten about the fear they had of getting on a plane. He continued his trend of thought, "And that's what Lisa and Gary did. They acted by going on that plane, and as a result they reaped the benefits of having that amount of faith, and those benefits were, as she put it, being in a place that was like heaven when they were with us yesterday on the beach."

--------AN AMOUNT OF FAITH--------

Erin hesitantly asked, "So, Bernie, how does that situation relate to me?"

"Well, I'll tell you," he answered. "You took the necessary action by deciding to come on and work for Sinbad even though you may have some personal differences as far as his lifestyle is concerned. Am I right about that?" Again, before she could answer, Bernie added, "That took a certain amount of faith.

"But getting back to what I know about the experience you and Sandra had back in Bermuda, you have to live your own life and make sure you're living it in the abundance that God designed for *you* to have. You can't live off the blessings that someone else may have received—like Sandra's healing. And I think by making the decision in moving to south Florida to follow your passion you're beginning to live that life of even more abundance.

"And I say that because I know you had a certain level of abundance in Bermuda, but I believe God always has more for us. No matter what we may be going through, whether good or bad, there are always more good things coming our way. And that's true for all of us. We just have to believe that and take that step—like the one you took when you decided to join us down here in south Florida."

Bernie continued, "And I'm saying all this because I grew up in church, and I saw a lot of believers forsake happiness in the name of being religious. I mean, as I told you earlier, as a family we could hardly do anything. As kids we couldn't go to dances; we couldn't socialize. In other words, we couldn't live the abundant life that God has for us all. And a lot of that mentality, one of a sheltered life, was ingrained in us at that time as young people, and it followed us into adulthood. But thank God I was delivered from all that stuff!

"And I know that you went astray early in life, and eventually you finally found the light of God's love for you. But sometimes it's so easy to go in the opposite direction, which apparently led you to that lifestyle in the first place. But then you found God and had another transformation. To be honest with you, Erin, I don't want to be someone with the kind of faith that limits the real joy that someone can have in life."

Erin reacted to what Bernie said, saying, "Well, that's certainly a mouthful, Bernie. And I think I understand what you're saying. You don't want to become involved with a prude, someone who's so religious that they can't have any fun. Am I right about that?" she asked.

He responded, "That's exactly right. And that's why I said that given your upbringing and how you were transformed into your faith, what you did in making the decision to work for someone you don't totally agree with in terms of values is a huge indication of spiritual maturity as far as I'm concerned."

Erin reinforced her own background in the faith when she said, "I know what you're saying has a lot of truth in it, but there is value in learning about the straight and the narrow way as it's sometimes called. And I'm not talking about straight in a sexual way!"

"I know that, Erin!" Bernie responded in jest.

Erin continued, "Well, what I was going to say is that I think it's important to learn those basic biblical principles as early in life as possible so that you can put them into practice later. Remember at some point what you may have learned early on will apply later in life. That's what it means in Proverbs 22:6; you can look it up when you get the chance."

Bernie responded, "Okay, I'll do that." He continued, "But, listen, I hear you! And that's what *I'm* saying, Erin. As long as you are not prevented from keeping your own values, those values established by that spirit within you, you'll be fine. And by making the decision to work for us despite questionable surroundings in your estimation, because of my brother's lifestyle, you're continuing in your passion, which is your purpose as I said before."

---------FAITH OR THE FLESH?--------

"Let me tell you something else, Erin. I'm not a churchgoer

although I was brought up in church. But to me, that's not a requirement for knowing God and allowing His power, as you put it, to work for you. And you can have fun and keep your faith too. And that's what I intend to do with us being together, to live that abundant life."

Erin tried to digest everything Bernie was saying and simply responded, "I think I know what you're talking about, Bernie. You know I've been in both worlds, the playground of the world where anything goes as long as it feels good, as well as life in the church and the strict upbringing that I had very early in *my* life—similar to your experience, I guess. But let me tell you, there's always competition between keeping our faith and giving in to the flesh. Believe it or not, I think there's a balance between the two if you live in reality. In other words, because we cater largely to a secular world, we naturally fall prey to fleshly desires, but our goal still should be to have the faith to resist whatever might come against us. So, I think there can be a balance between the two, faith and the flesh, without compromising those values. And, right now, I'm learning how to live more of an abundant life—one that God would approve of."

Erin added, "By balance, I'm not talking about doing some of the same things the world does but only doing those things that bring you fulfillment that God does not frown on. You know what I mean?"

Bernie replied, "I do know what you mean, and that's the kind of thing I want to hear from you!"

At that point they snuggled even closer together, desiring to live the life of abundance that they were talking about—mentally, spiritually, as well as physically. The flesh has its place in our lives so long as we recognize that it is the spirit that drives the flesh, and we allow that spirit, the Holy Spirit, within us to guide our actions. It's only in this way that the abundant life talked about in the scriptures can be attained.

----END OF A VACATION/START OF A NEW LIFE----

Erin's trip to Jamaica with Bernie and the boys would be one she would not soon forget. It was a time of reflection, and, thanks to Bernie, a time when she reevaluated her faith. An assessment that would include a greater focus on living the abundant life that God has for us all.

Erin was now more ready than ever to relocate and start a new life in south Florida, so she prepared to move and eventually did relocate. Erin's first few weeks on the job was certainly something she had to adapt to, but at least she was familiar with the resort management business. The real adjustment would come during an event to celebrate Sinbad's opening of the resort when Maggie and a group from the Chicago/Detroit area as well as the New York/New Jersey area would be there among those participating in the festivities.

Soon the third day at the resort arrived and the time came for everyone to pack up and prepare to return to Miami and end their little vacation.

CHAPTER SIX
STORMS OF DISCORD

Erin would soon have the opportunity for career advancement by transitioning from a resort management job in Bermuda to a similar one in south Florida. This profession is where she always wanted to be—in a tropical area she thought of as paradise.

Now, she would move from one tropical paradise, Bermuda, to another in south Florida. But Erin would have a challenge in adapting to a new situation as manager of Sinbad's resort. As it turned out, Bernie would be a new person in her life there. In her growing relationship with him, Erin would have continuing discussions with her new friend about his values and how those values might affect their relationship—possibly a long-term commitment to one another such as marriage.

-----MAGGIE AND FRIENDS GOING TO SOUTH FLORIDA-----

Maggie had already begun the planning for their trip to Miami while still at home in Chicago. She had ironed out the details earlier with Sandra, who had inside information about the event because of her new friend Freddie, Sinbad's cousin.

When Maggie awakened a few days before their journey, she said, "Fred, I'm so excited about this trip. Aren't you excited too?"

He replied, "Yes, Mag. I'm excited because you're excited. I can see the gleam in your eyes."

"Well, yeah, if that's the way you want to put it," she replied. "Anyway, I'm especially looking forward to the trip to New York to meet Katie. You do understand, Fred, that she and her teenage son Wynn agreed to come along with us. She has a friend in New Brunswick, New Jersey, right across the river from New York City, who would like to come too. And you know what I say—the more the merrier. Her name is Sheri and she has a daughter named Jeanie as well as a friend, David, who will be coming with her. David is a licensed lifeguard, so he should be helpful if there's a problem with all that water we'll be around down in Florida."

Maggie continued, "Anyway, you know Courtney and Gates will already be down there when we arrive because they will have taken a separate flight. But they'll be with us for all the festivities and will come back with us on our return flight to New York. And to put a cap on everything, I'll ask Gates to give a closing message about our trip at Katie's church on that Sunday evening before everyone returns home on Monday morning."

Maggie continued, "But I'll tell you, I still can't get over that dream I had when me and you and all the others went on a cruise. It seemed so real. To me, this trip coming up will seem like a reunion of sorts!"

--------MAGGIE'S FEARS--------

Maggie soon turned her attention back to her final intended destination, south Florida, and attendance at Sinbad's event. She said, "But I'll tell you something else, Fred. The only thing I'm uncomfortable about is Sandra coming along with us."

Fred interrupted before she could finish her statement and said, "Well, I thought you and Sandra were good friends, going all the way back to when she used to take care of your parents when you weren't around to take care of 'em."

"Yeah, Fred, I know. But she has Freddie as her friend now, and he'll be coming along with her," she told him.

Before she could offer an explanation, Fred responded, "Well, what's wrong with that? He seems to be a nice fellow. And Sandra seems to like him a lot." Fred added, "You know they seemed to be so comfortable with each other that night when Sandra and this other new hire at the law firm were being honored. You had stepped away, but Freddie assisted her back to the table after she made those emotional remarks. Then when the band started to play, he insisted that he be her dance partner; he apparently saw she didn't have one. I know I've been kinda cool towards him. But he seems to really like her."

That last statement affected Maggie, and it showed in her facial expression. Fred's mention of Freddie's desire for Sandra did not sit well with Maggie. She turned her head away from Fred briefly to compose herself.

Maggie knew that Freddie used to be with her. At the time of their relationship, she thought he really made her feel like a woman.

"You know, Mag," Fred continued, "I've noticed that you tend to tense up whenever his name is mentioned. But he's harmless. Just relax," Fred assured his wife.

Given their past relationship, Maggie certainly had reason not to relax with Freddie around. Maggie wanted to keep things as positive as possible. She did not want to remember the storms of discord with her first husband John that drove her to see Freddie.

Maggie's contentious relationship with John had reached its peak when he confronted Fred as he saw him about to have dinner with his wife at that hotel in Hawaii. Maggie certainly didn't want her intimate indiscretions with Freddie be revealed, so she changed the subject and began to talk about the time when they all would leave for New York later in the week in route to south Florida.

In changing the nature of the conversation, Maggie gathered herself from the devious thoughts she had about a past relationship with Sandra's new friend and said to her husband, "Okay, Fred, I hope you've been doing your packing because we're supposed to be leaving early Wednesday morning. We'll stay with Katie on the night we get to New York and then take an early morning flight to Miami the next day."

Maggie continued, "Of course, Sandra will meet us here at our house Wednesday morning, but she mentioned when I last talked with her that we could go in Freddie's new van. She said it should have more than enough room to hold all of us and our luggage. In that way, she said we wouldn't have to rent a larger vehicle. They'll be driving down from Detroit."

Fred conceded Maggie's apparently well-thought-out plan and saw justification for Freddie coming with them. He said, "That's sounds great, Mag; I told you it'd be fine with Freddie coming along with us."

"I believe you, honey," Maggie responded.

Maggie continued, "It's just unfortunate that I'll be missing out on my birthday celebrating with this trip. If we weren't going to Florida, I know that you would have something really special planned for me right here in Chicago. Now, wouldn't you, honey?"

"That's right, Mag," Fred replied.

Maggie had hoped that at least Fred would think about having some kind of elaborate birthday celebration before leaving for south Florida. Then she realized such a celebration couldn't happen because of all the planning and preparations to make the trip. She concluded her thoughts about that possibility by saying, "Oh, well, I'll let this trip be my celebration."

Fred responded, "That's my girl. Now we can concentrate on the trip!" Before going out to get a newspaper, Fred added, "Well, this trip will be so nice that you'll forget all about a birthday celebration here in Chicago."

--------DAY OF THE TRIP: LOADING UP--------

The day had come when Maggie and Fred would meet Sandra at their house to start the drive from Chicago to New York. Freddie would accompany Sandra, and, of course, he would use his van to drive them.

After planning for six days of being away from home, Maggie gazed out her living room window and saw Freddie's huge van roll up into their driveway. She yelled at Fred, who at the time was in another room but was on his way to where she was standing.

"They're here, Fred! Is everything ready to be taken out to Freddie's vehicle?" she asked as he approached.

"Yeah, I'm bringing some of our luggage in the living room now. This is just one of the items that I'll have to get. I'll go back and get the other things in a minute. After I do that, I'm gonna have to make one last check of the back of the house before we leave. It's not often we're away from home for such a long time," he told Maggie.

As Fred continued to gather their belongings and check for any missed items, both Freddie and Sandra got out of the van. As Freddie exited the vehicle, he said to Sandra, "I'm going to the back of the van to make room for all the luggage we'll get from Fred and Maggie."

"Okay, Freddie, you go ahead, and let me go over here and greet Maggie," Sandra said.

Sandra took the short walk to where Maggie was, who only moments earlier had left her living room and stood on the front porch.

As Sandra approached Maggie, she said, "Hello, Maggie. We're finally here and ready to go.

"Hello, Sandra. I'm glad you're coming along with us. It should be an interesting trip."

"Yeah, I'm really looking forward to it," Sandra responded.

Noticing Freddie was busy in the back of the van, Maggie asked Sandra, "Is Freddie making sure there's enough room to place everything we have in the back of the van?"

"Yeah, that's exactly what he's doing, Maggie," Sandra said. "Where's Fred?" she asked.

"Oh, he's in the back making a final check of everything before we leave," Maggie replied.

Freddie soon finished preparing the back of the van for their luggage and approached the porch where the women were, saying, "Hello, Maggie. I'm ready to put your things in the back of my van."

"Hello, Freddie. Fred only needs to get a few more things, and we'll have everything ready for you to place in your van in a little bit."

"All right then," Freddie replied.

During their brief conversation, both Maggie and Freddie tried as best they could not to think about the time they had spent together. Freddie had a plan to deal with that emotion, which was to focus on his new friend Sandra.

Freddie said to Maggie, "You know Sandra has really helped me a lot this morning cleaning up the van and getting it ready for this road trip."

In a less than exciting and even a derisive tone, Maggie replied, "Oh, how nice."

Soon Fred brought out the remaining luggage to be loaded. "Hello, everybody," he said. He added, "You have a nice vehicle there, Freddie. And, Sandra, it's good to see you again."

"Thanks, Fred," Freddie and Sandra replied in unison. Freddie continued, "You can help me load your luggage into the van now while the women finish their little talk."

"Good idea. I'll help you," Fred responded.

Remembering her own romantic interest in Maggie's husband, Sandra ignored what Freddie had said about loading the luggage and asked Fred about his work.

"Are you still writing, Fred?" she said.

"Yeah, I'm always writing something," he replied as he walked toward Freddie to help him as they agreed. Then he told both the women, "Well, you girls can continue talking, and I'll go and help Freddie start to load up the van with our luggage."

"Oh, yeah, as I said, I'll certainly help you, Fred," Freddie confirmed.

Sandra then said to both men, "Oh, me and Maggie will come along shortly. You guys know how us ladies are. We just like talking about a lot of things."

--------THOUGHTS OF THE SPIRIT--------

As the fellows began to load the van with belongings, Maggie and Sandra just stood there and continued to talk to one another.

Sandra said, "Yeah, it seems as though we just finished talking over the phone."

"Well, it seems we're always talking either on the phone or when we see each other, Maggie replied. "You know, girl, I do think we have a pretty good relationship," Maggie said in a joking fashion.

Maggie's behavior during her discussion with Sandra stood in stark contrast to the doubts she had expressed to Fred about having her come along on their trip to south Florida—all because of her connection with Freddie. But she soon came to her senses and realized what a genuine friend Sandra was to her.

Sandra showed her genuine affection to Maggie, saying, "Well, Maggie, you do know that you have a special place in my heart. Don't you? I mean, your parents practically took me in as their own child. I'm so indebted to Mensie and Matthew even though they're gone. I looked at them as being my surrogate parents. Oh, how I miss them! And, Maggie, you've been like a sister to me."

After those sentimental words from Sandra, Maggie responded, "Aw, you're gonna make me cry right here on my own front porch,

Sandra. But you know, they are still with us—in spirit—and that's because the spiritual part of them never died. I mean, they certainly lived as we all remember, and we certainly know they loved God. You know Jesus said in John 11:26 that 'whoever lives and believes in me shall never die.' Well, their physical bodies certainly died; they are no longer here with us in that way—physically. But their spirits are still here.

"But take note of what Jesus asked at the end of that verse, 'Do you believe this?' So, yeah, their spirits are still with us; you just have to believe it."

Sandra replied, "Well, Maggie, that idea is certainly out of the ordinary."

"You're right, Sandra. It's not ordinary; it's extraordinary! But then again everything about God is extraordinary—that's why He's God! When we believe, we're taken out of an ordinary to an extraordinary experience."

"That's very interesting, Maggie," Sandra replied.

Maggie continued with her trend of thought but attempted to make what she was saying more real to Sandra. She said, "Let me make what I'm talking about more practical. By spirit I mean the emotions they had—their attitudes, their likes and dislikes, how they treated other people, and so on. And it is not so much that these emotions are the spirit, but rather, they reflect the spiritual nature of the person. That's how we're still connected with them—with our spirits being like their spirits when they were alive physically.

"I can hear Mom now telling me, 'Maggie, you ought to go out with John more; he's such a nice fellow!' She would go on and on about that man. Well, at that time I thought she was digging too much into my business. But then again, Sandra…"

Maggie was unable to finish her thought because emotions overwhelmed her as tears started to fill her eyes. She gathered herself a little and continued as she tried to conjure up a smile, "She cared about me so much—a little bit too much, I thought at the time. Anyway, that part of her never died. And, you know what, Sandra, in some strange way, I thank God for that."

Sandra replied, "Yeah, I know what you mean, Maggie. You know the scripture says some place, and I'm not sure where it is, but it says that God has given each one of us our personalities as well as our physical appearance. It's up to us to use that part of our being to bear good fruit. You know, as humans, we've got that physical appearance down to a science, especially us women with all the makeup and everything. And, of course, the men eat it up, figuratively speaking.

"But you know what, Maggie, somehow God uses the fruit that we bear, those intangible personality traits, for our benefit," Sandra continued. "So I'm afraid we're stuck with ourselves, Maggie, with our personalities being displayed as an outgrowth of that spirit within us."

Maggie replied, "You're right, Sandra, but we can be assured that God made us in our unique ways for a purpose, and, like it says in Romans 8:28, we just have to believe that He made us that way to serve our best interests so that things will work out for our good—whether that might appear to be the case or not. And that's not to mention that the Good Book says He made all of us in His image, so as hard as it is to believe with our natural minds, we're like Him, and He's like us! Now that's amazing, Sandra! Yes, He is able to make all the billions of people on earth individually unique with our own personalities and proclivities."

Sandra replied, "Oh, Maggie, you don't have to use all those big words on me. Proclivities? What in the world, girl?"

"Well, Sandra, the word means simply our doing the things we like to do—on a regular basis. And we all have that trait," Maggie said.

To keep the conversation going, Sandra said, "Well, that's one way to look at it, Maggie, and what you're saying has a scriptural basis. I'm a witness to that because of what I experienced in Bermuda. I mean, I took seeing all those stars in the sky and grains of sand on the beach as evidence of my healing. And, Maggie, I believe all the sand and stars that exist represent each of us as human beings. So it's not impossible for God to make each one of them in His image."

Maggie replied, "Of course it's not impossible, Sandra; nothing is impossible with God!"

"Anyway, like I said, it's something we just have to believe regardless of how much these heavenly truths are over the heads of human beings to comprehend. And one more thing, that's why in the scripture it tells us not so much to understand it all but to simply believe."

--------FRUITS OF THE SPIRIT--------

"Here's something else you can chew on Sandra," Maggie said to her. Then she continued to say, "You know that scripture you couldn't think of where it talks about our personalities? Well, it's really addressing our fruits—like the fruit of the spirit that's talked about in the Bible. And I believe that it's Galatians 5:22 and 23. You can check it out.

"And, as Jesus said, those personal traits will continue to remain with us—even after the demise of our physical bodies. And by fruit in the verse of scripture I gave you, there are things like love, joy, peace, and being longsuffering. I can't remember what the others are. But anyway, we were taught that after we have transitioned will know one another by these fruits. So yeah, I remember the fruit of the spirit from way back when I attended Sunday school at Mark Methodist. I remember it as though it was yesterday when our teacher used some trees to illustrate his point."

Maggie continued, "But you know, Sandra, the truth about our spirit only becomes real when we remember and believe that truth— the truth about the spirit part of the ones we love being alive in the spirit even though they may no longer be with us physically."

"Now, Sandra, let me say this before the fellows return. The scripture says that fruit of the spirit can actually work in the opposite direction too. That is to say, a tree can bear bad fruit, which is what you don't want as a believer; you only want the good fruit as it says in that scripture I quoted. And in the worst case, a tree might not bear any fruit at all—it's just barren, useless to anybody. By the way, I just read it last night in my Bible reading before I went to sleep. It's in Jude 12."

"Anyway, it's just a matter of our remembering these things and believing that the spirit of our departed loved ones is still with us."

Sandra replied, "Well, I understand what you're saying, Maggie. But it's still hard not to miss them because they're not here with us in their physical bodies."

Maggie said, "Again, Sandra, you have to tell yourself that while their physical body is not here with us, their spirit is still all around."

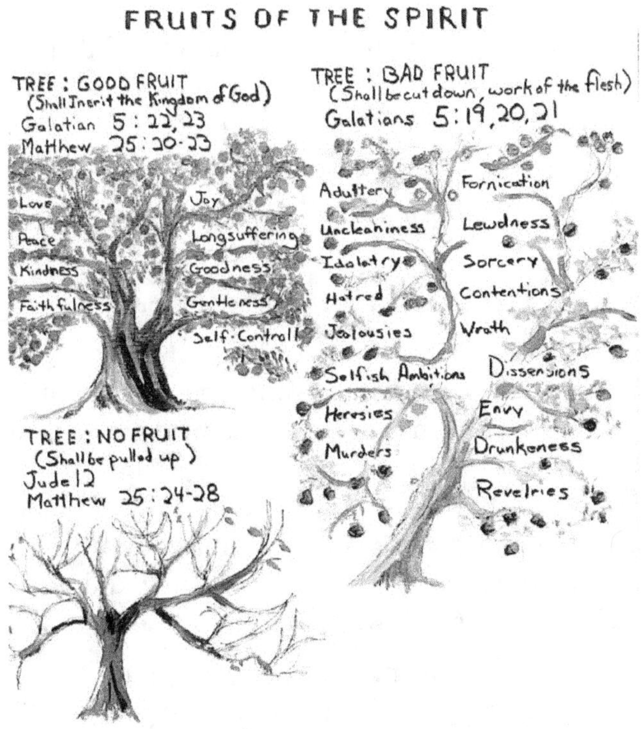

FIGURE 7 – FRUITS OF THE SPIRIT

"Therefore by their fruits you will know them."

- Matthew 7:20

--------THE STING OF A BEE--------

Maggie continued to discuss her loved ones who had passed on. She said, "You know, Sandra, the spirit of my parents and others who have passed on are alive and well. God is with them just as He was with you at that terrible time in your life back in Bermuda. Yes, you were at death's door, but somehow God brought you through the storm, didn't He?"

Sandra responded, "Maggie, I must admit, I didn't see how I'd ever get through that situation. I mean, as you said, I was at death's door, but God healed me along with the guidance of Erin, of course."

"Well, I hear you," Maggie said. "And I think you mean God alone was the one that healed you. Erin was only a conduit between you and that source."

Sandra responded, "Of course. She was there only to guide me through it all!"

Maggie went on, "And as far as missing my parents, yes, there *is* a degree of sadness that we can't escape when death comes, and that's because of what happened back in the garden with our original parents. You remember those Sunday School lessons? The disobedience of both Adam and Eve introduced death into the world based on what we were taught. But Jesus came and gave mankind hope, the hope of eternal life with God.

"So, yeah, we all still die physically, but as Jesus said in that verse you quoted earlier, if you believe Him, our spirit will live on. So my parents are right now totally in the spirit and I do believe that, Sandra. They're spiritually alive and doing quite well."

Sandra replied, "I know what you're saying, Maggie. In the scripture, death is described as a sting. But like the sting of a bee, although very hurtful when it happens, it dissipates with time, and usually it's not that long of a period. Sometimes after a while we have to remind ourselves that they *were* with us physically. But they're still with us now spiritually. That's what you're saying."

"You're right," Maggie confirmed.

Sandra added, "It's almost like our spirit is trapped in our own body!"

-------LIFE IN A PHYSICAL, MATERIALISTIC WORLD-------

Maggie paused for a moment to digest Sandra's comment; then she shared some more wisdom. "You know what, Sandra? After thinking about it, you might not want to use the word trapped because it implies something negative. But the spirit we have now in this present life—with all the emotions that I talked about before—is limited to the physical body we have.

"But according to the way we've been taught, at least what I learned back at Mark Methodist, the spirit within us will be released when our transition comes. And at that time our spirit will not be limited to the physical bodies we now have. Can you imagine that? Our spirits not being confined to our physical bodies? It's kind of like we can think about anywhere we wanna be and be there in our thoughts! But in this present physical life, we can't do that because our spirit is restricted to a physical body.

Maggie continued, "Let me give you an example of what I'm talking about. Like right now I can only imagine being in Florida. But it's so real in my thoughts. I mean, I can see myself right now on a beach chair – enjoying the sand all around, the incoming waves of the water, and the ocean breezes! Yeah, I'm there right now, in my thoughts. And yeah, it's in my thoughts because I'm eager to go there, but like the song says, it's just my imagination. Because our spirit is limited to these physical bodies, we can't experience Florida for real until we get there, physically, which will be very soon!

"But, anyway, when we transition from this physical body, we won't have that limitation. How exciting!" Maggie added.

Realizing they were about to take a long trip, Maggie said, "Well, enough of this deep spiritual discussion, Sandra. The fellows haven't returned yet, so let's go help them with the luggage, and I'm sure we'll be ready to go shortly."

Sandra agreed and they both went to where Fred and Freddie were. Soon all four of them would be off to New York.

--------EMOTIONS--------

Freddie was eager to test his new van on a long-distance drive. Fred would be sitting with him in the front passenger seat and would provide plenty of conversation. That's the way it was inside the vehicle as they started toward New York City.

Sandra and Maggie resumed their conversation in the back seat. Sandra said, "Maggie, it's so comfortable back here. Before meeting Freddie, the only place in a car that I knew about was behind the wheel. And I had an older car. But look at this vehicle. Wow! Sitting back here, you can even control the temperature and sound volume."

Maggie replied, "Yeah, Sandra, it's nice."

Maggie soon turned her attention to Freddie, saying, "I never knew you had a vehicle that was so nice, Freddie."

He replied, "Well, you know, Maggie, Sandra helped me make it this way."

Freddie leaned back as much as he could while continuing to pay attention to the road as he drove and said to Sandra, "Remember, Sandra? You cleaned it up a lot this morning."

With that comment, Sandra only shook her head and said, "Yes, I did do a little something to it."

Freddie added, "I only got it recently, Maggie. I'm kind of ashamed to say, but it came only because of my wife's death. You know you can do a lot with insurance money."

In response to that statement, Fred said, "For heaven's sake, Freddie, how could say something like that? It sounds like you're using your wife's demise for your own personal gain!"

While keeping his eyes on the road, Freddie retorted rather emotionally, "You know what, Fred? One thing that Maxie taught me was to be honest, sometimes brutally honest. She was a good woman. But sometimes I wasn't good to her.

"You know, Fred," he added, "I just get emotional when I remember the mistakes I've made. I wish I could say that I was as honest with her as she was with me while she was alive. And the same was true with my second wife. But I'm sad to say that I was not. I won't go into details, but I did some things with both women in my life that I'm not proud of."

Sandra responded, "You know, Freddie, you don't have to get into your marital history; you can keep a lot of that to yourself. We've all made mistakes."

Freddie responded, "No, Sandra! I need to get some of this off my chest. I know I did some things that I shouldn't have done. It took a dream one night of Peggy, my recent wife, and our son being killed in a car accident to shake me up. At the time I was not being completely faithful to her. She sensed something was wrong and ended up moving out and taking our son along with her. I think she moved to somewhere in Iowa."

Fred said, "At least you're being honest about your indiscretions." At the same time, inwardly Fred was thinking, *Are you kidding me? This man was untrue to two women?* But that opinion quickly left him.

Maggie also was listening to Freddie's accounts of his indiscretions while being married when Sandra commented, "Wow, Freddie. You sure are being transparent about your life story—at least your marital history. Like I said, you don't have to get into all that. But like you said, I guess it makes you feel better."

Freddie responded, "You are so right, Sandra. It's good for me to release a lot of my emotion. But I'm still not proud of a lot of things I did, and I'm not getting into more detail than that."

As Freddie spoke, the tears began to build in his eyes again. He added directing his comment to Maggie, "Maggie, you're the strongest woman I know."

At that point he couldn't go on any further because of the emotional, even romantic ties that he had with her. He managed to keep enough composure to control his driving.

Maggie could have scrawled under that back seat listening to Freddie's emotional expression, knowing that *she* was the cause of some of his guilt if not most of his issues with infidelity. After all, no one else knew about those shortcomings, so she quickly gathered herself as if his words had no effect on her.

Maggie was about as shaken as Freddie as he uttered some of the history involving his infidelities. She became uncomfortable as she sat there behind him, listening to what he was saying. She began to think about what Freddie would say next. She thought, *Oh my Lord. Is he going to bring up our relationship? I feel horrible! But he did say he wasn't getting into more detail. I sure hope he won't!*

Meanwhile, after Freddie's explanation of using insurance money to purchase his van, Fred wanted to lessen the impact of Freddie's response, desiring to keep peace with him. He said simply, "Well, Freddie, as far as your purchase of the van, I guess you did what you felt she would have wanted you to do."

While Fred and Freddie continued to deal with a storm of emotions during the drive, Maggie's feelings wandered all over the place, although she was successful in concealing them at least somewhat. Her anxiety about what Freddie was telling Fred, particularly about the time during the height of her relationship with him, was manifested by the perspiration that began to emerge from her forehead.

Sandra noticed Maggie's discomfort, and said to her, "Are you all right, Maggie? Many of the controls are back here; I can turn up the air."

"I'm fine," Maggie said. "I guess I'm too young to have those hot flashes that I hear some older women talk about. Like I said, I'm fine but I guess you could turn the air up a little."

Not being familiar with the controls in the back, Sandra said, "I can't seem to find the right knob back here, Freddie. Could you make the adjustment in the air on the front panel close to where you are so we can cool off back here?"

Freddie responded, "Yeah, I think *it is* getting a little warm in here."

"I second that," Fred said.

Freddie adjusted the air temperature to satisfy all the occupants of the van.

As the temperature was lowered, conversations continued among everyone. Freddie had driven from the local streets of Detroit and then to Chicago to the open interstate heading towards New York.

Fred continued to try to make up for the statement he made to Freddie earlier that caused such an emotional response from him. Fred asked, "So how long had you known Mag before we were introduced to each other, Freddie?"

Freddie responded, "Oh! We were at the same law firm together."

Then Freddie asked Maggie, "Hey, Maggie, do you remember those Christmas parties we used to attend? Not together, of course." He added the last part because, like Maggie, he didn't want either Fred or Sandra to know of their close relationship in the past.

Maggie replied, "Yeah, Freddie, I do remember. You know…"

Fred interjected before Maggie could finish her statement and said, "Oh no! One thing about Mag that I feel comfortable about is her conversation with men. I mean, just because you're talking to a guy doesn't mean that you're going out with him."

Relieved that her husband had entered the conversation at that moment, Maggie just sat there in the back seat with Sandra beside her, listening to Fred and Freddie continue to talk about such sensitive topics. She thought to herself, how in the world did they get on this subject, talking about relationships between men and women? Well, at least it's keeping Freddie alert while driving.

--------REMEMBERING HAWAII--------

Maggie didn't realize that the storms of discord among the four of them started long before Freddie asked her about attending Christmas parties. Maggie never got a chance to explain her answer to that question because Fred got involved in the conversation.

Fred continued talking with Freddie about another issue from the past that would affect the emotions of all of them. He said, "Yeah, I remember talking to Mag one evening over the dinner table in Hawaii when her late husband came up and really made a scene. I guess he behaved that way because he was thinking I was flirting with his wife. You remember that, Mag?"

Maggie, by now eager to say something more constructive, answered, "Yeah, Fred. But that was a long time ago." She wondered why Fred didn't just keep his mouth closed.

Maggie tried to deflect a discussion about that specific occurrence in the past, an occurrence that brought on anxiety that she felt was created by her husband Fred. So she started to initiate a discussion about the general nature of relationships when she said, "You know all relationships are funny. Sometimes we might care more about someone than is evident to someone else—if you know what I mean."

Sandra took the opportunity to gain more clarity about Maggie's comment by saying, "No, Maggie. I don't know what you mean! What are you saying?" Realizing how she once felt about Maggie's husband, Sandra quickly added before Maggie had a chance to answer, "Never mind, Maggie. This discussion is getting too complicated."

Wanting to offer Maggie her support, Sandra added, "But, yeah, Maggie, you couldn't be more correct; relationships can be very interesting to say the least."

-------STORMS OF DISCORD-------

Sandra desired to bring some sanity to the discussion. She wanted to let the men know how she felt about Maggie and said, "Well, fellows, I've known Maggie for some time now, and I can truthfully say that I've never known her to even look in a provocative way at a man—other than you, Fred, of course. And I'm sure you can appreciate that, Fred. Anyway, she seems so pure and faithful to you. Am I right about that, Maggie? You'd never cut out on Fred, now would you?"

As much as she wanted, Sandra was unsuccessful in bringing more sanity to the discussion they were having. It was unbelievable that she would put Maggie on the spot once more with a question about her fidelity.

Maggie started to respond, "Now, Sandra,…"

Again Maggie was interrupted before she could complete her sentence. Sandra was the culprit this time, not her husband Fred. Before Maggie could make her point, Sandra said, "And, Fred, I'm sure you can appreciate the kind of woman Maggie is."

Fred replied, "Yes, Sandra. Mag is a faithful wife. And let me tell you this, Sandra, I feel fortunate that me and Mag have a wonderful relationship and a great marriage, I might add," he said for emphasis.

It was not difficult for Freddie to keep from saying something, knowing his own relationship with Maggie before his earlier wife's tragic death—even while married to his second wife Peggy. He just tried to keep a focus on the road. Freddie tried his best to navigate the vehicle when Sandra finally asked him about the subject of relationships.

"So, Freddie, what do you have to say about all this? I know you were married for a while; then your wife died before you remarried. And I remember you telling me that both women were always faithful to you."

Before Sandra could continue, Freddie turned his attention slightly from the road, and said, "Can't we change the subject? I get the feeling that we're sowing storms of discord with the discussion we're having."

"Amen!" Maggie shouted.

Sandra responded, "Okay then. We're just having a little fun."

After that, things went quiet for a while as Freddie continued to drive towards New York, and everyone soon drifted off to sleep.

--------ARRIVING IN NEW YORK-------

After a few more miles of driving, Freddie decided to stop again, this time to fill up his gas tank. He turned on the radio loudly, which woke up everyone. Soon they came to another service station off an exit where they could rest a little before entering the Big Apple. After that they continued towards New York.

By this time Fred had taken over driving responsibilities from Freddie. Soon they would arrive at their destination, which was within an hour's driving time.

As the van continued into the New York City metro area, Fred had turned the radio to a station that was playing smooth jazz. Everyone needed the sound of relaxing music to calm down all the emotions stemming from their earlier discussions about relationships between men and women.

The sound of the radio as well as those emotional discussions did accomplish one goal, and that was to keep Fred alert after he took the wheel.

--------ON TO KATIE'S HOUSE-------

As Fred continued to drive, they came to the lower end of Manhattan and crossed Venzio Bridge over the Hudson River into Staten Island, where Maggie's friend Katie lived.

"Fred, I've been to Katie's house before, so I can direct you on how to get there," Maggie said.

Fred replied, "Okay, Mag, I'll go where you tell me."

Unlike Manhattan, Staten Island was not congested with people and vehicles and skyscrapers on every block. Here, the suburban environment was much more serene with large maple trees lining wide boulevards with single family detached homes and sidewalks being the rule.

Katie's house was not far from the main entrance to the neighborhood. After driving three or four blocks, Fred approached the entrance, where an assortment of flowering plants surrounded two large brick columns that were connected at the top by a wired arch. The arch was high above the street and had the name "Westwood" lettered across it to welcome residents and guests alike.

Knowing when they would arrive because of earlier discussions with Maggie, Katie and her son Wynn sat on the front porch of their two-story brick home, ready to greet them. Soon the van entered the driveway. Maggie, Fred, Sandra, and Freddie had finally reached their destination.

Everyone began to get out the vehicle and Katie approached them.

"Hello, everybody," she said. "Glad you made it here safely."

Being the first to get out of the vehicle, Maggie walked a short distance to where Katie stood and gave her friend a hug, saying, "How are you, girl? So glad to see you again."

Maggie waved her hand at and yelled to Wynn, who had remained on the porch. "Hi Wynn," she said.

Wynn reciprocated and said, "Hi, Miss Maggie."

Katie asked, "And your drive, how was it?"

"It was very nice—and you know that me and Sandra talked a lot."

Soon the others left the vehicle and stood with Maggie as she talked with Katie.

"I'm so glad to see all of you," Katie said to the rest of the group. "I'm really looking forward to our trip to Florida."

Maggie added, "Listen, Katie, we're so glad you and Wynn are coming with us to Florida. I told everybody I knew you would agree to go. And a bonus is that your son will be coming along too."

Then Katie finally got a chance to respond, "Yeah, I'm looking forward to it as I said, and I'm sure Wynn is too. But again it's so good seeing you, Maggie, and all of you."

For the next few minutes everyone just stood there talking to one another, enjoying the calm breeze on a pleasant, sunny Wednesday afternoon.

Soon after those initial greetings, Katie invited everyone into her house to get situated for the evening. They brought their belongings in for their one-night stay. Fred, Freddie, and Sandra, along with Maggie, followed Katie inside her home, where they passed Wynn, and everyone greeted him before proceeding inside. Once they entered the house, Katie guided them to the rooms where they would sleep for the night. Everyone was ready for a little relaxation and looked forward to the rest in preparation for the flight to Miami the next morning.

FIGURE 8: WESTWOOD

Even the sparrow has found a home, And the swallow a nest for herself, Where she may lay her young—Even Your altars, O Lord of hosts, My King and my God.

-Psalm 84:3

CHAPTER SEVEN
DREAMS

After everyone had situated themselves in their rooms in Katie's house, she invited them into the dining area for a late afternoon lunch. They were joined by David, Sheri, and her daughter Jeanie, who had arrived earlier. After introductions, conversations started again. They sat there partaking in an assortment of foods and casual chitchat, making sure to get more familiar with each other.

Katie mentioned to Sandra, "Maggie told me Sandra about your friend here." Then she turned toward Freddie and said, "So, Freddie, I understand that your cousin Sinbad's resort is where we're going in Miami."

Freddie replied, "Yeah, Katie, everyone down there is looking forward to our group coming from here in the New York City area as well as from the Detroit area. And from what I understand, that's because Sandra visited Erin's resort in Bermuda a while back."

Freddie continued, "And I don't want to forget Maggie and her husband Fred as well as Gates and Courtney over there in Chicago. Being a close friend of Sandra as well as yourself, she may have told you about the big event they're going to have this week in south Florida. We're all looking forward to what is being planned for us, including all of us here. We're looking forward especially to spending time with Sandra's special friend Erin, who will be honored for agreeing to run the resort down there for my cousin. So everybody seems to be excited."

Katie replied, "Yeah, Maggie told me about that. And when she invited me and Wynn to come along, I jumped at the opportunity—and I'm really looking forward to it."

After her last statement, Katie turned to all those assembled and said, "Listen, everyone. I want to give you a tour of my house in a few minutes. There's a large patio in the back that I think you'll like. We can go out there after we chat here a little longer."

Freddie replied, "Well, we don't have to wait and chat here. I mean, we men can go on the patio right now while you ladies continue to talk. Come on, Fred, and you too, Wynn and David. Let's go on the patio and leave the women to themselves for a while."

So that's what the men did. They left Sandra, Maggie, Katie, Sheri, and Jeanie around the dining room table and went out onto Katie's patio to chat among themselves.

--------SANDRA'S STORY--------

After the fellows departed, Katie turned her attention to Sandra. She said, "And, Sandra, Maggie also told me about a dream she had that seemed so real—a dream about a cruise she made to Bermuda to see Erin, who I understand had a great influence on your life."

Before Sandra had a chance to respond, Maggie interjected, "That's right, Katie. Erin has had a great influence on both me and Sandra."

Maggie stood there waiting to hear what Sandra would say. After some hesitation, Sandra finally said, "Yes, Katie, Maggie's right. Erin practically saved my life when I went to Bermuda and stayed at her resort." As Maggie nodded in approval, Sandra continued, "It was a life-changing experience. And, yes, Maggie told me all about that dream she had," Sandra added. "Yeah, I'll tell you, the level of detail she was able to remember was amazing. And the most amazing thing about it was that there was a spiritual aspect to it," Sandra continued. "I remember Maggie's late husband John, who was the pastor of the church I worked at, said in a sermon he gave once that God speaks to us sometimes through dreams."

Sandra directed her comments toward Maggie. "And, Maggie, I know you remember that sermon because I went to church with you on that particular Sunday."

Again, Maggie nodded her head in approval and said, "I certainly do remember that, Sandra."

Sandra continued, "And I believe that God spoke to Maggie when she dreamed about going on a cruise to Bermuda. Sometimes we just have to wait and see what those kinds of dreams really mean. But most of all, we have to believe that God is really speaking to us about something," she concluded.

Katie asked, "Exactly what kind of dreams are you talking about, Sandra? And what could God be speaking to us about?"

"Well, Katie," Sandra replied, "the kind of dreams I'm talking about are those where the people we know or have known are involved. Yes, even our loved ones who have passed on, I believe, speak to us through dreams.

"And to answer that second question, I believe the Master knows what everyone of us needs at any given time. And He uses people, circumstances, and, yes, dreams, to help us. And beyond that, if we are receptive to what He is saying to us, we can be assured that any desire we might have will be met. We only have to believe that."

Sandra continued, "And I believe that God spoke to Maggie when she dreamed about going on a cruise to Bermuda. Sometimes we just have to wait and see what those kinds of dreams really mean. But most of all, we have to believe that God is really speaking to us about something," she concluded.

Katie asked, "Exactly what kind of dreams are you talking about, Sandra? And what could God be speaking to us about?"

"Well, Katie," Sandra replied, "the kind of dreams I'm talking about are those where the people we know or have known are involved. Yes, even our loved ones who have passed on, I believe, speak to us through dreams.

"And to answer that second question, I believe the Master knows what everyone of us needs at any given time. And He uses people, circumstances, and, yes, dreams, to help us. And beyond that, if we are receptive to what He is saying to us, we can be assured that any desire we might have will be met. We only have to believe that."

As Sandra was explaining, Katie thought, *These ideas are really strange. Who would examine a dream like that! I know the dreams I have I forget about in no time after I wake up! Oh, well.*

Despite Katie's lack of understanding of much of what Sandra way saying, she didn't question those ideas because she realized that they were familiar to her from Bible study as well as in sermons she had heard. *Besides, it seems as though Sandra is confident in what she's saying, so I won't debate it,* she thought.

Maggie felt compelled to add, "Sandra, let me say this; then you can go back to what you were saying to Katie. You all know that what Sandra was saying is right—and I believe we can get what we want, as believers, if we truly believe that we will get it. That's what Mark 11:23 and 24 are all about. But it helps to know what your purpose is. And your purpose is tied to your talents—and that's what we're all called to take advantage of."

Maggie continued, "Now I'm not saying that it's a talent or anything like that, but it's amazing the level of recall and understanding of the dreams I have. I guess it's just something that I've been able to do ever since I can remember.

"But as far as our desires," she added, "God will give us whatever is deep down in our hearts that we want. But He only give us what is best for our unique situation, so only those desires that are in line with the purpose He has for our lives are most likely to be met.

"But let me tell you. If you venture outside of that purpose—the purpose God has for you—there's no guarantee that you will get what you want. Because what you want may not be in your best interests.

In the end you just have to pray that you'll be guided in the right direction. And God will always give you signs to guide you into the right direction in order for you to get those desires that He knows are best for you. That's what He did for Sandra when she was in Bermuda."

"Amen to that," Sandra shouted.

Maggie continued, "But you know, I don't want to be anywhere I'm not supposed to be and don't want anything that I'm not supposed to have—things that fall outside of His will for me. So in my opinion, it's a partnership when it comes to satisfying our desires," Maggie said.

Sandra replied, "That's a good way of putting it, Maggie."

-------LIFE IN THE SPIRIT--------

Katie as well as Maggie began to listen to Sandra as she chimed in more in the conversation. She said, "You know, Katie, I dream of Maggie's parents a lot. And I believe the reason for that is because I was so close to them. And, Maggie, whenever I dream about them, I believe they are telling me that they're okay in their spiritual dimension right now. It's a dimension, I might add, that we all will get to one day."

Katie responded, "Well, Sandra, that really is interesting and inspirational, I must say, even though I don't understand it all."

Maggie got back into the discussion, saying, "I agree with Sandra. I know that Mom and Dad are in a better place, as they say, but it still hurts a lot, not having them here with us physically. To me it just points to the finality of death, although I know better, because of what it says in the scripture—that if we believe in Him, we will never die; our spirit will live on.

"Nevertheless, regardless of how you look at it, it's just hard to get over losing someone you love—when they're no longer here. And as far as death is concerned, none of us wants to go to that 'better place,' at least not right now," Maggie said with a bit of laughter.

Sandra interjected, "The beauty of it is, Maggie, that if we leave our feelings out of it and just believe, we'll know that our love ones are still with us in spirit, we just have to believe what the Bible says about it."

Sandra continued, "And, Katie, you don't necessarily have to understand. Lord knows it's difficult sometimes to understand some of these spiritual truths that we are supposed to adhere to, but we are not necessarily called to understand but to simply believe—that is, in the case of departed love ones, to believe that they are still with us in spirit."

Katie responded, "Well, I certainly believe. And you know what? It makes your belief even stronger if you don't understand something. I mean, it's easy to believe if you understand everything. But if you put total trust in what the Bible says, then it's at least easier to accept some of the incredible things that it does say in there. I'm talking about the things that we as humans can't get our minds to understand naturally like what Jesus said about the fact that we will never die. Now a truth like that takes our spirit, the Holy Spirit, to help us to believe that even if don't understand it!

"And as far as dreams are concerned, I know I've dreamed about some of my loved ones that have passed on too, but until now I really didn't give it much thought."

Then Katie said something that she had thought about earlier. "But I have to admit, y'all, some of the dreams I have are so real, but when I wake up most of them escape from my memory. Anyway, thanks for that insight, Sandra."

--------RETURN OF THE MEN--------

The fellows returned to the dining room table after a short stay on the patio and immediately began to get involved in the discussion.

"So, what are you ladies talking about?" Freddie asked.

Sandra said, "We're talking life in the spirit and about dreams and what they mean."

188

Freddie replied, "Well, I certainly can identify with that." He referred to the dream he had about his wife and daughter's death in a car accident.

Sandra returned her attention to what she had been saying to the ladies before the men rejoined them. "Thanks, Katie, and you too, Maggie, for being so patient with me talking so much. And, Sheri and Jeanie, you all didn't say much, but thanks for your patience too. The Lord has given me so much understanding about things over the past two years. And I have Erin to thank for practically all of that."

Freddie entered the discussion, saying, "Sandra, I never knew you had such a spiritual side. I'm interested in knowing more!"

Sandra responded, "Well, all I can say is that I believe in the greater scheme of things, and by that I mean the way God sees things. But our life now is as human beings, physical beings that live on the earth with a spiritual component. A dream is something different. I guess it's like being alive but yet not conscious of your physical presence on earth. I guess another way of describing a dream is that it's another realm or dimension outside our conscious life, however brief it might be."

Sandra elaborated by adding, "Remember the scripture says that to God a thousand years is just one day? So, our lifetime of, say, a hundred years, if we are fortunate enough to live that long, is just like a fraction of a day to God—at least the way we as humans conceive of time like in days, months, and years. And the reason for that is because God is eternal and we are only temporal beings—affected by the physical laws of nature, like time as we know it.

"And I learned in school that time itself is a result of the earth's motion, its movement around the sun. That's what gives us our seasons." Sandra decided to inject some humor, adding, "Now, ain't you all proud of me and my knowledge of geography?!"

Maggie said, "Well, Sandra, remember I told you once that I took a geography class too during my time at MCCU."

Being caught up in the subject, Sandra continued, "That's right, Maggie. I do remember you telling me that. But going back to our discussion of spiritual things, I believe it's our destiny to be like God, to be in a perpetual, spiritual dimension where time as we know it is not a factor. That's where Maggie's parents are now."

"Wow, Sandra! You're so inspiring, but let's come back down to earth," implored Katie. Then she asked Fred, "How do you feel about all this, Fred?"

Fred replied, "What can I say? I don't know half as much about the Bible as Sandra, but it makes sense to me. And like Freddie said, I would like to know more."

-------REMEMBERING AND CONVERSATIONS-------

Then Katie changed the subject and asked, "Speaking of making sense, I know you're an author, Fred, who writes books that are interesting. Maggie sent me one of 'em—the one about how you two met back at MCCU and some other things. Are you still writing those books?"

Fred replied, "Yeah, I'm still writing, Katie. And I'm also holding down my corporate job too."

Katie added, "Yeah, I can remember as though it was yesterday when you met Maggie at that social at MCCU after a basketball game. It seemed you two hit it off immediately. And I just love the way you two serenaded to the song, 'Georgia on My Mind.'"

Maggie replied, "Yeah, I remember. That was a special night."

Katie turned her attention to the others in the room as she said, "Well, everybody, with all this spiritual talk, we may have ignored my son Wynn. Tell everyone 'hello,' Wynn."

In response, Wynn said simply, "Hi."

Katie said, "He doesn't talk much, but he's looking forward to south Florida too."

Fred said, "Don't worry about Wynn, Katie; the fellows talked to him a little while we were on the patio. You know, men's talk!"

Maggie was mystified at Wynn's demeanor. She remembered him when he was so active as a younger boy. She recalled that he had temper tantrums at that time. *Oh well, kids do grow up*, she thought.

"Fred, you mentioned men's talk. Well, I want you to know we have women's talk too, and that's what we did while you guys were on the patio," Maggie said.

While there was no response from any of the men to that last comment by Maggie, the conversations continued.

Maggie said, "Gates and Courtney will be flying separately to Miami. But they should arrive there at the same time as us, and they will meet us there at the airport. We'll meet them a little later after we've settled in."

Maggie added, "It's amazing that all of us were in the dream I told Sandra about, the dream of me taking a cruise to Bermuda. I just can't get over that!"

"Well, Maggie, I agree. That is amazing. Why, you hadn't even met Sheri, David, and Jeanie until today," Katie said.

Maggie replied, "Well, that's what I dreamed. I'm not kidding! It seemed so surreal, almost unbelievable. At least the part where now all of us actually will be in Florida together. Amazing!

"Anyway, this whole trip will seem like some kind of reunion of the characters that I knew in that mystical place where we all went in that dream. It'll be something special."

--------RETIRING FOR THE NIGHT--------

After a few more minutes of discussion, Katie suggested that everyone might want to retire for the evening and do any last-minute preparations they might have for the trip.

"We're having a quick breakfast tomorrow morning at 7:00," she said, "and since I'm your host, I'll fix it. After breakfast, we all can head to the airport at 8:00. It's only a half hour drive from here." Then Katie asked Freddie, "I understand, Freddie, that we'll be going in your van. Is everything good to go with your vehicle? I mean, with the luggage that Wynn and I have?"

Freddie responded, "Yes, it's all set—we've made room for your luggage."

"I agree with Katie, everybody," Maggie said. "We all should get as much rest as we can. It's going to be a long, busy day tomorrow. And as for as Gates and Courtney are concerned, as I said, they will be coming down on a separate flight, and we can meet them after we get settled."

Sandra said, "And, Freddie, isn't it right that someone from Sinbad's resort staff will be picking us up and taking us to our resort living quarters?"

"Yeah, that's right. Everything is all set for them to receive us once we get there, according to my cousin Sinbad."

With that, everyone retired for the evening. Morning soon came and, as Katie had mentioned, they had a quick breakfast then boarded the van and headed to the airport. Sheri, David, and Jeanie would follow close behind in the vehicle they had rented.

The plan was that upon everyone's arrival at the Miami airport, a chauffeur would take all of them to the resort where Erin and other eventgoers would be waiting.

--------TRIP DEPARTURE AND ARRIVAL IN MIAMI-------

The flight from New York was a smooth one, and, soon after landing at Miami International, everyone exited the plane and went through post-flight protocol, which included retrieving luggage and waiting in a designated area for pickup.

As he had done for Erin when she arrived from Bermuda, Bernie's brother Casey, a chauffeur, was there to take everyone to the Remington condominium. In the newly constructed condo, conveniently located across the street from the resort, was the first two floors; the remainder of a high rise contained mostly office space on the higher floors that had not yet been utilized. The structure would provide lodging during event festivities for the next few days. Casey, Sinbad's friend, was the lead chauffer at the resort and was designated to wait for Maggie's group in the lobby area of the airport for the guests to arrive.

After retrieving their luggage, Maggie, Fred, Katie, Wynn, Sheri, David, and Jeanie followed Sandra and Freddie to the area where they would meet the chauffeur. Casey was standing there, neatly adorned in his chauffeur's uniform. He held a name sign indicating that he was there to retrieve them and take them to the resort.

Having visited Sinbad on several occasions, Freddie knew Casey as one of Sinbad's trusted chauffeurs. As Maggie's group entered the terminal, Freddie was the first to recognize Casey from a distance.

As they approached him, Casey said, "Hello, Mr. Freddie. I see that this is your group here."

Freddie replied, "Hello, Casey, and you're right. These are some of the people that will be going to Sinbad's event over the next few days."

"I want you to first meet my friend Sandra," Freddie said as she stood by Casey. Then he turned and pointed behind him at the others and said, "And over here is Maggie, her husband Fred, her friend Katie, and her son Wynn." Freddie continued, "And these are Sheri, David, and Jeanie. Gates and Courtney arrived earlier, but we'll be meeting them later."

"I just can't wait to get there, so we all can begin to interact with one another and get better acquainted. And you know? We'll have three days to do it," Maggie concluded.

Soon they all climbed into the van so Casey could take them and their luggage to the resort to the Remington condo. Three days of associations and celebration awaited them at Sinbad's new resort.

CHAPTER EIGHT
THE EVENT

Day one of the stay in south Florida for attendees of Sinbad's event was Wednesday evening. Bernie had made all the arrangements including meals and the order of the program.

--------LODGINGS--------

The event's delegation from the northern cities had arrived at the condo where Casey directed two other bellmen to transport their luggage to the assigned guest rooms. Maggie and Fred, Sandra, and Freddie, were fortunate because their rooms, being next to each other, were on the first floor with a patio and direct access to the beach. Fred had requested these rooms be next to each other earlier. Maggie's group had accommodations on the first and second floors of the high-rise condo. Gates had reserved the entire first and second floors for his guests. The high rise building only had condos on the first two floors,, and Gates had reserved them all. The rest of the floors on this recently constructed skyscraper were reserved office space but were not in use during the time of their stay.

The multiroom lodgings were so large that someone could get lost in their own suite!

Sheri, David, and Jeanie were the only others who had first floor accommodations. Fred had requested that he and Maggie have a room next to Sandra and Freddie on the first floor with direct access to the beach. He and Maggie loved their spacious rooms, where sunshine flooded in through the glass doors to the patio and washed the walls and floor in golden light. Large windows opened to allow the ocean air to permeate the space, which was decorated in the colors of sea and sand.

Back to the first floor, Sheri, David, and Jeanie had the largest room, primarily because of three adults having to be housed, but, being situated on the opposite side of the hallway from Maggie and Sandra, they did not have direct beach access. And their suite had direct access to the second floor via a stairwell located not far from their back patio.

All the others in Maggie's group, including Gates and Courtney who had arrived earlier on a separate flight, had second-floor accommodations; their suites had balconies and a clear view of the beach and ocean. Being a man with connections and influence, Gates made certain that his party received the finest accommodations. All the rooms were appointed with mahogany furniture and tasteful linens, and the impressive view outside; both first floor and second-floor lodging quarters revealed a perfect strand of white sandy beach against an azure sky.

An extra feature on the second floor was a large gathering area – a lobby if you will, at the end of the hallway on that floor where people could assemble and mingle.

--------PRE-EVENT ACTIVITY--------

Prior to going to her room, Maggie said to Fred, "Well, I'm sure the event later will be nice, but I'm now ready to go to the room." She continued, "Maybe we can have our own little celebration there, honey. Remember? The celebration we didn't have for my birthday back in Chicago?"

Fred responded, "Okay, Mag. Don't make me feel guilty about that. Anyway, I wanna talk to some people before I head back to the room. Why don't you go to the main desk to get information about our living quarters and then go ahead to the suite. I'll see you there later. And don't worry about that birthday celebration."

Maggie reluctantly agreed with her husband, but she added somewhat in jest, "Well, okay. But it's not your birthday celebration we're talking about here. Anyway, don't worry about it. You go and do what you have to do."

Maggie really wanted to spend some time with her husband alone before they all met later to celebrate Erin's new position. She repeated, "Yeah, you go ahead and do what you have to do, and I'll go on to the room. But, like you said, I'll go to the front desk to get the information I need."

At that point Fred and Maggie went their separate ways as she started towards the concierge desk to get directions to their suite. On her short walk there, she thought, *I hope I won't have the same experience with Fred as I had with John when we were on our honeymoon in Santa Monica. He visited his friends and everything while I was left alone in that hotel room! And as far as my birthday celebration, I guess I'll just have to do something myself when I get to the room – like have some champagne—at least until he gets there.*

Just before Maggie arrived at the concierge desk, she thought, *Okay, gotta keep positive—gotta keep positive!*

By the time Maggie began to converse with the concierge, she had gotten rid of her negative emotions. She said, "I'm Maggie Mints and we're with Mr. Sinbad's delegation."

The gentleman replied, "Oh, yes! I have all the information here for you to take; the directions to your suite are in here as well. Go ahead and take this. And do you need any help with your luggage?"

"No, thank you very much. That has been taken care of," Maggie replied. Then she asked, "But one last thing sir, is there champagne in the condo?" "There sure is – it's in the cabinet just above the sink," the attendant told her. Then Maggie said, "Well thank you sir, you've been very helpful."

--------THE EVENT ROOM--------

Once the concierge gave Maggie the information she needed about their living quarters, she asked him, "Before I leave, could I see the conference room seating for the event?" "You sure can," the attendant said back to her, then proceeded to hand Maggie what she had asked for. He said, "Here it is Miss. This is the document showing the seating arrangements for the event tonight."

Viewing the document, Maggie saw that the names of each person would be on an index card placed on the seat of the chair indicating where they were to sit. Maggie was astonished that the seating was so similar to what she remembered in the dream she had about the cruise. *My, my*, she thought. *This reminds me so much of the dream.* Maggie saw that she and Fred were sitting together just as they were at dinner on the cruise.

"Thank goodness that Sinbad didn't split couples up," she mumbled to herself.

The condo staff had arranged the seating in a large dining room to accommodate Maggie's group where everyone would meet for an opening reception. Rows of seats for casual observers began a few feet from two huge circular tables that were located near the front of the room. Active participants in the day-to-day running of the resort, the staff, would sit at these tables. Erin, the one being celebrated as the new manager of the resort, would be located there as well as guests of the staff, including the delegation that came down from Chicago, Detroit, New York, and New Brunswick. Everything was set for the event to take place later that evening.

-------MAGGIE'S THOUGHTS-------

As Maggie began to leave to go to her suite, the concierge said to her, "Happy birthday, Mrs. Mints!"

She immediately turned around and said, "Thank you very much."

As Maggie continued to her suite, she began to wonder how he knew that information. Then she quickly figured it out. She thought, *Fred must have told him.*

As she continued walking to her suite, Maggie mumbled to herself, thinking about what Fred had possibly revealed to the concierge about them. "That man is always giving away personal information! And why would he give something as personal as my birthday celebration anyway? Oh well," she finally said to herself.

As Maggie neared their rooms, she began to contemplate what she perceived Fred had told the concierge. "That's the man I married, I guess; bless his heart. I need to talk to him about giving out our personal business." Without giving it any further thought, Maggie finally arrived at their suite.

-------FRED'S CONVERSATIONS AND EXCURSION-------

After Fred had talked to the folks he had told Maggie he needed to meet with, he took a short walk to the beach. "Maggie will be fine," he said to himself. "I'm going to take this opportunity to go on the beach and meditate a little bit." He planned to join his wife later in their suite.

Fred found a beach chair and just relaxed for a little while, listening to the ocean waves beating onto the shore. With few people around at his location, he could enjoy the seagulls flying in search of food. He thought about his relationship with Maggie, her business as a daycare provider, and, of course, his writing career. After a few more minutes of contemplation, he decided to go to the suite.

--------FRED GOES TO HIS SUITE--------

By this time everyone was situated in their lodgings. It was about 3:00 in the afternoon as Fred walked into their suite for the first time.

"Hey, Mag, I'm back!" he said.

Clearly somewhat perturbed that he did not come with her to their rooms earlier, she said, "Well, did you do what you had to do?"

Before he could answer, her demeanor became more positive and she added, "Don't worry about that now." In a more cheerful manner, she asked, "How do you like our suite?"

Fred replied, "It looks great—especially with the beach right outside our patio door. And that beach is really nice. I went out there for a little while. I mean, all the sand and those ocean waves—yeah, it's really nice out there."

Maggie wanted Fred to focus on their suite, not the beach. She said, "I know the beach is nice, Fred. But we're gonna be inside most of the time. Try to concentrate on our suite!"

"Well, okay! This place is so large; that's what impresses me the most about it. And I guess it has multiple rooms. Is that right, Mag?" he asked.

"Yeah, Fred, let me give you a tour. She began to show him the all the rooms in their suite. Then she asked, "And did you notice the furniture? It's really like nothing I've seen before. There's this nightstand with this huge picture on it of the beach and the ocean waves coming in. Now, this is really nice. I could just sit over here on this couch and stare at that picture for minutes at a time while listening to those ocean waves.

"You know, Fred, it makes me appreciate the ocean without actually looking at it while we're inside; it's almost like being out on the patio. Yeah, this is very nice," Maggie repeated. She continued, "And this couch—it looks so comfortable. Look here, Fred. It has some kind of pad on it, something you could crawl into and sleep really well."

Fred jokingly said, "Well, Mag, I might even sleep in it tonight!" Before she took him seriously, he quickly added, "I'm only kidding about that, Mag!"

Maggie said, "Okay! You're kidding. But you know, Fred, the arrangement of this furniture is the same in every suite. That's what Erin told me when she first moved here. She said she was assigned to a suite on the second floor above where we are now. Then she mentioned that she didn't want to be up there because she wanted to have direct beach access."

Fred replied, "Well, I'm so glad we're not on or near the top of this place. I mean, the building goes up to almost twenty stories – but the condos are reserved for the first two floors."

Maggie replied, "I guess that's true, Fred. But remember what Erin told me when she first came to this place—how the bellman, Casey, brought her luggage to the second floor, and she said she asked him to take it back downstairs to the first floor. Although he was very tired, he did it for her. Anyway, she said she ended going to lunch with him.

"We'll meet up with Erin later. But as far as the room, have you noticed, Fred, that large peep hole in the door, right in front of the couch I was telling you about? You can look and see everything that's out there in the hallway in front of the door. I'm sure it was installed for security reasons."

As Maggie and Fred continued to survey the suite they would call home over the next two days, they became quite tired. By then, it was mid-afternoon, and they took the opportunity to enjoy a short nap before getting dressed for the opening ceremony scheduled to start in about two hours. The event would be an opportunity to have dinner after a long day and also to have resort staff and special guests be introduced.

--------THE EVENT IS LIKE MAGGIE'S DREAM!--------

After their rest, Fred and Maggie felt refreshed and prepared for the evening's festivities. They soon ventured out into the condo lobby where they met Sandra, who was dressed in formal attire.

"Hello, Fred and Maggie," Sandra said.

After they returned the greeting, Fred stepped away for a moment. "Excuse me, ladies," he said, I'm going over here to look at the morning paper for a minute."

"Okay, Fred, we'll see you when you get back," Maggie said.

Maggie turned her attention to Sandra and said, "Hey, Sandra, I noticed you're sitting out here all alone. I guess all the others are still dressing. Where is Freddie?"

Sandra replied, "He's in the room talking to someone on the phone. He'll be out in a minute."

Maggie then commented, "Anyway, you look fabulous tonight, girl. Freddie had better be careful. Someone else may be taking a look at you."

"Aw, Maggie, come on now. No one else is interested in me. Besides, Freddie is all I need," Sandra responded.

Maggie turned her head away from Sandra briefly as if in denial that the man she once cared a lot about—at least in a physical way—was now in the grasps of her best friend. Maggie had certainly never told Sandra about the relationship she had with Freddie when they were at the law firm.

Katie had introduced Maggie to David as well as to his friend Sheri and to her daughter Jeanie, and they all ended up being a part of Maggie's group on this trip. Maggie had gotten to know David somewhat through sporadic conversations she had with him on the trip from New York. The discussions were general in nature—about life and about his relationship with Sheri and her daughter.

Maggie could not help but think about the dream she had of the cruise to Bermuda and especially the time when the group was having dinner one night. As she remembered from her dream, Sandra was sitting next to David at the dinner table. This time, now at Sinbad's event, Maggie saw that Sandra was sitting beside Freddie.

After a momentary trip back into the past when she thought about that dream, Maggie went on, "You know, Sandra, I looked at the room arrangement at the concierge desk and found that you and Freddie's suite is right next to ours, so I guess we'll be seeing a lot of each other over the next two days of our stay here."

Sandra replied, "Yeah, Maggie. That's great! At least we're not alone down here on the first floor."

Maggie said, "Well, you're right. Because everyone else is on the second floor except for Katie's friend Sheri, her daughter Jeanie, and her friend David. Yeah, they're staying directly across the hall from you, Sandra."

Sandra replied, "Well, that's fine."

During their discussion, Maggie's thoughts continued to be preoccupied with Sandra being in the dream she had. She did not tell Sandra about the part of the dream where David was all on top of her! *There's no telling what he would've done,* Maggie thought, *had it not been for the silver button she pushed on her bed's headboard in that dream.*

--------MAGGIE AND SANDRA DISCUSSIONS--------

Sandra added, "Well, you and Fred as well as me and Freddie are just fortunate to have direct beach access. I can hear the waves going back and forth on the sands of that beach right now. Maggie, the sound of the ocean is so soothing to me. It just makes me think about a lot of things. Just listen to it—you can hear it too!"

They paused for a few seconds as Maggie listened. Then Maggie said, "Well, Sandra, you sure do have the experience of being on the beach after spending time with Erin in Bermuda."

"Yeah, Maggie, you're right. But you have too, because of the cruise that you took there in your dream," Sandra said as she began to giggle.

Maggie replied, "Okay, Sandra, don't make fun of my dream!"

Sandra responded, "Okay, Maggie. It's just interesting how similar your dream was, as you described it, to this trip that we're on. Like I said before, it's just amazing!"

After she settled down a bit, Sandra continued, "Anyway, I just wish Erin would have gotten one of these rooms down here on the first floor. I mean a room that's located right here on the beach. All you have to do is to walk outside that patio, and you're practically on it."

Maggie replied, "Well, don't worry about Erin. She told me about the suite she got when she first moved here, and she said they're all the same, at least most of them. And even though they have rooms on the second floor, when her work starts here at the resort, she'll be able to get anything she wants. But all the suites are really nice! And the best thing is that they all have the same floor plan, so no one is at a disadvantage by being in a different suite. But after thinking about it, there is one exception: a few are a little larger to accommodate more people living in a suite.

"And you know, when we all leave south Florida, I understand that Sinbad has set Erin up for one of these suites like we have now—one with direct beach access—as her permanent lodging for as long as she'll be working here, which I hope will be a long time."

Sandra replied, "That's great because all of these rooms, excuse me, suites, are really nice."

-------THE PEEP HOLE-------

Sandra continued to talk to Maggie about the quality of their lodgings. "Have you noticed the entrance to these suites, Maggie? I mean, that see-through peep hole is larger than most, and you can clearly see outside the room into the hallway, and even from the outside you can see what's in front of the door on the inside, like if you're in there standing directly in front of it."

Maggie replied, "Yeah, I did notice that Sandra, but if you don't want someone seeing you from the outside at night, you just cut off the lights," Maggie said in a joking fashion. After Sandra took the time to giggle at the remark, Maggie continued, "You have to be careful too that you don't lock yourself inside the suite. The front door is kind of complicated."

Sandra, who was sitting on the couch right in front of Maggie responded, "Yeah, Maggie, be careful. You certainly want to be able to go outside, and you'll need to be able to get back in too. And don't forget about that pad on the couch – you don't won't to be caught in that thing."

Then Sandra returned to their discussion of the peep hole on the door. "My! What you said about that peep hole is funny, Maggie. Yeah, it's an advantage because of security reasons, but you sure don't need someone trying to peep inside!"

"No, Sandra, this whole complex is supposed to be pretty safe; it's only tourists down here, you know," Maggie replied.

Having an interest in going to the beach, Sandra asked, "Well, Maggie, being a tourist myself, I hope we'll have an opportunity to get into the water. Maybe tomorrow? What do you think?"

Maggie answered, "I think Sinbad will be talking about our schedule tonight at dinner."

Sandra said, "Well, hopefully we'll have time to go out there."

--------THE OCEAN FRONT--------

Sandra did have one concern, and that related to the resort's proximity to the ocean. She said to Maggie, "I know I said I wanted to get into the water, Maggie, but have you noticed how close the ocean seems to be? My gosh, it's almost on top of you! This whole condo tower is right on the ocean front! It'd be terrifying for all that water to be rushing into here where we are. Anyway, I guess being so close to the ocean is what makes this place so exciting."

Maggie replied, "I know what you mean, Sandra. Yeah, it's exciting all right. But it's also kind of creepy with all that water so close to us, especially at night when you can hear the roar of the ocean waves all night long. But you know it's kind of romantic too. I've told Fred that!"

Maggie continued, "You know, Sandra, before coming down here I read there was a structure at this very location before this tower was constructed and before Sinbad's resort was built that was totally destroyed by flood water because of a hurricane. I've heard that those storm surges can be very damaging. But anyway, that was a long time ago."

Maggie continued, "You know, Sandra, that roar of the ocean will provide for a night of tranquility. Like I was telling you before, the sound of the ocean can, not only be very peaceful, but also quite romantic. And listening to those roaring waves early in the morning can be so refreshing."

Sandra said, "Yeah, I know what you mean, Maggie. I have a machine that re-creates the sound of ocean waves and the wind—it really helps me to sleep at night. But you can't beat this; it's the real thing! And believe me, with Freddie, we plan to take full advantage of it."

That last statement did not sit well with Maggie because again she remembered how close she and Freddie use to be. She could only hope that those thoughts would not crop up as she and Fred anticipated a romantic evening themselves, being right next door to Sandra and Freddie. *Oh, who cares what they are doing,* she thought. Then she continued to ponder, *Me and my sweetie pie will be right here with a romantic rendezvous of our own, listening to those ocean waves.*

--------COURTNEY AND GATES--------

After a phone conversation in his suite, Freddie had arrived in the lobby.

"Hello, everybody," he said.

The group returned their greetings and continued to talk to one another. Fred had returned from looking at the newspaper.

At that point Courtney and Gates walked into the lobby and came up to Maggie and Sandra.

Courtney greeted them, saying, "Hello, Maggie and Sandra. And hello to you too, Fred and Freddie. It's good to see all of you."

Maggie said, "How have you two been? I know you two took an early flight down here to Florida. But we're all together now, and I know we're going to have a good time."

"We're fine and hope you all are to," Gates replied. "We're just tryin' to get used to the place down here. But it's real nice though. We can't wait to see what Sinbad has to say. I'm sure all of us are in for a treat!"

Maggie said, "Yeah, this place is wonderful. And, Courtney, I'm telling you, you look gorgeous in that outfit. For heaven's sake! I'd love to know where you got that. And, Gates, it looks like you're doing well."

Gates responded, "Like I said, Maggie, we're fine, trying to settle in around here. But we're enjoying everything so far."

Courtney responded, "Thanks, Maggie, for the compliment. And, yeah, I can tell you where I got it. But hopefully you won't get something exactly like it. Now you won't do that, will you?" Courtney responded in jest.

Courtney added, "And how are you doing, Fred?"

"I'm fine, Courtney," Fred replied. "And hope you two are well. And I know you and Gates are enjoying this nice Florida weather."

"We *are*, Fred," Gates replied simply. "Back in Chicago, I hear they're having an early snow."

Fred asked, "This early in the fall?"

Gates explained, "Fred, you know how the weather changes in Chicago. But I heard on a national forecast that it's only a flurry. But let me tell you, it's nothing like it is down here. I don't even think they get flurries in south Florida!"

Then Gates changed the subject to Sinbad's event and asked about Freddie. "And who do we have here?"

Sandra said, "Oh, Gates, this is my friend Freddie. He's also the cousin of Sinbad, the head person around here."

"How are you, and nice meeting you, Freddie," Gates said as he went on to introduce his wife Courtney.

"The pleasure is mine! Freddie replied. "Happy to meet you both."

With all the introductions out of the way, Gates commented, "I know you all are looking forward to getting into the water, but since I don't know how to swim, I'll just stay on the beach, taking in the sun and the breeze. You know, I'm hungry right about now and ready to eat."

"Okay, you all, let's go eat!" Maggie said.

Maggie and Fred and Sandra and Freddie started walking with Courtney and Gates towards the main dining hall for the opening program. All the others who flew into town for the event would soon join them as would Erin and Sinbad's other invitees.

--------THE DINNER--------

Soon everyone invited to the special event had arrived and taken their seats for the dinner. Maggie and Sandra seemed pleased that they were assigned seats near each other. Freddie was seated directly behind Maggie with Sandra sitting next to him. Maggie knew about this arrangement because she had viewed the seat assignments earlier.

Once seated, Maggie said a few words to Erin, who was sitting next to her. Then she leaned back and said to Sandra, who was sitting at the other large table, "Well, Sandra, we're not at the same table, but we're close enough to chat with each other."

Sandra replied, "Yeah, and Freddie is so close to you that your backs could literally touch."

Maggie responded, "Yeah, I don't know why they put the tables so close together, but I guess Sinbad has his reasons."

As the discussion continued, Maggie confessed, "Of course, Sandra, the main person we're celebrating tonight is sitting right here next to me."

Having overheard Maggie's discussion with Sandra, Erin said, "Thank you, Maggie. But let me say this. I may be celebrated tonight, but I realize that the reason I'm here is to control my emotions in what will probably be a very emotional event. God will take care of the rest – the fruitfulness of it all."

Sandra directed her words to both Maggie and Erin. "Oh, Erin, Maggie's right, and I understand what *you're* saying; but you *are* the person of the hour! It's your night girl!" Sandra said with a bit of excitement. "Yeah, I realize what we're all here for and you deserve it, Erin."

"You're so kind, Sandra," Erin responded.

Sandra added, "But, Maggie, don't forget your husband Fred; he's right there next to you too!"

While looking at her husband with a smile, Maggie said, "I'm not forgetting him, Sandra, not when he gives me everything I want!"

"All right now, girl. That's the way a woman ought to talk about her man."

Maggie said, "Well, Sandra, let me tell you, there *is* one thing that Fred didn't give me. And I think you know what that was."

"No, Mag, what was it?" Fred interjected, having heard her comment to Sandra. "I think I *do* give you everything you want—at least everything you ask for."

"You do, honey," Maggie replied. "But remember, you didn't give me a birthday party before we left Chicago. But I forgive you for that because we were so tied up in preparing for this trip."

"Well, I know he'll make it up to you somehow," Sandra said. "You know, Maggie, I'm sure if there were any way possible, Fred would've given you a party. Now, wouldn't you have done that, Fred?"

"I sure would have, Sandra!" Fred replied simply.

Sandra added, "Maybe you two can do something when you get back home—some kind of birthday event, I mean."

When Sandra made that last comment, she glanced at Fred and gave him a wink.

Maggie nodded her head in approval of Sandra's wanting to give her husband the benefit of the doubt in the situation. Fred, who was listening to everything being said between the two women, saw his wife's understanding in the matter and returned a

wink to Sandra. Fred and Sandra had always shared a special relationship, and those actions with their eyes gave more evidence to that.

--------THE RECOGNITION-------

During these discussions, Sinbad had been sitting by himself on the other side of the same table as Maggie and Fred. He had been busy looking over some papers but then finally went up to the podium to begin the evening's festivities.

Sinbad began to speak to the group, "Okay, people, we're ready to start. I'd like to say how happy I am that all of you could be here tonight. It's a special time for me because I've worked on this resort project for a long time. And every one of you will be a central part of it. My comments will be brief because, as some of you know, I'm not a big speaker. But I do believe in getting things done, which is the reason we're honoring our new hire tonight.

"Bear with me for just a little while this evening," Sinbad continued. "I'll talk briefly about three points. The first is the person that we are honoring tonight for her presence and her acceptance of the position as manager of the resort, and that is none other than Miss Erin Pearson. Erin, would you please stand up and be recognized?"

Erin did as Sinbad requested, and she received a loud applause.

After the applause had subsided, Sinbad continued, "We all expect great things from Erin as the overseer of the resort. She certainly has the experience because of her time in Bermuda running a facility there.

"The main reason for our having the privilege of working with Erin is her close friend Sandra, who befriended Freddie, my cousin. And Sandra is sitting here along with a faithful employee of mine, Bernie. Bernie was instrumental in encouraging Erin to 'follow her passion,' as he put it, and accept the position that was being offered to her."

"And I don't want to forget about Maggie, Sandra's close friend. Based on my understanding, she too had a lot to do with Erin being here tonight. Excuse me for a moment."

At that point, Sinbad left the stage briefly and went over to hand a note to Fred.

When Sinbad returned to the podium, he continued, "Sorry about that. But what I was going to say is thank you, Sandra, and you too, Maggie, for making all of us aware of the talents of Erin and her availability to help us."

Sandra nodded her head in recognition of Sinbad's thanks as well as his acknowledgment of her friend Maggie for their part in getting Erin to south Florida.

--------THE SCHEDULE--------

Sandra smiled as she continued to listen to Sinbad. She had gotten a glance at Bernie as he slipped Erin a note, and she wondered what that was all about.

Meanwhile, Sinbad went on, "The second thing I want to talk about this evening is the schedule of what we'll be doing over the next two days. After this dinner, you will be free to do anything you want. But try to retire early tonight because tomorrow will be a long day, beginning with breakfast at 8:00 and a tour of the facility beginning at 10:00. Then we'll have lunch right back here tomorrow at noon."

Sinbad continued, "What I'm really excited about is our venture over to the Island of Love, a facility that this resort was fortunate enough to obtain. And I'll let what we'll be doing there be a surprise to you."

"But, believe me, it will be an experience for everyone who has been in love—and I use that word loosely, because I not only mean love in a romantic sense but also love that only the Master above can give, and that is a genuine love for our fellow man regardless of how different they may be, for we all are the same in God's sight, that is, if we love and serve Him. Yes, He intended for us to love our physical bodies as well as our spirit, so I'll just leave it at that."

Sinbad went on, "And one last thing relating to this journey over to the island, which by the way should take about thirty to forty minutes, is that you need to make sure you get plenty of rest tomorrow after we eat lunch and before we leave for the island, which will be at 6:00 sharp. No latecomers will be accepted on board; in fact, we're leaving at six on the dot! Just before we set sail, a tour guide will be there to tell us what we will experience as we get off the ferry and venture onto the island.

"But before that we'll meet right back here again tomorrow for an early dinner at 4:30. And, just like for lunch, remember your seating arrangements; you'll be sitting where you are now."

Sinbad continued, "The last thing I want to tell you about is the possibility that a significant storm will be in the area in a few days. But according to the weather forecast, the first hurricane of the season is not due to arrive until later Friday, so we plan to get all the activities in before it arrives."

"The flight for our northern friends is scheduled to depart Friday afternoon, just prior to the storm's arrival, so you all don't have to worry about this storm, which is not unusual for this time of year down here in south Florida. With that in mind, bring on the food. I'm ready to eat!"

After Sinbad concluded his remarks, he returned to his seat. Everyone began to carry on casual conversation until the food arrived. When that time came, everyone was treated to a sumptuous meal. Casual conversation prevailed through the rest of dinner.

--------DISCUSSIONS--------

Among those chatting were David and Sandra, who were sitting next to each other.

"I'm looking forward to this trip to the Island of Love, aren't you?" David asked.

"Yeah, it should be fun," Sandra replied. After that she started to talk to her friend Freddie, who was seated on the other side of her.

Sinbad continued sitting alone at the table where the honoree for the evening, Erin, was. He talked to all of them at the table, including his associate Bernie and the Mints.

Not long after dinner the chatter around the head tables ceased, and people began to wonder back into the lobby for a little chitchat before retiring to their living quarters.

After a while Sinbad said to Maggie and Fred, "You two, come over here in one of the conference rooms. I want to talk to you about something." He escorted them into a separate room to talk to them, presumably, about business matters relating to the remainder of the trip. They left all the others congregated in the lobby to talk among themselves.

After a few minutes of conversation with Sinbad, Maggie and Fred left him to rejoin the group. As they were walking towards the lobby, Maggie said, "Fred, I'm really looking forward to our adventure tomorrow. I'll be praying that the hurricane won't mess up our plans."

Fred replied, "It won't; I can assure you of that, Mag."

Not fully understanding his certainty about the storm not affecting their activities, Maggie continued walking to the lobby to join the others with Fred by her side.

After talking briefly with another member of the group, Sinbad decided to speak to Fred once again—by himself. Having now left the dining area, he saw the Mints, who had returned to the lobby, mingling with other guests.

Sinbad walked up to them and said, "Maggie, you go ahead continue to talk with other guests, and I'm going to chat with Fred a little longer."

"Okay, have a nice evening, Sinbad, and I'll see you in a little bit, Fred," Maggie replied.

After Fred's brief private discussion with Sinbad, both he and Maggie got back together and headed toward their suite while the others remained in the gathering area.

Sinbad had a last word for them before they too went to their place of rest for the night. Then, everyone began to retire to their living quarters. They left one by one and, as Sandra passed Fred, she gave him another wink, which he reciprocated. The actions of those two went unnoticed by the others in the group. Before long, everyone had returned to their suites, looking forward to the next day's trip to the Island of Love.

CHAPTER NINE
VOYAGE TO THE ISLAND OF LOVE

The first day of Sinbad's event had ended and everyone had retired for the evening. For Maggie and Sandra, whose suites had direct access to the beach, it was tempting to go onto their patio and enjoy the calm night breeze despite their fatigue. The wind that brought the roaring ocean waves onto the beach was only a short distance away and too enticing to forgo.

Sandra and Freddie had said they would play a game of hide-and-seek in their spacious suite before retiring for the night. The suites were large with multiple rooms, and Sandra and her friend had planned to take full advantage of it. They got the idea from Sinbad earlier just before he had pulled Fred away to speak about something in private.

Maggie had a different plan for the evening, which was to get a good night's sleep. But she did not want to go directly to bed; she desired to transition into it. A more immediate interest was to get a glimpse of what Sandra had said she experienced during her time in Bermuda.

So, after Maggie and Fred returned to their suite, she said to him, "Let's go out on the patio for just a little while and see the ocean waves come in before we go to bed. And who knows—there might be a starlit sky too!"

Fred replied, "Sounds good. I just hope I don't fall asleep out there."

--------A STARLIT NIGHT--------

Fred and Maggie quickly slipped out of their formal attire and into their night clothes and sat on the patio sipping champagne they found in the kitchenette. As they sat on the patio absorbing the coolness of the ocean breezes, just as she figured, there was a starlit sky. It reminded Maggie so much of what Sandra had told her regarding her viewing of the celestial bodies on the last night of her visit with Erin in Bermuda.

Maggie decided to return to the kitchenette to get something to go along with the beverage they were having. She said to Fred, "Come on and go with me back inside to see what we can find to munch on as we sip this champagne."

"Okay, I'll go with you before I get comfortable out here," Fred said.

Maggie and Fred returned inside in search of something to go along with their beverage. They found a bag of chips.

"These chips would be perfect, Mag."

"Okay, Fred. This should do the trick," Maggie replied in approval.

As they returned to the patio, Maggie remembered she had a cell phone app that played music she enjoyed so much. She said, "Listen, honey, I remember on my cell phone there was a place that plays only romantic music, and I used to listen to it before going to sleep at night. It was like a sedative; it put me right to sleep. I think I'll get my cell and bring that app up, and we can listen to some nice music."

While Fred was in full agreement with their listening to music, he said, "Now, Mag, you *did* say that the music helps you to sleep. I hope that it doesn't put you to sleep out here on the patio. Because if it does, I'd have to carry you back inside."

Maggie replied in jest, "Well, dodo! That wouldn't be so bad. Remember, you carried me across the threshold of the door after we were married."

Fred was not able to argue with what Maggie had said, so they proceeded to walk out to the patio, him holding the bag of chips and her holding her cell phone, anticipating being serenaded with romantic music.

They sat down and began looking out over the ocean with that starlit sky hovering above it. And, oh yeah, listening to that romantic music.

Then Fred had an idea. He said, "Hey, Mag, while I was moving around the place for the first time, I saw an amplifier on one of the shelves. I think that if I can hook it up to your cell phone, it would increase the intensity and the quality of the sound."

"Oh, that's great, Fred. You go get that, and I'm sure that'll enhance the experience," Maggie said.

Fred then went to fetch the amplifier.

"Oh, Fred!" Maggie said after he returned. "What a night it must have been when Sandra received that last sign she felt she needed to confirm her physical healing while she was in Bermuda. And, Fred, that amplifier really works; the music sounds really good."

Maggie certainly could relate to the experience Sandra had that night in Bermuda. She said, "It's so pleasant and peaceful out here tonight, Fred. And look at those stars—such a starlit night! It's very romantic. In a way, it reminds me of when were on the 65th floor on your balcony in downtown Chicago. Do you remember that?"

"Of course, I remember, Mag," Fred replied. "Yeah, it was so peaceful up there on that balcony—close to the roof of the building."

Maggie replied, "But, of course, it's even more serene here with nothing but the ocean to distract us. Only it's not a distraction. Rather, it has a soothing effect on me, Fred," she said as they clung close together, enjoying what was before them.

After a few minutes of silence except for the smooth jazz playing in the background, Fred finally said, "Yeah, Mag, I sure do miss the hustle and bustle of the big city. And, yeah, the balcony I had in the condo near the top of the building where all of Chicago could be seen was really magnificent—the scenery, I mean. But I agree with you. It can't compare to this place."

"Well, you *do* know why it's so special, don't you?"

"No, Mag. Tell me," Fred said.

"It's because of you, dodo," Maggie responded to her husband in jest.

As Fred thought back to the time when he first moved to Chicago from Hawaii, Maggie's mind was on the present celestial wonders they were witnessing—that starlit sky—and the love of her life, Fred! But her thoughts also were on Sandra's experience with Erin.

"Yeah, Fred," she said, "I can appreciate where you lived in Chicago before we moved out into the suburbs. But, let me tell you, this environment we're in here is tough to beat. I mean, it must have been like this in Bermuda when Sandra was there the way it is right now here tonight in south Florida.

"For heaven's sake, Fred! Just look at those stars and tell me you don't feel anything. I know you do, honey. I love you so much. But you know? That night when Sandra was in Bermuda, love was in the air too! But on *that* night, it was God's love for her that she saw through that starlit sky. She told me as much by describing the thousands of stars she saw that night as well as the sands she saw earlier during that day on the beach; those two events gave her the sign she needed for her healing."

Maggie finally stopped chatting to Fred as they both just sat there, gazing upward towards the heavens.

After a little more silence as only smooth jazz played, Maggie continued, "Tonight, Fred, it's about me and you." She added, "And the background music being played on this cell phone, especially with the assistance of that amplifier, has added to the romantic atmosphere of the moment. Don't you think, Fred?"

"Yes, I do, Mag," Fred responded simply.

As they both continued to look outward toward the ocean and starlit sky, Fred said, "Yeah, Mag. Love certainly is in the air—my love for you, honey!"

Maggie could only respond by saying, "Oh, Fred, please, please tell me more!"

Fred responded by shifting his focus from the stars overhead to the glow that he saw in her eyes. They just sat there and stared at each other for a while before glancing back up at the night sky. The constant sound of the ocean waves provided its own background melody behind the music.

For Maggie and Fred, these moments felt like heaven on earth. They had no desire to speak and wanted only to drink in the scene before them in silence. Finally, they decided to go back inside to get some rest from a full of day of activity.

--------HIDE AND GO SEEK--------

While snugly in bed, Maggie heard a commotion in Sandra and Freddie's suite. This prompted her to say, "Sandra wasn't kidding when she said that they would play some hide-and-seek. Do you hear all that noise, Fred?"

"Yeah, it's hard for me to go the sleep because of it," Fred complained.

It was a while before Fred dozed off. They set the cell phone's alarm and placed it beside their bed. They were exhausted and did not want to take a chance on oversleeping and missing breakfast the next morning.

Maggie could not get over the fact that her best friend was having so much fun with the man she once passionately desired. She tossed and turned most of the night, and it also affected Fred by not allowing him to get the solid sleep he needed. Maggie finally fell asleep about an hour before daybreak, but shortly after that the alarm went off and woke her as well as Fred, who had only dozed off an hour or two earlier, giving him little sleep as well.

It was early in the morning when everyone arose, anticipating a long day. Breakfast was served and everyone partook and then prepared to attend the tour of the resort given by Sinbad. Maggie and Fred attended both the breakfast and the tour with all the others but struggled to stay awake because of the slight amount of sleep they got the previous night.

Jeanie and Wynn had gotten together and were the only ones not at breakfast. But they showed up on time for the tour.

Maggie and Fred were still tired because of a largely sleepless night; they were like zombies as they walked around on the tour, dazed and not attentive to what was going on. There was no rest for the weary for them because soon they would go to lunch.

Maggie and Fred managed to muster up enough strength to partake of a sumptuous meal that left them feeling even more fatigued. They could not wait to get back into their suite to the get the rest they missed out on the previous night and that morning. They both knew that for them to be alert for the big event in a few hours, the journey over to the Island of Love, they would need to get some sleep at some point in the afternoon.

--------ON THE BEACH---------

After lunch, Erin encouraged everybody to join her on the beach. It would be the only opportunity for the group from the North to experience the sand and water of the beach environment during their stay since their flight back to New York was scheduled for mid-afternoon the next day. Everyone would need to pack their luggage earlier in the day in preparation for that flight. Thoughts of the hurricane that was predicted lingered in the back of everyone's minds.

Erin wanted to make sure that everyone would at least take in some sunshine on the beach in the afternoon. She said, "Maggie, I'm telling everyone to come on out here to the beach. It will be so much fun. I know you and Fred are coming along. I overheard you two talking about how little sleep you got last night, but you gotta take advantage of this."

A weary Maggie replied, "Erin, I was looking forward to taking a long nap this afternoon, but I guess Fred and I will go ahead and join the fun with everybody and try to get some rest later before our trip over to the Island of Love."

"That's what I want to hear," Erin replied with much enthusiasm.

Katie weighed in on the issue. "Yeah, Maggie, you and Fred should at least spend *some* time on the beach." Then she asked Erin, "By the way, have you heard anything about what we'll be doing over there on the island?"

Erin replied, "No, Katie, I'm like everyone else. I guess Sinbad meant for it to be a big surprise—whatever it is."

Soon everyone returned to their suites briefly to dress in beach attire. Maggie and Fred also returned to their suite but resisted the temptation to remain there and rest; rather, they joined the rest of the group on the beach.

Courtney and Gates were already lying on a blanket that they had placed on the sand with an umbrella above them. Maggie saw Erin and her friend Bernie head to an available beach chair to sit while most of the others in the group attempted to find their own leisure accommodations.

Maggie said to Sandra, who was close by, "Hey, Sandra, you see Erin with her new friend over there? They seem to be getting along really well. She may have found someone already down here in south Florida, and she hasn't even started on her job yet!"

Sandra replied, "Yeah, Maggie, I'm really happy for her. Bernie seems to be a nice man from what I can tell."

After their sojourn onto the beach, Maggie and Fred finally got the opportunity to go back to their suite and get some rest. Back in the bedroom, Maggie said, "Fred, I can't wait to get into that bed. I'm so tired."

He replied, "Yeah, I could use some sleep now too, Mag."

Only two hours were left before they had to be at dinner prior to their journey to the Island of Love. Forgetting to set the alarm, they both went to bed and fell dead asleep.

--------THE MINTS MAKE IT TO DINNER?--------

Ring, ring! An alarm went off in Maggie's mind, and she was awakened from her slumber. She reached over to touch Fred, but he was not there lying beside her. "Fred, Fred, where are you?" she asked.

When she got no answer, she arose and began to look around the small bedroom of their suite, and he was nowhere to be found.

Maggie ventured out into the living area and saw Fred sipping some coffee. When she called his name, he looked around and saw her coming towards him.

"Hello, Mag," he said. "I guess you let the alarm wake you up. As for me, I couldn't sleep because of the wind. It's really picked up out there. Do you hear it?" he asked.

Maggie answered, "Yeah, now that you mentioned it, it *is* pretty windy outside. I guess it's a sign that the storm forecasted is on its way. I hope it doesn't affect our trip over to the Island of Love. I'm really looking forward to that."

"Yeah, me too," Fred replied. "I guess we need to get dressed and go to this dinner."

"Okay, Fred, I'll be ready in about ten minutes," Maggie assured him.

With that they both dressed for the dinner and headed out of their condo suite and over to the dining hall to enjoy a meal with the others. After that, the presumption was that everyone would be ready for the voyage to the Island of Love.

--------SINBAD'S ANNOUNCEMENTS--------

As everyone ate dinner, Sinbad got up to make an announcement. "Well, everybody, I hope all of you had a good rest last night and earlier this afternoon. Believe me, you are going to need it for the trip to the Island of Love right after we eat. We'll be leaving in about thirty minutes from now. At that time, we will board the ferry for the island. A van will be here to take us from the condo to the boarding dock. It's a nice little ride where you'll be able to do more sightseeing.

"Once we get there, you'll be given seat assignments. And these seats are assigned based on the information that each one of you mailed to me in preparation for the resort's opening event. It should be a lot of fun, so enjoy your food and, again, we'll be looking to see you over at the dock in about thirty minutes."

After returning to his seat, Sinbad remembered that he forgot something extremely important, so he stood again in front of the group and corrected himself. "I just remembered that I saw the weather report this morning and the hurricane that I first thought wouldn't arrive until tomorrow evening after you all, our friends from the North, have boarded your flight, now I understand that it might get here a little earlier than that. It shouldn't affect our trip to the Island of Love. But it could affect your flight tomorrow. I'll let you know more about that tomorrow morning at breakfast. Don't think about that now though. Just finish your food and we're gonna have some fun tonight!"

Sinbad had forgotten something else and began, "Let me correct myself about another thing. Although you will be leaving in thirty minutes as I just said, I won't be going with you. I'm going to the island right now and will be waiting on you all at the dock there, and the ferry boat will be waiting for you at the island dock over here. My guess is that you all will be finished eating in about twenty minutes, and then you will begin to make your way over to that dock.

"Meanwhile, I'll take a ferry ride over to the island to do some prep stuff, so it will be another hour to an hour and a half before I see you again over there on the island. Don't worry! Your ferry will be leaving on time. This is just a boat reserved for special assignments. I'm going to have to take care of some things. But I *can* tell you this much—we all will be over at, what's called, 'The Village' on the island. That's where all our activities will take place. And, believe me, you won't forget your experience at this place.

"Anyway, I'll see you there just before you get off your ferry boat on the dock."

While the sun had not yet gone below the western horizon, the warm, calm breeze that everyone had experienced earlier on the beach had transitioned into a brisk wind that brought the temperatures down considerably. Before he left early for the island, Sinbad made another announcement: "Listen, everyone. Before I leave, I would suggest that you return to your suites and get a light jacket. I think you will need it to adjust to the cooler air that's expected while crossing to the island on the ferry. I think it'll be quite breezy on there as you journey over. I'm going to the gift shop and purchase one now."

As he began to leave the group, he turned around and said, "Oh, yeah, it will be closer to 6:30 before your ferry leaves for the island. But when you do, just assemble at the dock and be ready to board the vessel at that time. We're looking at a departing time of closer to 7:00, and, like I said, in about thirty to forty minutes after you leave the dock you should be arriving at your destination, the Island of Love."

Sinbad left immediately, going ahead of the group to the dock where everyone would leave for the island. They would remain in the in the dining hall to finish their meal. They were taking their time, however, so it would be more than the twenty minutes Sinbad had indicated before they finished eating.

Sinbad took the private boat to the island to make final plans for the activities that awaited the group.

--------THE GAME OF LOVE-------

After about thirty minutes, the group had finished eating and began carrying on casual conversations. They went back to their rooms to collect their jackets and soon boarded a van that took them from the condo across the street to Sinbad's resort and then on to the part of the resort that bordered the bay and the dock. The waiting ferry would take them across the bay to the Island of Love, which was normally about a thirty-minute ride.

On this day, Sinbad had arranged for a special trip to one of the several tourist attractions on the island, The Village, a separate recreational facility that was directly affiliated with Sinbad's resort. Sinbad had managed to keep many of his plans for the group concealed. His secrecy about what they would do on the island prompted Maggie to say, "You know, Fred, I wonder what we all will do over there on this...*Island of Love*. And why does Sinbad have to be so secretive about it?"

Fred replied, "Well, most of us are coupled off, so I guess it'll be about love—us loving each other. But who knows? Who knows what games Sinbad has on his mind?"

--------THE DOCK OF THE BAY--------

Once everyone had gathered at the dock, Casey, whom Sinbad had designated to guide the people onto the vessel, was sitting on the dock of the bay awaiting their arrival. The group finally appeared, and everyone deboarded the van and gathered around him.

Casey then said in the midst of a light breeze, "Okay, it seems like everyone is here and ready for our short journey. By short I mean anywhere from thirty to forty-five minutes in duration once we get moving. Well, Sinbad usually says it's only about a thirty-minute ride, but I don't think he considered that the weather might hinder us a bit.

"We'll certainly have more than enough time to carry on casual conversations with our partners. From what I understand, this is all a part of the activity that we'll have once we get to The Village. Hopefully, you brought along a light jacket to combat the cool breezes as Sinbad suggested earlier."

Sinbad's special friend, Casey, carried out the orders he had been given, and that included handing out the assignment cards that would indicate where each person would sit both on the ferry and when they arrived on the island and entered the main entertainment venue, The Village. At that location on the island, they would sit together according to the devised seating arrangement that Casey would hand out to everyone.

Once in their seats, group members would play what Sinbad called "The Game of Love." He had been so secretive about exactly what they would do, and not even Casey had all the details.

-------THE BOARDING PROCESS-------

Casey took charge of the boarding process and called out the names of the individuals who would be paired for this fun excursion.

"Okay, everyone. Let's get close and as I call out your names you can board the ferry together—in pairs—according to the names on these assignment cards I have. Is everybody ready?" he asked.

Most of those gathered said in unison, "Yeah, we're ready."

Casey then proceeded to call the pairs of individuals who would be sitting together to claim their seats on the ferry. These same assigned pairs would remain together when they arrived at the island where this "Game of Love" would be played once inside The Village.

Casey proceeded to call the names of the partners who were to sit together on the top deck, going from front to back: "Sandra and David, would you please step forward to board and claim your seats?" He directed them.

This assigned pairing wasn't Sandra's idea, given that fact that she would much rather be with her new friend, Freddie. But she didn't want to rock the boat, so she went along with the idea. Besides, a part of her kind of liked the guy; she had learned that he was from New York as she was.

Then Casey continued to tell Sandra and David, "You'll take the seats in the front of the top deck. Here are your assigned cards, and, after you two board, the names of the others designated for the top of the ferry will be called."

"All right! Here we go," David said to Sandra and assisted her onto the vessel; Sandra seemed less enthusiastic about the pairing based on her facial expression, but she proceeded forward with him as she glanced at Freddie, who was standing among group members waiting for his name to be called.

After Sandra and David had boarded, Casey continued to call out group members who were to be paired together. He said, "The pairs following Sandra and David will take the next seats going from front to back. So, Gates and Erin, you're next and will sit behind Sandra and David. Courtney and Fred, you'll take the next seats."

"Then Katie, you and I will take the last seats in the back. That's right, Katie, you'll be paired with me in the back!" Casey emphasized to her.

Because she was standing the furthest from Casey, Katie yelled to him, "I'm fine with that, Casey," to assure him of her approval of the seating arrangement.

Casey replied, "Okay then, when I call your name just go up there behind the others and claim that last seat. I'll join you when I finish calling these names."

As Casey gave these instructions, he proceeded to give the assignment cards to the pairs he had called as they came to him. Each pair then proceeded to board the vessel and claim their designated seats as instructed.

After everyone had taken their seats on the top deck, Casey began to call the names of the other partners who would be sitting on the bottom deck, who had waited patiently to be selected for *their* seats. This time, it was those who had claimed their seats on the top deck who had to wait patiently until the boarding process was over.

Casey started calling the names of those who would be sitting on the bottom deck, beginning with those who were to sit in the back: "Maggie and Freddie, would you please step forward and get your assignment cards?" As they came up Casey told them, "You two will be the first to board the bottom level and will take the last seat there in the back. You will see a storage area for personal items right behind you."

"Bon voyage!" Freddie said in jest as he and partner Maggie boarded the vessel.

After Maggie and Freddie had taken their seats, Casey said, "The next pairs to board are Wynn and Jeanie; then Sheri and Bernie, who will be the last names I call, and you two will be sitting here right behind the captain of the ferry." He pointed to their seats.

After everyone was on board, Casey stood at the edge of the dock, looking over into the ferry with his light jacket flying in the wind. He then announced, "Okay, everybody, I hope everyone is correctly situated, because the way you're seated now will be the same when we get to The Village over there on the island. Just make sure you hold on to your assignment cards, and, in less than an hour, we'll arrive at the island."

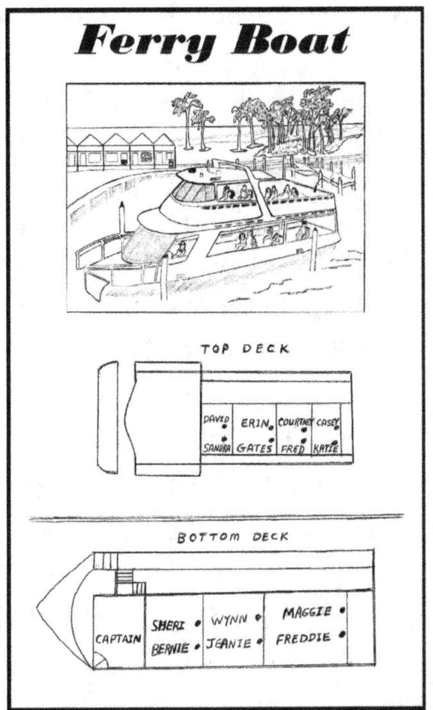

**Figure 9: Seating arrangement sketch –
On the ferry to the Island of Love**

--------SINBAD'S INSTRUCTIONS--------

Casey continued, "Sinbad wants me to explain to everybody what you will see as we approach the island. So here it is, the way I understand it. When we get to the island, we're to stay on the ferry and wait for further instructions directly from him. At that point he will give us a signal to get off the vessel, then meet all of us on the island's dock.

"Once we're all on the dock, he'll personally guide us onto the island. The Village will be to the right as we walk further on the island and a refreshment area will be to the left, where food and beverages can be purchased. And that's where we should go once we get on the island—to the left where we can refresh ourselves with food and drink. Sinbad will personally guide us over to The Village facility after that, and this is where we will have our activities.

"Sinbad told me to tell you no one is to go toward The Village without being assisted. At the time I talked to him, he said he will explain everything when he sees you there and will guide everyone to where we are supposed to be, which ultimately will be inside The Village. At that point you will be given more details about the planned activities.

"Based on my understanding, that's when you'll use the assignment cards you've been given to claim your seats."

Casey continued, "I do know that once you get inside The Village, there will be chairs arranged in a circular fashion. On the seat of each chair, you will see names on index cards. You simply go to the seat where you see your name."

Casey, who was standing on the edge of the dock overlooking the ferry boat and its occupants, then said, "Well, that's it. As all of you can see, everybody is on the ferry boat now except for me, but here I come!"

As Casey stepped off the dock and onto the ferry boat, he walked by the captain and said to him, "Sir, you can ramp up those engines and get ready for sail!" After that Casey walked up to the top deck, strolled to the back, and sat beside his partner, Katie. Then he said, "You ready to roll, Katie?"

"I am!" she replied.

At this point, everyone was situated in their seats. So the time had come to experience the voyage to the Island of Love.

--------SANDRA AND DAVID--------

Sinbad had warned everyone that there would be a breeze that could affect all on the ferry, especially those on the top deck. Being in the first seat where they faced direct exposure to the air flow as the vessel sailed forward, David and Sandra would be most affected by the constant winds. But this was only the beginning of the ferry ride; the breeze would increase in velocity, but everyone seemed so excited the weather went largely unnoticed.

The thing that most of the travelers *did* notice was the magnificent scenery as they sailed away from the Florida mainland and further into the bay. Sandra especially seemed to be amazed at the experience as she said to David, "It's so beautiful up here. You have a panoramic view of the whole area. Look, you can clearly see Sinbad's resort as well as that massive Miami skyline."

David noticed that Gates and Erin, who were sitting directly behind them, were carrying on a conversation together and realized an opportunity to pay a special compliment to Sandra. He knew the others were not close enough to hear what he would say and took advantage of the opportunity. In a lowered voice, assuring that Gates and Erin would not hear him, David said, "Yeah, like you say, Sandra, it looks nice up here, but not as nice as you!"

Sandra was astonished that he would make such a comment, and she rebuked his response. "Oh, David, don't get personal. You know this trip is not to develop personal relationships. Most of us are already in a relationship." Then she turned her head away from him and murmured to herself, "I don't know what Sinbad had in mind by pairing us up like this."

Having detected Sandra's whispered words, David replied, "Well, I'm glad he put us together—Sinbad, I mean."

Sandra replied, "You know, David, you have an excellent set of ears. I had no idea you understood what I just whispered to myself."

"Well, I pay attention to a lot of things, Sandra. And right now, I can't help but pay some attention to you."

--------A QUESTION OF FAITH--------

David continued, "You know, since being on this trip—coming from New York—I noticed that we seem to have a lot in common."

Sandra replied, "Well, I'll have to admit, you seem to be an outgoing, fun loving guy, the same as what I used to be as a woman of the world—*before* I was saved."

"Before you were saved?" David asked in a derisive manner. Then he continued, "Don't give me that! You know you still love the better things in life."

Sandra retorted, "Well, those better things in life are not what you think they are. You know, David, there are even better things that you can have in life than the things *you* apparently focus on."

"And what exactly, may I ask, are the better things *you're* talking about? Things that you say my mind is *not* focused on," David replied.

Sandra answered, "Well, I'm certainly not talking about those physical, material kinds of things. You probably don't even realize it, but some of the best things in life you can't see. They're spiritual kinds of things like honesty, love, and commitment. Now don't get me wrong, I'm still fun loving, but my purpose now is to do only what I think the Lord wants me to do."

David responded, "The Lord, huh? It's amazing how some of you who are in the church totally forget about the way you used to be. Lord, have mercy! You do know you have some of the same urges you used to have, Sandra, when you were a woman of the world as you put it."

"For one thing, David," Sandra replied, "you shouldn't use the Lord's name in vain like that. The Bible says that's the wrong thing to do."

"Okay, *for heaven's sake!* Is that any better? And why are you church people so prudish and judgmental?"

Sandra replied, "It's not being prudish, David, and I'm certainly not judgmental. But the feelings I have are for real. I mean, when the Lord touches you, it's something that's totally different than a physical touch; it's so much better, much deeper, much more inwardly gratifying. But *you* probably wouldn't understand that. I mean, anyone with a materialistic mindset."

David responded, "Well, *lookie here!* I don't know how to take being called materialistic; I can hardly say the word! All I know is that the stuff you all learn in church is almost like make believe—believing in things you can't see. Give me a break!" he said sarcastically.

David continued to question her faith again in a lower tone of voice. "And believing you'll go to heaven when you die? Have you ever seen a dead person, Sandra? Well, before you answer, I have and they're just lifeless. It's really kinda scary if you ask me."

Sandra responded to his last comment by saying, "Well, that's true, David. It is sad when someone you care about dies. And as far as a dead person being 'scary' as you put it, you probably have a point; it's not a very pleasant look. But here is the difference with us in the church—at least if you're a true believer. And that is while we see that a person's physical body is gone when they die—again scary as you say—we're taught that their spirit lives on with the Lord. What you see there in the casket is not the real person; it's their spirit that is the real thing about them, and that spirit is released from their physical body at the time of death—what we believers call the transition.

"But, David, let me mention something else. As far as my 'urges' as you call them are concerned, those things are so much more under control now. And I want to keep it that way, so don't think any wayward thoughts, buddy!"

-------FOR HEAVENS SAKE-------

"Um, I've never heard it put like that," David replied. "Most people don't analyze death like you just did."

Sandra admonished David by saying, "David, we're not most people; we're believers!"

"Okay, I respect you for that. But going back to what I said earlier about those urges, I'm just trying to be friendly."

Sandra replied, "I can do without that kind of friendliness. And one other thing, David. You made the expression 'for heaven's sake,' and asked me if that was an acceptable replacement for taking the Lord's name in vain. Well, my answer is that kind of expression is really not acceptable either, because heaven is a real place, so in my opinion you shouldn't use it unless you're serious about going there. And I don't think you used it seriously!"

"Wait a minute! Did you just tell me I'm going to hell?"

Sandra responded, "Those are your words, David, not mine."

Before David had a chance to respond further to her last statement, she continued, "But after thinking about it, in a way it really is acceptable because ...." She paused again, then asked David the question: "Have you heard of the scripture in Romans 8:28 that says that all things work together for good to those who love God and who are called for His purpose?"

Before Sandra allowed David to answer, she said, "Well, let me tell you. The expression 'for heaven's sake,' is acceptable in the sense that everything that happens, God allows. I mean, He's sovereign, for heaven's sake as you put it. So, whatever happens or whatever you're going through, there's always more good things coming! He's worked it out that way. Even Jesus' crucifixion, which was a very bad event to every believer, was actually necessary for our salvation."

Sandra went on, "You know, David, even in death there is more to life than what we know in this physical body because He has promised that all those who live and believe in Him will never die but will live forever in the spirit. It's our responsibility to believe that. So, whatever is happening in our lives, God has ordained to make something good come out of it—to fulfill His purpose. And the exciting thing about that is He's given us an opportunity to help that purpose come about. We only have to believe what He said and act on that belief."

By this point David just sat there, not saying a word, listening to what Sandra had to say. But after a brief period of silence, and not understanding much of what she was saying, he simply added, "Sandra, that was a mouthful!"

Sandra had one interest in David's questioning her faith. She asked, "And by the way, if you really don't believe in something you can't see, David, how do you explain the feeling you apparently have for me right now? I mean, I'm not going to call it love or anything like that, because I'm not interested. But it sure seems to me that *you* have an interest in me. Now that's something that's real—at least real to you—but you can't see that kind of emotion. But I bet you sure can feel it though, can't you, David?"

David replied, "Well, what can I say? I can't argue with that. But as far as that last statement you made, you do have a point. I mean, I can't deny feelings—what I'm feeling right now, for example. Yeah, there's something about you that's attractive to me. And you know that kind of emotion *is* real, I have to admit!" He continued, "Anyway, you're just a nice lady. Yeah, you're real nice."

--------TALK OF SHERI--------

After that deeply personal conversation with Sandra, David changed the tone of the discussion. "You know I have a nice friend in Sheri," he said, "and she reminds me of you a lot—except she's very quiet."

Sandra said, "Yeah, your friend Sheri *is* very nice. And my friend Maggie said that she had an interesting dream where she went on a cruise, and it's amazing that you two as well as Sheri's daughter Jeanie were on it. In fact, Maggie said a lot of us who are on this ferry were in the dream she had. It's really amazing."

David replied, "Um, that *is* interesting."

-------SEEKING TO BE WARM-------

Sandra changed the subject. "You know, while the view is great, that air is brisk, and it's kinda cool up here. This jacket I have is not helping much."

David said, "Come on over here, and I'll cover you with this blanket I have. I took what Sinbad said about having something to combat this breeze seriously, so in addition to the jacket, I brought along this blanket. But it won't be long now before we get to where we're going, I hope."

So Sandra scooted over closer to David, and he covered her with the blanket. Sandra felt odd being this close to someone other than her new friend Freddie, who was partnered with her best friend Maggie down on the first deck. But Sandra was comfortable being held by another man as long as it was only to keep warm and not romantically.

Sandra whispered to him, "David, what were you doing, tempting me to be so close to you like this?"

"Don't worry. It's only a 'holy hug,' as you might put it, being the religious person that you are, being *saved.* Is that what you call it?"

Sandra answered, "Yeah, that's what you call it. And the term simply means that Jesus saves us from our sins, that we are forgiven for the wrongs we've done." She continued, "And as far as a *holy hug,* exactly what is that?" Before he could answer, she looked back from gazing out across the water and said emphatically, "It's more like an embrace!"

Having finally finished his deep conversation with Erin, Gates witnessed David sitting close to Sandra. Because of the constant breeze, not to mention the spacing between the rows of seating, he could not hear clearly what they were saying to each other.

He said, "Hey, David, I know Sandra is kind of cool and everything, but you should refrain from any appearance of doing wrong, man, like embracing a woman when her male friend on the same vessel." Gates could not help but think of Freddie, who was on the lower deck sitting next to Maggie. Gates continued, "That's what the Bible says, you know, to avoid any appearance of evil."

David replied, "For heaven's sake, man, I thought you and Erin were in deep discussion back there. But anyway, what are you saying, Gates? That it would be okay to hold her like I'm doing if we weren't on the same vessel as her man? When does sincerity and just wanting to keep someone from the cold factor in? Like with what I'm doing with Sandra being over here?"

Gates did not answer, and his silence was deafening.

David perceived the irritation Gates had as reflected in his demeanor, so, after a brief pause, he attempted to explain by presenting a justification, saying, "And another thing, Gates, you may be right, but we're partners in crime, you might say, because she's the one who came over here where I am—and she's still here!"

Sandra then tried to justify her actions by saying, "David, that's true I'm over here where you are, but that's only because of that cool breeze that's blowing up in here, and now at least I'm warm."

At that comment from Sandra, David said back to Gates, "I rest my case, sir. I'm just providing a service."

--------THIS IS GOING TO BE SOME TRIP!--------

By this time everyone on the top deck was aware of what was happening near the front. Katie, who was sitting next to Casey in the back, said out loud, "I'm with Sandra! I don't blame her. I'd try to keep myself warm too!"

After giving her statement more serious thought, Katie looked toward Casey, who was sitting next to her, and said in a much lower voice, "Now, don't take that seriously, Casey. I don't have a problem with the temperature up here." She wanted to make sure that he did not get any ideas about being that close to her. Casey replied, "Don't worry, Katie. I don't have a blanket!"

Sitting directly behind the pair in the front, Erin by now had listened, however faintly, to much of what Sandra and David were saying to each other. She especially had noticed Sandra moving so close to David. She offered a response in validation of Sandra as her friend. "Listen, David, I can vouch for Sandra. Her life was changed when she came to see me back in Bermuda."

Realizing that by now everyone on the top deck knew what was going on, Erin turned around and raised her voice to share with everyone, "You all, this is going to be some trip!"

Fred, who was sitting behind Erin with Courtney next to him, also got into the conversation. "We're sitting a little farther back, but we can sense what you all are saying. And, Gates, your comments to David were spiritual in nature, but you weren't very spiritual when you confronted Maggie's husband John when I was about to have dinner with her at the Village Hotel that evening back in Hawaii!"

Katie, who was sitting directly behind Fred, said, "Fred, you and Maggie were seeing each other while she was still married to John?! Now you know that wasn't right," she rebuked him.

"Watch it, Katie," Fred responded to what he considered a condemning, judgmental statement. "We weren't doing anything wrong—just about to have dinner and chat a little bit. Remember what it says in Matthew 7:1-5 about not being judgmental? If you're not careful, you'll be judged the same way you're judging someone else!"

Then Katie responded, "Okay then, if you're quoting scriptures to justify your actions, I got one for you relating to being judgmental. It also says in John 7:24 that it's possible to rightly judge. Now what do you have to say about that?"

Before Fred had a chance to respond, Gates interrupted them both and said, "Okay, everybody, you all can leave this discussion of judging people to church and Sunday school. But I would like to say this, David, like I said earlier, God doesn't like even the appearance of evil.

"And by the way, Fred, that's why I reacted like I did when I saw Maggie's husband at the time confronting you and especially her. It was a righteous judgment, like Katie was talking about. But when I realized that you were sitting with a married woman, I backed off."

Gates continued, "But let me tell you, David, you still created what the scripture calls 'the appearance of evil.' I mean, you're not even supposed to look at a woman in a sensuous way unless it's your wife."

Fred responded, "Well, Gates, let me say this. I'll have to admit that you confronted John when he grabbed his wife, and I realize that you did not know at the time that *it was* his wife. But I also have to admit that I'm torn right now about you trying to calm the situation that night while at the same time interfering with a husband-and-wife issue. But like you said, you didn't know they were married. And the scripture says that you're not held accountable if you don't know—if you're ignorant about a particular thing."

"So now you're calling me ignorant, Fred?" Gates replied, partly in jest but also partly being quite serious.

Fred replied, "No, Gates. You know what I mean. Now, everybody, let us take Gates' advice and move on to another subject."

Gates responded, "Okay, Fred, as a minister I can't let you misquote the scripture. Before we move on, the Good Book also says that you reap what you sow!"

"Now, look here," David said, "at all this religious talk!"

Gates replied, "It's really serious talk, David. And as for you, Fred….." Then he hesitated and said sarcastically to the others, "You hear that everybody? He's let me off the hook." He continued, "Now listen, y'all, like Fred said, let's move on and talk about something else."

--------THE CONFRONTATION--------

After Gates' response, David turned around slightly in his seat to say, "Yeah, let's do that, Gates. Let's talk about something other than male and female relationships—like something totally different and that's religion." David directed his comments to all those on the top deck, "It's interesting how some people are supposed to be so religious but end up arguing more than most sinners do! That's what you all are doin'. Let's have some love around here! Remember, we're going to the Island of Love."

Casey, sitting in the back beside Katie, entered the discussion. "You know, David, we *do* have love. Speaking for myself, I know God has had nothing but love for me."

David yelled back at him, "How can you say that, Casey, when you're promoting the lifestyle that you're leading? And God don't like ugly. That's what I've always heard." Then he turned toward Sandra and said in a lowered voice, "As a matter of fact, that thought may have come from you, Sandra."

Before Sandra had a chance to respond, Casey, who was greatly offended, reacted to what David had said. He immediately stood up and started walking towards the front of the top deck, trying to resist the brisk winds that met him.

When Casey arrived to where David was, he confronted him. Putting his hand on David's shoulder, he said, "Get this down, David, speaking of ugly, you're an ugly person with an ugly attitude. And let me tell you, I'm not promoting nothing—nothing but the way I believe God intended for me to live."

When David didn't respond to Casey touching him, Casey bent down and got squarely in his face with his hand continuing to rest on his shoulder. Sandra was right there in front of them both and was startled at what was transpiring.

Casey continued his prodding of David by starting to place emphasis on what he had just said. "I said…"

But before he could say anything else, David pushed his hand away, looked toward Sandra, and said, "Excuse me, let me get up and get this guy out of my face."

Because of David's actions, Sandra let out a scream, fearing what might happen next. But then David assured her, "Don't worry; I'm not a violent person, but let me set this dude straight."

David then rose to his feet and now both men were nose to nose, staring at each other when he said, "Don't put your hands on me, dude," and brushed off his shoulder where Casey had just taken his hand away as if he were trying to decontaminate himself from Casey's touch!

In response, Casey said, "Don't call me that; I'm no dude! And don't talk to me like that either!"

David retorted, "I know you're no dude! I don't know what you are if you want to know the truth."

Casey responded, "Well, I know what I am—I'm a child of God! And don't you forget it!"

David replied, "A child of who? You know…"

Before David could finish, the confrontation got the attention of Casey's brother.

-------BERNIE'S RESPONSE-------

Bernie, who was sitting with Sheri directly beneath where David and Sandra were seated, got up to see what all the commotion above them was about. He decided to walk up the narrow steps to the top level.

When Bernie got there, he saw what he had suspected all along—that David and his brother were arguing. He said to them, "You guys keep the noise down. And what are you two talking about?"

"He called me a name that I didn't like," Casey said.

Bernie said to David, "Listen, David, let's just be cool. We all have to get along." Then with a lower tone of voice, he asked Sandra, "And, Sandra, what are you doing being so close to this man?"

Sandra said, "Oh, Bernie, he had a blanket and offered to keep me warm, so I'm just trying to keep warm."

Bernie replied, "Well, Freddie is down there in the back with Maggie, and you don't want to let him see you in this position."

Erin sat there absorbing everything, being proud of how her new friend was handling the situation.

Gates yelled at David, "I told you that, mister. God don't like ugly. And that's why we got all this commotion up here!"

"Hey, Gates, you're not a part of this argument," David told him. "That issue is between me and this *dude*—er, Casey."

Before more discussion, the one person who may have been the cause of all the conflict, Sandra, simply hung her head because of what Bernie had said. She knew Bernie was right; her friend Freddie was not far away down on the first deck.

Meanwhile, Bernie addressed everyone on the top level, "Listen, everybody, we should be on the island in a few minutes. I just want all of us to be civil."

Then he went back downstairs, and Casey, still fuming, returned to the back to sit next to Katie.

--------REMINISCING--------

When Bernie returned to his seat on the bottom level, Freddie yelled from the back at him and said, "Hey, Bernie, what's all the noise about?"

Bernie said, "Oh, it's nothing you need to be concerned with. We'll be on the island in a few minutes."

Freddie, who was sitting with his partner Maggie, had been enjoying the opportunity to talk with her about old times. He said, "You know, Maggie, since being on this ferry, we've talked a lot about this trip, but to reminisce a little, we had some good times seeing each other when we worked at the law firm."

Maggie replied, "Yeah, Freddie, we did. It's like what my husband Fred told me once, despite the mistakes a person may have made in the past, you have to at least try to forget and move forward into the future. But, yeah, I do remember. *Oh*, how I remember!" Maggie continued passionately, "And you know what, Freddie? Sometimes those feelings I used to have for you still come up from time to time. And I think now is one of those times!"

By this time the coolness of the air had permeated the lower level as well and had reached the back of the ferry where Maggie and Freddie sat, which had the effect of turning down the heat a little. Nevertheless, like Sandra and David above them, they took full advantage of the elements and snuggled close together to keep warm. At least for a moment, it was like it was in the old days.

--------APPROACHING THE ISLAND--------

Soon the ferry approached the dock of the Island of Love, and everyone was ready and even anxious to explore the adventures that awaited them—whatever Sinbad had in mind.

"What a beautiful place," Sandra said to David as they approached the dock, having largely forgotten the squabble that occurred only minutes earlier.

Overcast skies had replaced relatively clear conditions earlier as the wind had picked up and added to the chill of the air.

Down on the first level, Maggie said to Freddie, "I'm anxious to experience this Island of Love that Sinbad's been promoting. I'm talking about what he said in the letter he sent to you that you shared with Sandra, who in turn shared it with me. Remember that letter, the one about what we'll be doing on the island?"

Freddie replied, "Yeah, of course, I remember that letter. But Sinbad gave me only some of the details. Like everyone else, there's a lot I don't know about what he plans to do. Who knows what he might be planning in those woods? You *do* know the venue, The Village, is located in a heavily-wooded area on the island. But I guess we'll all find out."

Before Maggie and Freddie had ended their conversation, Sinbad came to the edge of the dock. He had just come from inside The Village where, presumably, he was making final preparations for activities for the guests.

--------DISCOURAGING ANNOUNCEMENT--------

Sinbad made an announcement to the group. "Hello, everyone. I'm glad you all made it safely over here to the Island of Love. And

I wish I had better news for you, but I heard on the latest weather forecast that because of the drastic change in wind direction within the last hour, the hurricane that was predicted for the region will be here sooner than expected. So, here's the plan. We'll have to postpone our activities in The Village and return back to the resort as soon as we can."

With that announcement, everyone let out a huge groan of disappointment. They seemed so anxious to participate in whatever Sinbad had planned. But at the same time, they knew the seriousness of being in a hurricane while on a vessel of any kind in the open water and were just as anxious to get back to the resort.

Sinbad added, "Before we make the trip back, you all can get off the ferry and refresh yourselves. But be sure to return on board as soon as you can so we can head back. I'll be going back with you this time on the ferry."

Sinbad also described what they would be facing once they get on the island. "There are facilities and refreshments, including snacks and beverages for you to bring back onto the ferry. But you need to keep to the left as you approach the entrance to the island. The Village facility is to the right, but you won't have a need to venture over there."

--------WELCOME NCSF--------

As the group got off the ferry and began their walk towards the front entrance, Sinbad returned to the vessel to get some additional information about the impending storm on the radar that was situated in the front panel of the boat.

By this time, Sandra had reunited with Freddie, and David was with Sheri and Jeanie. Everyone proceeded to the refreshment area as Sinbad had instructed while he went to the vessel checking on the status of the impending hurricane.

As everyone approached the place to purchase refreshments, David, being with his people who were in the back of the line, decided to venture over to the right near the front entrance of The Village facility, the place where Sinbad had instructed that no one should go.

"You two stay here in line, and I'll be right back," he said to Sheri and Jeanie. "I'm so curious as to what it is to the right of us."

Just before he left, Sheri said, trying to discourage him from going, "Now, David, you know Sinbad said not to venture over there."

But David, being contrary by nature, said, "Be cool! I'll be right back."

He started to walk toward the entrance to The Village facility, but after only a short distance he became entangled in heavy brush. He walked as far as the heavily wooded area would allow. Just as he had enough of what seemed to him to be a desolate area with nothing to be gained by going further, he noticed the entrance to the venue where Sinbad said the activities were to take place.

Just prior to David turning around to head back, he looked up and spotted a sign in the distance that was partially hidden by heavy brush. It read, "WELCOME, NCSF."

Because of the density of the wooded surroundings, he relinquished the thought at the time of what the sign may have meant and started heading back to the group. The whole way back, he had to negotiate the weeds and brush while still wondering what exactly was the meaning of the sign he had seen. Then he thought, *maybe those letters can give me information about it.*

Upon his return to the group, he found that the line had shortened quite a bit.

Sheri asked him, "What did you see over there, David?"

He replied, "Well, it was so wooded I just decided to come on back. But I did see a sign that was kind of interesting. It read, 'WELCOME, NCSF' over the entrance to The Village facility. I guess I'll have to google it later to see what it's all about."

It took little time before everyone had purchased what they wanted and had returned to the ferry. Couples had gotten back together while on the island, but they were separated again into their seating assignments on their return to the ferry.

The voyage to the Island of Love had become a big disappointment. Everyone wondered exactly what Sinbad had planned for them in The Village. What David noticed on that sign when he disregarded the instructions given by Sinbad to not venture toward facility could give a clue as to what the group was in for. As it turned out, no one would know for sure because they were prevented from experiencing that part of the excursion. Nevertheless, at this point everyone was more concerned about another experience they did not desire to have—being in the middle of a hurricane on the open water!

CHAPTER TEN
HURRICANE

As the ferry slowly left the dock of the Island of Love everyone was in their previously assigned seats and ready for the journey back to the resort. For the sake of time and order in boarding, Sinbad told everyone to keep the seats they had when they made the journey. The main concern now was getting back before the highest intensity of the storm hit.

--------EVERYONE'S CURIOUS: GAMES IN THE VILLAGE--------

Those sitting on the top deck were affected the most by the howling wind. As was the case in crossing the bay to the island, Sandra and David shared a blanket trying to buffer the wind and retain as much of their heat as possible.

Sandra said to David, "I wonder what it would have been like to play the games that Sinbad had planned over there at The Village?"

David replied, "I don't know, but I'm going to google what I saw on that sign when I walked away from the group and went over there."

Having overheard David's statement, Gates said, "Yeah, you do that, David. But listen. We were in front of you guys. You mean you disregarded the instructions given by Sinbad and went over to the right of where we all were standing?" Before David had a chance to answer, Gates continued to say. "Anyway, I for one was really looking forward to going over the right of the refreshment area where this "Village" facility was located on the island."

From the back of the top deck, Katie yelled, "Yeah, David, find out as much as you can about that place. I'm not going to knock you for going over there, because all of us are curious about that place."

Fred, smiling from ear to ear because of the discontent caused by David's actions, said to Courtney, who was sitting beside him, "You know, Courtney, this would be a great story for my next book."

Courtney replied, "Now, Fred, you're always looking for something to write about, aren't you? I could tell how dedicated you were even back when we were in Hawaii." Then she whispered to him so that no one else could hear, "You didn't even hit on me when you had the chance—when I was so aggressive towards you. Now, ain't that something?"

Fred replied in an equally lowered voice, "Yeah, that was something all right. But at that time my total focus was on my Mag, who was back in Detroit. And besides, Courtney, that was before you made a change in your life when you went with me to Queens Church. Remember that?"

Courtney replied, "Yes, I do! I'll always owe you gratitude for taking me there. Yes, it changed my life all right."

Fred was still eager to hear what David was going to do about getting more information about the Island of Love, so he raised his voice and said, "Hey, David, I want to encourage you to find out as much as you can about that island."

In response, David nodded in agreement and answered, "I will do that, Fred."

With all the chatter going on, everyone seemed to be more interested in what they may have missed on the Island of Love than the approaching hurricane. David continued to search on his cell phone for the meaning of what he saw on the sign at The Village.

"Let's see. I'm bringing it up now. NCSF, oh, here it is. It says," he started to read, but then paused, being surprised at what he saw. He then mumbled to himself a question, "Nudist Commune of South Florida?" He looked up, staring out into the water. Bewildered, he repeated in the form of a statement, "Nudist Commune of South Florida!"

Gates, who heard clearly what David said, also was surprised by what he had found. He said simply, "What?"

In a somewhat more subdued fashion, Sandra asked, "You mean we were going to a nudist colony of some kind? You gotta be kidding me!" she said in utter amazement.

"For heaven's sake," Erin said with great concern. "All of us are good moral people, and we were going to a nudist colony?"

She turned around and said to Casey in the back, "Hey, Casey! You're with Sinbad a lot. You must know *something*."

Casey said, "Well, Ms. Erin, I don't really get involved with a lot of Sinbad's business ventures. He's very secretive, you know, as most of you probably have figured out."

Courtney offered some encouragement to David, saying, "Well, David, since you've started to research the situation, I think you should continue and see what you can find."

"Well, unless he can get some more information about it, I guess we'll never know," Sandra said directing her statement to everybody.

David replied, "I guess I could just ask him outright—pulling no punches."

"Yeah, that's a good idea, David, Sandra replied. "Why don't you go ahead and ask Sinbad that when you get the chance? He's sitting right down there on the lower level."

"Okay then, I'll do just that," David replied. But I won't do it now —not on this trip back to the resort. But I will asked him," David reaffirmed his intentions.

There continued to be plenty of discussion on the top deck. Erin responded to what she heard Sandra ask David to do.

"That really is a good idea, Sandra, to find out what the activities we would have participated in back there. I'm sure everyone else is curious about that too. So, if you don't get a chance to find that out, David, before you all leave tomorrow, I'll be working down here, and I can get a lot more information on it."

-------DISCUSSIONS: BACK TO THE CONDO-------

"Thanks, Erin, for maybe filling us in on that. And by the way, we're so happy that you got the position. I'm sure you'll do very well down here."

"Thank you, Sandra," Erin replied. "And listen, I expect all of you from Chicago and Detroit to make it back down here on occasion. And you too, David and your crew. I know you're from New Jersey." Then she turned her head, looking toward the back of the top level of the ferry, and said, "And I didn't forget you either Katie, the New Yorker among us."

"You go, girl!" Katie replied.

The wind continued to howl as the ferry boat made its way back to the resort dock. Upon its return, a van that had been reserved was waiting to take them back to the condo.

Everyone eventually exited the ferry and boarded the van. The short trip to the condo was a bumpy one. By this time rain was coming down harder and the wind was gusting. At least they were back on land and not on the ferry when the weather got worse.

After a short ride, everyone had returned to their lodgings. Maggie was so glad to be back in their suite, although, like everyone else, she was disappointed that they didn't get to play the games Sinbad had planned at The Village. At least they made the voyage to the Island of Love and had something to tell people once she returned to Chicago.

The bonus of the whole trip for Maggie was the opportunity to be close again with her former workmate and lover, Freddie. She could tell he was a changed man, having gone through the loss of a spouse as well as a separation from another whom he wed shortly after the death of his first wife. Married life had not been kind to Freddie. Maggie saw an opportunity to relive some old times within an apparently unfulfilled marital situation that she knew nothing about at the time. At least she was unwilling to reignite some of those old flames; she was content and had rededicated her love for Fred.

Everyone eventually had returned to their living quarters including Fred and Maggie. It was when they were back in their suite that Maggie was most comfortable in asking Fred about the trip.

"Fred, I know I haven't had a chance to talk to you much about your experience on the ferry. I know you had Courtney as a partner. So how was that?" she asked.

Fred answered, "Well, Mag, it was fine, but I was more interested in listening to what Sandra and David had to say. You know they were sitting not far from us on the top deck. Only Gates and Erin separated us from them."

Maggie said, "Oh, so Gates and Erin were in front of you?"

"Yeah, they were," Fred replied. "And Casey and your friend Katie were behind us."

"By the way, what was all that noise about up there?" Maggie asked.

Fred replied, "Yeah, there *was* quite a bit of commotion up there for a while on the way over. Casey had a disagreement with David about something."

Maggie replied, "Well, that's nothing new. It seems like David rubs a lot of people the wrong way."

"I guess you're right, Mag," Fred replied. "But Bernie came up and kind of cooled things down a bit. But what about you and Freddie—how did you two get along?" Fred asked.

Maggie replied, "Yeah, it *was* nosey up there for a while. But as far as me and Freddie, to be honest with you, Fred, me and him were carrying on our own little conversation, and even though we heard the noise, as I said to you earlier, we didn't pay much attention to it. I just figured that it would calm down after a while, which it did."

Fred responded, "So, what *did* you two talk about —old times at the law firm?"

"Yeah, that's exactly what we did; we talked about our time there," Maggie told him without getting into the details of their intimate relationship.

Maggie went on to divert attention from her conversation with Fred about Freddie. "You know, Fred, while I'm sorry we didn't get to go to the venue that Sinbad had planned, I'm glad we returned to the resort when we did because the wind is really picking up out there. And like I said when we first came into this suite, the ocean seems to be so close to the building—so close you could almost take a dip in it from our patio. I hope the storm surge that I heard about in the weather forecast doesn't occur because if it does this place might become totally flooded."

--------EMERGENCY!--------

One of the special features of Sinbad's resort was that an intercom system was installed to transmit important messages from the front office. The system served its purpose on this day when Sinbad received the news that the group's flight would be delayed a day later because of the impending hurricane, so for the first time Sinbad utilized the system.

Along with everyone else, Maggie and Fred heard the message from Sinbad over the system. After three buzz sounds, Sinbad began:

This is a special message from me, Sinbad Warren, to all of you, our guests who arrived by plane two days ago from New York. Unfortunately, your flight scheduled to depart tomorrow from Miami International at 4:00 will be delayed one day because of the storm. I received this information directly from the airport's weather center.

So, your departing flight will not be until Sunday at 4:00. I'm very sorry for the delay. My only advice is to hunker down and ride out the storm. Its highest intensity is predicted to take place sometime tomorrow morning, so I don't know how much sleep you'll get tonight. Just be vigilant and try to relax. All the buildings around here are designed to withstand some of the strongest hurricanes. And while this one is reportedly one of the strongest that we've had down here in quite a while, let's pray that God will keep us safe.

When Sinbad finished speaking from the main office of the resort, he walked the short distance from there back to his condo on the edge of Gator Bay. What a magnificent scene. On one side stood Sinbad's condo on the bay and on the other side a line of condos along the Atlantic Ocean were visible. Structures on the ocean side were directly exposed to the waves rushing onto the beach, and, more dangerously, possibly into the condos where Sinbad's friends from the north stayed.

When Sinbad returned to his condo, he found that Casey was not there and had apparently ventured out onto the beach. Sinbad took a look through the kitchen window, and, with a clear view of a part of the beach where he usually went, he saw that Casey was not just on the beach but at quite a distance out in the water and apparently was having problems staying afloat. The waves by this time were violently beating onto the shore because of increasing winds speeds, which were propelling the ocean waves even higher. Sinbad saw that Casey's arms were swinging everywhere, apparently in order to stay above the water.

Not a swimmer himself, Sinbad knew that his friend needed some help—immediately! But it had to come from someone other than himself.

"Oh my God! I have to get somebody out there to help him. Otherwise, he's going to drown!" Sinbad said frantically to himself.

In desperation, he utilized the intercom system for a second time, this time in his condo. It was the same system he had used earlier in the resort office, which also had been installed in his place of lodging. But unlike before when the message was about a flight delay, this time it was an emergency! He needed to call for assistance.

Sinbad's thoughts immediately turned to some of the guests from the north; he hoped some of them would have experience in swimming in rough waters to save his friend. After three short buzz sounds, his anxious voice spoke through the intercom:

Hello again, everybody. I don't have long to give you this message, but I need your help—and I need it now! I saw my friend Casey out there in the ocean and he appears to have a problem staying up above the water. I'm not a swimmer, so I need those of you who know how to swim in rough water to come and try to save him. Now, I'm speaking mainly to my male guests from the north—to come and give him the assistance he so desperately needs right now. There's literally no time to lose! Just change quickly into your swim attire and go out to the beach area. It's a few feet to the right along the ocean front from where you are in your condo. I can meet you there as soon as you arrive, hopefully within five minutes. At least I will be able to give you moral support. Again, because I'm not a swimmer, that's about all I'll be able to give you."

And by the way, everyone that's on the first floor should start moving upstairs to the second floor to avoid a possible storm surge. There's a lobby at the end of the hallway on that floor where you can assemble. Thanks.

Figure 10: OCEAN VIEW

One thing I have desired of the Lord, That will I seek: That I may dwell in the house of the Lord All the days of my life, To behold the beauty of the Lord, And to inquire in His temple.

-Psalm 27:4

--------THE RUSH TO HELP--------

"Did you hear that, Fred?" Maggie asked.

Fred had just come back into the room from another part of the condo. "Yeah, I heard it," he replied, "and I'm on my way out there to that part of the beach where Sinbad said Casey is. I just have to put on my swim trunks, and I'll be ready to go. It's been a while since I've taken a swim, but I'll see what I can do to help. We can start moving up to the second floor when I get back."

Before Fred rushed out of the condo, he had the idea to grab a beach towel. *Maybe it can help in some way*, he thought. As he was running to the bathroom to get the towel, Maggie asked, "What are you doing?"

"We may need a towel," he said. "I'm goin' to get it then be on my way."

"Well, I don't know what you would need a towel for—but go ahead and don't waste time. Yeah, and why would you need a towel anyway?"

"Who knows? I'm gone now and will be back and soon as I can."

"Okay! Be careful," Maggie said.

Towel in hand, Fred quickly left the condo through the patio door. Once outside on the beach, he looked to the right and then sprinted to where he thought Casey would be. Before too much time had elapsed, he got to the area where Casey was. As Sinbad described in his announcement, Fred saw Casey struggling to stay afloat in the water.

Fred soon saw Freddie, who had also just arrived at the location where they could see Casey well out in the ocean.

"Hey, Freddie, I need to get out there and help Casey so I can get back to the condo and help Maggie up to the second floor."

"Yeah, I left Sandra in our condo too! So, we both have to get back soon."

Both men anticipated it would not take long to rescue Casey, so they felt comfortable in leaving the women in their separate living quarters on the first floor with the intent of returning soon.

Like Fred, Freddie had only limited experience as a swimmer but had been much more active in the water than Fred. With the wind howling, in a loud voice Freddie said, "Fred, I'm gonna swim out and give Casey some help. I've never done a rescue before, but I guess we don't have much of a choice at this point since you said you haven't taken a swim lately."

David, who had heard the same announcement, was a bit hesitant about going out at first, especially since he had a major argument with Casey on the ferry crossing to the Island of Love. Apparently realizing how serious the situation was, Sheri got in his face and told him, "Now, David, you've got to go out there and help that man and give those other guys some help too. I know the other fellows are responding. And you should be able to help a lot since you've been a lifeguard.

"While you're gone, Jeanie and I will go on up to the second floor to the lobby area like Sinbad said to. So when you get back, we won't be here. We'll already be up there with the others—just like Sinbad instructed."

"Okay, Okay! I'm going," David responded to Sheri's urging. As he headed out the door, David saw that Sheri and Jeanie were in the process of heading out as well, going to the second floor as Sinbad had instructed.

David said, "Before you go up, make sure you take some snacks just in case if you two get a little hungry. I'm goin' out now. But before I do, I'm gonna run to the van and get some items from my lifeguard kit—a couple of towels and some rope. It's all in the back of the vehicle. I think that should help."

Sheri responded, "Okay, David. I'll go back and get something for us to snack on while we're up there." Then she said to her daughter, "Just wait here, Jeanie, and I'll be right back." She added to David, "You go ahead out there because we'll be fine."

David headed out first to get some items from his utility kit in the van and then to meet Fred and Freddie and assist them in getting Casey out of the water. Not having thought clearly about the crisis at hand, he rushed out of the condo without changing into swim trunks. He was still wearing the same clothes from their boat ride—a shirt and slacks with boxer shorts beneath. Nevertheless, he rushed to help the other men.

--------SAVING CASEY--------

Within practically no time, all the men of the group who were on the first floor had gone out to where Casey was. Gates, who could not swim, and Wynn, who had little experience around water, stayed in their second-floor condos.

Following the instructions he heard in the announcement and at the request of his friend Sheri, David went to the area of the beach where Casey was having problems in the water. Freddie had already gone out to help Casey while Fred remained on land.

Fred raised his voice over the howling wind and said, "Hey, David, we're so glad you're here. As you can see, we can use all the help we can get. I mean, Casey's out their struggling to stay afloat. And you see Freddie has already gone out there to help him. Freddie has more experience in the water than I have, so he went on out there to try to rescue him."

"Yeah David, glad you're here," Sinbad said to him.

"Listen!" David shouted over the wind and surf. "I was a lifeguard and have the experience in dealing with situations like this, so I'll go out and help Freddie; we both should be able to bring Casey back."

"Wow! That's great!" Fred responded.

David, who had not changed into beach attire as Sinbad had asked, proceeded to take off his shirt and pants, leaving only a T-shirt and boxer shorts on his slender body. He began to shiver in the brisk breeze that was blowing. He then pointed to his shorts and said to Fred, I hope they stay on me!" He continued, "Anyway, you two can stay here and help me and Freddie when we bring him to shore.

"Before I go, I'm going to take this rope I have to secure all of us out there. I'm leaving enough of the rope to tie around both Casey and Freddie as well as me. Then I want you Fred to hold the other end of this rope and help to reel all of us in when I give you the signal."

"I gotcha," Fred responded in approval.

Fred remained on the beach with Sinbad awaiting David and Freddie's return, hopefully with Casey still clinging to life. As David swam out, the waves relentlessly crashed against him, and he had to combat fierce winds. The gusts and the rain had increased due to the oncoming hurricane.

In almost no time, David caught up with Freddie, who had just left and swam toward Casey.

As they continued to swim, they neared Casey, who continued to struggle in the raging waters. By the time they reached Casey, David recognized that he had lost consciousness and was just bobbing back and forth slightly above and then just below the surface.

Fred tried to yell above the roaring waves, "Looks like he's given up trying to stay above the water."

David knew time was short to save Casey. *Just let me do something here*, he thought to himself. In his lifeguard days, he had learned a technique that would at least help them get Casey to the beach, where they could try to revive him. The main thing was to tie the rope he brought around his waist and make sure the rest of it was tied around Casey. Fred had the other end of the rope and when David gave him the signal, he would pull them in."

Within seconds David was able to grab Casey and place a thumb on his nose to prevent more water from entering his lungs. His lifeguard training taught that this would keep the victim alive, though unconscious, until CPR could be applied.

As he treaded water, David shouted to Freddie, "Take this rope and tie it around me and Casey, then around yourself. The rope I'm handing you should be enough to do that. When you finish, I'll give Fred the signal to pull us in."

Freddie did what he was instructed to do by David, while trying as best he could to keep himself afloat amidst the roaring waves.

"Okay, I've just tied the rope securely around all three of us," Freddie yelled. "Now are we ready to roll?"

"All right then, we're ready!" David bellowed. "I'm going to try to raise his body. When I do, I'll need you to help me get him on my shoulders."

With Freddie's assistance, David was able to maneuver Casey's arms around his shoulders and back, helping to secure Casey to his body as he continued to tread water. "Okay, I've got him now!" David shouted to Freddie.

Waving his arm, he motioned to Fred on the shore to begin pulling.

"Okay, I'm pulling!" Fred yelled.

It took all the strength David had to corral Casey and swim amidst the roaring waves, now seemingly moving in all directions, but the surf was crashing towards the shore, thankfully pushing the three men closer to the beach as Freddie swam next to David. With Casey over his shoulder and one arm stroking the waters and with Fred pulling them inward, soon they got back to shore.

With help from Freddie, David staggered from the water with Casey on his back. It took all his effort to walk through the wet sand beneath the swallow waters. But soon he was able to reach the dry area on the beach where Fred was standing with Sinbad.

Almost exhausted, David tumbled onto the sand still holding Casey. He said with a loud voice, "For heaven's sake, we're back on solid ground.

--------**CPR**--------

After realizing a need to cover himself as they had just gotten out of the water, David did just that with a towel that Fred gave him—he had lost his shorts! At that point everyone turned their attention to Casey.

Seeing that Casey had not regained consciousness, Fred said, "Hey, David, I have experience in CPR; I do it on a regular basis at Mojco where I work—it's required of every employee."

"Well then, get to it!" David shouted.

Fred quickly jumped into action and did CPR on Casey. After a little while, he had no positive results. Casey was not responding to Fred's efforts.

David said, "Let me try for a while. I know you're getting tired, Fred."

After a short while, David began to see some positive signs that Casey was coming around. Within seconds, a rush of water came out of Casey's mouth, and he began coughing and gasping for air— seemingly uncomfortable but conscious nonetheless at that point.

The one person Casey saw first after regaining consciousness was David, whom he had a big issue with on the ferry ride to the Island of Love. He said, "How long was I out?"

David answered, "You were unconscious for quite a while and were about to go under. I don't really know whether you would've come back up if you had gone under again, but you're here now. And it looks like you're okay. But listen, Fred was the one who started your track back to life. I just stepped in at the right time. You owe a lot to him. And don't forget Freddie; he's the one who helped me get you back on the beach from the water."

Casey replied, "I owe a lot to all you guys."

While David tried to deflect the credit from himself to Fred as well as to Freddie, in helping Casey during his time of distress, he and all the men involved had performed heroically that day. In the end, it was David who was responsible for getting Casey to where Fred could help revive him, and David was the one to finish the job.

--------THE STORM SURGE--------

Despite the heroic actions of David with assistance from both Fred and Freddie on saving Casey's life, there was no time for celebration. As David completed CPR on Casey, Freddie was the first to notice the potential effect of the weather on the first floor condo where Sandra and Maggie awaited their return.

As Freddie looked down the beach, he was amazed to see the roaring ocean waves surging dangerously close to the suite where his friend Sandra was. Within a few seconds the waves were beating on the patio door. Freddie imagined it would be only a matter of moments before the whole area would be inundated by water. A horrifying thought.

The guys knew they had to get the women to the second floor as Sinbad had instructed right away.

Both Fred and Freddie understood that the strength of the water could easily seep through the huge glass door of the patio and, if not take the door down entirely, at least overflow the interior of the dwelling. They were aware the storm surge was no joke! With a significant surge of water from the ocean, the buildup of water within the condo would be life-threatening to anyone inside.

Freddie feared Sandra's life was in imminent danger, and Fred had the same thoughts about Maggie. The two women were in the same predicament.

Knowing how urgent the situation was, Fred said to David and Sinbad, "Freddie and I need to get back to see about the women since we left them on the first floor. We've gotta run."

"By all means!" Sinbad said. "You guys need to go see about Sandra and Maggie. Don't worry about David and me. We have things covered here. We can get Casey back to my condo; it's not very far from here."

David said, "Yeah, Fred and Freddie, you need to go and see about those women. We'll take care of Casey. Sheri and Jeanie went up to the second floor just as I was leaving to come here, so they should be fine. You guys just make sure that Sandra and Maggie get on that second level.

"And by the way, the easiest way to get there is right through our suite. The door should be open. Once you all go in just head to the patio door in the back; there's a stairwell over to the right when you walk out, and it leads directly to that second level.

-------A RETURN TO THE CONDO-------

While stormy conditions persisted, Fred and Freddie rushed back to the condo through the driving rain and howling wind. During their brisk walk, Freddie said to Fred in a loud voice, trying to overcome the sound of the raging weather conditions, "We've got to get back there. The water from the ocean is moving so fast toward the condo; I think we might have a flooding situation on our hands!"

Fred replied, "Yeah, this storm must be reaching its highest intensity now, not later tomorrow morning like Sinbad said he had heard on the weather forecast. And you're right, Freddie, we have to get back to see about the women."

The wind was picking up by the second. David and Sinbad were making sure that Casey made it back to his place of lodging.

David assured Sinbad, "We're gonna get Casey back to your place and do it pretty quickly because this weather is getting worse by the second."

"You're right, David. We need to get goin' with Casey. And by the way, I really appreciate what you guys have done."

David replied, "No time for thanks. Fred and Freddie have gone to get back to take their women to safety, and we need to get inside too."

"I'm with you!" Sinbad replied.

The wind continued to howl as rain had shifted from light to heavy, then back to light again as it came down intermittently. David, a former lifeguard who clearly had experience in carrying those overtaken by water in one fashion or another, was now ready to help Sinbad get back to their suite.

Just before getting Casey in a position to be lifted, David said to Sinbad, "I'm sure glad Sheri and Jeanie went up to the second floor as I was leaving to come here, so they should be okay. And I know that Fred and Freddie will take care of Sandra and Maggie once they are back. And we'll be in the safety of your suite soon!"

"I'm with you David," Sinbad assured him.

With Sinbad's help, David securely positioned Casey over his shoulder again and began carrying him as Sinbad led the way to their condo on Gator Bay. On the final leg of their travel back to Sinbad's condo, they had to cross a short walkway over a narrow stretch of water. Getting on a ferry boat nearby was out of the question because of the thunderous waves.

As the weather continued to intensify, it was evident that a storm surge would threaten all the condos along the beach. Suites in the condo tower on the first floor where Maggie's group resided were particularly vulnerable to the incoming waves from the surge. Sinbad and Casey's condo, which was located away from the ocean on the bay, was high enough off the ground so as not to be affected as much by the raging ocean waters.

--------FRED AND FREDDIE AT THEIR SUITES--------

Fred and Freddie rushed back to the suites in their condo along the same route they came to the beach to help save Casey. The wind continued to wail as the dark gray clouds moved swiftly across a light gray background of a rain-laden sky.

By the time Fred and Freddie arrived, they were fearful of what they might find. As they entered the condo and walked through the lobby, they looked down the hallway and could see water seeping beneath the doors from the suites on the ocean side into the hallway.

"Do you see what I see, Freddie?" Fred asked him.

"Yeah, I do, and I'm afraid to think how much water is inside the suites where Maggie and Sandra are."

"Yeah, we just got to get in there," Fred said.

They approached Freddie's suite, which was the first one they got to. "Fred, I'm going inside and check on Sandra. You can go ahead and see about Maggie."

Freddie quickly opened the door to his suite, and immediately excess water began to spill into the hallway. The force of the flow pushed him back a little as he tried to walk into his lodgings. When he pushed through the water, Freddie saw Sandra lying unconscious on the couch with a large picture frame beside her.

He grasped and said, "For heaven's sake, Sandra! Sandra!" At that moment, the thought came to him: *That frame must have hit her head and knocked her out as the wind blew inside.* He wasted no time in carrying her out of the suite in ankle high water, and by the time they both were outside in the hallway, Sandra had regained consciousness and had become aware of where she was.

Now safely outside their suite, Freddie found a spot in the hallway that was not too wet where he and Sandra could sit with their backs propped up against the wall. Still somewhat disoriented, Sandra looked at Freddie and asked, "Oh, Freddie, what happened? I was near the couch looking out the patio door and saw all this water come rushing in. It was so frightening!"

Trying to control her tears, Sandra continued, "Freddie, I was so scared, seeing all this water rushing in like that. Then I just passed out, I guess."

Freddie said, "Well, Sandra, you're fine now. What really happened apparently was that the picture frame hit your head as it was blown away from the nightstand by the wind, and you were knocked unconscious for a while. You're fortunate to still be here! But, hey, we have to get up to the second floor."

Sandra then asked Freddie, "How about Casey? Were you all able to get him?" "Yeah, but don't worry about Casey. He's fine now thanks to David. He's the one who brought him to shore. Casey was unconscious out there in the water, but we were able to revive him," Freddie answered.

"And how about Maggie next door?" she asked Freddie.

"Don't worry about her either. Fred will take care of Maggie. He's over there now. Don't you see him there?"

--------HORRIFIC FINDING!--------

As Freddie and Sandra were carrying on conversation, Fred was a few feet from them in front of the door to their suite. He was trying desperately to open it to get to his wife.

Both Sandra and Freddie could hear Fred mumbling as he clearly became more and more frustrated that the door wouldn't budge. After several attempts, he gave up trying to open it and yelled at Freddie and Sandra, who were leaning against the wall.

"Hey, Freddie, Sandra, I've been trying to get inside our suite where Maggie is, and I can't get this door open! Come on over here, Freddie, and see what you can do. And, Sandra, I'm glad you're okay."

"I'll be right there, Fred," Freddie responded. "Have you looked through that huge peep hole on the door to see inside?"

"Freddie, I was so involved in trying to get this door open, I didn't even think to do that."

"Sandra is okay now, so I'll be right there," Freddie said as both were now standing against the wall. He turned toward Sandra and said, "You continue standing right here, Sandra. I'll be back."

Still disoriented, Sandra said, "You all see about my girl!"

By this time, the wind was blowing fiercely against the building. It seemed as though the structure could hardly withstand its force. But this high rise wasn't going anywhere. The real problem was the water coming in on the first floor!

As soon as Fred was reminded that he could look through that peephole, he peered inside and saw what appeared to be water that had risen to well above the peephole. And he saw a figure through the water snuggly wrapped in a couch pad, apparently having struggled to become free to escape the rising water in the room. Trying to keep his composure, he realized that the figure he saw was Maggie who just lay there, eyes open and bulging wide, staring through the water towards him.

Freddie asked, "What do you see, Fred?" With much emotion, Fred turned away from the door and told him, "Well, Freddie. It's horrible! It appears to me that she had struggled to get out of the couch pad when she was apparently overwhelmed by the water."

"Now wait a minute!" Freddie said. "What do you mean, 'she *had* struggled,' using past tense to describe the situation in there? Is she all right?"

Barely able to control his emotions, Fred replied, "Take a look for yourself. I saw Mag in that couch pad. I saw... I saw..."

Figure 11: Maggie Submerged in Water

Man who is born of woman Is of a few days and full of trouble.

- Job 14:1

Get a hold of yourself, Fred!" Freddie told him. "Now tell me what you saw before I look."

Trying to calm himself a bit, Fred continued, "I saw her head lifted while still lying in that pad, bobbing up and down without the ability to control her movements. We got to get in, Freddie! We got to get in! To save Mag! To save Mag!" Fred repeated, having stepped away from the peephole to yell those words.

At that point Freddie rushed towards the door to take a glimpse inside; he was equally horrified to see Maggie in that condition.

"Don't worry, buddy. We'll get inside somehow."

Realizing what was going on, Sandra shouted, "You two get Maggie outta there!"

Freddie was aware of Sandra's concerns and now tried *his* hand at opening the door. He struggled with the knob as Fred did before him, trying to open it but had no success.

--------TO THE RESCUE - AGAIN--------

Just at that time, David entered the hallway. He had just returned from taking Sinbad back to his condo. That's when both Fred and Freddie turned toward David, and Fred said, "David, Mag is in the suite, and we can't get that door open. Maybe you can help."

David replied, "Well, is she alright?"

"No, no! We have to get inside!" Freddie repeated.

The wind was howling as loudly as ever as David said, "Okay. I'll see what I can do. I see Sandra over there, standing next to the wall. She seems to be in a daze. Anyway, she needs to go upstairs where the others are. There's a convenient passageway and stairwell outside our suite, and a stairway where she can easily get up on the second floor."

David continued, "Freddie, why don't you go ahead and take her up there now; just go inside our suite next to where Sandra is standing and continue out the back through the sliding glass patio door, and you'll the passageway leading to that stairwell as you look to the right. And that stairway will take you straight up to the second-floor lobby. And when you get to the second floor, you'll see everyone assembled there.

"Don't worry about water being in our suite; we're on the side of the hallway away from the ocean, so it's perfectly dry in there. I'll stay here and help Fred get inside where Maggie is."

"Okay, we're going up," Freddie said to David. "Just get Maggie outta there!"

"Get her out! Get Maggie out!" Sandra yelled as she just stood there, seemingly mesmerized and hardly believing what was happening.

Freddie went to Sandra and said, "Okay, Sandra, calm down now. Everything's gonna be all right. Let's go up through David's suite to the second floor. We'll be good there until the storm is over. Fred and David will take care of Maggie."

As they were leaving, Freddie yelled back to David and Fred, "We're going on up, but I'll be back down once I get Sandra settled up there."

After briefly describing to David what he saw through that peep hole, David said to Fred "Forget about that peephole right now. Let me get to the knob on the door and try to get it opened. We have no time to lose based on what you just said."

David continued, "I used to be a locksmith and still have some of my special keys. Let me run into our condo and grab them from my wallet. I believe I can open this door."

David rushed into his nearby condo and found the wallet where he left it before going to rescue Casey. After returning as quickly as possible, he worked with the knob using the special keys he had. He inserted one key, then another, then a third key, trying to unlock the door without success. With the fourth key, it worked, and he heard the lock turn.

As David opened the door, water began to rush out of the suite where Maggie had been trapped. David and Fred, who was right behind him, were met by a wall of water that had enough force to knock Fred back against the wall on the opposite side of the hallway. It subsided slowly after it spilled over into the hallway but continued to gush out into the outer area near where Freddie and Sandra had stood moments earlier.

After the initial impact of the rushing water, Fred rushed back to David, and they both went inside to assist Maggie.

--------SAD CONFIRMATION--------

Maggie had been totally submerged before David was able to open the door. As the level of the water subsided in the room, it was easier for Fred and David to enter the suite to check on Maggie. When they finally reached her, it was apparent that Maggie did not survive.

David did a quick check of the artery on her neck and found no pulse. He turned toward Fred and shook his head.

Tears flowing from his eyes, Fred mumbled, "She's gone; she's gone!"

David simply lowered his head, not wanting to believe what he was witnessing.

Both Fred and David knew Maggie had drowned. Ever so gently, Fred embraced her and rocked her body back and forth. "She's gone," he repeated.

"We need to move her body, Fred," David whispered putting a hand on Fred's shoulder.

It was some time before Fred was able to compose himself enough to move. Finally, they brought her lifeless body out into the hallway.

By that time, Freddie had returned from taking Sandra upstairs. He saw Fred holding what appeared to be Maggie's lifeless body. "Oh, no, oh, no!" he said. "Is she… Is she…" He did not have the courage to finish the question and to hear that she was gone.

David said, "Yeah, Freddie. We were able to get her, but I'm afraid she didn't make it. She's dead."

Freddie just stood there, trying to contain his own emotions.

-------GRIEVING A LOSS-------

By this time Fred was sobbing ceaselessly.

"Stay here with her," David said, "and let me get a blanket from my suite to place on this damp carpet; then we can lay her on it."

Fred could only say, "My Mag, my Mag!"

While holding Maggie's body delicately, Fred waited for David's return. In less than a minute, he brought the blanket. Fred had noticed an alcove at the end of the hallway that was almost secluded from view. It was hidden by a thick curtain and apparently an area reserved for storage. He went down the hallway and pulled the curtain back and saw there was nothing there. Unlike most of the other places in the hallway that had been flooded, it was dry, and it seemed to him that the spot was reserved just for him—and for Maggie, a place where he could comfortably lay her body.

Fred said, "There's an area at the end of the hallway that I think would be a good place to lay Maggie. I'm going to take this blanket down to that area and lay Maggie on it."

"That's good, Fred," David replied, "and I see a wheelchair near the front that we can use to make it easier for us to get her down there."

Fred agreed with what David proposed, so David retrieved the wheelchair and said, "Go ahead, Fred, and place Maggie in it so we can take her down to the alcove."

They proceeded to move Maggie to that spot where her body could lie in rest.

"Yeah, this is a good spot, David. It seems to be completely protected from any wind or rain that may intrude into the hallway during the night."

"Yeah, it looks like you've found an ideal spot to lay Maggie down, Fred."

Fred replied, "Yeah, we can lay her here."

Fred gingerly laid Maggie's body inside in the alcove behind the curtain. After securing Maggie's place there, Fred sat against the wall outside the area where he laid her and began to grieve his loss.

--------A LONG LONELY NIGHT--------

During the early part of the night, Freddie went back upstairs to see about Sandra, and David left Fred there with Maggie to go upstairs to be with Sheri and Jeanie. Fred continued to sit next to the curtain that had Maggie behind it. The howling wind and persistent rain had decreased in intensity from only minutes earlier.

Total quietness was betrayed by a breeze that stirred outside. Its continuous whirring helped Fred to doze off a few times. Remnants of the hurricane lingered as Fred contemplated thoughts Maggie had expressed to him about the reality of the spirit. He recalled her reciting Acts 2:2, 3, and 4, speaking about the spirit being invisible like the wind as the Apostle Paul described it and saying that spirit will always live. He envisioned her as she so often recounted the teachings from the Scriptures she had learned back at Mark Methodist Church—that God is not just the epitome of truth; He is Truth. Fred clung to these comforting thoughts as he sat with his back against the wall during those moments of relative quietness and reflection with only the faint sound of the wind stirring outside.

Fred knew he could not erase the pain he was feeling, and tears continued to flow as he softly called out her name, "Mag, Mag, Mag."

On the second floor, Freddie, overwhelmed by the day's activities, lay asleep on one of the couches in the gathering area. As her friend slept, Sandra could not resist the temptation of going back downstairs to assist Fred in his grief and to be with her dear friend Maggie.

--------A VOICE FROM BEYOND--------

As the night transitioned into early morning, Fred had drifted off to sleep. While still sitting there, on occasion, he would pull the curtain back and rub Maggie's forearm as she lay there as though asleep. Fred had only the howling wind and the faint raindrops beating on the exterior of the building to keep him company.

After comforting himself with those small gestures of touching his wife, Fred closed the curtain back as a shield between her and him as if to give Maggie more privacy. He was about to drift off to sleep again when Sandra arrived before slumber totally consumed him. As he wandered in and out of sleep, he wondered if he was dreaming.

When he saw Sandra approaching, Fred said, "Sandra, what in the world are you doing down here on the first floor? You know it's much safer up on the second floor where I guess you came from."

Sandra replied, "Yes, I know, Fred, but I had to come down and see Maggie for myself. She has been like a sister to me, and I couldn't pass up the chance. Freddie's sound asleep, so I had a chance to come down. You know he had a long day along with you and David. I mean, the way you guys saved Casey." Sandra began to focus on Maggie. "Oh, Maggie, Maggie!" she whimpered.

Despite his own grief, Fred tried to console her. He said, "Well, I know that Mag would have wanted you here, Sandra. She cared a lot about you. I could always tell it when she was talking about you and especially about how Erin helped to change your life."

Sandra sat down beside Fred, leaning her back against the wall as he was and sharing in the grief of such a tremendous loss. Just as Fred was about to turn around to talk more with Sandra, he heard the curtain suddenly begin to flap—at first smoothly and then moments later more violently. It was as if Maggie had control over its movements. The curtain waved for several seconds. Their movement was so sudden and so real—at least Fred thought so.

After a brief period, the fluttering of the curtain stopped. Fred then asked Sandra, who was herself somewhere between waking and sleeping, "Did you hear that? I know there's no one behind that curtain but Maggie's body. Plus, there's no wind blowing about inside the building right now."

Sandra replied, "Yeah, I've been dozing off and on and was thinking maybe I was dreaming. But, yeah, *I did* hear that curtain flap. I guess I thought *I was* dreaming. But now that you've confirmed that it wasn't a dream, Fred, I believe that it was her voice! Yeah, a voice from beyond in that special spiritual realm. Beyond where we are now in this physical world."

Sandra continued, "But I truly believe it's even more personal than that, Fred. I think it's Maggie telling you—and me—that she's all right. In fact, she's more than all right now that she's transitioned into her spiritual body!" Then Fred replied, "Thanks for that insight Sandra, it's a great comfort to me."

Soon after that experience, Sandra left Fred to return to the area upstairs to be beside Freddie, whom she found still asleep.

It was a long night as the hurricane resumed its force with sustained winds and persistent rain that again flooded large portions of the first floor. Miraculously, the area where Fred was with Maggie behind the curtain remained relatively calm and dry. He only heard an occasional burst of wind that persisted outside around the resort.

Soon Fred would drift off to sleep again and dream that a beam of light shone upon him; he later would perceive that it was a sign from God-giving comfort he so desperately needed in the most trying of circumstances.

Many of those on the second floor would not even realize what had happened below them during the night until sunlight exposed all the damage both inside and outside the building. The hope was that the fierceness of hurricane winds and water would be history by morning, and once again a calmness in the air would persist over south Florida—a peace that Fred would not have for a long, long time because of the fate of his wife.

FIGURE 12: A LONELY NIGHT

Blessed are those who mourn, For they shall be comforted.

- Matthew 5:4

CHAPTER ELEVEN
VISIONS OF HEAVEN

Maggie had always wanted her life to end in what she considered a tropical paradise. What she had seen in south Florida at Sinbad's resort appealed to her. Maggie missed her parents, Mensie and Matthew, so much. She knew that her faith would allow her to meet them again. She would be going to her spiritual home.

This time Maggie would be in a spiritual dimension, a place that was more real than anything she experienced during her sojourn in her physical body on the earth.

"Hello, Mama and Dad," Maggie said to her parents on one occasion when she had returned home from college.

Mensie replied, "Oh Maggie, you come on in here and get something to eat. I know you haven't had a decent meal since you've been at college."

Matthew added, "You come here first and give me a hug, little girl."

When they met each other again beyond this world, they carried on a conversation much as they had done countless times during their lives in Flint when Maggie was growing up.

The difference that Maggie found in this dimension was that now she could explore places and personalities in her spirit that her physical body while on earth would not allow. One place she fantasized about—as in a dream—was the tropical paradise of south Florida.

Maggie found herself in a glorious dimension, reconnecting with friends and loved ones like her parents, her younger sister Sadie, and her first husband, John Jr., who had themselves transitioned, and she could explore places she had always wanted to visit in her natural lifetime but could not because of the limitations of her physical body. Maggie experienced again the whole trip to south Florida to help celebrate her friend Erin's new job as a resort manager.

The exciting thing was that her spirit could always return to that physical body whenever she desired. She had the best of both worlds—one was a new heavenly existence while the other was an opportunity, if she wished, to return to a time long past, seeing herself as she was when she was growing up, for example.

All the personalities of past acquaintances and loved ones were still intact; their fruits of the spirit were on full display as expressed in Galatians 5:22 and 23. Maggie was reminded of a sermon she heard back at Mark Methodist in which the pastor described the spirit part of existence as being like good fruits on a tree—love, peace, and joy among them.

--------MAGGIE AND PASTOR JOE--------

What was especially pleasing to Maggie was her connection with the Reverend Joe James. Pastor Joe, as he was affectionately called, was John Jr.'s grandfather and patriarch of his family. He was the person who started Maggie's home church, Mark Methodist, back in Flint. Pastor Joe's son and John Jr.'s father, the Rev. John Sr., was pastor of the church throughout most of Maggie's childhood.

In Maggie's vision, the spiritual dimension she had apparently transitioned into included discussions with Pastor Joe.

He said, "Young lady, you are so bright, and I always knew that you'd be doing great things in life."

Pastor Joe continued, "And one more thing. I remember dreaming that you were going to meet three men that would totally transform your life! And my goodness, that is exactly what you did."

"Oh, Pastor Joe, I wasn't even born yet when you had those dreams of me, and you mean you were there all the time? With me when I married your grandson, John Jr.?" Maggie asked.

Pastor Joe replied, "Of course I was. Remember, by that time I myself had transitioned and was right there in spirit. Maggie, remember, spiritual beings like us are not affected by time. If anything, we influence time—the time we wish to apply our spiritual fruits. You do remember those fruits of the spirit, don't you, in lessons taught in your Sunday school by my son John Sr. while you were growing up at Mark Methodist back in Flint?"

Maggie replied, "Okay, now I remember, now that you mention it."

Pastor Joe continued, "And remember when you said that prayer the night when John was late coming home, after you two were married?"

"Yes, I remember," Maggie answered. "I was so disappointed when he didn't return home earlier. I suspected that he was being unfaithful. And when he did finally come home, he seemed so distant. When we went to bed, I just cried and cried—ended up saying the 100 Psalm and that's when I went to sleep."

Pastor Joe then said, "Well, little girl, I was there to comfort you and was the reason why you went to sleep when you did. Otherwise, you would have cried all night long."

Maggie replied, "Oh, Pastor Joe, you called me 'little girl!' That's what my father used to call me a lot. And Pastor Joe, I've seen some pictures of you at Mark Methodist, and my goodness, you were so young and handsome – I saw you as being a carbon copy of your grandson, John, Jr. And now, you haven't changed a bit!"

The Pastor Joe replied, "Well little one, the Lord had blessed me to live to a ripe old age in the natural realm. And I'm sure there are some pictures at that church that showed me in my advanced years.

"But you know, in this dimension we're all in the prime of life – and there are no age differences. It reminds me of our Lord, when He was crucified in His natural body – His was only thirty-three years old you know. And when he appeared to the disciples that time after He had been glorified by ascending to the Father, He retained all His physical characteristics – even the holes left in His body from the crucifixion were still there! And although the disciples were terrified when they first saw Him, because they were safely tucked away, they thought, in a room behind a wall of stone. But they quickly came to realize that it *was* Him, so that's when they believed.

"Only Thomas *didn't* believe – because he wasn't there at first. But about one week later, when Jesus appeared again in His glorified body, Thomas *did* see Him then, and that's when he finally *did* believe.

"And you know what little one, all that is recorded in the Scriptures, I believe, to show what you too will be in mid-life after transitioning into *your* glorified body. Now we who have arrived already are still learning baby girl – and we don't know everything we will eventually know about the kingdom. But we're getting there."

As Pastor Joe continued to impart wisdom to Maggie, as she saw in the dream, he began to drift away. That's when Maggie uttered, "Pastor Joe! Pastor Joe! Come back! Come back! Don't leave!" But he simply said, "Go back little girl, go back – you don't belong here now. And besides, others are waiting to see you. But don't worry, we'll meet again." At that point Maggie drifted into oblivion.

Conversations like these made it so special for Maggie in the spiritual dimension when she spent time with those not necessarily a part of her physical life on earth but now intimately connected in spirit. In the case of Pastor Joe, without her awareness at the time, he was with her at a critical time in her marriage to his grandson Pastor John Jr. Now she understood that Pastor Joe was essential to her overcoming adversity in her marriage in those days, and especially that time when John, Jr. came home late one night.

Maggie felt a deep connection to her spiritual mentor, Pastor Joe, of like spirits across generations despite being separated by decades apart in their physical existence. But their spirits were now united with one another. As Pastor Joe commented, their spirits were connected even that night when she recited Psalm 100 when John, Jr. came home late from work.

His wisdom seemed prophetic as well, because the three men that Pastor Joe told Maggie about did mean so much to her during her physical lifetime—her father Matthew, first husband John, and current husband Fred. They all were there with Maggie in the spiritual realm. She felt such a peaceful and enlightening awareness.

--------A ROOMMATE NOT FORGOTTON--------

In this spiritual realm, Maggie's spirit spanned across time to past generations like the one that Pastor Joe was a part of, and she also reconnected with those she knew in her physical existence on the earth but were spatially separated for some reason. Over the last several years, she had received greeting cards from her old roommate, Cody, at MCCU at Christmas time. Although her other former roommate, Katie, was still her close friend, those greeting cards came from Cody, who had roomed with Maggie and Katie during some of their time in college. Maggie had learned that Cody ended up living far away from home after graduation. Most of that time when she was away, Maggie found that Cody had been on the West coast of the country.

Maggie and Cody certainly were not on the friendliest of basis during their time at MCCU; in fact, at that time Maggie desired to be friendly with her, but Cody appeared anything but welcoming towards her. Cody just wasn't interested in developing a relationship with Maggie at the time.

After college, Maggie's secret desire was to be friends with Cody—through phone calls, emails, or writing letters; but that never came to fruition. Even Katie, who also roomed together with Cody along with Maggie in college, thought that Maggie had severed ties with their former roommate. Meanwhile, Maggie forged a genuine, long-term relationship with Katie—the kind of relationship that did not develop with Cody.

Eventually, it was apparent that Cody had changed along the way. She somehow found Maggie's home address and began mailing greeting cards to her at Christmas. One year, Maggie opened a card and read, "Hi, Maggie. Thinking about you and all my friends in college. God has been good to me over the years, and I trust you've been blessed abundantly as well. Sincerely, Cody."

Maggie never thought of Cody as being a spiritual person, not even necessarily approachable in college, which was why they never really connected at that time.

"Things sure do change over time," Maggie said to herself. After that, Maggie often told herself that at some point she needed to reconnect with Cody. But she never did that in their physical life. But in her spiritual dimension, they *did* meet and there was nothing but hugs and kisses and reminiscing about their time in college.

In addition to her unlikely reunion with former roommate Cody, the whole experience of Maggie's dream was like a gathering of friends and relatives. It was those that she lived a life with, in a spiritual realm, as she perceived in the dream. She communicated freely with the ones she knew in her own physical existence on the earth. But she also conversed with those who had not connected with her at that time, either because, like Pastor Joe, they lived in a previous generation or because of being physically separated by distance as in the case of her former roommate Cody, who ended up living in a different part of the country.

--------THE POWER OF DECISION--------

Maggie's sense of peace continued until she heard cries of sadness in the distance. She was able to view her physical body as it was laid in a casket with mourners passing by and weeping for their loss. She wanted so badly to tell them that they should not mourn for her, because she now was in a place of peace and joy, which started the moment she tried to escape the rising water in a south Florida condo where she and husband Fred resided. But the hurricane changed all that, and her physical demise was a result.

Maggie was gone from the tangible world, but her spirit was as alive as ever, having even a greater awareness than when her spirit was restricted to a physical body before her transition. Maggie wanted to tell everyone at her service not to mourn, but she knew she could not return to them at that time to make them aware of her joy. Her spirit was with some of them, the ones that exhibited what the scripture calls "a peace that passes all understanding" for the believer. But for others who did not have that spiritual foundation that gives us hope in the Lord, it was such a devastating moment that showed in their demeanor with cries of anguish and pain.

Nevertheless, remembering what she was taught at Mark Methodist Church in Flint, Maggie knew that the penalty of sin, which was introduced into the world by Adam and Eve in the garden, was physical death and was still in effect among those she saw mourning over her lifeless physical body. The scripture called death a "sting" that challenges even those strong in the faith.

But Maggie's spirit could reconnect with those who did believe that she was still with them. She had reconnected with her deceased mother, Mensie, that day on the beach during her physical lifetime. Maggie had the power of decision at that moment, the ability to decide to focus either on that time of bereavement that her friends and relatives had for her or to concentrate on other realities of the spiritual realm—realities such as those promised in Revelation 21:7, where all her desires are met. Those desires included the acquisition of the fruits of the spirit identified in Galatians. She knew this meant to inherit all that God offered, including love, peace, and joy.

--------A TRANSITION TO SPIRITUAL LIFE--------

Maggie's life had changed in an instant during a hurricane in south Florida. Being unable to breathe because the water had overtaken her, she desperately tried to free herself from within the pad on that couch where she had wrapped herself and was thus attached to the couch. It was comfortable at first—to the point of leading her into slumber. But when she awakened, the rushing water overwhelmed her, and she failed in her efforts to escape the grip of the sofa. She only could gaze at the front door, eyes wide open, unable to reach it to escape her impending demise.

In an instant Maggie was taken to that spiritual realm where every believer hopes to be—where Jesus and all the saints reside until that day of His second coming to the earth. There she was in the company of what appeared to be heavenly hosts with Christ appearing as a flaming fire as the scriptures described in the book of Revelation. The dynamic voice coming forth from Him seemed to be instructions to those assembled about their assignment once that day comes.

Maggie saw the period where the saints will reign with Christ for a thousand years, a time of learning and teaching, of God's way and government as she had been taught in Bible study back at Mark Methodist. She knew this would be the ultimate destiny for those who loved the Lord as expressed in Revelation 20:6.

This heavenly meeting that Maggie envisioned was tempered when she detected the loudest cries during her homegoing service came from David. He was among those she saw in the vision and who had gone with her, among others, to south Florida to celebrate Erin's new job as resort manager. Thank God Maggie had the power of decision, which led her to that other place in paradise, one that entailed love, peace, and joy.

CHAPTER TWELVE
"I WANNA GO HOME"

--------END OF MAGGIE'S DREAM--------

David's cries woke Maggie from her slumber. That was when she realized it was all a dream. As Maggie became more fully awake, she reached over to touch husband Fred and said, "Fred, Fred!"

Maggie tried to wake him. They both were so tired that she felt that they had overslept the trip Sinbad had planned to the Island of Love. She only remembered that she had not set the alarm clock as she had done before.

Fred finally stirred and saw Maggie lying beside him, staring up at the ceiling as she had done when she viewed the stars through their bedroom sky window at home.

He asked, "What time is it?"

"According to my watch, it's 8:30.

Fred replied with a short question and then an elaboration, "8:30? We were supposed to have been at dinner at 4:00 and take off with the group in a ferry for the Island of Love at 6:00. I'm sure everyone has left by now and gone over to the island. It's pitch dark outside, and we may be the only ones here. Maybe we need to go out and see if anybody is still here in the condo with us, which I doubt."

--------MAGGIE DESCRIBES THE DREAM--------

"I just had the strangest dream, Fred!" Maggie said. "I know you want to check on the others, but you won't believe this dream."

Fred continued, "Since we've probably been left here at the condo anyway, tell me more about the dream you had when we took that nap."

Maggie obliged and began, "Well, let me tell you this much, Fred. You know, we did get to go to the Island of Love—and all of us were there. It was so real! But I know that it was only a dream because I envisioned a loud alarm waking me up from that nap, and I know that we didn't set the alarm before we went to sleep."

"And, Fred, there were other indications that it was only a dream like me ending up in the arms of another man while on the voyage over there. Now, Fred, like you told me once, I only have eyes for you; I wouldn't be so bold."

Fred asked, "Well, who was he?"

"Now, Fred, you don't need to know that," she said. She was unwilling to give him more information because the other man was Freddie, and she had always tried to conceal her past relationship with him. "But anyway, more than even that, I woke up from an alarm going off, and I knew I had not set an alarm."

Fred confirmed that, saying, "Yeah, I can verify that because we don't even have an alarm clock, only the alarm on our cell phones. And I was so tired I know I didn't set my phone alarm, and I know you didn't set yours either. For that matter, I didn't think to call the front desk to have an attendant give us a ring to wake us up in time for that dinner. Oh well. What's past is past," Fred added sounding somewhat disappointed.

Being curious about her dream and especially the trip to the Island of Love, Fred asked Maggie to describe more of what took place. He said, "Don't keep me in suspense, Mag. Don't tell me what happened after you woke up; tell me more about what happened in your dream," he implored her.

Maggie replied, "Well, it's so much more than we probably have time for. But I'll give it a shot. I dreamed that we all went on a ferry ride to the Island of Love, the trip we probably overslept. But we were not able to participate in a planned event there because of a storm."

Maggie continued, "We ended up coming back to the condo. And let me tell you, the wind and rain came so hard that the suite we were in filled up with water. And let me tell you, I was caught in the padding of the couch in there Fred and ended up drowning! It was horrible!" Maggie said as tears began to flow.

She paused to regain her composure and continued, "At that point it was so terrifying. And the worst part was that, as I said, I ended up drowning in the front room of this suite. Yeah Fred – I saw myself drowning! And Fred, I tried to get to the door but was constrained somehow on the couch, in that padding, totally overcome by and submerged in water! In the dream, the person we befriended on the trip, David, was the one who got me out of the suite, but I was already gone—lifeless. It was so sad.

"The strange thing is that in the dream it was not all sad. I mean, while drowning was certainly terrifying, at that very moment I envisioned the spirit part of me rise out of my physical body to see the whole thing as it unfolded. In other words, I knew I had died, but nonetheless I was very much alive! I saw myself through that little peephole in the door as I was lying there, lifeless, on the couch, bobbing and weaving up and down on that thing. All the fellows were in an uproar over it; none of you knew what to do. But thank goodness, in the dream David came to the rescue!

"I even saw my own funeral, Fred, and I tried to comfort those who were mourning for me, but they didn't know I was there because

I was in spirit. They only saw my lifeless physical body lying there in a coffin. And, yes, even in the dream I envisioned that I was in a spiritual dimension." Maggie continued, "I can't get over the fact that I was in my spiritual body and reconnected with my parents and other friends and relatives—those who had passed on themselves. That was the part that was so peaceful, even glorious! I even reconnected with someone I had not seen in years, my college roommate."

Fred said, "Wait a minute, you've seen Katie a lot."

Maggie explained, "No, Fred. I mean my other roommate, the one that I didn't get along with. Her name was Cody. You remember Cody, don't you?"

"Oh, yeah," Fred said. "Of course, I remember Cody. You know, I remember her making a nice comment about me when we first meet at that social after the basketball game at MCCU. But I made it clear that I wasn't interested in her. My eyes at the time were only for you, Mag, like you just said about me."

"Well, that's nice of you to say, Fred. But, anyway, I had a secret desire to befriend Cody during all these years because that was a time when I just wanted people to like me—to be friends. But no! She didn't want anything to do with me at the time. And that's why I developed a relationship with Katie, and, as you know, we've developed our relationship over the years."

Maggie continued, "You know, Fred, I believe that God granted me that desire I had all those years ago to befriend Cody, which was something I kept to myself for so long. And it actually happened in the dream. I mean, it was only then when we finally experienced a joyful relationship with one another; we were just hugging and kissing and everything just like we've been friends forever!

"But like I said, although there were those joyous times in the dream, there were the sad ones too like, as I said earlier, when I witnessed my own funeral.

"But even that wasn't as sad a feeling as you would think, because, in the spiritual body of my dream, I had the ability witness the extend in which people really loved me in my physical existence through their grief. These emotions I didn't see much in my physical lifetime. And I also was able to focus on more joyous aspects of where I was in that heavenly dimension. I simply refocused on a place of peace and joy. And although those mourning me were so sad, I realized that at some point they too would be in a spiritual dimension upon their own transition. At that time, I knew that they too eventually would experience that life of joy and peace that I was having in the dream."

"But again, Fred, in that dimension I was able to make decisions that let me escape from that sad situation—and as much as I wanted them to see me with the joy I had, I knew that wasn't possible, not in their physical state of existence.

"Somehow, at that point I felt they eventually would understand the joy I had apart from my physical body. I knew they had the faith that at some point they would see me in a perfectly constructed spiritual dimension, where all of us again would be together!

"Now, ain't that exciting, Fred? To know that at some point all of us will be reunited—and certainly to see my mom and dad again as well as my sister Sadie and my other siblings in that spiritual dimension when I transition from this physical life? And, yes, all of us will be able to see our friends and relatives too, to see even those with like spirits that we never had an opportunity to know in this physical life!"

Then Maggie continued with the description of the dream she had, "And you know Fred, our being reunited someday was confirmed when I had a discussion with Pastor Joe, the grandfather of John, Jr. and the one who started my home church, Mark Methodist, back in Flint. It was so real, even though I never met him. But then he began to drift away. And I said don't go! But he continued to drift away, nonetheless. Then he said I didn't belong where we were, and that we'll meet again. And he said something else Fred! He said that others are waiting to see me. I now realize that he was talking about all those I may have known in my physical life with a like spirit—that spirit that the Apostle Paul talked about in the scriptures as the Fruit of the Spirit. I can't wait 'til that day Fred. Anyway, let me snap out of it. I'm getting all into this dream again. Don't get me wrong Fred, I don't wanna rush things. God gave us this physical existence and I want to be here as long as I can!"

In her excitement, Maggie continued to said to Fred, "But let me tell you this. I remember telling Sandra once that despite all the teachings I've had about Jesus being with us always, even in death, it's hard for the human mind to be comfortable with that reality. Thank goodness, despite how we feel, as believers we're only called to do just that—believe.

"And as people of faith, I know we all believe that the Bible is true, but I think it really has to seep deep down into our spirits for us to have the joy that is revealed in the scriptures, especially in the face of death and all the bad things that may happen to us."

"And the truth, Fred, is that God will be with us at our transition because of that belief."

"But getting back to that homegoing service, I envisioned that David was the most expressive about seeing my body like that, motionless within that casket. He started to cry uncontrollably, and that's when I woke up."

--------STING OF DEATH--------

Fred interjected with what Maggie was saying with his own words of wisdom. He said, "Well Mag, that was sad, being able to see your lifeless body like that, and you envisioning David with all that grief—waking you up. What he experienced, while still in the physical realm, at least in your dream, is what the Scripture calls the sting of death. I'm afraid that's something we never get use to in this physical dimension—when someone we care about dies."

Then Maggie responded to what Fred had said, "You're right Fred. We never get use to death being around us."

"But as far as that dream? It was so detailed, and horrific; and I guess with death being a reality of life, we just have to stay 'prayed up,' as they say—and believe—believe that the end of this physical life in death is not the end of our spiritual being."

--------BACK TO REALITY--------

Fred replied, "Mag, that was some dream. Maybe at some point you can tell the others about it. But we need to get back to reality and go out and see if anyone is in the lobby."

Maggie said, "Now, Fred, you know no one's out there. They're all gone on the ferry over to the Island of Love, remember? We've overslept."

Fred replied, "Well, we won't know for sure unless we go out there and find out."

Maggie said, "Okay, if you insist, we can go. I just don't want you to be disappointed. As for me, I'm looking forward sitting on that couch in front of the fireplace and just celebrating my birthday with you, honey, with just you and me. We'll see the others when they return from the voyage over to the Island of Love."

"Are you sure you want to sit on that couch?" Fred asked. "You know that's where you lost your life in that dream!"

"Oh, Fred, don't be superstitious now. We're back to reality!"

"Okay then. We can go out," Fred replied. "But we need to get dressed and can dress like we're going out on the town."

"Oh, Fred, I like that idea! Let me tell you, we can go ahead and dress, but it's going to be just us two out there because everybody's gone. I'm agreeable with what you're saying though. I'll be ready in ten minutes."

A few minutes had passed before they were dressed and ready to head out the door. Maggie couldn't wait to spend a nice quiet time alone with Fred in front of the fireplace. With all the activity of the group since they arrived in south Florida, she really anticipated a peaceful and romantic evening alone with the love of her life.

She said, "We can just sit in front of that fireplace and cuddle until the group returns from the ferry trip." In Maggie's mind, the Island of Love would have to wait for another time.

When they finally arrived in the lobby, they were astonished at what they saw and heard.

--------CELEBRATING MAGGIE!--------

"Surprise, surprise!" Everyone shouted in unison as Fred and Maggie entered the lobby. "Happy birthday, Maggie!"

Everyone in Maggie's group was there, apparently waiting on her and Fred to arrive. Maggie had no idea they would be there; she just knew they had gone on the ferry to the Island of Love.

They began to chant her name with emphasis being on the last syllable: "Maggie! Maggie! Maggie!"

They all were there to celebrate Maggie's birthday! Maggie was speechless. She uttered words in the form of a question, "What in the world?" Then she looked around the lobby at the decorations – decorations designed to honor *her*. Then said to her husband, "Look at all the balloons and the banners Fred!"

She was astonished at their apparently remembering she had just celebrated her birthday recently back in Chicago prior to the trip to south Florida. While all the attention was being lavished on her, Maggie thought, *Fred must have told them about the small celebration we had had in Chicago. Lords knows we didn't have time to do anything larger because of planning for this trip.*

Tears began to build in her eyes, and Maggie was about to lose control emotionally. She wondered if her husband had a part in planning this celebration.

She said, "Fred, did you have anything to do with this?"

With everyone watching, she got her answer when he did not respond to her question; he just looked at her and smiled, then said, "Happy birthday, Mag!"

After things settled down a bit, Maggie got her chance to address the group. "I'm just flabbergasted, simply overwhelmed by all of the attention you guys are giving to me. I'm so undeserving of receiving all this love. And it's a total surprise. I was thinking that you all had left to go over to the Island of Love."

"Now, do you really think we would have left here without you, Maggie," someone shouted from the group.

Fred was not the only one responsible for the group knowing about Maggie's birthday. She had mentioned to some group members that she and Fred had a modest celebration prior to making the trip by going out and having dinner at a restaurant in Chicago.

But whether she expressed a desire for something more than a simple dinner at a restaurant or not, deep down inside she wanted more—and Fred knew it. Nonetheless, there was no clear indication from her husband that he was a part of any planning for *this* celebration—in the lobby of a condo in south Florida.

--------REMEMBERING A MORE MODEST CELEBRATION--------

After everyone had finished recognizing Maggie for being there taking part in her own birthday celebration, someone shouted, "Say something, Maggie. We want to hear from you."

Maggie then tried to clear her head and give some kind of sensible response to all the love being lavished on her. Finally, she started to speak. "You all shouldn't have gone out of your way to do this. I'm just overwhelmed by it all.

"I remember as though it was only yesterday when Fred took me to this restaurant to have dinner back in Chicago. Well, I guess it wasn't that long ago, just last week before we all boarded a plane and headed down here to south Florida. Anyway, at that time, it would be only a few days before we took off on this trip.

"It was an eloquent but quiet affair—just the two of us. And I received a nice gift from Fred—a greeting card with some cash in it."

Fred interrupted, "Let me tell all of you this. I don't want you to think that I was cheap by giving her only that for her birthday. Shortly after that modest celebration, I began strategizing how I could contact as many of you as I could to make this possible. And thank God I was able to talk to most of you about it, and we were able to pull it off.

"I knew that the trip was mainly about the celebration of Erin's new job at Sinbad's resort, but I also wanted to have a celebration for Maggie, not just a birthday celebration but a celebration of what she means to all of us."

--------THE IMPORTANCE OF MAGGIE---------

The celebration in the gathering room of the condo was more than a birthday observance; it was a recognition of how important Maggie was to all those assembled. After Fred made his remarks, the group again began to chant, "Maggie! Maggie! Maggie!"

Everyone there on this occasion had felt the positive effect of Maggie's presence in their lives in some way. Even Wynn, the son of her college roommate, Katie, expressed his gratitude when he stepped forward and said, "I want to say something, everybody." Wynn looked down as if being embarrassed.

His mother Katie said, "Go ahead, Wynn."

With her encouragement, he continued, "Ms. Maggie, you told me once when you visited my mother to hold down my temper and not to get too excited about things. Well, I think I've been able to do that—thanks to you." Wynn then stepped back beside his mother and leaned his head on her shoulder.

Most of those in attendance then let out a collective, "Aw!" A few, like Maggie, had gotten teary eyed. Soon the tears were freely flowing from her eyes.

After a few moments, Maggie gathered her emotions and replied to Wynn's comments. "Yeah, Wynn, I do remember that. And from what I've seen, you've done a good job in controlling that temper. And I think you can see the results of your actions, because you've developed a fine relationship with your friend Jeanie over here."

Those comments made Jeanie's mother Sheri proud and prompted her to say, "Maggie, I appreciate those words. Wynn has been so special in my daughter's life, and you have definitely had an effect on all of us in our household."

David shouted, "Amen to that!"

Maggie got the opportunity to tell many in the group about the dream she had—about actually experiencing everyone going on the ferry over to the Island of Love. It made them even more interested in making the trip another time when they would not have a hurricane to contend with.

--------MAGGIE'S INFLUENCE--------

Wynn certainly was not the only one in the group to have been influenced by Maggie. Everyone in attendance had been affected by Maggie's presence at one time or another in their lives—no one more than Sandra, who had been crying with Maggie as her friend was being recognized. Maggie had played such an important part in her life and had contributed to her simply being alive. She was healed from a near fatal health condition due largely to Maggie's support.

But Maggie also was with Sandra when her parents took her in as though she was their own child, and Maggie had become like a sister to her.

Sandra's brief romantic interest in Maggie's husband Fred was remedied largely with the help of Erin, who steered Sandra onto the right track. Nonetheless, she found time to spend with Fred quite a bit during the gathering in the lobby after the dinner, giving him signals by the wink of an eye about all the plans that were being made for this birthday celebration. But she had long gotten over Fred as a love interest. She was just thankful that the whole Bermuda experience led to a healing of her physical malady with the assistance of Erin. Her tears of joy said it all!

Erin herself felt the same emotions as Sandra; she knew Maggie had a lot to do with her even being there in south Florida working as a resort manager.

Maggie had never mentioned anything about her relationship with Freddie to anyone, not even to her husband Fred. Keeping that deviant behavior within herself took a toll on her psyche; nonetheless, she was slowly getting over that past relationship despite a brief reconnection she had with him in the dream on the voyage to the Island of Love.

Gates and Courtney knew of Maggie's effect on their lives because they had met with her and husband Fred every Sunday evening to socialize after attending church earlier in the day. On this day, Gates had something else in mind to honor his friend.

--------GATES' MESSAGE-------

Gates began, "I have something to say about our friend Maggie, but first I'd like to thank the organizers of this event—and you know who you are—for allowing me to speak about Maggie. But before I get to that, I'd like to congratulate Erin, who we all have been celebrating over the past three days for her new position here.

"Now, Maggie, I'll get to you in a minute. But as I get started with my brief message, if you don't remember anything else, I want all of you to remember this: each one of us as human beings is made up of two dimensions—our physical body that we all pay a great deal of attention to and our spirits that live within this physical tabernacle. The scripture even tells us that this body is the temple where the spirit resides. Well, I want you to know that it is that spirit that drives all of us; it drives our physical body to move and respond to stimuli as well as to initiate good or evil actions towards others—to make wise decisions.

"On this trip I've seen evidence of both good and bad spirits in all of us. And the reason for that? We're all human or, to put it in religious terms, we're all sinners. But thank goodness we're all saved by grace through our risen Savior Jesus Christ."

"I'm sure we all recognize that our physical bodies are different, and they are driven by our unique personalities. God recognizes everything about us—both the physical as well as our spirit. But because of our natural tendencies, we pay a lot more attention to our physical bodies than the spirit that is within us. But it's that spirit part of us that will live on even as the physical body perishes at some point—something none of us want to talk about—the subject of death.

"Well, I will not talk about death now but about life and how God wants us to live more abundantly. I *will* say this. I've noticed the evidence of both body and spirit of many of you who have been with us on this trip. And, as I've just said, we all have different personalities, and our histories are quite different as well.

"Our individual spirits—our personalities—certainly drive our physical bodies. But the one unifying factor within all of us is the Holy Spirit. This is the third head of the trinity, which causes us to be one body in Christ, and it's a blessing I hope all of you will remember. In doing so, you can move confidently into the future, knowing who holds the future, and therefore we will be eternally a part of it.

"I want to emphasize that we should increasingly let our spiritual self be more in control. And, if we do that, we'll end up making better decisions that will increase our joy while in this present life and will improve our physical presence on the earth.

"While this event put on by Sinbad is about Erin, I can't end my message without saying a word about Maggie, the focus of *this* celebration. I'm so happy for you, Maggie. Let's face it, you're the reason why we're having this gathering today to celebrate your birthday. Maggie, you're dear to Courtney and me because of how you contributed to us coming together.

"I want all of you assembled here to understand that when Maggie brought Courtney and me together it was very unintentional. You see, this is what I mean. I understand that Fred left college early to come to Hawaii where both Courtney and I were living at the time. Courtney has always said that she was knocked off her feet, as she puts it, when she first met me. Well, she may have been knocked off her feet when she met me, but let me tell you, I was taken off my feet too when I met her.

"But anyway, Maggie, you gave Fred your blessings when he left you for Hawaii. It was a sacrifice for you because you loved him dearly. But at the time he felt he could not pass up a job opportunity on those islands in the Pacific. Well, he did go there, and that's when he met Courtney, my wife who is standing right here.

"Courtney was in a bad place when Fred first met her, and she confessed as much. I mean, being a pole dancer was not the most honorable profession you can have to say the least. But that was what attracted me to her at first. She was really kind of wild, you know, out there in the world. And I know she doesn't mind me being transparent about her history because, for heaven's sake, I have a history too. Yeah, I was out there in the world doing everything *I thought* I was large enough to do, so I guess we kind of were made to be with each other.

"But Fred was an honorable man, and Courtney, being completely honest with me, later in our marriage let me know that she was really attracted to Fred to the point of her wanting to develop a relationship with him.

"But Fred was true to you, Maggie, at that time even if he was thousands of miles away from where you were back in Michigan.

"Now I realize that you continued your life by getting married to your childhood friend John and went on to have a nice life together with him, notwithstanding how brief it was. While Fred was devastated after you made that decision to marry John, he held out hope that he could be happy without you in his life.

"So, while all that was going on back in Detroit, Fred took the opportunity to show Courtney a better way of life in Hawaii than the one she was living at the time—the right way—one of knowing the Lord. So, when they visited Queens Church, that did it for Courtney; she was converted and was never the same again.

"Her change of life was a puzzle to me. I didn't understand it at first and didn't necessarily like it. I was an atheist at the time and didn't want anything to do with God—didn't believe in Him. But Courtney showed me the way, and that's how we are connected to Maggie—through Fred and how he affected Courtney's life and eventually my life through Courtney.

"What is the moral of this story, our story, everybody? Well, it just shows that whatever you're going through, whether good or bad, there's always more good things coming your way. You just have to believe that despite the circumstances you may be in. And whatever trials you're going through, each one of those challenges is for a purpose—even if you created the trial—like Courtney and I did, being uncontrolled out there in the streets!"

"So I can truthfully say that if it wasn't for Maggie, I wouldn't have become a minister. But more important than that, I wouldn't have learned what the scripture has to say about life in general and about each one of our lives. And in knowing that, we all can build a productive, joyful life.

"And do you know what the most joyful life is? Well, it's being able to help someone else along the way. Now that's where the real joy is—in helping someone else in some way. And, Maggie, through your husband, Fred certainly has done that because he provided a way for me to meet the Courtney that changed me from a life being in the world to one as a believer.

"Let me end by saying that all of us are different; we bring different things to the table because of our unique personalities, our likes and dislikes. I've been noticing all of you. There are a lot of differences among us. But despite those differences, we've come together and have what Sinbad called a successful celebration down here for Erin. The key is to utilize those differences with whomever we decide to be close to for our own benefit but to realize that everyone may not be a good fit for us for whatever reason. And that's okay.

"And I'm sure many of you have found that out being together as we have the last three days. Who to connect with and who to avoid is something we all must figure out.

"But, Maggie, we certainly believe in you and your ability to have a positive effect on others. And, Maggie, your parents and others who have transitioned are waiting for you; you'll be going home someday. Thank you all for listening. And I'll turn the program back over to the leader of this event, Sinbad."

--------SINBAD'S GRATITUDE--------

Sinbad spoke after Gates' rather lengthy remarks. "Thank you, Gates, for those encouraging words. I don't know what to say after that. But I have to say, Gates, Maggie told us that you've been selected to give a sermon on the night you all return to New York at Katie's church. Well, I think you've just given a sermon down here in south Florida. I think you all understand now why Gates became a minister; he's never at a loss for words.

"By the way, what will be your message at Katie's church, Gates?" Sinbad asked.

Gates replied, "Well, Sinbad, since you haven't told us what the experience over on the Island of Love will be like, I don't feel led to tell you what I'll talk about in my sermon," Gates answered with a smile. "But I will give you this much. The title of my message will be 'For Heaven's Sake.'"

Sinbad replied, "That's an interesting title, Gates. What made you choose that?"

"Well, Sinbad, I've heard that expression used so much on this trip, I decided to talk about what it really means. Usually when people use it, it's just a cliché, something that people say in normal conversation."

Sinbad replied, "Okay, I can live with that. Just send us back here in south Florida a copy of the manuscript of the message."

To that, Gates simply said, "Okay! Will do!"

Sinbad continued addressing all those assembled, "But in all seriousness, everybody, I'd like to thank all of you for helping this event be as successful as it has been over the past three days. Everyone knows the hurricane is coming. Well, let me rephrase that. Everyone knows except for Maggie. I'm sure she's talked to some of you about the dream she had of already having experienced it."

David shouted out, "Hey, Sinbad, you mentioned the success of this event we've had. But tell us what we would have done over there on the Island of Love? I'm curious—especially after hearing Maggie talk about her dream of going over there. I really want to go, maybe the next time we're down here, and I do hope we come here again *soon!*"

Sinbad said, "Well, David, Maggie can tell you all about the trip in the dream she had. Yeah, she's already been there at least in her dream." He paused, then said, "At some point, we can go over there for real—at least at a time when there is no threat of a storm.

And by the way, when Maggie described the dream she had to me, she mentioned the fact that David was the one who saved my friend, Casey, from drowning. And he also was the one who brought Maggie out of her condo when she … Well, I'm not going to get into all that. Maggie has described the dream to many of you, and I'm not going to repeat a lot of what many of you already know. I'll just say, thank you David, for saving my friend, even if it was only in a dream," Sinbad said with a smile.

Sinbad continued, "But to answer your question about what we will do over there, David, that's still a secret like I just told Gates. But I agree with you. I'd like all of you to come back down here at some point to finish what we didn't get to do this time because of the storm."

"All I can say is that when we finally get to go to the Island of Love, whenever that will be, it will be quite stimulating. But as you know, we can't go this time because of the hurricane."

David said, "Well, that's fine, Sinbad. This is a nice resort you've got here, and everything about it is stimulating. I think it makes all of us want to come back."

With the statement that Sinbad made about the activities on the Island being exciting and stimulating, Maggie wondered what in the world Sinbad was talking about. She remembered in the dream how David saw a sign on the island that suggested the existence of a nudist colony. She finally concluded in her mind, *Well, I guess we'll just have to wait to find out.*

--------RECOGNIZING ERIN AND MAGGIE--------

Sinbad finished the evening's event by thanking Erin for coming to work at the resort and added that everyone was expecting great things from her.

He said to Maggie, "I know you didn't get hardly any sleep last night, and sorry we asked Sandra and Freddie to be sure of that by making the noise sound effect machine be directed towards your suite. They made it appear as though they were playing hide-and-seek as they had said earlier in the evening."

Maggie turned toward Sandra and Freddie, seemingly in denial that they had played such a trick on her. She simply said, "I can't believe it!"

Sinbad continued, "No! They weren't really playing hide-and-seek, Maggie, as you were led to believe. They only made sure that the machine was positioned so that noise from it would be directed to you and Fred's suite so you two *couldn't* get any sleep. They ended up in another part of their suite where the noise wouldn't affect them, so they, like all the rest of us, got the sleep we needed.

"I know you were like zombies when we asked you to be with us today, and when you finally took that nap two hours before dinner, you simply overslept and didn't wake up until you came here.

"We knew that we wouldn't be going over to the Island of Love because of the storm, so we used the time you two were sleeping to prepare for this celebration for you, Maggie. All the banners and the signs – that was the work of all of us. And I must say, I think we did a pretty good job, and it was well worth the wait!

"Yeah, the idea was to get you to oversleep the time I said we would leave for the island. We knew eventually you would come here as you did—and it worked thanks to Fred's help. We even had Fred smuggle a bogus alarm clock into your room, which you really didn't need because you were so tired. Well, to be frank about it, it couldn't alarm anyway because it had a defect.

"So, everything worked as we had planned. It gave us ample opportunity to prepare for your surprise party, Maggie."

Maggie turned to Sandra and said, "Oh, Sandra, for heaven's sake! So you were in on it too. No wonder you were talking with Fred as much as you did when we left the dinner and assembled in the lobby. And I did see you wink at him! Yes, I did! I saw you, girl!"

As Fred had done, Sandra just smiled after Maggie made these remarks, but then she added, "That wink was only a confirmation that we understood the plans being made for this celebration for you, Maggie—nothing more!"

Maggie said, "Okay. I believe you."

--------MAGGIE'S GRATITUDE--------

Maggie then turned to the rest of the group and said, "I think you all know that Sandra and I go way back. And I care so much for everybody here tonight. I think all of you know that too. But I cannot even imagine that you all never had intentions of going over there to the island. Well, I guess we have the storm to blame for that. And, Fred, I can't believe you were in on this too! I just can't believe it!"

"Well, Maggie, would you have rather been caught in a hurricane on a vessel in the middle of the water?" Courtney said being facetious.

At that point Maggie thought about the dream she had and how she drowned in her suite during a storm surge. Then Maggie answered Courtney's question and said with all the emotion she could muster, "No, no! Forget about that hurricane. I wanna go home! I wanna go home! We can do the Island of Love thing the next time we're down here. And let me say this, I'm so happy for Erin. I know she'll do a great job at your resort Sinbad."

Sinbad finally said to Maggie, "Well, thank you for those remarks Maggie. And all of you will be flying home tomorrow." Then he turned toward David but addressed everyone in the group, saying, "And to all of you, as far as the Island of Love is concerned, you just have wait to see what's over there and what I have planned for you. But I promise you that's what we will do when you all come back. I'm sure Maggie will be communicating with all of you about that.

"Until that time, we'll be taking good care of your friend Erin, who in turn will be taking good care of us in her service as resort manager.

"And, David, you, Sheri and Jeanie just keep in contact with your friend Katie about the specific time you all will return. I know she'll be in contact with Maggie about that. I certainly want the contingents from the New York City area, including nearby New Brunswick, as well as those from the Chicago and Detroit areas represented at that time.

"Well, you all have a good night sleep and have a good flight tomorrow morning back to New York. I know all of you have had a good time here, but I also believe that you're anxious to be going home."

At that point everyone retired for the night, and finally Maggie and Fred got the sleep they so desperately needed. And yes, tomorrow, they all would be going home!

William Porter

Heaven's Sake Word Search Puzzle

```
M  S  Q  T  D  B  M  L  P  F  N  K  V  E  Y  S  N  N  L  Z
C  F  E  X  M  A  Q  O  N  E  S  N  E  J  T  O  C  N  I  X
F  H  I  T  G  F  H  C  M  D  Z  C  L  X  I  T  C  R  H  R
M  Z  U  G  A  U  B  K  A  I  X  F  N  T  C  Z  O  N  I  I
M  A  I  R  J  G  E  H  E  P  Y  J  C  H  H  S  G  L  N  P
Z  E  N  O  C  L  R  A  B  K  L  U  I  J  O  I  A  G  R  W
G  Q  E  I  H  H  N  R  D  W  R  C  A  D  M  S  T  M  A  A
S  R  A  B  K  K  I  T  X  T  A  M  N  A  E  O  G  R  T  M
K  M  U  J  D  I  E  B  S  G  A  O  H  B  N  D  D  H  R  L
D  S  T  I  N  G  N  N  O  I  M  F  M  N  N  Y  M  D  H  G
S  R  N  F  S  I  I  S  C  F  F  K  J  I  Y  K  M  T  U  D
P  J  O  T  R  E  P  A  O  C  E  A  N  S  W  R  A  L  B  E
I  X  I  C  B  E  L  I  E  V  E  R  D  Y  O  E  Q  T  T  T
R  R  T  L  S  F  D  E  H  T  I  A  F  T  D  X  V  A  I  D
I  P  I  S  T  I  O  R  T  E  D  R  S  G  S  H  A  U  N  E
T  L  S  A  K  J  D  K  S  X  D  K  V  O  U  Y  Q  O  N  L
U  O  N  N  O  B  T  C  A  S  E  Y  I  N  C  Z  C  S  A  F
A  V  A  D  U  L  E  V  C  G  R  I  E  V  I  N  G  G  P  C
L  E  R  R  G  V  E  S  O  R  F  B  R  Q  D  U  E  U  D  P
A  Q  T  A  O  Z  F  O  C  N  S  W  F  K  S  J  D  G  Q  A
```

BELIEVER	BERMUDA	BERNIE
CASEY	CHARLOTTE	CHICAGO
CHURCH	CODY	CONDO
CRUISE	DAVID	DEATH
DETROIT	DISCORD	DREAM
ERIN	FAITH	FRED
FREDDIE	GATES	GRIEVING
HOME	HURRICANE	INSTRUCTION
JAMAICA	JENSEN	JOE
KATIE	LISA	LOCKHART
LOVE	LUGGAGE	MAGGIE
MANIKINS	MCCU	MIAMI
NCSF	OCEAN	REMINGTON
REWARD	SANDRA	SCRIPTURE
SHAUN	SINBAD	SPIRITUAL
STING	STORM	TRANSITION
VILLAGE	WYNN	

About the Author

William Porter is the author of inspirational books. The current book, *For Heaven's Sake: The Dreams Continue*, is the fourth in a series of novels that continues to examine the saga of lead character Maggie in her quest to obtain a "heaven on earth" in this physical life on earth. Three other volumes in this series include: *Heaven Can't Wait or Can it? Dreams of Love, Deceit, and Hope, Heaven Can't Wait or Can It? THE SEQUEL*, and *Heaven Can't Wait or Can it? THE FRUITION*. The next novel in this series is entitled *Wonders Of The Spirit*, with an anticipated release date of late 2022 or early 2023.

INSPIRATIONAL BOOK CLUB
JOIN US IN OUR DISCUSSION

Where the spirit IS reality!
A meeting where believers can
share their experiences
AND
Review books written by Dr. William Porter,
Author of Inspirational Books

MEETING DAY: Every First Saturday of the Month

START TIME: 6:00pm eastern; END TIME: 7:00pm

LOCATION: Zoom – ID & Access Code will be provided

AGENDA: Part One: Review of Dr. Porter's book

Part Two: Personal Testimonies

For more info: email: waporter4995@yahoo.com

Website: WilliamPorterLife.com

Don't miss other volumes in the *Heaven Can't Wait or Can It?* series

Heaven Can't Wait or Can It? Dreams of Love, Deceit and Hope

This novel is the first in the series as lead character Maggie and her friends seek their "Heaven on Earth." However, while making their earthly journey, there are many pitfalls in pursuing this goal.

Heaven Can't Wait or Can It? The Sequel

This novel is a follow-up to the first in this series. Maggie and her friends continue the saga of trying to find "Heaven on Earth" while living in an imperfect world.

**Heaven Can't Wait or Can It?
The Fruition**

Maggie and her friends seek the fortunes of a happy life through relationships, adventure, and faith as they take a cruise from New York to Bermuda. Unfortunately, the trip did not go without conflict, danger, and misfortune.